PAGES OF THE PAST

DIANE GREENWOOD MUIR

Cover Design Photography: Maxim M. Muir

ISBN-13: 978-1511425926
ISBN-10: 151142592X

Don't miss all of the books in
Diane Greenwood Muir's

Bellingwood Series

All Roads Lead Home – Bellingwood #1
A Big Life in a Small Town – Bellingwood #2
Treasure Uncovered – Bellingwood #3
Secrets and Revelations – Bellingwood #4
Life Between the Lines – Bellingwood #5
Room at the Inn – Bellingwood #5.5
A Season of Change – Bellingwood #6
Tomorrow's Promises – Bellingwood #7
Through the Storm – Bellingwood #8
A Perfect Honeymoon – Bellingwood #8.5

Look for a short story based
on the Biblical Book of Ruth (Kindle only)
Abiding Love

CONTENTS

ACKNOWLEDGMENTS

There is nothing more fun than writing - at least for me. It takes a lot of solitude – a perfect life for this hermit. One little black and white cat named TB (The Beast) lives with me to remind me that there's a bigger world than what's going on in my head. I love that little bugger, even when he pesters me while I'm desperately trying to finish a chapter.

Thank you to Rebecca Bauman, Tracy Kesterson Simpson, Linda Watson, Carol Greenwood, Alice Stewart, Fran Neff, Max Muir, Edna Fleming and Nancy Quist for all they do to make these books happen.

Continuity issues, typos, odd grammatical issues, missing or extra words get caught because they spend time reading this when it is still pretty raw. I take all of their input and use it to help me build a better book. I couldn't do this without them.

The Facebook iteration of Bellingwood had a contest to choose the name for the new coffee shop and bakery. Great names and lots of fun.

Jancie Ter Louw's "Sweet Beans" was the winning name and Sal is so thankful to have that dealt with. Other awesome names were offered by Pam Weaver, Kay Pflueger, Phyllis Mescia, Kate Hickson, Nola Knowles, Cathy Callahan and Brad Hickson.

CHAPTER ONE

"After thirty years of marriage, I don't know what's happening with him," Lydia said. "He keeps telling me it's nothing, but it's been over a month. He mopes around the house and doesn't come to bed until long after I'm asleep. I don't hear from him during the day unless he's responding to a specific question. I don't know what's going on."

"What do you think?" Polly asked. "Surely not..."

"No, no, no," Lydia said, her head snapping up to look Polly in the eye. "Aaron wouldn't do that. At least I don't think he would. For heaven's sake, Polly. I guess I don't know anything right now."

Everything that was bright and cheerful about Lydia Merritt had evaporated in the last month. She'd lost weight and the small amount of makeup she usually wore wasn't enough to cover the dark circles under her eyes.

"Is there anything I can do?" Polly asked. She smiled as little Han tried to jump up on the sofa between the two women. He'd grown, but his cute puppy face still captured her heart. Han and his littermates were settling in to life in Bellingwood after being rescued by Polly and Henry on their honeymoon. Kirk and Khan were having fun out on the farm with Eliseo and Padme was in seventh heaven at the Donovan's. Andrew adored her, Jason was in love with her and even Sylvie talked about her like she was a member of the family.

Polly reached down, picked Han up, and put him on her lap.

Lydia sagged into the sofa beside her and reached out to scratch Han's head. "I don't think so." She looked up again and gave Polly a weak smile. "Unless of course, you could find a dead body or two to kick him back into gear."

"Does he talk to anyone?" Polly asked.

"It's always been me. I listen when work is stressful, when he's annoyed with people in town, or just mad because his deputies make poor decisions. So much has to be kept confidential and he's trusted me with it all." She rubbed her hands on her pants, then went back to wringing them in her lap. "We did that for each other. No one else needs to know how we feel about their idiocy. But now I don't know what to think."

"Is he at least talking to you about regular things?"

"Not unless we're with the kids. He's almost normal when he's with the grandkids, but then we get in the car and he clams up again."

"Lydia. I'm so sorry. I can't believe you've been dealing with this alone for so long."

"It's only been a couple of months. In the beginning, I pressed him pretty hard. He never said anything, so pretty soon all I was doing was nagging." Lydia reached over and took Polly's hand. "I feel like I'm losing my husband and I don't know why."

Tears flowed from her eyes and Polly pulled her in close.

Lydia pulled back and said, "I'm sorry to dump this on you. I wasn't going to and then you asked like you really meant it and I couldn't shut up."

"Have you talked to Beryl and Andy?" Polly was really hoping that someone else had advice for Lydia. She'd known them for just a few years, but if there were two people that were her rock, it was Aaron and Lydia Merritt. To have their lives fall apart meant everything was upside down.

"They know something's up. How could they not? I'm with them every day. Neither of them know what to think. But then, they're more my friends than Aaron's. Beryl thinks she should spy on him, tracking his every movement. Andy wants to host an intervention."

"How far did Beryl get with the spying thing?"

Lydia chuckled and brushed tears from her cheeks. "No further than talking about it. She's terrified that she'd get caught without a good explanation for being where Aaron was. Especially if he was working on a case."

"Could it be a case that's bothering him?"

"No, that's what doesn't make sense. Aaron has told me about some incredibly delicate cases. He says that having someone listen to him think out loud helps him hear the details and they come together to make sense. I've been through the very worst of what he's dealt with, day in and day out."

Polly shuddered. "I can't believe that hearing about those things doesn't upset you more."

"Oh honey, I learned early in our marriage that Aaron's job was who he was. I could either be part of it or ignore it. I had friends who told their husbands to leave the job at work. That's just baloney. If we're going to be a team, I have to be able to accept every part of him, even the fear of having him out there *and* the gory stories." She winked at Polly. "Because I expect him to accept every part of my life, too. Even the crazy little old ladies."

"If you look ahead six months," Polly started, "do you think things will be back to normal or do you feel like this is going to last longer than that?"

Lydia pursed her lips to one side, pondering the question. "I don't know what to think. Fear tells me this is a new normal or that something horrible is going to happen and our lives will turn upside down. I'd like to think that it's short term and Aaron will pass through it and come out on the other side, but I just don't have any confidence right now."

"I wish I could do something more for you," Polly said, patting

Lydia's arm.

"You listened. That's enough. But I wanted you to know why I've been so distant. I felt awful when we didn't come up for the Christmas party and I hid during January. You've probably needed me and I wasn't here."

Polly nodded. "I wondered, but assumed you were busy. I'm glad you said something."

"I should have trusted you earlier, but I've always protected Aaron's reputation, no matter what. He's a wonderful man."

"You're very patient, Lydia Merritt. I'm afraid that by this point, I would have strung him up by his toenails until he talked."

"Maybe that's what I should do, but I'm not ready for extreme measures yet."

"When you are, let me know. I'll be glad to help."

Lydia's phone chimed and she swiped it open. "Oh my goodness, look at the time. I have to be at church in fifteen minutes." She leaned over and hugged Polly. "Thank you for listening and please, don't be angry at Aaron until we know what's going on."

"I'll do my best," Polly said. "But if he doesn't realize that he's hurting you, he's the idiot."

Lydia smiled. "Thank you. I have to believe that it's all going to work out." She reached over and stroked Han's head again. "Maybe I need a dog to keep me company."

"You wouldn't have time for that. You're never home." Polly stood up with Lydia and put the puppy back on the sofa. He stood at the edge and looked down at the floor, then yipped at Polly.

"I know, I know," Polly said. "But you're going to sit there while I say goodbye. I still don't trust you to stay on this side of the door."

"Has he gotten out?"

"He tries to go out the front door whenever it opens," Polly puffed out an indignant laugh. "The only problem is that he's terrified of the steps, so he doesn't get very far. I want to start training him to go up and down steps independently, but right now this is safer for everyone." She opened the front door and walked out with Lydia. "Maybe it's time for us girls to get together. I should call Beryl."

"I'm up for a girl's night out any time," Lydia responded. "Just let me know."

"Now I can put you on the floor, Mr. Cute-ums," Polly said when she was back inside her house. "And you have to be pretty darned cute to inspire Lydia Merritt to consider owning a dog. In all the time I've known her, pets haven't interested her." Polly sat down on the sofa and put Han on the floor, then picked him back up when he whined. Obiwan jumped up and settled in beside her.

"How could a person not have animals?" Polly asked them. Sometimes you're the only sanity I have."

Polly's phone rang and Jeff Lyndsay's face popped up at her.

"Hi there," she said. "Aren't you just downstairs?"

"No, Miss Smart-Aleck, I'm not. If you ever checked your calendar, you'd know I'm in Ames this morning at a gathering of area Bed and Breakfast owners."

"Are you telling them how to make money?"

"I might if they'd listen, but this group is talking about things that don't have much to do with us."

"What's up?"

"I have a favor to ask. I thought Rachel was available, but she has a doctor's appointment and I need you to go over to the hotel."

"Sure, what time?"

"Can you be there by eleven? People are coming in for the weekend."

"I'd be glad to. Anything I need to know?"

"No, everything's on the computer. All you have to do is..."

"I know how to work the system," she said, interrupting him. "Just because I don't pay attention to the calendar doesn't mean I can't do this. I mean, really. How many times have I been over there checking people in and out?"

"Okay, okay. You're right. I feel bad asking you to do this, though."

"One of these days you're going to hire someone to run that

place, right?"

"Soon. I promise. Soon. So far, it's not been a lot of trouble, but I do hate putting you out."

"You can just get over that. I own the place and a little work hasn't turned me into mush yet."

"Thanks, Polly. I'll be back in the office this afternoon."

"Then I'll see you later. Be nice to the little old B&B ladies."

"You have no idea. I'm their favorite. Two of them want me to meet their sons."

Polly sighed with laughter. "You're really something, Jeff Lyndsay. I just love you."

"Will that get me a raise?"

"Only if you're a very good boy."

"What does that mean?"

"Whatever you want it to mean. You know I can be bribed."

"Yeah. That's what worries me."

"Okay, I need to take Obiwan outside if I'm leaving for the hotel. I'll see you later."

Polly took her dogs down the back steps. Obiwan ran for the tree line and sniffed the snow, then ran back to Polly and Han. The puppy was doing better on the leash and paid attention to Obiwan. Having the older dog made house training much easier. She opened the door for Obiwan to go back upstairs and carried Han to her truck. He could spend time at the hotel with her today.

There weren't any cars parked at Sycamore Inn yet, so Polly pulled in behind the caretaker's cottage. Once inside, she hooked Han's leash over a drawer pull behind the counter. Today was going to be busy. The wedding in town must be bringing guests in, many of the last names were identical. She looked up when a burst of cold air came through the front door.

"Hi," she said. "Welcome to Bellingwood."

For the next three hours, Polly checked people in and sent them on to their rooms. Rachel called and offered to come over, but Polly enjoyed meeting people. She was so proud of what they'd done at Sycamore Inn, it was a joy to show it off.

Han had fallen asleep on a blanket she'd brought from the

truck, but when he got up and started to pace, Polly figured she had time to take him outside for a walk. They went out the front door, just in case the last guests arrived.

She walked with him across the parking lot, practicing some of the commands he'd been learning, until they stopped at the grassy area under the sign. Han sniffed the pole and the flowers underneath a thin layer of snow. When he finally stopped to piddle, Polly bent down to tell him what a good boy he was.

An old pick-up truck pulled in under the canopy and a man got out.

"Hi there," she called across the lot. "I'm your host. I'll be right over." Han wasn't in any hurry to leave the grass, but before Polly could bend over to pick him up, the man walked to greet her.

"He's pretty young, are you training him?"

"I am," she replied and put out her right hand. "I'm Polly Giller, the owner of Sycamore Inn."

"Nice to meet you, Miss Giller. My name is Albert Cook. I should have a reservation."

"You sure do." Polly bent at the knees and scooped Han into her arms. "If I let him, he'll stay out here nosing around all day. Let's go inside."

She started across the parking lot and heard a thump. Turning, she was surprised to see her guest slumped on the ground.

"Mr. Cook! What happened?" Polly rushed to him and put her hand on his shoulder in order to turn him and see his face. "Oh my god! What?" A small hole in his forehead was seeping blood. It took her a moment to grasp what had happened. This was insane. This was Bellingwood. Her heart started to race and she broke into a cold sweat. Han tried to reach out from her arms to sniff at the man's body and she clutched him even tighter to her.

Polly glanced around and realized that she was still exposed. Did the shooter miss? Was she the target or had he gotten the person he intended to kill. She didn't see anyone and didn't hear squealing tires from a getaway car. She ducked behind a parked car and realized that since she had no idea where the gunshot had come from, there was really no safe place. She hunched down as low as possible, holding Han to her chest, and duck-walked to get between two other parked cars.

Polly fumbled in her pockets, trying to get to her phone. Her fingers felt as if they were completely disconnected from her body and she couldn't make them work as they trembled uncontrollably. When she finally got her phone out of her pocket, it fell to the ground underneath a car. She gulped and tried to swallow, then blinked her eyes a couple of times in order to clear her head, leaned on the car door and felt on the ground with one hand for the phone. Her thumb brushed across its slick surface and Polly concentrated on controlling her hand in order to pick it back up.

Han squeaked, telling her that she was holding him too tightly, but that didn't matter. He couldn't be allowed to escape. Polly pressed her face into his neck and took a couple of deep breaths, hoping to think straight, just for a moment.

There was only one person to call. She didn't care what he was dealing with. He was the only one who would know what to do.

"Hello, Polly," Aaron Merritt said. There was no friendly banter, no question about a body.

"Aaron, a man was just killed in front of me." Polly was whispering, desperately trying not to draw any more attention to herself than necessary.

"It's not enough that you find bodies that have been dead for a while, you're bringing me fresh ones?"

"That's not funny." Polly's voice shook with fear. "I don't know if there is still someone with a gun out here or not. I'm hunched down between two cars at Sycamore Inn because someone just shot one of my customers. I have more people that are supposed to check in, my dog is with me, and I'm scared out of my mind."

"Okay. Don't you dare move. Was there more than one shot?"

"Just one, I think. I didn't even hear it. All of a sudden, the man dropped to the ground. I thought maybe he'd just collapsed until I saw the hole in his forehead."

"I'm in town. I'll be right there. Please don't move."

"I don't think I can. I feel like I'm stuck to the pavement."

In less than two minutes, Aaron's SUV drove past where she was crouched. She waited for him to circle the lot and he came back, stopped, and rolled down the window. "Can you climb into the back seat? Stay low."

Polly made her way over and after putting Han on the floor of the vehicle, climbed in and did exactly what he asked. Aaron drove to the back of the caretaker's cottage and pulled in beside Polly's truck.

"Do you know who that is out there?" he asked.

"He said his name was Albert Cook. Can I sit up yet?"

"No, not until we know what's going on here. I've called everyone in. Can you just stay there?"

"Aaron, he was walking right beside me."

"I know, honey. I'm so sorry."

"What is the world coming to when it isn't safe to walk around in Bellingwood?"

Aaron turned in his seat and looked at her. "Polly, this was personal. It's not about Bellingwood or Iowa. If you didn't hear the shot, this was someone who knew what they were doing."

"Like a sniper?"

"I suppose so."

"I watch television shows, you know."

Aaron gave her a weak smile. "I suppose you do. The teams are starting to arrive. You stay here until I send someone for you. We'll fan out through the neighborhoods and find out where the shooter was located. As soon as I know it's safe, you can go home."

"I have a hotel full of people who are here for the wedding this weekend and a few more who will be checking in."

"We'll knock on doors. We want to talk to them anyway. Don't worry." He opened his door and got out. "Please stay put for a few more minutes. I need you to be safe."

"It isn't very comfortable back here."

"It's not meant to be. Stay there, though."

Polly picked Han up and turned on her side, snuggling him against her chest. "This is turning out to be a very strange day, Mr.

Han." He licked her face. "The scariest thing? I know that once it starts, I'm in for a couple of weeks of pure insanity. You've never experienced this part of your mama. It gets hectic. That peace and quiet we've had going on for the last several months has finally come to an end."

Stu Decker, one of Aaron's deputies, finally opened the door beside Polly's feet. "Hi there," he said, grinning down at her.

"Can I come out now?"

"Let's go inside. You'll be safer there anyway."

"This is more excitement than I was looking for today, you know," she said.

"It always is with you. All of us down at the station are trying to figure out how you aren't institutionalized with these odd things that happen around you. We're paid to deal with the world's madness and none of us like it very much, but you keep stumbling on it. How are you not paralyzed with fear every day?"

He walked back into the front room with her and waited while she sat down at the desk behind the front counter. The front parking lot was filled with sheriff's cars and even the local police were there. A black van that she recognized from the State Department of Criminal Investigation (DCI) had just pulled in. It did seem strange that she recognized so many people.

"Fear? Fear is the mind killer," she muttered.

"What?"

"Oh nothing. I'm just being flip. I don't know why I'm not scared all the time. Maybe I just don't have time to think about it. I'm always surprised, but once I absorb it, I hug an animal or cry on Henry."

She looked up at Stu. "Henry! If he hears about this from anyone but me, he'll be really upset. Do you mind if I call him?"

"Call your husband and tell him that we're taking care of you. Tell him that he can't come over here, though, okay?"

"I'll try."

Polly dialed Henry's number and before he could speak, she blurted out. "Before anyone else tells you anything. I'm fine. There's been a murder at Sycamore Inn. A sniper shot one of my guests while he and I were walking back to the hotel. I was outside with Han when it happened. Stu wants me to assure you that they're taking care of me and you're not supposed to come over here."

"Stop. What? Slow down and repeat yourself. What in the hell are you talking about? A murder? At Sycamore Inn?"

She took a deep breath and said. "I'm okay. Do we have that clear first?"

"I'm clear. You're okay. That shouldn't even be a question. But I guess that since it's you, I should always be worried. Now, what happened?"

"I went outside with Han. He needed to go to the bathroom. And by the way, he's getting really good at this. We went out to the grassy area under the big sign and he went right away."

"Whatever. I don't care about the damned dog's peeing habits."

She pursed her lips. This wasn't going to be easy. "Anyway, a man pulled in under the canopy. He walked over to greet me. His name was Albert Cook. There were only a few more people who were going to check in, so I was waiting for them to arrive. We talked for a couple of minutes and then went back toward the hotel. I heard a strange thump and turned around. The man had fallen to the ground. I thought maybe he'd just collapsed, but there was a hole in his forehead."

"I can't breathe," Henry said.

"As soon as I realized what happened, I grabbed the dog and got beside a car, then I got in between two other cars and called Aaron. He came along and I got in his back seat and he went to the back of the caretaker's house. Stu came and got me and now I'm inside. The place is full of cops and emergency vehicles. Stu said you aren't supposed to come over here to get me. They'll make sure I get home."

She waited a few moments in silence and said, "Are you there?"

"Barely. So what you're telling me is that there's a sniper in town, he shot a man that was walking beside my wife and I'm supposed to stay away from the scene."

"Pretty much."

"I need a drink. A big drink. With Valium or Novocain or something."

"That's not a good idea."

"I know. I know. I'm just jabbering words because I don't know what to do or say."

"I'm sorry."

"Don't be sorry. You didn't do anything wrong. But I'm at a loss."

"Henry?"

"Yes Polly."

"Go home. Take Obiwan and go for a walk. Go down to the barn. Anything."

"I'll go get Obiwan, but I don't know what I'll do after that. I want to hold on to you and make sure you're all in one piece."

"I promise you that I'm fine."

"Polly, a man was shot right beside you."

"I know that and when you and I are quiet in bed tonight, I'm going to fall completely apart and you're going to have to hold me until I quit freaking out. But there are too many people here right now and I can't lose control."

"Oh honey, I love you."

"I love you too. I'll be home later."

CHAPTER TWO

Although the sun was shining, Polly still didn't feel like getting out of bed. The bedroom door was closed, there were no animals anywhere, and Henry had disappeared.

She smiled to herself and texted him, *"Where are you?"* Technology was awesome.

"In the living room. Are you awake now?"

"Come hug me."

Once the door opened, two dogs and two cats came running into the room and jumped up onto the bed. Han tried, but he couldn't quite clear the mattress yet. Henry picked him up and dropped him beside Polly.

"How are you feeling this morning?"

"Like I've waded through mud with weights around my waist. I'm sorry I had such a hard time sleeping last night."

"It's to be expected. I can't believe you don't have more of these nights."

After answering questions from the different law enforcement groups at Sycamore Inn, then had come home and done her best to be pleasant and calm around Jessie and Rebecca. When she'd finally relaxed in their bed, she shook and sobbed. Henry held her until she calmed, but Polly spent the rest of the night tossing and turning. Every time she drifted off, her mind would flash back to the image in her mind of the man with a hole in his forehead and she'd wake up again. It wasn't until four thirty that she'd exhausted herself enough to fall into a dreamless sleep.

"What time did you get up?" she asked.

"About seven. Jessie was up and Obiwan decided he'd waited long enough. Everyone has been fed and watered, so you don't need to hurry out of bed."

Polly smiled and reached out to touch his arm. "Thank you. I need to take Rebecca over to Beryl's for her lesson this morning."

"I can do that for you."

"No. I've got it. You and I both know that this is just the beginning of things spinning out of control. I might as well wrap my head around it and buck up. Besides, I want to talk to Beryl."

"What's up?"

"Lydia is stressed because Aaron is upset about something and won't tell her what it is. I think it's time for a party. Or at least an opportunity for us to wallow in ice cream and chocolate sauce."

Henry leaned over and kissed her forehead. "That sounds perfect. I like the way you take care of your emotions."

"It's the same way you take care of my emotions - ice cream and chocolate."

"I know my girl," he said, standing back up. "If you have things to do this morning, I am heading over to the shop. Jessie is already there."

"On a Saturday?"

"Yeah. Someone had to open the place. We've got a load of barn wood coming in today that needs to be sorted."

"You're sorting it?"

"Sure. Some of the guys will be in to help, but I might as well be there if you won't be here."

"Okay. Is Rebecca up?"

"She sure is. She's had breakfast and I believe she's downstairs in her mother's room, sketching the horses."

"So there's no one here?" Polly asked coyly.

He stammered. "Uhhh. Uhhh. This isn't fair."

"I know. I was just teasing. Who knows when she'll come back. I should start my day anyway." Polly pushed the blankets away, swung her legs over the edge of the bed, and stood up. Little Han came scurrying behind her, trying to leap into her arms. She grabbed him up and put him on the floor. "Don't do that, you silly thing. You scare me to death."

Henry walked to her side of the bed and gave her a hug. "Do we have plans tonight?"

"Not that I know of. Why?"

"Just wondering. Let me know when you've figured out what they'll be."

"Why do you say it like that?"

"Because you're about to tear through town today and that means that we'll be busy tonight."

"I don't understand."

"You dealt with another dead person yesterday. You're worried about Lydia. You're talking to Beryl in an hour or so and that will only be the beginning of you coping with all that's coming at you. I've learned to just strap in and enjoy the ride."

Polly pursed her lips and wrinkled her nose at him. "I was kind of thinking we might ask Joss and Nate to bring the babies over."

Henry's eyes lit up. "What if Joss brought the babies over and I spent the evening with Nate in his garage?"

"We might be able to do that for you. I'll call her. Now you get out of here while I shower and get ready. Are you taking Han to the shop?"

"I can. He's getting pretty comfortable over there."

"You told me that he was going to be your dog."

"Come on, you rug rat," Henry said, bending over to pick up the pup. "When are you going to grow to full size? I'm tired of carrying you." He gave Polly another quick kiss and left the room. She pushed the bedroom door shut and went into the bathroom to start the shower.

~~~

"Mom was good this morning," Rebecca said. "She said she's coming to the Valentine's Day dinner. She promised."

"That's great news," Polly replied.

"If I do some extra things around Sycamore House, can I make some money?"

Polly slowed down as she prepared to turn the corner. "What do you need money for?"

"I want to buy her a nice dress for the party. She's lost so much weight that nothing fits her right."

"We could help you buy that."

"No, I want it to be from me."

Polly slowly nodded her head, and bit her upper lip as she thought. "Let me think about this. We'll certainly find some things for you to do. Do you want to help in the main house or down at the barn?"

"I'll do anything. I found a really pretty dress uptown."

"You did. When did that happen?"

"After school last week. Kayla and I walked to the library after school and there was this yellow dress in the window at Osborn's."

Polly knew exactly which dress Rebecca was talking about. The only problem was that it wasn't anything Sarah Heater would wear - lemon yellow, and sleeveless with a very low cut back. She wasn't sure how they kept it on the mannequin in the window.

"Let's talk to your mother first."

"But I want to surprise her."

"I will think of some things you can do to earn money. You go on in to Beryl's for your lesson and I'll be back for you in an hour." Polly had pulled into the driveway and waited for Rebecca to jump out of the truck.

Beryl came running out of the house and Polly rolled her window down.

"Go on inside, honey," Beryl said. "You can get started. I'll be right there."
~~~

"What's up?" Polly asked.

"I wanted to ask how you were doing. Lydia called this morning to tell me about your experience at the hotel yesterday. We're all worried about you."

"Thanks. I think I'm fine. Did she say anything else? About the man who died or anything?"

"You don't know?"

"Know what?"

"Aaron knew him. That's why the guy was in town - to see Aaron."

Polly frowned. "He didn't say a word yesterday."

"He's been kind of quiet about everything lately. I'm worried about our girl." Beryl put her hand on Polly's arm. "What are we going to do?"

"I don't know," Polly said. "But I think it's time for another evening like the old days."

"Tell me about it. I miss you guys. We haven't had a good slumber party in a long time."

Polly laughed, thinking about the only other slumber party she'd attended with these women. It had been the craziest introduction to Bellingwood she could ever have imagined and it had been perfect. "Are we ready for that much excitement?"

"Maybe not." Beryl grinned. "But it's time to plan a party. I'll talk to Andy. Do you have any evenings this week that we should avoid?"

"Nope. Not that I know of."

"We'll plan, you'll come, and we'll tell our girl how much we love her. Maybe that will return a smile to her face."

"Perfect. Thank you."

Beryl pulled her shawl tight. "I'd better get inside before I freeze to death. I'm glad you're holding up. We can't lose you to the insanity of your calling."

"Calling-schmalling. Stop it."

"You're the girl with the bodies. Everyone knows it. We just wait for it to happen." Beryl leaned in and whispered. "You know, people perk up when you come around. They just wait to see if you'll discover anything while they're watching."

"Stop it. That's not true."

Beryl shrugged. "It's kinda true. I always do. I always leave you just a little disappointed."

"Get inside," Polly said, waving her friend away. "I'll be back later for Rebecca."

"We'll be the ones having fun." Beryl turned and danced back toward her front door, then turned and waved while Polly backed out of the driveway. The woman was a complete nut.

Since no one expected her to be anywhere for the next hour, Polly turned and headed toward Joss Mikkels' house. She felt guilty for just showing up with no notice, but laughed an evil laugh and pulled in. She listened at the front door to make sure there was no screaming or crying and knocked softly. When no one came to the door, she backed up and looked in the window to the front room. Joss was sitting forward on the sofa, picking things up from the floor. She glanced up and saw Polly, then jumped to her feet and ran toward the front door.

"What are you doing here?" she asked, before the storm door was even open.

"In the neighborhood. I dropped Rebecca off at Beryl's and thought I'd see what you two were doing tonight."

"Come in." Joss stepped back. "It's cold out there."

"Where are the kiddos?"

"They're downstairs with Nate. Sophie stood up the other day and he thinks Cooper should be doing the same thing. He's decided that help from Dad can't hurt."

"Okay," Polly looked at Joss's face. "How do you feel about that?"

"Him pushing Cooper to keep up with his sister at this age? Oh, I'm thrilled." The sound of sarcasm rang through Joss's words. "But I didn't get any sleep last night, the house is a mess and to be totally honest, if he wants to spend time doing anything at all with those two… fine. We'll have that argument later. All I want to do this morning is pick up and take a nap. Nate's in charge for the next three hours."

Joss dropped back down on the sofa and pointed at one of the rocking chairs. "Sit. Talk to me."

Polly sat down and bent over to pick up a book beside the chair.

Joss leaned forward and took it out of Polly's hand. "I heard about your escapade last night. How are you?"

"I was a complete and utter mess all night long - no sleep, just dreaming about what happened. I don't know why this one bothers me more than others. Maybe it's because I don't have any concept of why it happened. He was standing right beside me and someone shot him. They could have just as easily shot me. Why didn't they? Why him? What if the shooter had missed and hurt me?"

Joss shuddered and shook her head. "Do they know anything yet?"

"Beryl says Aaron knows him. What's that about? Is Aaron the next target? Does he know why the guy was killed? He was so nonchalant when we were going through everything. I had no idea that he knew the guy."

"That is odd. Have you talked to Lydia?"

"Not today."

Joss twitched when one of the babies started to cry, but didn't move.

"You can ignore that?" Polly asked.

"If he needs me, he calls. He's got it."

"So here we are, eight months later. Does this feel normal to you now?"

"You have no idea. It's so normal, I can't imagine any other life. What are you going to do when Jessie has her baby?"

"That's at least a month away," Polly said. "And I don't know. We've talked about what her next steps are going to be. I know that she's been saving money."

"You'll be okay with her moving out?"

"I'm not her mother. I'll be fine with it. In fact, I'm ready for it to happen any time. But, nothing will happen until she's ready. And if that means that she needs to stay with us, I guess that's what it means."

"You're a good woman."

"Yeah. Whatever. I committed to this and it's not like she's hard work or anything. She helps out and she's there for the kids when Henry and I want to go somewhere, but she's an adult and really needs to be on her own."

"Has she started looking for an apartment?"

"Not that I know of." Polly gave her head a quick shake. "I shouldn't be like this. I told her that she had a home as long as she needed it and that we'd be there for her when she had the baby. And I've been through all the childbirth classes with her." She rolled her eyes. "I know that you want babies in your life, but after that, nothing at all makes me want to be pregnant and give birth."

Joss laughed out loud. "Hey, I'm fine with someone else bearing my children. I was never one of those girls who thought that the whole pregnancy thing was a glorious experience."

"Jessie is really digging it."

"That's fabulous. If you're going to be pregnant, I think you should enjoy every minute of it."

"She keeps telling me that she's never felt better in all her life. Because she's been so focused on the baby, she eats really healthy and doesn't drink anything that's bad for her. She's been doing yoga and meditation to keep calm. The baby turned her into a different person."

"Wait until that child shows up, live and in person. That will turn her into crazy bat-shit lady in a hurry."

Polly laughed at her friend. "You're hilarious. You aren't that bad. I haven't seen much bat-shit crazy stuff from you in the last few months."

"Uh huh. You might want to get her out of your house sooner rather than later, or you're going to see her crazy side show up when she doesn't get enough sleep and the baby wants one more thing or starts crying even after she's met its needs."

"You're complaining."

Joss sighed. "I am, aren't I. Sorry about that. See. Not enough sleep."

"Because I know how much you love those two."

"More than anything else." Joss glanced at the stairway leading down to Nate and the twins. "It's not that bad and I wouldn't trade my life now for anything."

"But, Jessie needs to make her own life. You're right. We'll see what happens."

"Joss?" Nate's voice came from downstairs. She jumped off the sofa and ran for the top of the steps.

"What do you need?"

"Has Polly asked you about tonight? Henry's on the phone."

Joss turned and looked at Polly. "What's up for tonight?"

"Those boys don't even give a girl a minute. I was going to ask if you wanted to come over this evening. Rebecca and Andrew would love to play with the babies and I'd like to spend time with you. Henry thought maybe he and Nate could work on their cars."

"Why don't you bring your kids over here? That way I can put the babies to bed. I'll cook dinner."

"We'll bring pizza."

"No, I'll cook. Nate and Henry can eat with us and then go out to the garage."

"Joss?" Nate asked.

"We're working out the details, but yes."

"Cool."

Joss came back into the living room and sat down again. "That will motivate me to get moving."

"You'll be cooking for a lot of us. Are you sure?"

"Absolutely. I'll make a lasagna."

"Then let me bring bread and salad. Rebecca and I can work on that this afternoon."

"How's her mom?"

"Okay for now. She told Rebecca that she wants to go to the Valentine's Day dinner, so we're on the hunt for a new dress."

"She won't be able to wear it very often, am I right?"

Polly shook her head. "I guess if she only wears it once and that creates a memory for Rebecca, that's enough."

"You're right. That wasn't very nice of me."

"No, it's fine. It's the truth. Sarah won't like the idea, she'll think it's wasteful, but Rebecca wants to raise the money on her own and pay for the dress."

"I'll pay her and Andrew to keep an eye on the kids tonight."

"You don't have to do that."

"We'll be right here. They can play with them and pay attention to them and make a little money. It would be a start."

"Thank you," Polly said and then gave her friend a grin. "Rebecca wants to buy that yellow dress in Osborn's window downtown."

"That flimsy thing with no shoulders?" Joss chuckled. "Poor Sarah. What are you going to do?"

"I have no idea, but we have to fix this for Sarah." Polly stood up. "I should probably get back to Beryl's."

"Thanks for coming over." Joss stood and bent over to pick toys up from the floor.

"I felt a little guilty about dropping in."

"You should. The place is a mess."

Polly looked around. The toys and blankets that were in the living room were part of a home with active children. There was no mess. "If I didn't have three other people who were relatively clean and neat living in my house, I'd never let anyone come in. This is pristine in comparison to how I lived before Henry married me. Stop worrying."

"It will be better when you come over tonight."

Polly gave her friend a hug and ran back out to her truck. She hoped she hadn't been inside long enough for it to completely cool down. It felt like it was getting colder as the day went on. She was really tired of winter.

CHAPTER THREE

Rebecca was standing next to Polly in the kitchen, drying dishes after Sunday breakfast. "Can I ask a question?"

"Of course, sweetie. What's up?" Polly rinsed another plate and put it in the drying rack.

"Well, I have a friend at school..."

Polly's heart jumped into her throat. This was a first. It was an exciting first. She tried desperately hard not to react and plunged her hands back into the suds.

"Can she come home with me tomorrow afternoon?"

"Sure?" Polly had so many questions, she didn't know where to start.

Rebecca stopped and turned to face Polly. "She always goes to the library to wait for her sister to pick her up and they aren't open on Mondays anymore."

That decision had nearly destroyed Joss. But the city had cut back funding and though she was fine with spending more time at home with her babies, she hated its impact on the community. Tomorrow was the first Monday they'd be closed.

"Sure, she can come here. What's her name?"

"Kayla. She's really nice."

Polly remembered Rebecca mentioning that name. "How long have you two been friends?"

"For a while. She's my table partner."

Polly smiled inside. Mrs. Hastings had done her very best to seat Rebecca next to someone who would befriend the girl. It looked like her plan had finally worked.

"I'd be glad to host your friend tomorrow. Maybe we should call her family today so they know where she's going to be. You wouldn't want her sister to go to the library and not find her there."

Rebecca looked at the floor. "We kinda talked about it on Friday and I told Kayla you wouldn't mind."

"You were absolutely right. I don't mind. But I still think that I should talk to her mother."

"She doesn't have a mother. Just a sister."

Polly wrinkled her brow. "Just a sister? No father either?"

"No, something happened to them, so it's just Kayla and Stephanie."

"Do you have Stephanie's phone number? I would like to just talk to her so that I'm sure she knows Kayla will be safe here."

Jessie came into the room from doing laundry. "Stephanie Armstrong? She has a sister named Kayla."

"You know Stephanie?" Rebecca asked.

"Sure. She works at the convenience store. I haven't talked to her in a while, though. Not since I left there."

"Do you have Kayla's phone number, Rebecca?" Polly asked again.

"No. Can't we do it tomorrow and then you can meet Stephanie when she picks Kayla up tomorrow night? Please?"

"That will be fine. Of course."

"Can I show her the donkeys?"

"You know who has to answer that," Polly said.

"I know. Eliseo. But he'll say yes, won't he? And Jason will be down there, so he can show us around."

"We'll see how the day goes tomorrow. If Kayla isn't dressed to go down to the barn, we'd hate to mess up her clothes."

"We won't get dirty. We'll just look."

Polly patted Rebecca's back and turned back to the sink. "Let's wait and see."

Rebecca put another dried plate onto the stack. "Why don't we ever use the dishwasher?"

"Because I like hanging out with you," Polly said, laughing. "Honestly, once I got started today, I couldn't quit."

"That was my question too," Henry said, coming around the corner. "You hand wash a lot of dishes, Polly."

"I never got used to a dishwasher. We didn't have one while I was growing up and my apartment in Boston didn't have one." She shrugged. "I just wash dishes, I guess."

Henry took the towel out of Rebecca's hand. "You go play. I'll deal with the tyrant."

Rebecca smiled and ran out of the kitchen. "Jessie! You wanna play a game?"

"She has a little friend," Polly whispered to Henry.

"Yeah. I know, she looks ready to pop. What do we have, another month?"

"Not Jessie, you dope. Rebecca. She's bringing a friend over after school tomorrow."

He stepped back. "No kidding. Imagine that. And you didn't have to get involved or anything."

Polly flicked suds at him. "Leave me alone. I'm just happy she has someone other than Andrew. He's a wonderful boy, but she needs more friends. So does he, for that matter."

"I spoke too soon. You're about to get involved, I can tell."

"Joss has to close the library on Mondays now. I was thinking that since kids probably went there until their parents picked them up, we should use the classroom and computer room for Monday afternoon homework sessions."

"Yep. I knew it."

Polly elbowed him. "It's a great idea!"

"Talk to Jeff before you do anything rash, will you?" He opened the cupboard doors and put stacks of plates and glasses where they belonged.

"So you didn't say last night. How are things going with those cars? What are they? Woodies?"

"Yes. Woodies. And you already know that. You pay attention to everything."

"Whatever. Anyway, how far are you?"

He put his hand on the counter and looked at her, puzzled. "You do know that this is going to be a very long project, don't you? They aren't going to be ready for you to drive this summer."

"Yeah, yeah, yeah. How long are they going to take?"

"It could be a year or more. We have a lot of work to do. The engines are a mess, there's no upholstery, and the bodies were completely rusted out."

"I get it. I'm sorry I asked."

"No, that's not it. I just don't want you getting excited. This kind of restoration is labor intensive and since we don't get to spend a lot of hours doing it, well..."

She scowled. "Am I supposed to feel guilty about not letting you work over there?"

"That works for me. But no, neither of us has a lot of time. It's just something fun to do."

"Okay. Just checking."

He kissed her cheek. "And thanks for acting interested."

"At least you aren't carousing at the bars every other night."

"Who has time for that?"

"I know!"

They walked into the living room to find Rebecca standing behind Jessie, brushing and braiding her hair, the older girl sprawled out on the sofa. She looked terribly uncomfortable. A pile of folded laundry sat on the table in front of her.

"I'll put it away in a minute. This just feels so good," Jessie said. Obiwan was stretched out beside her and Han had curled up on her chest, his head resting on her belly as she stroked him.

"You know I don't care. It looks as if you have the full-on doggie spa thing going on."

Henry went on into their bedroom and pushed the door closed.

She heard the television come on. Football. It was his Sunday afternoon escape. He didn't want to go to anyone's house to watch it, he didn't even particularly care to watch it on the big screen in the media room. He just liked to sit in the big, comfy chair with his feet up. More often than not, one of the cats or Han was in his lap, but he preferred being alone.

Polly had taken to napping on Sunday afternoons. She'd discovered that if she relaxed her body, she could consider the sounds of the game as white noise. Henry had tried to talk to her about the teams that were playing, but when both of them discovered that first of all, she didn't care, and secondly, he didn't really want to chat during the games, they gave up and let the other do their thing.

She went in and waited while the two cats darted in the open door. Without saying anything to Henry, who was already seated and watching the television intently, she crossed to her side of the bed, pulled her shoes off and stretched out, nestling her head into the pillow.

~~~

"I'll see you all later," Polly said as she went down the back steps. She and her friends rarely missed a Sunday evening at Pizzazz downtown. Henry was still watching football, while Rebecca and Jessie were making spaghetti for dinner to take down to eat with Sarah and Evelyn Morrow.

She opened the back door by the garage and waited while Sal Kahane pulled in. She'd texted Polly earlier that she would pick her up. Polly usually walked to the pizza place, it was only a few blocks, but the temperatures were low enough that the wind chill was quite bitter.

Polly darted to Sal's car and jumped in. "Thanks for picking me up."

"Nobody should be walking in this. It's awful."

"No worse than what we dealt with in Boston."

"I know. You're right. I keep thinking that maybe I should
~~~

move to Hawaii or southern Florida or somewhere warm. I don't know that I'm cut out to be a Canuck."

"We don't live in Canada."

"There is only one state between us."

"A long state! Stop complaining."

Sal laughed. "I'm going to bet you a pizza that before the end of this winter, you're going to tell me at least once that you hate winter. You always complained when we were living together."

"I don't complain anymore. I love living in Iowa." Polly wasn't about to admit that she'd silently been complaining for days.

"Uh huh. We'll see." Sal pulled into a parking space across the street from Pizzazz. There were plenty of spaces in front of the pizza place and she'd gone around the block to get the right angle.

"What are we doing on this side of the street?" Polly asked.

"I want you to look at the empty building right in front of us."

"Okay. Very nice empty building."

"Take a good look at it. Look closely."

Polly rolled her eyes to the side. "It's a building. What about it?"

"Have you taken a good look?"

"As much as possible."

"Fine. We'll talk about it at dinner."

"Tell me." Polly glanced at her friend and saw a wicked gleam in her eyes.

"Nope. You have to wait until everyone is there."

"You're just mean."

Sal backed into the street, then did a sharp turn and pulled into a space directly in front of the restaurant. "I love small towns," she said. "You can do this kind of stuff and everyone expects it. The first time someone turned in front of me to grab a spot on the other side of the street, I nearly collapsed. You'd never get away with that out east. But here, it's just what you do."

"It seems like you've perfected the move."

"Only if there are no cars for three blocks in either direction."

Sylvie pulled in beside them and as they were getting out, Joss pulled in on the other side of her.

"Things are really quiet here tonight," Sal commented.

"Wonder what's up?" Polly asked.

They went inside and saw only two other tables with customers. "This is eerie," Joss said.

As they made their way to their regular table, Bri put drinks down in the center and smiled at them. By the time they'd chosen a seat and grabbed their drinks, she put two baskets of cheese bread down.

"Your pizza is in. It should be out in a few minutes," she said.

"Thanks. You're awesome," Sylvie responded.

They'd tried several different pizzas over the last few months, but each time came back to their regular order - a Pizzazz Classic with everything on it. Bri perfectly timed the pizza's arrival as the first basket of cheese bread was emptied.

"Why is it so quiet tonight?" Sal asked their waitress.

"Dylan thinks it's because of the cold. But we've had colder days than this and the place is full." Bri shrugged. "I got nuttin'."

Polly made a show of drumming her fingers on the table in front of Sal.

"What?" Sal asked.

"You know what. Why did you want me to see that building across the street?"

"I'm going to buy it."

"You're what?" All three of them looked at Sal and then turned to look out the window.

"You're buying a building?" Sylvie asked. "To do what?"

"That's why I want to talk to you three. I need a place to write."

Polly burst out with a laugh. "You can't write at home?"

"Yes, I can write at home. But it's so quiet. Sometimes it's deadly quiet. I do my best work in hustle and bustle."

"I doubt that you'll ever find hustle and bustle in Bellingwood," Joss said. "Even downtown, you're doing well to have a little hust ... never any l-e." She spelled the last two letters out.

Sal nodded. "On any given day in any city in the country, creative types make their way to coffee shops, where caffeine and sugar stir their imaginations. They're inspired by everyone else who sits at a table working away at their computers or in their notebooks. It's like a perfect competition. You see other people working and can't help but imagine their projects and it brings out the best in you. I need my coffee shop."

"So, you're going to build a coffee shop?"

"That's what I want to do. I'm meeting Henry tomorrow afternoon to talk about remodeling the place and then..."

Polly frowned. "You're meeting Henry? He didn't say a word."

"That's because I made him promise to keep quiet. I wanted to be the one to tell you. I just found out Friday afternoon that the sale was really going to happen."

"I can't believe he didn't tell me." Polly growled at Sylvie. "And he didn't tell me when you bought your house, either. That man is going to be in serious trouble one of these days for not letting me in on his secrets."

Joss patted Polly's leg. "Shhh. Tell us more about the coffee shop, Sal."

"Henry said that you are genius with interiors, Polly. I want lots of wood like Sycamore House. I don't know. Maybe a coffee bar with cool stools and tables or booths. I don't know any of that stuff. So, can you meet us here at one thirty tomorrow? I want to know what you think."

"Hmm," Polly responded. "Maybe he won't be in trouble after all."

"What are you going to do with the apartments upstairs?" Sylvie asked.

Joss grinned. "Apartments? Are you going to be a landlord, too?"

"There are two apartments," Sal said. "From what I can see, they're not in terrible shape. They need some work. They've been empty a long time, but I think they'd make cute places to live."

"Do you really think you can make money at this?" Polly asked.

"I don't know, but it can't hurt to try. You've become an entrepreneur and you're really good at it." Sal's eyes lit up. "I want to be just like you - renovating and remodeling and making a go of it."

Sylvie sat back and shut her eyes. Her fingers were moving and every once in a while, her tongue crept out and licked her upper lip.

"What are you doing over there, Sylvie?" Polly asked.

"I'm concentrating," was the response.

"Well you look weird doing it."

Sylvie's eyes popped open and she stuck her tongue out at Polly. "If you're going to do this, Sal, you need more than just coffee. You need bakery items, but I don't have the stoves at Sycamore House to do that much baking. I could help you in the beginning when you're just getting started, but if you're successful, things will have to change."

"There is a ton of space in that building. Maybe we put a bakery in later. Oooh, wouldn't that be fun?" Sal was bouncing in her seat when Bri brought the pizza to their table.

"You can't bake," Polly said.

"I know I can't, but Sylvie can. It could be an extension of her catering business."

"It's Sycamore House's catering business," Sylvie interjected quickly.

"We can work that out. Maybe Sycamore House Catering needs two locations. It won't all happen at once. It's going to take some time before we are big enough to do that."

Polly's brain began whirring. This was a great idea. "Do you think that would work, Sylvie?" she asked. "How strange would it be for you to have two locations?"

"It's not the worst idea in the world. There are details that need to be ironed out: personnel, all of the appliances. We haven't done many cakes because I don't have a good place to build them." She looked off into space as she thought about it. "I've had people ask about cakes for special events."

"If we put a bakery in with your coffee shop," Polly said, "that would bring business in for both of us." She took a bite of pizza and then breathed through her mouth to cool it down. "Every single damned time. You'd think I would learn. Pizza cheese is hot!"

Sal waved her hands in front of her. "You guys are turning this into a bigger deal than I planned for. I just wanted a busy place where I could write and get a decent cup of coffee without having to make it myself."

"What did Mark think when you told him?" Polly asked.

"He's the one who found the building. Well, Dylan did. He and Mark's sister, Lisa were over for dinner a few weeks ago and he was complaining about the empty building across the street from this place. It wasn't a half hour later and I was whining about needing a barista of my own. The next thing I knew, Mark and Dylan were talking about how I should bring a coffee shop into Bellingwood. Joe only makes regular and decaf at the diner."

"I didn't even think about that," Sylvie said. "You'd be competition for him."

"Not really. I wouldn't want to serve food." Sal shuddered. "Can't you see me slinging hash with a greasy apron on and a hair net over these pretty locks?"

"Hey!" Sylvie said, laughing.

"Yeah. Like any of your aprons are ever greasy."

"They are after a long day, but I'll give you a break. You totally wouldn't fit in any kitchen I know."

Joss hadn't said much and Sal finally asked her, "What do you think about all of this?"

"I could get a White Chocolate Mocha? In town?" The yearning in her voice made the rest of them giggle. "I love you, Sal. Like the sister I never had. And if you want more than that, I will love you more than that. This is the best idea ever!"

"I guess that's another vote for the coffee shop. Now all I need is to figure out what to call it."

"How about Sal's Joe?" Polly said.

"That's too weird," Sylvie replied. "Maybe Java Sal, though."

"Maybe we don't go any further with this tonight," Sal said. "Think about it, though. You girls are my best bet for a clever name. And anyone who wants to come up tomorrow to walk through the building with me and Henry," she looked at Polly, "and you too, just show up. I don't know what I'm doing. I just know that I want it to happen and I want it bad enough to do something about it."

"I get white chocolate mocha," Joss said dreamily. "I might cry."

CHAPTER FOUR

Opening Jeff's office door after a light knock, Polly gave him a sweet smile. "Do you have a minute?"

"Good lord, what do you want now?"

"What do you mean by that?" Polly wanted to be offended, but inside she was laughing.

"I recognize that smile. You want something. Woman, I've given you my blood, sweat and tears. My first born is already promised to that man at the crossroads who was playing the fiddle. I've got nothing else."

"You think you're funny."

"I'm a little funny." He gestured to a chair in front of his desk.

Polly dropped into it and leaned across. "I need to talk to you about lots of things this morning."

"Do any of them include a raise?"

"You must have had a good weekend."

He shrugged and grinned. The running joke on his raise was one they were both quite comfortable with. Jeff was paid very well and they had already negotiated his yearly salary increases along with his bonuses. It seemed the joke was never going to grow old, though.

"It was a good weekend. I had dinner with a friend last night."

Polly perked up. "A friend or a *good* friend?"

"I don't know," he smirked. "But her daughter loves her very much."

"Oh," she said, slumping back down. "I thought it might be a date."

"No. It's just a friend who needed a shoulder to cry on. So we ate expensive steak and I flirted with the waiter. He was adorable. Maybe a bit too young for me, but the flirting was fun."

"You're a nut."

"And you love me. What's happening in Polly-world?"

"Before I stir Sylvie up, I want to know what you think about a coffee shop and bakery coming to downtown Bellingwood."

He sat back and nodded slowly while he thought. "It's not a terrible idea. The Chamber would love to see a business like that. They're always looking to fill those empty buildings. Are you planning to buy and remodel down there?" Jeff glared at her. "Why don't you ever talk to me before you start doing these things?"

"I'm talking to you now and no, it's not just me. Sal is buying the building across from Pizzazz. She wants to put a coffee shop in, but then we were brainstorming and before I knew it, I had an entire bakery to dream about while I slept. We don't have room for additional equipment and supplies here at Sycamore House."

"Yes we do."

"You're not helping."

"Really. If Sylvie wanted to do it here, we could put ovens and racks on that back wall. We'd have to yank the table out, but mixers could sit on the counter back there and..."

Polly waved her hand to stop him. "Sylvie started getting excited about putting a bakery in Sal's building."

"She really wants to work out of two separate kitchens?"

"I think she sees the potential for bringing on more employees. And we really don't have room in this kitchen. Besides, a bakery and coffee shop seem to go together, don't you think?"

"So Sycamore House Bakery downtown?" he asked.

"Sure. It expands our reach and both of those small businesses would be a draw for the other one."

Jeff leaned forward on his desk and rubbed his forehead with both hands. Looking up from under his fingers, he sighed a deep sigh. "Why can't anyone just be satisfied with growing the businesses we already have?"

"You can hardly blame Sylvie. She wants to use the heck out of what she learned. And you and I both know that she doesn't have room here to bake wedding cakes like she wants. Just think of all she could create. And think of all the people she could hire as the bakery grows."

"What if it doesn't?"

Polly curled her nose at him. "Who are you and what did you do with my Jeff? First of all, you'll be promoting the place..."

"I will? Who said I'd do that?"

"Don't make me pull out the boss card on you. And secondly, this is Sylvie. She's amazing in the kitchen. People already ask about her breads and pastries. And that's just what she does on a small scale for wedding receptions."

"So, Sal's buying the building and putting a coffee shop in. I suppose Henry's doing the remodel."

"Well, duh."

"And you want me to tell you *what* about the idea of a bakery?"

"I want you on board with this. I'm meeting everyone at one thirty, and then Henry and I are going to talk to Steve."

Steve Cook was Polly's financial advisor. His firm had worked with her father and he'd been involved with her decisions since the day she decided to return to Iowa and buy an old schoolhouse. He had yet to say no to her and Polly was hoping that she never presented him with an idea that he thought would fail.

"You know that if you and Sylvie decide this is what you want to do, I'll be behind you all the way."

"Good. I'll let you know."

"What were the rest of the lots of things?"

She was confused for a moment and then said, "Oh! Those. It's mostly about hiring more people. I can't handle all of the bookkeeping that is going on with Sycamore Inn and catering and if the bakery gets busy, it's going to just get worse. And ... I think we need a full-time receptionist."

Jeff shut his eyes and shook his head back and forth. "I kept hoping that Sarah would be able to do more, but that poor woman seems to be hanging on by a thread. She comes into the office every once in a while, but after an hour, she's exhausted."

"I know." This was a hard conversation to have. Polly kept having it in her head, but she didn't want to deal with the reality.

"I don't want to have to tell her that we're replacing her."

"I'll talk to her. There will always be something for her to do if she has the energy, right?"

"Of course," Jeff said.

"That's all she needs to know. But I think we need someone else here in the office. And you have *got* to hire someone at Sycamore Inn. Rachel can't keep going out there to clean rooms. Especially if Sylvie gets busy with another kitchen."

"Are you yelling at me?" he asked.

"No. I'm just telling you that I think it's time we finally admit we are no longer a four person operation. We need more help."

"Maybe you just need to rescue a few more people."

She laughed. "You're a brat."

"That's where your best employees come from. Am I right?"

He was right. Sort of. And that made Polly a little crazy. If Henry wasn't giving her trouble about rescuing the whole world, Jeff was."

"It's time to look," she said. "Would you put together some job postings?"

"I hate interviewing."

"So do I. Do you remember your interview? I stunk at it and you hired yourself."

He grinned. "I learned that closing line from a friend of mine and to be honest, I couldn't believe it worked. But I also knew that I wanted this job. As much as I might want to tell you that we're getting too many businesses..."

"It's only three and maybe four," she interrupted.

"Anyway, it's the best fun I'm ever going to have in my life, so you do what 'cha gotta do and I'll find people to support you."

"You really will?"

"I'll get on it right away. But don't forget you have to talk to Sarah."

"It might take a day or two, but I'll make sure she's comfortable with whatever happens."

~~~

Polly pulled in beside Henry's truck and jumped out. He was standing with Sal and Sylvie just inside the glass front door. Sylvie pushed it open when Polly approached.

"So what do you all think?" she asked as she walked in. Then she stopped talking and looked. The place was a complete mess. Dressmaker's dummies were scattered around, some on their sides, others still standing erect. It looked creepy. Boxes and bins littered the floor. A pile of filthy old furniture was shoved up against the interior wall and counters and cabinets were piled against a back wall.

"Wow. Did you know about this mess?" she asked Sal.

"Of course. I've been in here a few times. We just need to bring in a dumpster and empty the place."

"We? That includes you?" Polly asked. "Wouldn't that mar your latest manicure?"

"Don't be smart," Sal scolded. "Of course not me. But your husband says it's no big deal."

"Now Polly. You need to look beyond the mess and see the entire space. Just like you did when you began creating Beryl's art studio or the apartment at Sycamore House." Henry took her arm. "Look at the windows and the walls."

"Is that the wall that separates this from the back room?" she asked. "Is that where the bakery could go?"

"It's not a load bearing wall, so it can be moved anywhere. We
~~~

just need to leave these beams in place." Henry knocked on a steel beam that went from floor to ceiling."

"Can you wrap those with wood?"

"We can do anything."

Polly spun around. "What kind of style are you thinking about, Sal?"

"Hell, I don't know. I just want coffee. You tell me what I want."

"I think it should be comfortable and cozy. Use reclaimed wood and stain it really dark. Hang lamps from the ceiling and sconces from the walls. None of that fluorescent stuff." She pushed some fabric out of the way with her feet and bent over to look at the floor. "What kind of shape is this in, Henry?"

"I haven't had a chance to really look at it yet, but most of the floors in town were laid by the same people and they're generally in really good shape."

"So we clean the floors. Those could be beautiful." Polly paced off a section. "Here would be a dark wood bar - like a dark walnut. Henry's dad could so make this. It would be gorgeous. Put comfortable wooden chairs in front of it. Then, the tables and chairs on the main floor would all be different. We could hit thrift stores and find tons of those things. Different shapes and textures. But I'm sitting in every single chair. I hate uncomfortable chairs at a coffee shop. And bookshelves. Lots of bookshelves. Because books warm the room."

Sal and Sylvie stood back and watched her dream out loud.

"And you need to talk to Jerry about re-wiring this place," Polly said, gesturing at the walls.

"We'd have to do that anyway. Nothing in here is up to code," Henry said.

"Smart wiring. And there should be outlets all along the wall and maybe bring some into the middle of the room somehow. Can you put them in the floor?" she asked Henry.

"Running lines under an existing floor won't be easy."

"If people needed to plug in, they could take a table along the wall. But there need to be tons of outlets. No one should have to worry about whether they have access."

"And you could have coffee pots on a big round table here in the middle of the room. Customers could buy their cup at the counter and for just plain coffee, they can get free refills. Any of the special stuff, that's done by the barista. And tea out here, too. This could really work. You could have specialty coffees and teas every day along with familiar brews."

She looked at the three of them. "Whatever! I'm just saying things out loud. Step in if you want something else."

"It sounds great to me," Sal said. "Do you want to see where the bakery will be?"

"Yes. Have you seen it yet, Sylvie?"

"Not yet."

Polly walked past the area where she'd paced out the bar. "There would be racks of bread right here. Rolls and baguettes. It will smell so awesome. And a glass counter here for pastries and cakes. And we should construct a booth here for you, Sylvie, so you can talk to people who want to place big orders. Tall backs so your conversations don't bother anyone else. We'll install a tablet in the table and network it with your computer. You can be completely high-tech about it all. This would make a really fun office for you."

Sylvie nodded at her, obviously having no clue what Polly was babbling about. She whispered loudly to Sal, "All I'm hearing is bake, bake, high techy-techy." The two laughed while Polly walked through an opening into a large space.

"We need bathrooms," Polly said. "Don't forget the bathrooms."

"Do you want an open window to the bakery?" she asked Sylvie. "Because how cool would that be? Customers could watch bread come out of the ovens and see you decorating cakes."

"You're kidding, right?"

"No. I'm not kidding. It would be awesome."

"I don't want them watching me. That would be really intimidating."

Polly was confused. "But people can stand at the counter at Sycamore House and watch you cook."

"We'll talk about this later. If you can give me a good reason why I should show all of Bellingwood how much flour and sugar I pour down my front, maybe I'll let you talk me into that."

"Have you looked online at ovens and mixers and refrigerators and coolers?" Polly asked.

"Not yet," Sylvie gave a little laugh. "We only started talking about this last night. Just because you're making plans doesn't mean I have everything put in place four hours later."

Polly rolled her eyes.

"Are you really going to do the bakery?" Sal asked. "I thought last night we were talking about it happening in the future... maybe. That Sylvie would bake things at Sycamore House until we got bigger."

"If this is going to happen, why shouldn't the whole thing happen at once?"

"Because it's a big investment."

"We'd take on the bakery investment and rent this space from you."

Sal nodded and then shook her head. "That's crazy."

"That's kind of what Jeff said. But I think it can work. If anyone can make it happen, it's Sylvie."

Sylvie took Sal's arm and dramatically wobbled back and forth. "I'm feeling pressure here."

"She's frightening when she starts dreaming, isn't she."

Polly waved them off and wandered back into the front room. "What's this door here?" she asked.

"That leads up to the apartments," Sal said. "Do you want to see them?"

"Do you want me to fix them up?" It was almost as if Polly were daring her to respond.

"Yes? No?" Sal turned to Henry in desperation. "Do I want her to see them?"

"Why don't we focus on this level," he said. "We'll clear out the junk and look at the floor, then take measurements and think about where you want walls. I'll bring Jerry in to look at the electricity and we need to find out where water comes in to the building. There is plenty of foundational work ahead of us before we let Polly loose. But now that she's seen the place, her mind won't turn off until she's created the perfect coffee shop and bakery. Isn't that right, honey?"

"What?" Polly asked. She looked over her shoulder at them.

"What are you thinking about?"

"A little stage."

"A stage?"

"For performers. You know, singer-songwriters, poets, jazz combos."

"Like I told you," Henry said. "Her brain isn't going to leave this alone for a long time now. We've created a monster."

Sal looked over at Polly, "Do you really think this could work?"

"Why not? Once we get it in place, the only thing you have to do is keep the quality high, the place clean and prices reasonable. As long as your customers can count on you being consistent, they'll keep coming back and they'll tell their friends."

"And you think Bellingwood can handle it?"

"I don't know what the population numbers are doing right now, but Bellingwood isn't a back water community, going stale and lifeless. Things are happening here. The boys at the winery are doing well and Sycamore Inn is getting busier. You aren't the only person who is buying empty space. That new boutique that opened up next to the general store is bringing in customers and the screen printing shop by the bank is opening sometime next month."

"They're talking about repaving Washington Street this summer," Henry said, walking across the floor. "The downtown is going to look really nice. Now's the time to start."

"No time like the present, then," Sal said. "You must think I'm the most foolish person you've ever met."

"Why's that?" Polly asked.

"All I wanted was a place to serve me some really good coffee. No one else was going to build it, so I had to."

"Jeff and I talked about it last year and we just couldn't make a decision. We weren't ready to expand beyond Sycamore House, so buying a building downtown didn't make sense. But we also knew that we weren't a good location for a coffee shop. There's no drop-in traffic over there."

"Did I steal your idea?" Sal asked her. "Because I can back off. I haven't signed the papers yet."

"No, I love that someone else is doing it. That lets me off the hook."

"Except for the bakery," Henry said, nodding at Sylvie.

"That's going to be the most amazing part." Polly rubbed her hands together. "Sylvie are you ready to do this? You're going to have to start training more people, you know."

Sylvie gave a little shudder. "This is so much more than I'd ever expected when I told you I was going back to college. I'm in charge and it scares the life out of me."

"Are you going to train my baristas and manage the coffee shop too?" Sal asked with a grin.

"Not on your crazy, coffee-loving life. That's all on you."

Sal turned to Polly. "Will you do it?"

"Nope. You're going to have to get involved."

"I'm spending money. Isn't that enough?" This time she turned to Henry for support.

He backed away. "Don't look at me. I'll take your money, but I'm not getting involved with the business of this place."

"Fine then. I'm going to go flirt with your manager."

"Jeff? Good luck with that."

"He loves me."

"Like I said. Good luck with that."

CHAPTER FIVE

Not wanting the kids to walk home in the bitter cold, Polly drove to the school. She watched for them to come out and as Rebecca pulled her scarf around her head, Andrew looked up and saw Polly's truck. They were with a girl whom Polly had seen a few times before. That had to be Rebecca's friend, Kayla. She followed her friends to Polly's truck and Andrew jumped in the front seat.

"I called shotgun," he said. "Don't make me sit in back with the girls, okay?"

The two girls clambered into the back seat and Polly waited for them to all belt in. "Are we ready?" she asked.

"Thanks for getting us, Polly," Rebecca said. "This is Kayla."

Polly turned in her seat and put her hand out. The girl took it in her left hand and looked at Polly in confusion. "Hi," she said.

"I'm glad to meet you, Kayla. How was school today?"

Kayla simply said, "Fine."

Andrew, on the other hand, was wound up. "It was fine, except for that stupid Perry. He got us all in trouble again. Mrs. Hastings told him four times to sit down and quit playing, but he wouldn't. Then he got some of the other boys all riled up and when we went out of the room for lunch, he started a fight."

"Were you in the fight?" Polly asked.

"No!" Andrew was shocked at her question. "But Mrs. Hastings said we were all talking too much today and he really made her mad, so we had to write letters to the principal telling her that we were sorry for misbehaving in the hallway and making too much noise."

"You had to write a letter?" That didn't sound like horrible punishment to Polly, but maybe the kids saw it differently.

"That's the time when I get to read my book," Andrew complained.

"And I get to draw," Rebecca chimed in. "If we get our work done, we get fifteen minutes to do whatever we want at our desk as long as we're quiet."

"I see. And you had your work done?"

"The stuff that we were supposed to hand in today."

"Do you have homework tonight?"

Andrew's sigh was loud and dramatic. "So much! She must have been really mad. We have math and social studies and science and then we're supposed to write a poem."

"That's all due tomorrow?" Polly asked.

Rebecca swatted her hand at Andrew. "No, it's not all due tomorrow. The math is due tomorrow and so is the poem."

"It's a lot of homework," he said. And just like that, his focus shifted. "Is Han there today?"

Polly took a breath so that she could shift with him. "No, he's with Henry. Would you two like to introduce Kayla to Obiwan, though, and take him on a quick walk? He's going to need it."

Andrew nodded at Polly and then turned to say to Kayla, "Han is the brother to my dog. Her name is Padme. You know, from Star Wars? Do you know Star Wars?"

She shook her head.

"You haven't ever seen Star Wars? I've watched it a thousand times!" he said. "Polly, can we watch Star Wars?"

"You know the deal. Homework and then play."

"But we have so much homework! We'll never get to play."

She scowled at him and he sat back in his seat. "Here's the deal," Polly said. "I'll make brownies while you work at the table on your homework. We'll see who finishes first."

"But we have so much," Andrew whined.

"Really? You're whining?"

He grimaced and slumped lower in his seat, then sat up again. "Can we take Kayla down to see the animals?"

Polly's laughter rang through the cab of the truck. "Andrew Donovan, you're wonderful. You'll try anything, won't you? Homework first, then you can decide whether you want to watch Star Wars or go down to the barn."

"Okay," he said sheepishly as Polly pulled into the garage.

"Take your books upstairs and bring Obiwan back down," she said. "Don't stay out too long with him. It's cold."

She waited at the door while the three kids got out of the truck with their backpacks. As they passed in front of her, she put her hand on Kayla's shoulder. The girl flinched at Polly's touch and ducked enough to avoid it. She kept her eyes focused on Rebecca's back and followed her up the steps into the apartment.

Polly grabbed Andrew before he could go up with them.

"What? I'm sorry. I was just excited," he said.

"No, that's not it. You're fine. Do you know Kayla very well?"

He shrugged. "I suppose."

"Does she have very many friends?"

"No. She isn't popular. They call her Trayla Kayla because she lives in the trailer park. They call her other things too but those are really mean."

"Have you ever met her family?"

"She doesn't have parents. She only has a sister. The kids say mean things to her about that, too."

"Okay, thanks. And thanks for being nice to her."

"She's just another kid like me."

"There is no other kid like you," Polly said and pulled him into a hug. "I think you're wonderful."

Andrew grunted and waited limply for her to release him.

"You don't like hugs much, do you?"

"You do it a lot," he said matter-of-factly and headed for the doorway to her apartment.

"I guess I do," Polly retorted and went into the kitchen.

"Thanks for picking up the kids," Sylvie said.

"Rebecca brought a friend home - a Kayla Armstrong. Do you know her?"

Sylvie thought for a moment and said, "I've seen her. She's a little chubby and lives with her older sister?"

"Yeah. I just tried to touch her and she flinched. Do you think there's a problem?"

Sylvie took Polly's hand and led her back to the table. "No, it isn't with the sister. Rumor has it they escaped from an abusive home, that when the sister turned eighteen, she took Kayla and ran because the dad was starting to... you know."

"But the flinching? I'm a woman."

"I heard that he beat them all up too."

"Where do you hear this stuff?" Polly asked. "Do the parents live near here?"

"No," Sylvie's spoke quietly and Polly had to lean in to hear her. "Who knows how much of it is true, but you know how kids talk and sometimes things get out from teachers and other parents."

"It seems to me like those are the people who'd want to keep her safe and not gossip."

"I know. Half of what I told you might not be true."

"Poor thing. Well, it looks as if I've trained Rebecca in the rescue and keeping of people. She's the one who asked to bring Kayla home." Polly saw the three kids running and romping with Obiwan through the back window. "Since they closed the library on Mondays, Joss and I thought about opening the classroom and computer room here for kids to do their homework."

"Who's going to watch them?" Sylvie asked.

"We haven't gotten that far. What do you think, though? Would you consider making snacks if we start this?"

"I'm going to really need that bakery, aren't I?"

"Isn't it just the best idea?"

"You don't do things in a small way, do you?"

"Not if I can help it. Why wouldn't we go for it? I know that I won't have to be involved in the actual work, but if you think it's doable, then why not?"

"It's going to be hard work and early hours. I'm not sure if I'm ready to be working early mornings and then late evenings on the weekends."

"Then you'll have to hire and train good people."

"But until we get busy, it's just going to be me."

"We'll figure it out. And speaking of baking, I told the kids I'd make brownies while they worked on their homework. What are you working on in here this afternoon?"

Sylvie gave Polly a grin and dropped her head. "I'm actually catering a dinner out at Secret Woods tonight and a breakfast meeting in the morning for them."

"What's going on?"

"It's some leadership retreat thingie. I have no idea. They're staying at the Inn. Didn't you know about it?"

"No, but that's not surprising."

"Jeff's been in and out all day. They checked in last night, had breakfast at the Diner this morning and Davey's catered lunch. I'm doing dinner and breakfast tomorrow."

"Do you need anything from me?"

"Nope, it's not a large group, so Rachel and I have it."

"You're amazing," Polly said. "How late do you need Andrew to stay here?"

"Eliseo said he'd take the boys home after Jason's done. They're old enough to be on their own now. At least that's what I've been told by my eldest over and over."

"Okay, well let me know." Polly went up the steps to her apartment and found the three kids sitting at the table in the dining room. Rebecca and Kayla each had a glass of water beside them and Andrew had poured himself a glass of milk.

"Is it okay we got something to drink?" he asked.

"Of course it is. Thanks for asking, though. Do you need anything else?"

"Just those brownies," he said. "Any time now."

Polly ruffled his hair as she walked past the table. "You'll notice that these two are very comfortable here, Kayla. If there's anything you need - anything at all, be sure to speak up."

She nodded and went back to the work in front of her, whispering to Rebecca about one of the problems.

"It's okay," Rebecca said quietly. "Polly doesn't care if we talk about our work together. Sometimes she even helps us if we have trouble. Don't you."

"If I can figure it out, I do." Polly pulled out the cocoa and other ingredients. "Do you all like nuts in your brownies?"

"I'm allergic," Kayla said.

"Then brownies with no nuts. Smooth brownies, we'll call them. How about frosting?"

"I love frosting." This brought the first smile Polly had seen to Kayla's face.

"Smooth brownies with chocolate chips and chocolate frosting. How about that?"

"They won't be smooth," Andrew said.

"Smart-aleck. So, chunky brownies with chocolate chips and chocolate frosting."

The kids were still working through math problems when Polly put the brownies into the oven. She cleaned up the kitchen and opened the refrigerator door to look for supper ideas. There was some left over pork loin in a container, but not enough for a whole meal. She opened the freezer. There was nothing in there that could be defrosted in time for dinner.

She texted Henry. *"I'm a failure as a mom and have no idea what to cook for supper."*

"We need to buy a crock pot and try to plan better in the mornings."

"You know I'll never remember to do that."

"I might."

"Uh huh. I'm tired of pizza and sandwiches. What if we take the girls to Davey's tonight?"

"That's always fine with me. I'll be home about five thirty or six. Okay?"

"Great."

Polly leaned over the peninsula and asked, "What time will your sister be here to pick you up tonight, Kayla?"

"She gets off work at five thirty on Mondays. Is that okay?"

"You bet. I was just checking. How are you guys doing?"

"I'm working on my poem," Andrew announced.

"You finished your math?"

"Yeah. It was no big deal."

How about you girls?" Polly asked. She walked around the peninsula to stand between the two girls and put her hand on Rebecca's shoulder, carefully avoiding Kayla. Bending over to see what they were working on, she said, "You're almost done, too. Right?"

"We only have to do the even numbered problems."

"Do you ever do the odd numbered ones too?"

That stumped Kayla. "Why would we do that?" she asked.

"For practice. To make sure you know what you're doing."

"No," Rebecca announced and firmly set her pencil down on top of her paper. "I'm done. I don't want to do any more."

"Are they right?" Polly asked.

"Isn't that why the teacher grades them, to see if they're right?" Kayla asked.

"Rebecca?" Polly asked again.

"Polly says we're supposed to do our very best and sometimes she makes me redo problems if I mess them up."

"Why?"

"Because I'm learning, I guess." Rebecca didn't sound too confident of her reason.

"Because learning is more than just getting a grade," Polly said. "Learning is about the whole process. Let me see your sheet, Rebecca. Yours too, Andrew."

Both kids handed her their work. As far as Polly could tell, Rebecca's was pretty much right. She put Andrew's back in front of him and pointed at number six. "Are you sure about that answer? Check your subtraction."

He peered at his answer and then looked up at Polly. "Thank

you. I'd have gotten it wrong."

Kayla's eyes bounced back and forth between the two kids and then she timidly held her paper up. "What about mine?"

Two of her answers had errors in the calculations and Polly put the sheet back down in front of her. "You need to look at your answers for number two and number ten. The others look good." The timer on the oven rang and Polly said, "Rebecca, do you want to get the brownies or help Kayla with her work?"

"I'll get the brownies."

"Hot pads. Don't forget the hot pads."

Rebecca slipped out of her seat and Polly took it and sat down. She leaned back and grabbed a notepad from the corner of the counter behind her.

"Let's work through these numbers and see if you come up with a better answer," Polly said. She turned back around. "Just put that on the cooling rack for a few minutes. I'll cut it."

"Okay," Rebecca said.

Kayla had taken the notepad and was reworking problem number two. Polly saw her eyes light up and she worked through it to the right answer.

"Good," Polly said. "Now try number ten again, using the information you just learned."

"That was easy," Kayla said when she finished the second problem.

"Sometimes you just have to slow down and think it all through. We have plenty of time, so why don't you three take a break. Andrew, do you want to put Star Wars in and I'll bring brownies over? You can watch it for half an hour and then come back and write your poems."

He ran across the room to queue up the movie and dropped into the chair beside the sofa. Obiwan jumped up to join him.

"Come on," he called as familiar music played into the room. "This is the best movie!"

Kayla followed Rebecca and the two girls curled up on the couch. Rebecca took a blanket off the back and threw it over their laps.

"Hit play," she said. "We're ready."

Polly cut brownies and poured milk, then took the treats into the living room and waited until the opening scroll had finished before passing them out.

"This is in space?" Kayla asked.

"Yes, it's awesome!" Andrew declared. "Just watch."

"It's my favorite movie in the world," Polly whispered. "I make him watch it all the time."

"It's my favorite too," he agreed. "But there are six of them and they're all good."

Polly rolled her eyes. Thank goodness he was young enough to appreciate the movies, no matter what. She had decided that complaining about Jar Jar Binks was not necessary around the kids. They didn't know they were supposed to hate the character.

"You should see her office," Rebecca said. "She has Star Wars everywhere."

Kayla nodded, caught up in the plot. When the image of Leia was projected from R2D2 and said, "Help me, Obi-Wan Kenobi. You're my only hope," Kayla's eyes jumped to the dog. The image repeated the phrase and Kayla pointed to the dog.

"Polly is Star Wars crazy," Andrew said. "Keep watching. This is a good part." He directed her eyes back to the screen.

Polly interrupted them after the half hour was up and though there was moaning and complaining, she insisted, and they settled back in to work on their poems. She went into the living room while they worked and opened her laptop. There were so many things spinning in her mind that she wanted to get them into her notes program while they were still fresh.

Ideas about the new bakery and the possibility of an afterschool kids club at Sycamore House gave her lots to think about. The most frustrating thing was the fact that she didn't have enough employees to make it all happen easily.

Jeff would tell her that was the least of her problems. She didn't have any business for the bakery and she was already trying to hire more employees. Heck, she didn't even have a finished building. It wouldn't come together for months. But it was so exciting to think about starting a new project, she could hardly contain herself.

"I'm done," Andrew said, coming out to the living room. "Can I turn the movie back on?"

"What do you think?" she asked.

"Not until everybody is done," he grumped.

"Exactly. Get your book out and read quietly or something."

"I just wanted her to see the whole thing before we have to go home tonight."

"The movie will be here the next time Kayla comes over and I'm sure you'll remember where you left off."

"Okay. Can I go down to my desk?"

"Why do you want to do that?"

"I dunno. Just something to do."

"Where's the book you're going to read?"

"In my backpack."

"The girls won't be that much longer. Why don't you bring your book out here and read with me. You and Obiwan can have the other couch."

"Fine." Andrew slopped his feet across the floor back to the dining room and then came back, dragging the backpack behind him.

"If you scratch the floor because you're being a poop, I'm siccing Henry on you," she said.

He picked the pack up and carried it to the sofa and sat down.

"What's up with you, anyway?" Polly asked.

"Nothing."

"Nothing really? Or nothing you don't want to tell me about it."

"Nothing."

"That's helpful."

He whispered at Polly, "Is she coming here every day?"

That was it! He was jealous of Rebecca's time. Polly wondered if he noticed the crush Rebecca had on his older brother. That would just kill him.

"Who knows how often she'll come here, but wouldn't you rather she had a safe place to go after school than wander around town by herself?"

"I guess. But ... oh nothing."

"I get it, Andrew. But trust me. More friends are more interesting than just one friend. You might find that you really like her."

"I like her fine. She's just a girl, but she doesn't know all the stuff that Rebecca and I do here."

"Then you'll have to teach her."

A knock at the front door of the apartment startled both of them.

"I got it," Andrew said and ran to open the door. Rachel was standing there with a slip of paper in her hand.

"What's up, Rachel?" Polly asked. "Come on in."

"You're supposed to call Kayla's sister at the convenience store. She didn't know how else to get in contact with you." She walked over to hand Polly the piece of paper. "That's her cell phone."

"Did she say anything?"

"No, she just wanted you to call her. She said it was important."

"Okay, thanks for bringing this up to me. When are you heading over to the winery?"

Rachel smiled. "In an hour. I can't wait. I haven't seen the whole place yet. Billy said we could go some Thursday night during the summer. They're going to have musicians and wine tastings and stuff."

"That will be fun. Okay, thanks for this. I'd better find out what she wants."

Polly took out her phone as Rachel pulled the door shut behind her. After dialing the number, she waited for someone to answer.

"It's Stephanie," the girl said.

"Hi, Stephanie, this is Polly Giller over at Sycamore House. You called?"

"Yeah. I'm so, so sorry, but I have to work another shift tonight and I don't know what to do with Kayla. Maybe she could just walk over here and stay while I work?"

"She can stay with us and you can pick her up when you're done. What time will that be?"

"Not until eleven thirty."

"She won't get home until eleven thirty?"

"I know. It's bad, but there isn't anyone else to work here. I have to stay."

"I get that, but wow. Eleven thirty?"

"I don't know what else to do. I'm sorry."

Polly bit her lower lip, trying to think through the evening. They could take Kayla to dinner with them. Maybe she should just offer to let the girl spend the night. At least she would get to sleep at a reasonable hour.

"Would you mind if I ran over to meet you?" Polly asked.

"Sure. But why?"

"Because I'm going to see if you want to let Kayla spend the night with us and I'll take her to school with Rebecca in the morning. But I want you to meet me first."

"I know your husband. He always comes in for ice cream sandwiches."

"Yes. I guess he does. But I'd like to put a face to your name. What do you say to her spending the night so she can get to bed at a normal hour?"

"Sometimes she doesn't go to bed until ten thirty or eleven. Tonight wouldn't be too late."

"I see."

"That's bad, isn't it?"

"No. Don't say that. I'm not trying to give you trouble. Let me come meet you. I'm serious about her spending the night, though. You can pick her up after school tomorrow."

"I have to work until five thirty. She usually goes to the library until I'm done. I've never gone a whole day without seeing her."

Polly took a breath. "Then I'll bring her and Rebecca with me right now. But if she's staying here until after eleven thirty, I can guarantee she'll be asleep. I'll probably be asleep."

"Okay. Come on over. I'm really sorry about this."

"You don't need to apologize. It's okay. We'll work it out. I want to make it easy for you and if you're really uncomfortable with her spending the night here after you meet me, we'll figure out how to fix it for you."

"Thanks. I have a customer." Stephanie Armstrong clicked off and Polly walked into the dining room.

"How are you girls doing on your poems?" she asked.

"We're close," Rebecca said.

"It's time for another break. Put your shoes and coats on. We're going to run over to the convenience store to meet Kayla's sister. She has to work a late shift tonight and Kayla's going to hang out with us for a little longer."

"Yeah!" Rebecca yelled and jumped up. "You'll get to meet Henry and Jessie and see their other dog, Han. And I'll take you down to meet my mom."

Rebecca usually spent a couple of hours in the evenings with her mother. The amount of time was perfect for both of them. She came back upstairs to get ready for bed before her mother completely ran out of energy and before Rebecca had to watch Evelyn Morrow help Sarah through her own evening preparations. Sarah did her best to rest up for the weekends when Rebecca was able to spend a great deal of time in her room. They'd found games they could play together and sometimes Sarah just watched as Rebecca drew all she could see from the large windows in the room.

"You girls get ready to go. Andrew, do you want to come, too?"

"No, that's fine. I'll stay here and read."

"Are you sure?"

"Yeah. Whatever."

"Boys," Kayla said with feigned disgust.

"Boys," Rebecca huffed.

CHAPTER SIX

Stephanie Armstrong was a nice enough girl. She seemed too young to have the stress of raising a younger sister, but the two interacted well. Kayla hugged Stephanie when she got to the convenience store and after hellos, they were discussing Kayla's day and her homework. Star Wars took a few more moments and then Stephanie asked Kayla to show Rebecca the puzzle magazines.

When the girls were out of earshot, Polly smiled at the young woman and asked about Kayla spending the night again.

"Don't feel like I'm insisting," Polly said. "You just tell me what you'd like to do and I'll help you out."

"I know that I'm keeping you all up late, too," Stephanie replied. "That's not fair. I've never had to do two shifts in a row. Usually I get some time to take her home and make dinner before I have to come back to work, but Brian is out of town and he couldn't cover for me."

"I get it. It's hard to make things work when you're alone. My best friend has two boys and I know how hard it's been for her, trying to go to school and work. Luckily her sons get to hang out at Sycamore House."

Stephanie screwed her lips up and twisted them as she tried to make a decision. "She doesn't have any clothes for tomorrow."

"That's right," Polly agreed. She needed to let the girl figure this out for herself.

"But she does have a key to the house..."

"We could take her there after dinner."

"It's going to be so weird to be alone. We've never been apart at night."

"Stephanie, please. If you want to come get her when you're off work, that will be fine."

"She really likes Rebecca. It could be like a slumber party. She's never done that before."

"Rebecca likes her too and I'm glad they're friends. Rebecca has needed a good friend."

"Really?"

"That's a story I'll tell you some other day. But trust me when I say that they're good for each other. Mrs. Hastings did a great thing when she put them together."

Stephanie nodded. "She's been a good teacher for Kayla. I wasn't sure how my sister would adjust to a new school. It's been a rough year for her."

"I know you don't know me very well, but I really only want to make this as easy as I can for you."

"Everybody in town talks about you. I can't believe I've never met you before. Your husband comes in all the time."

"Tell me he doesn't explain why he's buying all those ice cream bars."

"He just said they're your favorite."

"Yeah. And he buys them for me when I'm stressed out or upset. He's a smart, smart man."

"Well, we stock more since you two got together," Stephanie said with a grin. "At least that's what Brian said."

Polly laughed out loud. "Great. We're changing the economy of the convenience store."

"Yeah. Just don't stop eating them. You'll kill us."

"Not any time soon. Don't tell Henry, though. I quit buying them at the grocery store so he can pick them up whenever he wants to do something nice for me."

"That's funny," she said with a slight smile.

"Just don't say anything. I don't want him to know I'm on to him."

"Okay," Stephanie said.

"Great. He's one of my favorite guys in the world."

"Okay. She can stay with you tonight."

The transition was abrupt, but Polly accepted it. "Do you want me to bring her to you in the morning before school? Is it going to be hard on you two if you don't see each other until later?"

"No, that's okay." She gave a laugh. "I wouldn't hate sleeping in one time, but don't tell her I said that. I never want her to think that she's a problem for me."

"Got it. We'll keep each other's secrets."

"Kayla?" Stephanie called out. They waited until the two girls joined them at the counter.

"Yah what?" Kayla asked.

"What do you think about spending the night with Rebecca since I have to work so late? You could go home and get clothes and your toothbrush and stuff. They'll take you to school and I'll see you after I get off work."

Rebecca was practically vibrating with glee. She waited to see what Kayla's reaction would be before she got too excited. When her friend looked at her with big eyes, the two girls jumped up together and then did a quick high five.

"Awesome!" Rebecca said.

"Give me a hug," Stephanie said and reached out for Kayla who ran into her arms. "And promise to be good."

"I will. I promise. Thank you."

"I love you and I'll see you tomorrow. Okay?"

~~~

It had only taken a minimum of chaotic organizing to get
~~~

everyone ready to go to dinner. By the time Henry and Jessie arrived, homework was completed and the kids were settled in on the sofa watching the end of Star Wars. Jason came up to get Andrew before the movie was over, causing no small amount of consternation for the boy, but knowing Eliseo was waiting, he got his things together and left with his brother.

A flurry of activity occurred as everyone got ready to go. Polly took the dogs out for a quick walk in the back yard. Han was learning to negotiate the stairs, but since she was in a hurry, she picked him up and called for Obiwan to follow.

The hostess at Davey's smiled when they all walked in. She counted heads and said, "Table for five?"

Polly nodded. She automatically reached out to put her hands on Kayla and Rebecca's shoulders in order to move them forward ahead of her, but drew back, remembering Kayla's initial response. "Go ahead girls, follow Mariah." She nodded to Jessie to go ahead and then took Henry's hand.

"There are a lot of females at this table tonight," he said.

"You're good for us all," Polly said. The restaurant was busy and Mariah led them to a large room in the back. Polly waved at Lydia Merritt, trying to catch her friend's attention, but Lydia was staring at her salad, unaware of the activity around her. However, the only large table available was right next to Lydia and Aaron.

Polly slipped in beside them and said, "Looks like you've got company tonight."

Both Lydia and Aaron glanced up from their plates in surprise. Lydia jumped up and hugged Polly. "I wish we'd have known you were coming. You could have joined us."

"We practically are," Polly said.

Aaron had stood with her and shook Henry's hand, then took Polly's. "How are you this evening?" he asked stiffly.

"I'm good. How are things with the case? Rumor has it that you know the man who was killed." Polly sat down and continued. "Why didn't you say something to me? There I was acting all girly and scared and it was someone you knew."

"You were alive and it was too late to do anything for him.

Simple priorities," he said.

Polly hadn't seen much of Aaron after he'd escorted her to the back of the caretaker's house and now that she had a chance to look at him, she was shocked at what she saw. He'd lost weight and he looked drawn and exhausted. His eyes were dark and his skin sallow. Gone was the easy laughter that came to his face. His entire demeanor had changed. She didn't know the man standing in front of her and was glad that Lydia had said something earlier so she was at least prepared.

"What's good tonight?" Henry asked. "I'm feeding a crowd."

"I'm sure the kids will find something that interests them," Aaron responded and sat back down.

Lydia took a deep breath and gave Polly a sad smile. "It's just a salad for me tonight. I don't feel much like eating. Benny's your waiter. He'll tell you the specials. I've forgotten what he said. I think there was a chicken strip meal, but I must not have paid much attention."

Polly took her hand, squeezed it, and gave Lydia another hug before the woman re-took her seat. "You two enjoy yourselves and forgive us if our table gets too loud. I think poor Henry is about to find out what it means to take four women out to dinner."

"Enjoy your evening," Aaron said, effectively dismissing her.

Henry held Polly's chair for her and sat down. He took her hand under the table and squeezed it, his eyes asking what he couldn't say out loud. She gave a slight shake of her head and turned to the table.

"Okay girls, what'll it be? Shall we get some appetizers?"

Rebecca nodded furiously and Kayla took a cue from her and asked "What do they have?"

"We like the platter. It has onion rings and fried mushrooms and cauliflower, cheese sticks and a cheesy dip with veggies. How does that sound?"

"Great," Kayla said.

"Jessie? Anything else?"

"No, that's wonderful."

Kayla and Rebecca pulled their menus down in front of them

and chattered about the various offerings.

"Should we order off the kids menu?" Rebecca asked.

"Do you see something there you'd like to have?"

"I want chicken strips, if that's okay," Kayla said. "I can share with Rebecca if it's too much."

"Oh no," Rebecca assured her friend. "Polly and Henry will let you order your own meal, won't you, Polly?"

"You bet. If we have that big appetizer platter, maybe I should order off the kid's menu, too."

Polly tried to ignore the uncomfortable silence that had settled between them and the Merritts. It was completely unnatural. Any other time they would have all been laughing and telling stories, mostly to entertain Jessie, Rebecca and Kayla, but tonight Polly and Henry both felt the deathly quiet behind them.

Fortunately, the rest of the table had no idea that things weren't normal. Jessie's baby was wide awake, turning and kicking, so she let Rebecca and Kayla touch her belly. Kayla was in awe and for quite some time, kept watching Jessie, hoping for more movement.

Before they'd gotten through with their appetizers, Lydia placed her hand on Polly's shoulder, bent over and gave her a quick hug.

"It was good to see you tonight," she said. "I hope you have fun with the rest of your evening." She smiled across the table. "It was nice to see you again, Jessie. Be sure to let me know if you need anything."

Jessie nodded and smiled as Lydia left with her husband.

~~~

"It's that one," Kayla said, leaning forward to point out the front window.

Henry pulled into the driveway of an older model trailer.

"Do you need any help?" Polly asked her, turning the overhead light on in the cab.

"No, I can do it. I just need pajamas and a shirt for tomorrow."
~~~

"Don't forget fresh undies and socks," Polly said.

"I would have forgot that."

"And your toothbrush and hairbrush."

"Yeah. Okay."

"And do you have your own shampoo?"

"No, I use Steph's."

"Then you can use Rebecca's. Do you need your own pillow or anything?"

"I don't think so." Kayla sat back. "Maybe you should come in and make sure I don't forget anything. I've never done this before."

"Can I come too?" Rebecca asked.

Kayla was startled by the question and Polly understood right away. "Why don't you and Jessie keep Henry company. We won't be very long. I promise."

The porch light wasn't turned on, so Kayla fumbled with the lock. Once inside, Polly wasn't surprised to see a very spare living room. They had an old sofa with worn spots that someone had attempted to cover with blankets. Two plastic TV trays sat in front of the couch and an old television sat on a rickety stand.

The carpet was vacuumed and things were clean and neat, but the walls were dingy and the curtains hanging in the windows were thin.

Kayla went into the kitchen and dug under the sink before coming up with a plastic grocery bag.

"My room's back here," she said.

Polly followed her and glanced into what had to be Stephanie's room. It contained just a bed with a few knitted blankets piled on top for warmth and crates stacked neatly that held her clothing. A lamp and clock rounded out her possessions.

Kayla's room was just as spare. The blankets were bright and cheery and they'd found a set of sheets that were decorated with clouds and flowers. More crates stacked on their sides held the girl's possessions, from clothing and shoes to books, dolls and a few games and puzzles. A lamp sat on a card table in the corner and two chairs were pushed in neatly.

"I didn't want Rebecca to see my room. Hers is pretty. She has so many nice things," Kayla said as she sat down on her bed.

"Oh honey, Rebecca wouldn't mind. You should tell her about your room. I suspect she understands more than you realize."

"Since you're an adult, you have to be nice. My friends aren't very nice when they know how poor I am. But Steph does the best she can and I think she's amazing."

"She is amazing and you two have done very well here." Polly picked up a teddy bear from Kayla's pillow. "Who's this?"

"That's Silver," she said.

"Interesting name."

"She listens to me when I'm upset. Steph told me to tell her everything, even things that I don't want anyone else to know."

"Do you talk to Silver every night?"

"You think it's weird, don't you?" Kayla was trying to decide between a couple of shirts she'd pulled out.

"No. I was being serious. I think it's a great idea." Polly shrugged her right shoulder. "I tell my cats and dogs much more than I tell any of the people around me. Even my husband. When I'm mad at him, they get to hear about it first."

"I'll take this one." She chose a pair of pajamas, then put a blue checked shirt into the bottom of the plastic bag, and pulled out a pair of socks and underwear. "Anything else?"

"You're good with the pants you're wearing?"

"Yeah. Sometimes I wear them a couple of days before we do laundry."

"That's cool. Now, what do you need to take from the bathroom?"

"I'll be right back. My toothbrush and hairbrush, right?"

"That should just about do it."

Kayla ran out of the room and in a flash, was back with the necessary items. She put them in the bag on top of her clothes and grabbed the handles. "I'm ready."

"Do you want to take Silver tonight? It would be okay."

"Can I?"

"Sure. I'll drop Silver and your bag of clothes at Stephanie's work before she picks you up at the library tomorrow."

"I had fun today. Thank you for letting me come over."

"Honey, you can visit any time. Work it out with Stephanie and Rebecca and you're always welcome."

Kayla hesitated as she stepped forward and then stopped. "Thank you."

"Can I hug you?" Polly asked.

The girl rushed in to Polly's open arms, hugged her tight, then held on for a few extra moments."

"Shall we?" Polly gestured to the door when Kayla stepped back. She let the girl walk through and flipped the light off in the room, then followed her to the front of the trailer.

"I want to turn the outside light on for Steph," Kayla said. "I always do that when she comes home late and it's dark."

"That sounds like a good idea. Which one?"

Kayla flipped the living room light off and the outside light on and they pulled the door shut behind them. Polly waited for Kayla to climb up into the back seat, stepped up on the running board and into her own seat.

"Who's that?" Jessie asked, pointing at the teddy bear.

"That's Silver."

"I think Silver should meet my Durango."

"You have a teddy bear?"

"No, Durango is a purple horse. But he sleeps with me every night."

"Really?"

"Oh yeah. I'd be lost without him."

When they got back to Sycamore House, Rebecca took Kayla upstairs to drop her things off and then they ran down to spend time with Sarah.

"I'm totally worn out. I just want to get into sweats and die," Jessie said, once she'd puffed her way up the steps.

"You get comfortable," Polly said. "Henry and I will take care of the animals. If you need anything, just holler."

Polly sat at the top of the steps snuggling with the cats while Henry took the leftovers to the refrigerator. Obiwan and Han had followed him, hoping they might be rewarded for simply being dogs. He came back with Han's leash.

"I don't know why I'm so tired," he said. "But this has been a long day."

Polly nodded. "That was weird at the restaurant tonight with Aaron and Lydia."

"Yeah. What's going on?"

"I have no idea." She shook her head. "But I can't imagine Lydia is going to let this go on much longer."

"Maybe it has to do with the guy who was killed the other night."

Polly wrinkled her forehead and looked back at him as they went out the back door. Henry put Han down on the ground. He tried to surge ahead to follow Obiwan, but had quickly been learning that the leash was stronger than his desire.

"Makes sense to me." Polly mused.

Obiwan had stopped to smell a clump of grass and Han ran over to help him make sure that it was safe.

"How far are you planning to go to rescue Stephanie and Kayla Armstrong?" Henry asked.

"I have no idea what you mean." Polly walked away from him and nudged Obiwan to keep moving. This conversation could only go badly for her.

"I mean... what's the next step in making their life better?"

"We do need more employees. I don't know what Stephanie can do or what she'd want to do, but surely we pay better than the convenience store and our hours are more stable."

"Uh huh."

Polly spun around to see Henry grinning at her.

"You're the one who set Jessie up to work at your business," she said. "Don't you be giving me trouble about this."

"I just tell everyone that I'm in training. You're the master."

"I'm not going to do anything right away, but if something comes up..."

"That'll take about a week, maybe two, I'm guessing."

Polly gave a low whistle and Obiwan ran to her side. "Come

with me, big dog. We're going back inside and leave the man and his little dog out here in the cold."

CHAPTER SEVEN

Polly startled awake at Han's yip. Then she heard a knock at the bedroom door.

"Polly?" Rebecca called quietly.

"Come in, honey," Polly said.

Rebecca opened the door and came in to the bedroom and walked over to Polly's side of the bed.

"What's up?"

"Kayla's upset. She had a bad dream and now she won't stop crying."

Polly's feet were already finding their way out from under the pile of animals on her bed and she put them down on the floor, then swiped open her phone to check the time. It was only eleven fifteen. The girls had gone to bed at eight thirty. She'd heard chattering and laughter until after nine, but after taking the dogs out for one last walk, she checked the room at ten thirty and they were sound asleep.

"Do you need me to do anything?" Henry asked.

"I've got this. No worries." Polly pulled her robe on and went into Rebecca's bedroom.

Kayla was curled into a ball on one side of the bed. She didn't make any noise, but it was obvious that she was upset. Polly flipped the light on and sat down beside the girl. She started to reach out and touch her, but hesitated.

"Honey? Kayla? It's me. Polly. Can you tell me what has you so upset?"

The girl gulped back a sob. "No-o-o-o." she said.

"Will you let me put my arms around you?" Polly took her silence as acquiescence and bent over to hold her. Kayla didn't relax, she held herself tightly as she cried.

"Sweetie, did you get frightened when you woke up in a strange bed?"

"Uh huh."

"Did you have a horrible dream, too?"

"Ye-e-e-es." Kayla's voice hitched as she tried to speak through her tears.

"Do you want to talk about it?"

"No-o-o-o."

"Okay then. We'll be quiet for a while until you realize that you're safe and it's all going to be okay." Polly turned to look at a very freaked out Rebecca. "Honey, would you get a small glass of water from the kitchen? And bring tissues back with you, too."

Rebecca seemed thankful to be able to leave the room.

Polly saw the teddy bear lying on the floor and scooped it up with her foot, tossing it behind them onto the bed. With one hand, she stretched to grab it and then pressed it into Kayla's hands, hoping the girl would unclench long enough to be distracted by something she recognized.

The girl clutched the bear, but didn't relax a single muscle and Polly began stroking her back. Then she realized what time it was. Stephanie was still at work.

"Kayla? Honey? Would you like me to call your sister and have her pick you up so that you can sleep in your own bed for the rest of the night?"

That got her attention. The sobbing stopped and Kayla went limp, then sat up beside Polly. "Would you?"

"Of course I would, if that's what you'd like. You don't have to stay here."

Rebecca walked in with a glass of water and tissues. Seeing that Kayla was sitting up, she came around the side of the bed and handed her friend the water first.

Kayla took a sip and said, "Thank you."

"You were scared," Rebecca said. "You had a really bad dream. Did you know you talk in your sleep? I tried to wake you up, but you wouldn't."

"What did I say?" Kayla asked.

"You kept saying 'No. You're hurting her.' That must have been a really bad dream."

The look of shock on Kayla's face startled both Rebecca and Polly. Her hand trembled and water sloshed out on to her pajamas. Polly took the glass from her and brought the teddy bear back up so Kayla could focus on it.

"Give her a tissue, Rebecca," Polly said. "I'm going to call Stephanie. You two relax as much as you can. I'll be right back."

Polly went back into her own bedroom and shut the door.

"Is everything okay?" Henry asked.

"No. That poor thing is scared to death. I'm calling her sister. She should just be getting off work. There's no reason for Kayla to go through any more trauma tonight."

He sat up and reached for a pair of sweatpants to pull over his shorts. "Anything I can do?"

"No, just a second." Polly swiped the call and waited.

"Hello?" She recognized Stephanie's voice.

"Hi, Stephanie. This is Polly Giller."

"Is everything okay?"

"Yes and no. Kayla hasn't hurt herself, but she just woke up from a nightmare and Rebecca came to get me because she was huddled in on herself sobbing. The poor girl is pretty scared and I suspect that she might feel safer if she was in her own bed and at home with you."

"I'm so sorry she did this to you."

"She hasn't done anything to me. I'm sorry that she's

frightened. Rebecca is with her right now and we'll get her things packed up. I'm not going to have her change, just put a coat on."

"Tell her I'll be there in ten minutes. I need to close down a few things before I leave. Will that work for you?"

"Sure. Do you know how to get to our back garage door?"

"Yeah. I've seen it."

"Then come around back and we'll be watching for you."

"Thank you so much, Mrs. ..."

"It's just Polly. And I'm glad this happened while you are still at work and can come get her. I'll tell her you're on the way. That will help a bunch."

"Thank you, Polly."

"Thanks for coming over. We'll see you."

"She's coming here to get Kayla," Polly said to Henry. "Would you want to turn lights on in the media room and kitchen?"

"Finally. Something to do," he said. "I was feeling really inadequate."

Polly went back into Rebecca's room and picked up the bag that had held Kayla's clothes. "Stephanie will be here in ten minutes. Your timing was perfect. She hadn't left work yet."

"I'm sorry," Kayla said. "I didn't mean to be a baby."

"You're not a baby," Rebecca insisted. "It's okay to be scared. Right, Polly?"

"Absolutely. The first slumber party I ever went to was when I was in sixth grade and my friend's mom had to call my dad to come get me because I threw up. I wasn't sick. I was just scared."

"Really?" Kayla's eyes brightened and she relaxed her death grip on the bear.

"Really. Dad didn't say anything at all. He just gave me a hug and two weeks later, told me that I could invite my friends AJ and Dev to spend a night at the farm. He took us out to dinner and gave us a ride on the tractor and told us we could stay up all night if we wanted."

"You stayed up all night?" Rebecca asked.

"No. We were asleep by ten thirty. He knew that all we needed to do was get exhausted. But those two girls lived in town and they had sisters and had done sleepovers before. He wanted me to find out that they were fun so I'd get comfortable."

Rebecca patted Kayla's arm and said, "Maybe we can try again sometime,"

"Maybe you can spend the night at Kayla's house one of these days," Polly offered, ignoring the look that Kayla gave her. "Friends figure out how to spend time with each other."

"I've done a lot of sleepovers," Rebecca said. "But most of the time they're at Andrew's house."

Kayla looked at Rebecca in surprise. "You had a sleepover with a boy?"

"I get my own room, but we stay up late making up stories and stuff. It's only on the weekends, though."

"Okay girls, we need to pack Kayla's things. Make sure you get all her school clothes in there and then be sure that everything is in her backpack, too."

Kayla held out her pants. Should I put these on?"

"If they'll go over your pajama pants, you can. Otherwise, you can just wear your pajamas. But put your shoes and socks on. You'd best hurry," Polly said. "Come into the media room when you're ready. Stephanie is coming to the back door."

She left the room and strode across the living room. Henry was in the kitchen. "How do I pack Kayla's leftovers up with more food so Stephanie doesn't think we're just being charitable?" he asked.

"Good heavens, I love you. Let's not worry about that tonight. I have a feeling we might see more of Kayla." Polly hugged him. "I'm glad that Rebecca has a new friend, but it's going to make Andrew jealous. He liked having all of her attention."

"That boy just needs to learn that having two girls pay attention to him is much better than one. All he needs to do is redirect it so that he's in the middle rather than on the outside."

She patted his right pectoral muscle and winked at him. "If I have trouble explaining that to him, I'll send the boy in to learn from the master."

"I ain't no master. I had enough trouble getting one girl to pay attention to me."

"Oh baby, I was paying attention."

"Maybe I wasn't talking about you."

Polly chuckled. He was so much fun. She started to respond when Rebecca and Kayla came into the room. "Are you ready?" she asked, checking the time on her phone. Stephanie was probably already downstairs.

"I have everything and Rebecca said she'd bring me anything else I forgot."

"Then let's go downstairs and see if your sister is here. Rebecca, if you want to head back to your room, I'll be in before I go to bed."

"Okay, but I'm wide awake."

"What does that mean?"

"I don't know."

"I've got this," Henry said.

"Okay. I'll be back."

The dogs were confused with the whole situation, especially when Polly headed for the back door. As Kayla and Polly headed down the steps, the two animals stood at the top, hoping to be called down. Polly looked up and shook her head just before closing the door on them.

She opened the back door and saw a car in the driveway. Kayla ran over to the passenger seat and got in. Polly pushed the door shut and made a motion for her to turn the window down.

Stephanie leaned across her sister. "Thank you again for taking care of her tonight. I'm sorry we woke you up."

"Please don't worry about it," Polly said, resting her hand on the open window. "I hope you'll spend more time with Rebecca, Kayla."

"I will."

"Did you tell her thank you?" Stephanie asked her sister.

Kayla looked up. Her eyes were still red-rimmed from crying, but she had finally relaxed. "Thank you. I'm sorry for waking everybody up."

"It's no problem. I'm glad this worked out and I hope you sleep well tonight." She backed away from the car and pulled her robe around herself while she waved at the car backing out of the driveway. Polly gave a quick shiver as she ran back inside and up the steps.

The dogs weren't sitting at the top of the stairs when she got there and she soon discovered why. They were sitting beside Henry, Jessie and Rebecca at the dining room table.

"We thought we should have snacks since everyone was up," Henry said. "Join us."

"I'm sorry we woke you, Jessie," Polly said.

"It's okay. I had to go to the bathroom anyway." She took a bite of a brownie. "This is good. I'm going to have to work so hard to lose weight after the baby comes."

Rebecca was slowly nibbling at her brownie when Polly sat down beside her.

"You have five more minutes, little girlfriend," Polly said. "Then it's time for all of us to go back to bed."

"She was really scared," Rebecca said.

"Yes, she was and you did exactly the right thing by coming to get me. You were a good friend to her tonight."

"Will she come back sometime?"

"For after school stuff, I hope you invite her to come any time you'd like, but for overnight stays, it might be a while before she wants to try that again. Just keep being her friend. It will get easier for her. Remember how weird it was when you moved in here?"

"I tried to tell her that my room wasn't always like this. She didn't believe me. She told me that her place was a dump and I said that I didn't care because she was my friend."

Polly glanced at Henry. She knew she couldn't fix everybody, but there had to be something she could do about that.

"Just keep telling her that she's your friend. It will get better."

~~~

Polly was in her office the next morning when she looked up to see Lydia walk in the front door. It was quite obvious that she'd
~~~

been crying, so Polly jumped up and out of her chair and met her friend outside the office.

"Lydia, what's going on?"

"I shouldn't be here, but I need to talk to someone."

"Do you want to go upstairs?"

"Could we?" The poor woman looked like she could fall apart at any moment.

"Would you like coffee or tea or anything?" Polly asked when they entered her apartment.

"Coffee would be nice."

"You sit down. I'll be right out with it." Polly went into the kitchen and quickly texted Jeff that she was upstairs and didn't want to be bothered. She poured out two cups of coffee and went back into the living room, snagging an opened box of tissues with her little finger as she passed by a table.

Sitting in the chair next to where Lydia was seated, Polly handed her the coffee and dropped the tissues on the table in front of them. "What's up?"

"First of all, I'm so sorry about last night. I didn't have the energy to cook supper and thought that if we went out for dinner it might help him relax, but it just made things worse."

"You don't need to apologize for anything. We were worried about you two."

Lydia shook her head. "I don't know what to think. All of these years he has been the most stable man I've ever known and now things are falling apart and ..."

"He's still not talking about it?"

"Not a word. I've quit asking. It only makes it worse. He didn't even want to go over to Dayton to see the grandchildren on Sunday. He's never missed that. I couldn't tell Marilyn what was going on. She has enough stress with those three active little ones. But she knew something was wrong."

Polly reached out and took Lydia's hand.

"He slept in the guest room last night, Polly. Even when we're sick, he doesn't do that."

"This is the first time?"

Lydia nodded. "He didn't say anything, just put his pajamas on and left the room. I shut the door and cried all night long. He was up and out of the house before I went downstairs. I heard him taking a shower at five o'clock. And you know he's never up before seven."

"Maybe it has to do with a case."

"No. It's not that." Lydia shook her head. "I know it's not that." She thought for a moment. "Okay, I don't know for sure since he's not even talking about those anymore either."

"What do you want to do? Do you want to leave the house?"

'No!" Lydia declared. "That's our house and I'm not leaving it because some alien has taken over my husband's body."

"Okay, then what?"

Lydia deflated. "I don't know. I want to tell you that I'll fight for the marriage, but if he wants something else out of life, I guess I want him to be happy."

"Do you mean that?"

Lydia nodded, then she shook her head and then she nodded again. 'I don't know what I mean. I've never had to do this before. We have always been a team. No matter what came at us, whether it was external or internal to the family, we talked until we were on the same page and then presented a united front. All of a sudden, we've been separated for some reason and I don't know what to do next."

"I think the first thing you need to do is figure out what's going on."

"I don't even know where to start. I can't talk to anyone at his office."

"Why not?"

"Because I don't want to screw with his work life. If it isn't about work, they don't need to know that we're having trouble in our marriage. If it is about work, they don't need to know that he isn't coping well with it."

"Do you really believe they don't see this?"

A shrug was Lydia's only response.

"Does he have any family here?"

"Not here. His sister and a brother live in Georgia and another brother is in Birmingham, Alabama."

"He's from down south? How come he doesn't have an accent?"

Lydia smiled. "He'd lost that by the time we met. He always said that us northerners had too much trouble understanding what he was saying and he didn't need that when he was trying to arrest someone. His sisters and brother have thick accents."

"Have you talked to them about this?"

I doubt they'd know anything."

"No friends that he talks to?"

"Just me. And I guess not even that."

"What about Ken Wallers or the guy from the DCI - what was his name, Digger?"

"Darrell ... yes, Digger. They're friends, but I've never known Aaron to confide in either of them. Honestly, Polly, that's what I've always been around for. He can't trust people because of confidentiality. He trusts me." She started to weep. "And now he doesn't even have me. I wish I knew how to break through whatever is going on."

"How can I help you?"

"This is enough. I just needed someone to talk to this morning."

Polly didn't dare ask why Lydia was talking to her and not Beryl or Andy. Who knows, maybe she already had and just needed someone else to listen.

"Has Beryl talked to you about getting together?" Polly asked.

"Uh huh. Are you free Thursday night?"

"Absolutely." Even if there was something else, Polly would change her plans for this. "Where are we going?"

"I told Beryl that I didn't want to do any silly artistic stuff if we went to her house, but she was going to talk to Sylvie since we haven't had a chance to christen the new place yet."

"That sounds like fun. You'll love it."

"It's a beautiful home. I was in there several times when the Glau's lived there."

Polly smiled. Of course she had. Lydia had probably been inside every house in Bellingwood. "Sylvie's been working on updating things in the house. The boys' bathroom didn't have a shower, just a cool claw foot tub. Eliseo and Jason changed that out."

"I'm glad she has him. Are they ever going to get together?"

Polly smiled. "I don't know. I wanted her to figure it out before she invested in a house, but I wasn't about to say anything. She was so excited to finally be able to make this happen for her boys."

"Today I'd tell her to hold on to all of the independence she can. When you rely on someone else for more than thirty years and find yourself all alone, it just..." Lydia glanced around the room as if to make sure no one heard. "It sucks."

"You aren't all alone, Lydia. Until you know what's going on with Aaron, you can't make those assumptions."

"I go back and forth between falling apart because he's pulled so far away from me to being absolutely furious and wanting to kick him to the curb. My heart really needs me to either make a decision about which path to take or at least find a happy medium. I don't know how much more of this I can take."

"This is killing me," Polly said. "I want to do something... fix something... even break his neck. I feel helpless." She gulped. "I'm sorry. I know it's not about my feeling helpless. I really can't imagine what you're going through."

"Maybe we should call in an emergency from Sylvie's on Thursday night and tie him up until he talks to us," Lydia said. "Who knows, maybe you guys would get more out of him than I can."

"Do you want me to talk to him?"

That gave Lydia pause, but she shook her head. "No. I don't want him thinking that I'm airing our dirty laundry all over town."

"So he's allowed to mope around like Eeyore, but you aren't allowed to ask for help? That's crap."

"I know. I just won't stop respecting his position."

"But..."

Lydia stopped Polly by lifting her hand. "No. I have to give him the benefit of the doubt."

"No you don't." Polly was furious. "He's been giving you absolutely nothing for over a month now, right? And yet he wants you to act as if nothing is different?"

"I know," Lydia said through an intake of breath. "It's not fair to me, but it's where I am right now. Let me have more time. If it doesn't get any better, I'll find another way to confront him."

"I hope it does get better, but it seems to keep getting worse, right? How far down are you going to let this go before you stop it?"

"Maybe we'll find bottom soon."

"Okay. You do what you have to do and trust me, I will always be here for you."

"But?"

"No buts. Just - I will be here. Even if I think you're making the wrong decision, I still support you. It's your life and your marriage."

"Thank you, sweetie." Lydia checked her watch. "Look at the time. I need to be at the nursing home in a few minutes." She stood up and ran her fingers through her hair, fluffing it up.

"I love you, Lydia. I wish I could do more."

"You've done enough. You gave me back some energy so I can face today. That's all I need. One day at a time."

Polly walked with her to the front door, then down the steps to the main door of Sycamore House. She stood and watched as Lydia crossed the parking lot to her Jeep, got in and drove away. Aaron Merritt's easy life was forfeit now. The first time he crossed Polly's path and was alone, she was ready to take him to the ground and pummel him until he told her what was going on. How could he do this to his wife?

She chuckled. Pummeling Aaron wouldn't be an easy task, but he'd best hope he didn't have a reason to be at Sycamore House. Avoiding Polly might be the best decision he could make right now.

CHAPTER EIGHT

As Polly tried to sneak her legs out from under the animals, Henry's breathing changed. She went still, hoping he'd drift back to sleep.

"What time is it?" he asked, his voice raspy from sleep.

"It's five thirty. Don't get up. I just feel like going down to the barn. It's been a couple of weeks and I need some horse hair and hay on my clothes."

"Okay." He rolled to his other side and tucked the blankets under his chin.

She slipped into her jeans and a flannel shirt, pulled a sweatshirt over that and picked up her boots. "Come on, Obiwan. You're with me." She'd tried taking Han down to the barn a few times, but neither he nor the horses were any too happy with that. Obiwan stood beside her as she opened the door and darted into the living room.

Polly went down the front steps with him and took a breath. It was quiet this early in the morning. Once they got outside, she took a deep breath in the crisp air and swiped her phone's flashlight on to make sure there was nothing on the path. Obiwan raced to the fence and waited for her to catch up.

Lights were already on inside the barn and she wondered what it would take for her to beat Eliseo down here in the mornings. It used to be enough to arrive at six thirty.

She pushed the door open and Obiwan followed her inside. "Hello?" she called out.

"Good morning!" Eliseo's voice called out from somewhere in the back.

Tom and Huck must have been with him, because both donkeys came out to greet her. "Hello you gorgeous young men. How are you this morning?" Tom nosed at her pocket, hoping for a treat. "Oh no you don't, you beggar. Stay out of my pocket."

Eliseo came out of the donkey's stall. "What are you doing down here so early?"

"I missed my animals and since things move so fast in the mornings, the only time I have is before everyone gets up."

He nodded. "I get that. I have two at home that love mornings."

"I'm here to work. Can I just start in Daisy's stall?"

The horse heard her name and snorted. Polly stepped up and rubbed her head. "Yes, pretty girl, I'm talking about you. Are you ready for me?"

Polly walked over to Demi's stall. She could usually find Hansel and Gretel sleeping with him. He was the most patient of all the horses and let them sleep on top of him, around him, anywhere they wanted. Sure enough, the two cats were snuggled in. He didn't move anything except his head when he saw Polly.

"You are amazing," she said. "Do those cats really deserve your good will?"

Eliseo came down the center alley with the wheelbarrow and rakes. "Do you really want to do this?"

"Hey," she said, laughing. "It hasn't been that long."

"It's been a while and you certainly don't *need* to help this morning. Jason will be here at six."

"When do I start paying him for the work he does?"

Eliseo handed her a rake and opened Daisy's stall. "Not any time soon. We can talk about it this summer, but for now, he's just fine."

"Are you paying him?" Polly asked, lifting muck out of the stall.

"His mom and I worked out an allowance so he has spending money. He works on the farm and helps in the barn. He's fine."

"Has he said anything about saving for a truck or a car?"

"He isn't even fifteen years old yet. He can't drive for another year. There's plenty of time."

"Okay, I won't push anymore. But..."

"We've got this, Polly. Don't worry."

She went back to work, muttering to herself. Daisy goosed her in the back and Polly spun and said to the horse, "What? Do you want to tell me what to do, too?"

The horse pushed at her again. "What?" Polly asked.

Eliseo walked in with a bucket of grain. "She wants her breakfast. You're doing things out of order."

Polly laughed at him. "You're right. I forgot. I guess it has been too long since I've spent any time down here.

He patted Daisy's neck. "That's okay. We'll forgive you. Do you want to stir Demi and the cats?"

"Those three are awfully lazy in the mornings."

"You have no idea. He lets them do anything they want. I caught Hansel crawling up his neck the other day to use his head as a launching point for the beam up there. None of the other horses would tolerate that behavior, but Demi just puts up with it."

"He's my boy," Polly said. She opened his stall door and the cats leaped up from their nest and scattered. Tom had been waiting for the door to open and stood in the doorway as Demi came to his feet. Once the horse was up, Tom brushed past Demi's legs. He stood, waiting in front of the grain trough.

"What are you doing?" Polly asked.

"Demi is so easy going that the donkeys think they can eat his food."

She grinned and put her hand on top of Tom's head. "That's not fair."

"Nope. We don't let them get away with it, but they don't stop trying." Eliseo snapped a lead rope on Tom's halter and gave it a tug. When the donkey refused to move, Eliseo grinned. "It's usually a contest.

"Who wins?"

"Who do you think?"

"My money is on the donkey, but you're no slouch."

"No donkey will ever get the best of me, no matter how hard they try. However, it usually takes bribery."

"I'm here." Jason's voice rang throughout the barn. Tom lifted his head and started out of the stall to see who was speaking.

"Or a distraction," Eliseo said. He followed the donkey out and handed the lead to Jason. "Deal with him until Demi eats."

"Got it," Jason said. "What are you doing down here this morning, Polly?"

"Just spending time with my equine friends," she said. "I need to do this more often so it isn't such a surprise."

Eliseo came back with another bucket of grain and poured it into Demi's trough. The horse nudged Gretel out of the way after she jumped in to see if anything interesting showed up.

"I'll take care of the cats, too," Jason said. "Come on, Hansel and Gretel. You know where your breakfast is." He clicked his teeth and the two cats ran ahead of him to the feed room.

"It's a regular party down here in the mornings, isn't it," Polly said to Eliseo.

"We like watching them wake up. They each have their routines."

"And I've messed with them this morning. Sorry about that."

"It's no big deal and they all love you."

"Tell me what to do and I'll do it. Don't let me get away with opening doors and getting in your way, okay?"

"Stop it. You're fine. Here. Start mucking Demi's stall. Jason and I will take care of Nan and Nat. Then we're almost done."

Polly went to work and was headed back up to the house before the sun had started to rise. Obiwan followed and when she got upstairs, Henry was in the kitchen.

"I'm going to take a quick shower. Would you feed Obiwan?" she asked.

"Food is already down and coffee is brewing. What do you want for breakfast?"

"I can do that. This will only take a minute."

He looked at the counter, then back at her. "I could start something."

"You wanna start something in here?" she asked, winking at him and nodding toward the bedroom.

"Of course, but you have a couple of girls who are going to be waking up in a few minutes."

"Well, that's no fun." Polly stopped in the door to their bedroom. "I was going to make French toast. You made coffee... that will help.

~~~

Polly was in her office later that morning when Rachel came storming in. The girl started to slam the door, but thought better of it and turned to Polly, "Can I close this?"

"Sure. What's up?"

Rachel plopped down into a chair and flipped her hair. It was jet black with hot pink tips today. "I'm going to break up with him. He's an idiot."

"Billy?"

"Yes. Him and that freakishly idiotic friend of his. They're joined at the hip and he can't make a stupid decision without talking to Doug."

"What decision do you want him to make?"

"We're all in our early twenties."

"You're twenty."

"Close enough. Anyway, I don't see why they think it's a bad idea for me to move in."

Polly sat back, a little surprised. "Move in? Above the garage?"

"Sure. I don't take up much room. I'm there all the time anyway."
~~~

"What was his reason?"

"He said it wouldn't be fair to Doug and they didn't have room."

Polly pursed her lips, trying hard not to allow a laugh to escape. "Have you talked to your mom?"

"No, not yet. But she'll be fine with it."

"Really? You're twenty."

"She was twenty when she had me."

"Uh huh, and you're exactly the same person as she was back then?"

"What do you mean by that?"

"I mean, you've made all of the same exact decisions that she made through your childhood and teenage years?"

Rachel didn't understand yet. "No. But what does that matter?"

"Because you two aren't the same twenty-year-olds. You're two very different people and you should be talking to her about these big decisions."

"But that doesn't let Billy off the hook." She huffed and slammed her arms across each other on her chest. "Maybe I should just break up with him."

"Do you want to break up with him?"

"No, but I'd like to separate him from the idiot who lives with him sometimes."

"I get that, but those two have been friends for a long time."

"Maybe they should just get married then."

Polly put her hands down on her desk and leaned forward. "Okay. When did this whole moving in conversation happen?"

"Last night and this morning."

"You spent the night with him."

"Sure. I do all the time."

"And he told you that he wasn't ready for you to move in."

"Pretty much."

"Did he tell you that he didn't love you?"

"No."

"Did he say anything about breaking up?"

"No." Rachel started unclenching her fists, coming to grips with reality. "I pushed too hard, didn't I?"

"Maybe a little. These two guys have just figured out what it means to live on their own away from their moms. They're having a ball and by the way, they're including you in the fun."

"It's not so much fun anymore," Rachel said. "They quit playing video games with their buddies."

"Why did they do that?" Polly asked. "They had fun."

"I think it's my fault." Rachel's voice got quieter. "I told Billy he was like a kid with all the 'dudes' and the games."

"But you played those games with them."

"I know. I miss it too. But now that I'm working all the time I need more sleep. I can't do those all nighters like we used to do and I work on Friday and Saturday nights. Those are the best nights to game because no one has to work the next day or go to school."

Polly smiled. "So how mad at Doug are you really?"

"I don't know. He really doesn't want to grow up and I think he's holding Billy back."

"From doing what?"

"Going out on his own."

"But it was those two who went out on their own together and that was only last year."

"But Billy has grown up so much."

"Oh Rachel, I'm going to ask you a crazy, crazy question."

"What?" Rachel set her jaw.

"What made you fall for Billy in the first place?"

"I dunno. He was funny and did crazy things. He always made me laugh. He wasn't afraid of anything. If people laughed at him because he was a geek, he just blew it off." She dropped her head.

"All of the things that you've been training out of him this last year? All of the things that Doug is still doing?"

"But I love Billy more now that he's acting like an adult."

"Is that really true or do you kinda miss the Billy who dressed up in a robe and painted a light saber? I know I miss that boy."

"But he can't be that way for the rest of his life. He has to grow up sometime."

Polly slowly shook her head back and forth. "I don't think so. He's responsible. He goes to work and does a good job every day. He pays his bills. I know that he spends time with his parents. He enjoys his friends. He loves you and apparently will do anything to make you happy. He's kind and good to his dog and he's wonderful with Andrew and Rebecca. Tell me how growing up will make him a better person."

"But..."

"No buts. You fell in love with an amazing young man. Let him be that person until he chooses to do something differently. If he isn't ready to have your girly stuff in his apartment, let that be okay. He wants you there. Learn to fall in love with his best friend, because I'll tell you right now, if you separate those two boys, you'll be the one who pays in the long run. He'll let you get away with it, but someday down the road, it will come back to haunt you."

"Why am I the one who has to change everything?"

"Because you're the one thinking about it and asking the deep questions. This matters to you right now and this is the time when you can do the right thing."

"Crap."

Polly laughed. "What did you think I was going to tell you when you came in here?"

"I don't know, but I didn't think that I was going to be the one who was wrong. How do you make Henry fall in line all the time?"

"What?" Polly looked at her in shock. "Henry falls in line?"

"Everyone talks about how perfect he is. He never does anything wrong. He's always doing stuff for you. I heard someone say that he was whipped."

"Henry Sturtz whipped. That's a good one. It's occurred to no one that he does what he wants to do? If I ask for help, he does what he can to be there, but that goes both ways."

"Nobody else would bring puppies home from their honeymoon. He did that for you."

"Tell me another man out there who would have ignored those

puppies, leaving them in the street to die."

"Well..."

"Henry does the right thing. And you'll notice he never apologizes for it either. He thinks about the things he's going to do and then he does them. People don't have enough on their own plates if they're worrying about my husband."

Rachel put her hands up defensively. "It wasn't me. I was just trying to figure out how you get him to be so nice to you."

"Mostly I don't ask him to do things I know he doesn't want to do. And if I am going to ask him to do something like that I make sure there's a darned good reason for it. If I asked him to drive off a bridge, he'd tell me I was nuts, but if I asked him to run the car into the river because the trunk was on fire, he'd figure out a way to get us both to safety and then send the car into the water. He's not a stupid man and I'm not a stupid woman. We listen and we talk and we respect the other person's ability to make good decisions."

"Maybe that's what I need to do."

"What's that?"

"Let Billy make good decisions."

"If he isn't ready for you to move in, you have to respect that."

"You're right. I'm just so ready to get our lives started. He isn't."

"He will be someday and if you let him get there on his own, it will make it easier."

"What if it takes ten years?"

Polly chuckled. "Okay. That might be a bit much, but I doubt Billy takes that long. He's only been out of his parent's house for a year. Let him have this."

"What am I going to do with Doug?"

"You might find him a girl to date. That's always a good distraction. And why don't you be the one to work with Doug to set up a game night. Do it on a Friday night after one of your early wedding rehearsal dinners. Make great food and invite their friends. Let him know that you aren't trying to separate him from his best friend. Encourage their fun."

"Maybe we could do it this Friday night." Rachel jumped up.

"Thanks for talking me down, Polly."

"Where's Sylvie this morning? Don't you usually talk to her?"

"She had a delivery coming to the house. I think she's getting new living room furniture."

"She's what?"

Rachel shrugged. "I don't know. She didn't say much yesterday, just that she was going to be late."

"Huh. That's weird. She didn't tell me about it."

"Maybe she wants to surprise you and I wasn't supposed to say anything."

"No, she'd have told you."

"I'd better get back to work. Thanks again."

"No problem."

Polly watched her leave, took out her phone and dialed.

"Good morning, sweetums. Miss me already?" Henry said.

"Of course I do."

"So why are you calling?"

"I just found out that you are the perfect husband. People talk about it in town, you know."

"I didn't know that. Who let the cat out of the bag?"

"Apparently you do everything I want you to do, so you're whipped or something."

"Hmmm," he said. "I think you were doing everything I wanted you to do last night and I certainly don't remember whips."

"Stop it," she giggled, a flush rising through her face.

"So I guess that I've lost all my man points in town, eh?"

"Yep and I've taken them from you."

"Does this bother you?"

"A little. But on the other hand, as I was talking to Rachel about it, I realized how amazing you were and how much I love you. You're so danged smart and reasonable."

"There. That's the right way to look at it. Smart and reasonable. And completely smitten, by the way."

"Still?"

"I told you last year that there would never be a time I wasn't completely in love with you."

"Me too, Henry. Me too. I really am the luckiest woman in town."

"And don't you forget it. So was that the reason for your call or do you need something else, because I'm in a room full of men in hard hats and..."

"You're not!" Polly felt her entire body flush all over again.

Henry laughed out loud. "No. I'm not, but they are in the next room and I need to get back to work."

"Oh my," she breathed. "Scared me to death. No. The real reason I called was to tell you that I love you because you are amazing."

"I love you too."

CHAPTER NINE

"So what was that about?" Jeff asked, poking his head in Polly's door after Rachel left.

"Nothing," Polly said with a shrug. "What's up?"

"Are you going to be here for a while? I just got a confirmation on an interview and she has some time before heading to her job at ten thirty. She'll be here in fifteen minutes."

"Nothing like giving a girl a warning."

"If you're busy, I can do this. No worries. We'd talked yesterday and I called her this morning and she had time right now."

"I'm kidding. Of course I'm available. I'll finish up what I'm doing here and meet you in the conference room, right?"

"Thanks." He left her office and Polly turned back to her computer. She looked at the screen and back at the pile of bills on her desk. Then she lifted her upper lip in a snarl. She hated this part of the job. Jeff had all the fun. He got to deposit funds. She had to make it go away.

Little by little the pile was whittled down and the stack of checks in her printer grew.

"Polly?" Jeff asked from her door.

"She's here? I didn't see anyone come in."

"You must have been concentrating. She came in the front door."

Polly took a notepad and pencil and followed him into the conference room, then grinned when she saw Stephanie Armstrong seated at the table.

"I didn't know it was you," Polly said.

"I saw the ad come up and thought I'd take a shot. You don't have to give me an interview just because you know me, though."

"Oh no. Jeff is the one who put this together. He had no idea we'd met before. You're good."

"How do you know each other?" Jeff asked.

"Stephanie's sister is in Rebecca's class at school and spent the evening with us on Monday."

"Okay." He gestured to a chair and Polly sat down. He sat and leaned forward. "Do you have a resume?" he asked.

Stephanie handed him a manila folder. "I'm sorry. I don't have the job at the convenience store on there. This came up so fast and I didn't have time to get to the library and update my resume."

"No problem," he said, opening the folder. After a quick glance, he pushed it to Polly. "Tell me what interests you about this position?"

Polly put her hand on his forearm. "Which position are you talking about here today?"

He looked at her and pursed his lips. "I don't know. Either one."

"I can do anything," Stephanie jumped in. "You'll see that I worked a hotel front desk when I lived in Ohio. I did everything and that was when I was still in high school. I know that I'm not a manager at the convenience store, but I do most of the office work. I prepare the orders and check things in, stock shelves, clean, get deposits ready, schedule employees."

"What does your manager do?" Jeff asked.

She shrugged. "I don't ask anymore. He's a nice guy, but ..." she let the rest of the sentence trail off.

"Would you like to work here in the office as my assistant or out at the Inn?"

"Either position would be great. If I worked here, would it be regular hours? I only ask because of my sister. Polly took care of things the other night when I couldn't take her home. I'd like to have a little independence to make sure that she's safe after school."

Jeff nodded and Polly glanced up when she saw Sylvie come into the office.

"You two go on," she said. "I'll be back in a few minutes."

She shut the door behind her when she left the conference room. "Hey, Sylvie, what's up?"

"I'm sorry to bother you. Nothing really. I just wanted to let you know where I was. Are you interviewing?"

"Yeah. Jeff and I finally caved. We have to hire someone at the Inn and he's looking for someone else to work in the office here."

"That's cool. Who's the girl?"

"Stephanie Armstrong. Her sister Kayla is in Rebecca and Andrew's class."

"Oh, her!" Sylvie said, a grin taking over her face. "Andrew was so jealous of her, he sputtered and fumed the last two nights. He's still not over it."

"Poor boy. But he's the one who showed her Star Wars."

"But then she wanted to do girly things with Rebecca and he hated that. He's terrified that Rebecca won't want to be his friend anymore."

"Like that could happen. Those two are inseparable. I wish I'd had a friend like that when I was in elementary school. So, Rachel told me you ordered some new furniture."

"She did, did she? I was going to surprise you with it tomorrow night. There was no way I wanted you to come to my house and sit on that dingy old stuff we brought over from the apartment. It's all moved down to the basement. Jason and Andrew are going to love having a place to hang out."

"I can't believe you did that for us. You're a crazy girl. We don't care what it looks like."

"I care. It's the first time in my life I can afford to dress up my house and I want it to look nice for my inaugural party."

"I can't wait to see it. What did you buy?"

"Not telling. You have to come over and experience it."

"Have you planned the menu? Will you tell me what to bring?"

Sylvie scowled. "I'm a chef. You will bring nothing. How embarrassing would that be?"

"We have to bring something. That's the plan for these parties. Beryl and Andy won't let you get away with that."

"They already have. I know how to be firm."

"And Lydia?"

"She caved in just moments. There's something really wrong with her. Have you seen her lately? Her eyes are dark and she looks like she's going to cry at the drop of a hat. Is something going on with one of her kids..." Sylvie's face grew grim. "Or one of her grandkids? That would destroy her."

"No, that's not it. Maybe she'll talk about it tomorrow night."

"So... payback for me not telling you about the furniture?"

Polly chuckled. "No. She's just so private that until she talks about it, I don't want to be a gossip."

"You're a good person. Better than me." Sylvie took Polly's arm. "And I'll let you get away with it because you shamed me."

"Sorry?"

"Yeah. No." Sylvie took a breath as if she were steeling herself. "I'd better get to work. I'm sure Rachel is wondering where I've gotten to."

Jeff stepped out of the conference room as Sylvie left. He shut the door. "Got a minute, Polly?"

"Sure. Your office?"

"Okay."

They sat down in the chairs and he said. "I like her. She's smart and willing to learn and the price is right..."

"You don't have to sell me," Polly said. "If you want to hire her, I'm all for it. She's a nice girl. Henry says she's pleasant and decent to customers. He sees her when he's buying ice cream to keep me tranquil, I guess."

"Then my next question is where should we put her?"

"Where do we need her the worst?"

"It's really six of one, half dozen of the other," Jeff put his hands out and lifted each as if they were a balanced scale.

Polly sat back in the chair. "I don't want to tell you what to do," she said.

"Do you have an idea?"

She sat forward again. "Okay, hear me out and don't get all 'Polly's a busy-body' on me, okay?"

"Whatever. You are who you are. Pointing out the obvious seems like a waste of time."

"Jerk."

"Yes, boss. I am."

She laughed. "I was thinking that she and Kayla live in a really dingy trailer. They have no money to make it nice. Barely any money to buy furniture. We could take some of the furniture from my Dad's house to the caretaker's cottage and they could live there."

He thought for a moment and then shook his head. "I only hesitate because with the people that are in and out of there, I can't guarantee they'll be totally safe. I'd really like to put a married couple in there."

"Sexist much?"

"I know. It's horrible," he said. "But they're right on the highway and who knows what kind of creeps would show up in the middle of the night."

"Turn the vacancy light off."

"But still. Creeps. She's so young and if her younger sister is there with her. It's just too scary for me to do that to her."

"Then you've already made your decision."

"I know we don't help her living situation right away, but I'm going to pay better than the convenience store, so she'll make more money and other than special events, she'll have normal hours. And maybe..." He looked at Polly.

"Maybe what?"

"Maybe her sister could come here with Rebecca and Andrew

after school. She'd have a better place to be and could leave with Stephanie at five."

"You're so smart. You should tell me what you're thinking before I start babbling."

Jeff grinned at her. "It's so much more fun when you babble. I'm going to offer her the job. Did you talk to Sarah Heater?"

"I think she's relieved that we aren't counting on her. It's settled. Go hire yourself an assistant."

He stood up and patted Polly's shoulder as he walked past her to go talk to Stephanie again. "Thanks."

~~~

When Polly's stomach rumbled a third time, she turned her monitor off and pushed back from her desk. The stomach wasn't going to feed itself. Sylvie and Rachel were serving a lunch meeting in the auditorium and she didn't want to bother them today. The last thing she wanted was to have to forage for food upstairs.

"Hey," she said, poking her head in Jeff's office. "I'm going to the diner for some food. You want anything?"

"Nah. I'm good." He held up an apple.

"Are you dieting again?"

"Go eat your lunch and leave me alone."

She shook her head. "You're a good looking man. Don't be silly."

"Dating, you know."

"If he doesn't love you for who you are right now, he isn't worth it."

"Easy for you to say, you svelte wench, you. And you're happily married, too."

"Maybe you should get a big dog that needs a lot of walks. You'd be surprised at how many calories you can use up."

He seemed to ponder the possibility and then laughed. "No, I think I'll just suffer and feel sorry for myself."

"I'm having a pork tenderloin," she said, tauntingly.
~~~

"Now you're a nasty wench. Get out before I throw this apple at you."

"Okay, you're sure you don't want me to bring anything back for you?"

Jeff gripped the arms of his chair dramatically and threw his head back. "Begone! You are my devil!"

Polly laughed at him as she walked out of the office.

Once she got in the truck, she texted Henry. *"I'm heading to the diner for lunch. Do you want me to bring you anything?"*

"That would be great!" he texted back. *"Can we call in an order and have you bring it to the shop?"*

"Sure. I'll be over after a while."

"Thank you. You're the best wife I've ever had."

"Uh huh. That could be an interesting conversation."

He sent back a heart emoji and she drove out and headed downtown.

Lucy smiled at her when she went in. "Are you here to stay?"

"No, Henry is going to call in an order for takeout. Could you add a pork tenderloin with fries to that for me?"

"Sure, honey. Have a seat. I'll get you a Dew."

"Thank you." Polly looked around the diner and saw Aaron Merritt sitting by himself in a corner. "Lucy?"

"Yeah, hon."

"I'm going to talk to the Sheriff. Skip the Dew."

"I can bring it to you over there."

"Nah. I'll only be a few minutes. Wave at me when the food's done."

"Got it." Lucy swung around with a pot of coffee and headed for a table filled with young men.

Aaron hadn't looked up to see her coming and was shocked when Polly sat down across from him. "Hi, Polly," he said.

"How are you today?" she asked.

"Fine."

"Any news on that murder? It seems to me that a sniper in Bellingwood wouldn't be that difficult to find."

"Unless he was in and out."

"I suppose. So, nothing?"

"We're investigating. I'm just not at liberty to talk about it."

"I see." She screwed up all her courage and finally blurted out. "You're not at liberty to talk to anyone about anything these days. What's going on with you, Aaron?"

He raised tired eyes to look at her. "Nothing."

"That's a flat-out lie," she said, lowering her voice. "You're a wreck. Your body is screaming that there's something wrong. Do you think no one notices?"

"Polly, this is none of your business."

"You can tell yourself that, but you're my friend and Lydia is one of my best friends. Do you have any idea what you're doing to her? Shit, Aaron. Are you seeing someone else?"

The shock on his face told Polly that she'd missed the mark. She was so grateful for that, she immediately felt weak all over.

"Why would you even think that?" he asked.

"Because you are a completely different person than the man I've known for the last two years. And your poor wife doesn't have a clue what's going on. You two have never kept secrets from each other. Of course we're going to think that's the reason."

"Lydia doesn't think that," he said.

"She's not saying it, but trust me when I tell you that there isn't a woman alive who doesn't worry about it when their husbands behave like you've been behaving this last month."

"I would never betray her."

Polly reached out. Her heart hurt so badly for him she wanted to cry. She touched his arm. "I wish you would talk to someone. Whatever is going on is destroying you and Lydia. She doesn't laugh, she doesn't play, she's numb."

He put his arm down on the table and Polly slid her hand back so that she was holding his fingers. "Aaron, I love you. So much, but you can't keep this up."

"I..." he sat there, shaking his head. "I can't talk about it."

"When I saw you here, I wanted to come over and give you a piece of my mind," Polly said. "But you look like a dog who has been abandoned by its owner and left to fend for itself in the middle of winter. I want to fix this for you."

"There's nothing for you to fix." He was shaking his head again. "It can't be fixed."

"Then you have to get out of your funk and put it behind you. You can't live like this. You're killing yourself."

"Maybe," he said and pulled his hand out from under hers.

"Aaron..."

"No, I'm not suicidal. Don't read anything into that. I'm sorry. I shouldn't have said that."

"You have to talk to someone. Isn't there anyone you trust?"

"Not with this. Please stop pressing, Polly. I can't talk about it and even now I've probably said too much."

"Do you love your wife?"

"Of course I do."

"Then tell her that. At least make sure that she's on your side, no matter what comes at you. The two of you have spent a lifetime creating a foundation that's solid. Don't start kicking at it because of something you can't control."

Both of them saw Lucy give a quick wave to Polly and point at three plastic sacks beside the register.

Aaron spoke first, "That's your order. Thank you for taking time."

"Aaron, you're scaring us all. If nothing else, find a way back to your wife."

"It won't be..." he started to speak and then stopped.

Polly stood up and in a moment of complete insanity, she bent over him and hugged his neck, then whispered into his ear. "We love you, you old fool and we need you to come back to life. If you won't let us help and you won't talk to us, get over your damned self and figure it out on your own. You don't live on an island."

He patted her arm and gave her a weak smile. "I hear you," he said. "Take care."

Polly walked away from the table and when she reached the register, realized that she was gritting her teeth. She paid for the meals and carried the bags to her truck.

Once she was belted in and the doors were shut, Polly slammed the palms of her hands on the steering wheel. "Damn him all to hell."

She took a deep breath, checked her mirrors, backed out of the space and headed for Henry's shop. The smell of sawdust and a hug from the man she loved might help her get past this moment of fury.

CHAPTER TEN

There was no one left in the house by the time Polly left for Sylvie's. Jessie was out with friends, Henry was heading to his shop, and Rebecca was spending the evening with her mother. Sarah Heater was feeling good enough that when Rebecca asked if she could spend the night, Sarah was overjoyed to be able to say yes. The girl paid close attention to her mother's health and seemed to know when it would be okay to even ask.

Polly offered to arrive at Sylvie's early in order to help her friend get ready for the evening, but Sylvie refused, saying that she wanted it to be a surprise for everyone and no one was to show up before six thirty - she wouldn't let them in. Polly pulled into the driveway right at six thirty and was still the first to arrive. She sat in her truck and waited... not long, before Lydia's Jeep pulled in behind her. Andy, Beryl and Lydia got out and Polly jumped down from her truck to meet them.

"What do you think Sylvie's up to?" Andy asked. "She was pretty insistent we all come together."

"I think she's going to meet us at the door dressed in nothing but Saran Wrap," Beryl said.

Lydia shook her head. "Why in the world would she do that?"

"Because it's fun!"

"Don't you dare tell me that you ever did anything as crazy as answering the door dressed in nothing but plastic wrap."

Beryl sashayed up the sidewalk and up the front steps to the porch. "Okay, I won't, but it certainly surprises vacuum cleaner salesmen."

Andy gulped. "You aren't serious."

"Oh for the love," Beryl said, cackling madly. "Of course I'm not. You know me better than that."

"None of us really know what you might do," Polly said. "You're wild."

"I'm not all that wild. I just like people to think I am."

"You're plenty wild for Bellingwood," Lydia said, reaching up to ring the doorbell. "No one is ever sure what you'll do or say."

Sylvie opened the door and held it as the four women walked into the foyer. "May I take your coats?" she asked.

Polly shrugged her jacket off and started forward.

"Oh no you don't," Sylvie said. "You can wait."

"You're no fun."

"That's what my boys tell me every day. If I can take it from them, trust me, you're easy." She hung coats and jackets in the closet and then said, "Okay. I'm just beginning to decorate, so I don't have things on the walls or my knick knacks out yet. All you're seeing is the furniture I've been looking at and finally just bought. Okay?"

The other four nodded and Sylvie stepped forward and into the living room.

"Oh my," Polly said. "That's not at all what I expected."

"Do you like it?" Sylvie asked.

"It's gorgeous! How did you do this so quickly?" Polly turned to Lydia, Beryl and Andy, who were fanning out across the room.

"Once I found the right pieces, it was just a matter of filling in."

"You've done a beautiful job, dear," Lydia said. "This looks very comfortable."

"Beryl?" Sylvie turned to her friend. "I know it's not blasting with color, but..."

"You shouldn't apologize. This is very nicely done. You used a specific palette and fleshed it out with textures. Girl, this is beautiful."

"I wanted furniture that the boys would feel comfortable in, and I wanted it to be easy to accent."

Andy picked up a pillow and stroked it. "So many different looks here and then the coffee table. I would never have seen these together."

"Is it comfortable?" Polly asked.

"Sit! I'll be right back."

"You aren't bringing food out here. What if we spill?" Polly was horrified.

"Please. I have two young boys. They've already climbed across everything."

Polly sat down on the edge of the overstuffed gray sofa. It was filled with pillows in black, white and various shades of gray. At one end, a darker gray settee stood apart, creating a corner in which she'd placed a rustic end table which matched the rustic barn board plank coffee table. Two wing chairs, one in a gray plaid and the other in very different hues of gray stripes finished the seating arrangement, another end table between them.

Sylvie had lit small white candles, adding a warm glow to the room.

She came back in, carrying a tray filled with crackers and baked Brie covered in raspberry sauce. Sylvie placed it on the table and said, "Wine all around?"

They nodded and made themselves comfortable and she returned to the kitchen.

"Are you sure we can't help?" Lydia called out.

"No. I want you to relax and then I'll show you the rest of the house." Sylvie poked her head back out, holding a bottle of wine while she twisted the corkscrew into it. "I haven't bought the dining room set yet, so we're eating in the kitchen, but I think you'll like it out there."

They sat and looked at the Brie, no one willing to say anything.

Then Sylvie called out, "Polly? Could you come here?"

Polly jumped up and ran into the kitchen. "What do you need?"

"I was so nervous about showing you the new living room furniture that I seem to have lost my mind. Could you take these plates and napkins out?"

"Sure," Polly said, giggling. "How about a knife or two. And can you manage the wine glasses?"

"Hush. You're laughing at me."

"A little bit. It's just us."

"It's the first time I've been able to host an evening and I wanted to make it nice."

"It is nice. You've done a beautiful job with your living room and you have confidence in your food, right?"

"Well, yes."

"Then relax. It's just us."

"Okay, then. Just a second."

Sylvie reached down into the back of a cupboard and brought out a big wooden tray. "Put the plates and things on here. The glasses will fit, too. You can carry the wine and I'll take this."

"This is beautiful. Why haven't you used it before?"

"Because I forgot I had it until we moved."

"It would look great on that coffee table."

"Do you think I should just leave it there and put decorative things in it."

"You should do whatever you think looks nice. Now come on. We need to get wine in all of us, don't you think?" Polly grabbed two bottles of wine and followed Sylvie back into the living room.

"Now we're talking," Beryl said and stood up. "Tell me how I can help you."

Sylvie put the tray down and passed out small plates. "Sorry about that."

"Don't worry," Lydia said. "You're fine."

"I was so flustered at having you here." Sylvie handed the cork screw to Polly, who opened the second bottle and began pouring. "I've been running since I walked in the door after work. Thank goodness I put the meal together during the day today."

"Where are the boys?" Andy asked.

"Eliseo took them. And he took the dog. He thought that the three of them should do obedience training, so every Thursday evening, they go down to Ames."

"I wouldn't have thought he needed obedience training," Lydia said.

Sylvie smiled. "Of course he doesn't, but the first time he watched Andrew try to walk with Padme on the leash, he knew he had to fix it. They have a great time. The boys get McDonalds or whatever they can talk him into eating for supper and if the class goes well, he treats them to ice cream."

"When are you going to figure this out, girl?" Beryl asked quietly.

"Figure what out?"

"That the two of you should be together."

"Don't start. We're just friends."

"And those kisses haven't meant anything?"

"Kisses. As in plural?"

"You're telling me that you've only kissed once."

Sylvie's entire body flushed red.

"You've kissed more than once!" Beryl exclaimed. "I knew it. Methinks thou doth protest too much."

"Fill me back up," Sylvie said, holding her empty wine glass out to Polly. "I won't make it through the entire evening if I'm not a little loose. Not with this woman in my house."

Beryl shrugged. "At least it's out there on the table. It isn't like we haven't all been wondering if you're going to finally let him in your bedroom."

Sylvie's mouth dropped open and the other three flipped their faces toward Beryl, in shock.

"What?" she asked. "Are we supposed to be prudes now?"

Lydia was the first to speak. "I think our bedrooms should be off limits."

Beryl finished her wine and held it out to Polly. "Whatever. Just because you haven't been getting any for the last couple of months."

Lydia put her glass down on the table and reached for her purse, then pulled out a tissue. She dabbed at her eyes and turned away.

"Oh, honey, I'm sorry," Beryl said. "I didn't mean to make you cry."

"No, it's okay. Just leave me alone for a few minutes. Talk about anything else, but leave me alone."

"I have the biggest mouth." Beryl scowled at Andy. "Why don't you throw things at me before I get myself in trouble?"

"Because sometimes you surprise the heck out of me. I wasn't expecting you to start down this path tonight. Poor Sylvie. She wants to be independent and you have to give her trouble. When was the last time you entertained a man in your bedroom?"

Andy started to laugh out loud and snorted through her nose. "I can't believe I just said that. We're giving Beryl trouble for her big mouth and I went too far." She slapped her knee. "I crack myself up."

"Well?" Sylvie asked.

Andy was confused. "Well what?"

"Not you. Beryl. When was the last time you had sex?"

"We're out of wine here," Polly said quietly. "I'm going to need more really soon."

Sylvie jumped up and ran out to the kitchen and returned with two more bottles. "Who is coming to get you all if you're too drunk to drive?"

Lydia finished the wine in her glass and set it firmly down in front of Polly. "I'm spending the night right here on this sofa if I'm too drunk to drive. Screw it. This is my night to have fun." She turned to Beryl. "And just so you know, it hasn't been two months. So there."

Beryl shook her head slowly back and forth. "Nope, not talking about that one anymore." She pushed the glass in front of Polly who was still trying to unscrew the cork. "Lord, Sylvie, next time buy the cheap crap with tops that unscrew. It's so much easier."

"You've neatly avoided the question, old lady," Andy said.

"I didn't hear no damned question."

"You've had sex! With who?"

Polly quickly filled Lydia's glass and then her own. Things were spinning out of control and all she could think was how glad she was that none of this conversation was about her. She was going to sit here quietly and not make eye contact as long as possible.

Lydia took a long drink, winked at Polly and then took another. "This is good stuff," she said. "Fill me back up."

"Ladies, don't you think we should have some food before we finish off these bottles?" Sylvie asked.

Beryl scooped up a hunk of cooling cheese with a cracker and handed it to Lydia. "Eat that and then have another. You don't need to be out of control tonight."

Lydia's eyes flashed. "What if I do? I never get to be out of control. I'm always good ole Lydia. I make sure everyone else is taken care of. I drive you all over, hell, I drive half the old ladies in town all over the place. I get up early and make breakfast. Does anyone care? No! I run all of the meetings that no one else wants to handle. Do I get a thank you? No! If the pastor needs something done, he calls me. If anybody in town needs something taken care of, they call me. I never get to be out of control. And now, damn it, I want to be out of control tonight. Won't you let me?"

"She swore," Beryl stage-whispered. "I think she's serious."

"Of course I am. Do I have to be in control when I'm with my best friends?"

They all shook their heads no.

"Good. Then fill up my glass. And if I pass out, don't bother calling Aaron, because he won't even know that I'm missing." She looked at each of them. "And I don't want to talk about it, so don't ask."

"Got it," Beryl said. "No talking about the big ole elephant in the room. Because no one here is even thinking about him. Am I right?"

More silence as everyone nodded in agreement.

Lydia curled her upper lip. "Well, unless that elephant is shitting on your shoes, I don't want to think about him."

"More swearing." Beryl picked up an empty wine bottle. "Sylvie, do you have enough of this stuff to get us through the night?"

"Ummm, not sure."

"Better start chilling whatever you have left."

"It already is. But dinner will be ready in just a few minutes."

"Oh, thank god!" Beryl exclaimed. "This deteriorated much more quickly than I expected and we need to get her back to normal."

"Me? Normal? This is as normal as you get tonight," Lydia said. She unbuttoned the sweater that she'd been wearing over her blouse, pulled it off her arms and flung it across the room. "If I can't be a little wild and crazy with you girls, what good is my life? My kids don't need me, my husband doesn't want me, and the world just uses me. Drunk is a good place for me to be."

They sat in stunned silence.

"That's right," she said, her tone getting angrier and angrier. "I'm tired of being happy and nice. I want someone to take care of me and it would be nice if I could at least count on a few of you to do that."

"Honey, we'll do whatever it is that you want. If you want to come stay with me for a few days and let me cook for you and do your laundry, just say the word." Beryl moved over to sit beside Lydia on the couch.

"I can pick up some of the errands you run for the old ladies in town," Andy offered.

Sylvie jumped in. "And I'm glad to call Pastor Boehm and offer to help with some of his tasks."

They all looked at Polly.

"I'll do whatever. I could go find a dead body and when Aaron showed up, push him in the creek or something."

Lydia started to laugh. "That sounds perfect." She patted Beryl's knee. "I know that if I need to come stay with you, I'm welcome. Thank you. If I get too drunk tonight, I just might do that. As for the rest of it, I..." She shook her head and looked at the floor. "I do like my life and wouldn't live it any other way.

Sometimes I just get tired of it."

"That's what we're here for," Andy said. "You can fall apart on us any time and we won't..."

Polly held up her glass as she interrupted, "We probably won't even remember it tomorrow."

A bell dinged in the kitchen and Sylvie jumped up again. "I have to check on dinner."

"We'll all help. None of us are individually worth much right now, but maybe as a team we can get the meal on the table," Polly said. She looked down at the cheese and crackers and stuck her finger in the melted Brie, scooped some up and popped it into her mouth. "What?" she asked, looking around. "It's not like the rest of you were diving into it."

Lydia buzzed her lips. It didn't work. "They're numb," she said, starting to giggle. "Look, I can't make a raspberry." She tried it again.

Polly put her finger in the raspberry sauce and rubbed it on Lydia's lips. "It's raspberry. Does it help?"

Lydia attempted another buzz of her lips. "Have I lost my mojo? Will I be able to give my babies raspberries? Oh, what have I done?" She finished the third glass of wine and held it out to Polly. "Here, take this. I don't want to drop the glass, but I want it full by the time I sit down at the table."

She grabbed Beryl's arm. "Where the hell's the table? I need to sit down. Polly's bringing me more wine. And by the way, you had sex?"

When they got into the kitchen, Sylvie had pulled a large casserole dish out of the oven. She was reaching in for a second when Lydia slapped her bottom.

"What?" Sylvie asked.

"It was just so cute, sticking out there. I'm sorry. Should I have not done that?"

"Put her in a seat right now," Sylvie commanded Beryl, pointing at the table in the small sunroom just off the kitchen.

"She's right. It is a cute bottom. I'll bet Eliseo thinks so too."

"When did we revert to junior high? Now get going. Are any of you sober enough to help me put these dishes on the table?"

"I haven't finished a single glass," Andy said. "Let me help."

Polly stood in the middle of the kitchen holding two wine bottles and two glasses. "Lydia wants more wine. Should I let her?"

Andy nodded. "Let her do whatever she wants tonight. She hasn't tied one on in years ... decades. Just keep filling her glass."

"Okay!" Polly took the glass and the bottles over to the table, filled Lydia's and put it down in front of the woman. "You're kind of a lightweight," she said. "Three glasses of wine and you're soused."

"This is good stuff," Lydia said. "What is it?"

Sylvie came over with a hot dish and set it down on a trivet. "It's Secret Woods, of course. Whenever I cater for them, they offer me a bottle of wine. That's why I don't know how much I have here. I just keep bringing it home."

"Eliseo should make you a wine cellar," Beryl said.

"Poof," Lydia interrupted, flicking her hands at Sylvie. "You're a wine cellar."

Sylvie and Andy continued bringing food to the table until Polly stood up. "I feel guilty, I should help."

"No, that's it," Sylvie said. "The bread was the last thing." She uncovered the first dish, revealing a baked cheesy dish. "Spaghetti squash with ricotta and spinach."

Andy drew the foil back from the dish in front of her and Sylvie said, "I'm sorry. More wine. Chicken stuffed with goat cheese and asparagus." She gestured to a gravy boat. "With wine sauce. And cheesy mashed potatoes and am I forgetting anything?"

"Lordie, I hope not. You're going to kill my buzz with this food," Lydia said. "Sit down."

"Oh! I have a salad. It's in the refrigerator."

Lydia laughed. "I don't want no stinking salad. Serve that to skinny wenches who have a husband who will have sex with them. Polly? You want salad."

"That's okay," Polly said.

"Yeah, yeah, yeah." Beryl said, grinning at her. "You'll just go home and work off everything you eat. You two must be awfully quiet to be having first year married sex with people living in your house."

"I knew this conversation was going to get to me," Polly said. "So really. You aren't going to tell us who you've been having sex with?"

"You're having sex with someone?" Lydia asked, draining her fourth glass of wine. "Why didn't you tell me?"

"I'm not!" Beryl protested.

Andy shrugged a shoulder, "After all of that and now is when you deny it? I think you're the one who is protesting too much."

"How did this turn on me? I was fine with it being about Sylvie and Eliseo."

"Well, I wasn't. I'm the cook and provider of alcohol tonight," Sylvie said. "Deal with it. And tell us about your sex life."

"I'm not talking. Now pass that chicken over here. We need to put food in your mouths and stop them all from babbling."

CHAPTER ELEVEN

Polly's head hurt. A lot. And she couldn't figure out why it was so dark. Then she moved her feet. No animals were tucked in, restricting her movement. Where was she?

Then it came back to her. Sort of. Her phone had to be here somewhere. Polly patted around her body and ran out of bed. No. Sofa. She was asleep on Sylvie's new sofa. Good heavens, she hoped she hadn't been drooling on one of those new pillows. She turned over on her side and her cheek rubbed on a smooth ... yes, that was a pillow case. She was still drunk and she didn't feel good. What time was it?

A moan alerted her to the fact that there was someone else in the room. She remembered now. They'd inflated a blow-up bed and Beryl was sleeping on it. Lydia and Andy were upstairs in Jason and Andrew's rooms.

Last night would have been embarrassing if it hadn't been so terribly funny. They'd laughed and polished off several more bottles of wine before Eliseo and the boys arrived. He walked in and saw what was happening and sent the boys up to their rooms to pack for a night and for school the next day. He moved those boys in and out so quickly, they didn't have time to ask questions, even though Polly was sure they would have plenty.

While the boys were packing, he made phone calls. His first was to Henry. Polly shut her eyes again. No wait. She hadn't opened them yet. They felt like they were stuck together. Henry had actually come by on his way home from the shop. He'd asked if she wanted him to drive her home, but they weren't finished with their evening yet and if she remembered right, she'd actually gotten down on her knees in front of him and begged for him to let her stay a while longer.

Oh good heavens, she'd begged him! She hadn't been this drunk since college.

When Eliseo called Aaron, Lydia started to cry. The poor man didn't know what to think of it and oh, good heavens again. Polly had gotten on the phone with Aaron, telling him that there was no dead body, but he was killing his wife. Eliseo grabbed the phone back and made each of the women promise that they wouldn't try to go anywhere. The last call was to Len, who was quite confused with the entire situation. Andy just didn't drink all that much.

The truth was, none of them really drank all that much, but easy access to bottles and bottles of wine, a good meal, and the fact that they really hadn't spent time as a group together in months was a recipe for disaster. Lydia's problems with her husband were the tipping point and to avoid really talking about it, they just kept pouring until Sylvie passed out... at the kitchen table. Andy had barely gotten the plate out from under Sylvie's face. She'd been leaning on her hands, they were all laughing, and then she was gone.

The rest of the evening had been chaos as the women looked for sheets for the sofa. Sylvie had come awake enough to tell them where the air bed was.

Beryl ended up dragging it down the steps and flopped down on the floor with it, starting to blow it up herself. Fortunately, Lydia found the foot pump and they took turns inflating the bed.

Polly tried to open one eye. A street light was shining into the room, but her eye didn't want to stay open. She tried opening the other eye, but since it was pressed into the pillow, she failed and started to giggle.

"Shut up, whoever you are," Beryl said.

"It's me. Polly."

"Shut up, Polly."

"What time is it?"

"Damned if I know. We're too old for this."

"Uh huh. Where's my phone?"

"You were all worried about it last night. You kept trying to call Henry to tell him to take care of the animals. And then you had to call him to tell him that you loved him. And then you had to call him to remind him to take Rebecca to school. We finally had to take it away from you."

"Where is it?"

You cried when we wouldn't let you have it. Pat the table in front of you. It has to be right there. You threatened to post pictures of all of us on Insty-book or whatever it is that you youngsters use."

Polly felt for the table and began to pat the top of it until her hand landed on something that felt familiar. It was her phone. She swiped it open and shut her eyes tightly against the bright light.

"Turn it off!" Beryl moaned. "Why would you do that?"

"Because I want to know what time it is."

Polly opened her eyes to a squint and peered at the phone's screen. "It's four fourteen."

"Okay, so it's four fourteen. What does that mean to you?"

"Nothing."

"We don't have to be awake. Shut that thing off, shut your eyes and leave me alone."

"I have to pee."

"You're in your mid-thirties, you don't have to pee. I have to pee." There was rustling as Beryl moved on the air bed. "Damn it, why aren't you in this bed on the floor. How are these old legs supposed to haul me up in time so I don't wet my pants? Why didn't you wake me up earlier?"

"Do you need a hand? I think I can help."

"No. Leave me alone." There was a thud. "Crap. I'm on the floor."

"Do you need help now?"

"I need some light. Can you turn that damned phone back on?"

Polly swiped her phone open again and found the flashlight app, then shone it around the room. The place was a complete mess. She finally found Beryl on the opposite side of the air bed. "Are you okay?"

"Get yourself over here and help me up. This is ridiculous."

"I can't believe you fell out of bed." Polly was trying not to laugh. Her head really hurt.

"I can't believe I didn't wet myself. Will you get over here now?"

"Are you hurt?"

"No. I'm not hurt, but there isn't a limb on my body that is capable of independent movement right now. This is why I don't drink."

"I feel like I might still be drunk."

"Ya think? We stopped four or five hours ago and at that point none of us could remember how much we'd had."

Polly bent down and tried to reach under Beryl's armpits to lift her up."

"What in the hell are you doing?" Beryl cried out. "You weirdo. Just give me your hand."

"I didn't know how broken you were."

"Not that broken. And you're going to make me laugh. We don't want me laughing right now. Trust me on that." She took Polly's proffered hand and lifted herself to a standing position. "Look at that. Steady as a ... nope, not steady at all. Let's find that bathroom."

"It's right through here." Polly shone her flashlight ahead of them so they could walk, and turned the light on in the bathroom.

Beryl weaved backwards and then forward into the room. "That's too bright. They should make drunk woman lighting levels. Stay here. If I don't come back, break the door down."

"Don't lock the door. I don't want to wake everyone upstairs,"

Polly said.

Beryl leaned backwards and yelled, "Hey, upstairs drunks. We're up and peeing. Do you want to join us?"

"Beryl!"

"Well, if you hadn't gotten me up I might have wet the bed. Wouldn't it be embarrassing if someone wet a bed upstairs?"

"No one is wetting any beds. Now go do your thing."

"Think she's got aspirin in here? And water? I should probably rehydrate. We should both rehydrate. Imagine that. Tomorrow morning when we all get up, you and I will be just fine and they'll all be hung over."

"Go to the bathroom."

"Right." Beryl leaned into Polly. "I really gotta pee."

"This is the right place. And will you hurry? Because me too."

Beryl went into the bathroom and shut the door, then started singing *"Old black water, keep on rollin,' Mississippi moon, won't you keep on shinin' on me."*

"What is she doing?" Polly jumped a foot to the side when Lydia asked the question right beside her.

"She's peeing. You scared me to death. What are you doing down here?"

"I have to go to the bathroom and Andy is using the toilet upstairs."

"Well, I'm next."

"Well, if it rains, I don't care, don't make no difference to me."

"You're not helping, Beryl. Stop singing that song. It has too much water in it." Polly said.

The singing stopped and was replaced by a hideous giggle. "I wanted to help. Here, I'm washing my hands now." The faucet turned on and Beryl opened the door. "Lydia. Are you down here to play with us too?"

Lydia grabbed Beryl's arm and pulled her out of the bathroom. "Get out. There's a line!" She winked at Polly and slipped past them and shut the door behind her.

"Hey!" Polly said. "Not fair."

"I might be old, but I'm wily," Lydia said. "You're too trusting."

"What is going on down here?" Sylvie asked, standing on the bottom step. Andy was right behind her.

"We're sorry," Beryl said. "Did we wake you up? It's Polly's fault."

Lydia opened the bathroom door. The faucet was still running and Polly grabbed her hand, tugged her out, ran in and shut the door.

"It's not my fault," she called out. "I just wanted to know what time it was."

"It's four thirty," Sylvie said. "Is everyone as messed up as I am?"

Polly remembered to wash her hands and turned off the faucet and then went back into the hallway where everyone was standing. "Were you all waiting for me? That's so nice."

"Is anybody hungry?" Andy asked.

Lydia nodded. "I could eat."

"I kind of remember cleaning things up in the kitchen," Sylvie said. "But I'm afraid to look." She flipped on the light in the hallway and they wandered into the kitchen.

Food had been put away and plates had been stacked in the sink. "See, we weren't so bad," Andy said.

"You're the one who made us do this," Beryl accused. "You wouldn't let us go to sleep until we picked up. And there was Sylvie sleeping on the table."

Sylvie shook her head. "I got hammered. I have never, ever done that before."

"Do you have eggs?" Lydia opened the refrigerator and then quickly closed the door. "Okay, that wine sauce wasn't covered and it's making me ill."

Polly was arranging the wine bottles on the counter. "There are eleven empty bottles here," she said and pointed around the room at each of them. "There are five of us."

"We're old enough to know better." Lydia was opening cupboard doors.

"What do you need?" Sylvie asked.

"Glasses. I need water. And do you have aspirin?"

"Polly the aspirin is in the bathroom cupboard. Can you get it?"

Polly nodded and left the room. She came back with a bottle, trying to get it open. "This is child proof. Since you all are older than me, one of you should open it."

Andy finally took the bottle and popped the top off. The five of them stood in the kitchen, leaning on counters while they each took a couple of aspirin and slugged down a full glass of water. Beryl was filling hers again when Lydia started to laugh.

"What's so funny?" Polly asked.

"Look at us. Just look at us. If anyone else in the entire world saw us right now, they wouldn't believe it. We got smashed last night and then kicked Sylvie's boys out of their own beds on a school night so we could have a drunken slumber party. Who does this?"

"Apparently we do," Sylvie said. "I don't know how I'm going to explain this to Jason and Andrew, though."

Polly nodded. "It would have been fun listening to Eliseo try to explain it. He was so funny when he saw us. The poor man paced back and forth, wanting desperately to get out of here with the boys and trying to figure out how to take care of us." She and Lydia were laughing hard at this point.

"You begged Henry!" Beryl said. "The look on his face was priceless!" She started laughing so hard, she squatted down on her knees and then sprawled her legs in front of her on the floor. The rest of them sat with her as they howled with laughter.

"I'm so glad I peed," Andy said, causing another round of uncontrollable laughing.

"I don't want to go home," Lydia said in the middle of it.

Everyone turned to look at her.

"I've had such a wonderful night. I haven't been this relaxed in a long time. Thank you for taking care of me." Her face screwed up and tears began flowing from her eyes. "This has just been the worst new year and I don't know when it's going to get better."

Beryl scooted close to her on one side and Sylvie slid over to sit on her other side. Andy and Polly both moved in so they were all touching her.

"I don't know what to do anymore," she said through her tears. "I'm tired of fighting. I just want to know if it's worth it."

"It is, honey. It is," Beryl said. "Whatever he's going through, he'll figure it out and then things will go back to normal. I promise."

"But what if they don't? What if he just pulls so far away from me we can't ever find our way back again?"

"That isn't going to happen sweetie," Polly said. "We'll wear him down."

They sat in a huddle on Sylvie's kitchen floor while Lydia cried. When she was finished, she patted Sylvie's knee. "Maybe we need more sleep."

"No food?" Beryl asked.

"Are you really hungry?"

"No, but if you were going to cook, I was going to eat." Beryl held her hand out to Polly. "Will you pull me up again? I can't believe I'm back on the floor."

Polly stood up and helped Beryl stand, then one by one they were all upright.

"Let's try to get some more sleep," Andy said. "We'll help you clean in the morning, Sylvie."

"I want those empty bottles gone before Jason and Andrew see them. It's bad enough that they think I was drinking. I don't want them to know how bad it really was."

Beryl picked two of them up. "I'm going to have a chat with those boys at the winery. If they're going to make such good wine, they can't be giving it to you for free. That's called feeding an addiction."

"I believe they thought I'd use them as gifts or maybe I might spread their use out across, oh, I don't know, a year or so," Sylvie said. "Who would have thought we could drink that much."

"Everybody scoot," Lydia said, making shooing motions. "Back to your beds. Whoever wakes up first starts the coffee and deals with that wine sauce in the refrigerator."

When Polly and Beryl were alone in the living room again, Polly sat down on the air bed.

"What are you doing? That's my bed."

"Only because I didn't know what I was doing. You take the sofa. It's comfortable and I won't have to worry about you falling on your butt in the morning."

"You're a sweet girl, Polly Giller. No matter what they say about you downtown."

"What do they say?"

"That you're a sweet girl, of course. Turn off that light, would you? I'd probably crack my shin on this heavy table if I had to do it."

Polly flipped off the overhead light and swiped her phone open and to the flashlight app as she made her way back to the air bed. She put her head on the pillow and closed the phone.

"What are we going to do about our girl?" Beryl asked quietly.

"I don't know. I talked to Aaron the other day at the diner. He was trapped and I sat down with him."

"What did he say?"

"That he couldn't talk about it. He's as miserable as Lydia. I wanted to be mad at him, but Beryl, he's a wreck."

"He should be. What a jerk. How could you treat that wonderful woman so badly and not be a wreck?"

"There's something else going on."

"It better not be another woman."

"I don't think so. He was upset that I would even think that."

"Good. I'd take a shotgun to his nuts if he did that."

Polly chuckled. She was sure that if Beryl got angry enough, that might actually happen.

"Don't think I wouldn't."

"I know."

"I love that man, but he's gone too far this time."

"It's pretty bad, but I'd like to get the whole story before I start calling for tar and feathers."

"If only he would tell someone what that story is."

"You're right."

"Of course I'm right. Now quit talking to me and go to sleep. Lydia will probably be down here at six thirty in the morning making all sorts of noise."

"Good night, Beryl."

"Good night, sweet Polly. You know I love you, right?"

Polly smiled to herself. Every night she went to sleep after exchanging those words with Henry. She couldn't imagine not hearing them. But Beryl didn't get to hear them every night.

"I love you too, Beryl. You're a wonderful woman."

"Now, shhh."

CHAPTER TWELVE

"Up you go, sweetums."

Polly knew it was Henry's voice and struggled to come awake.

"Would you like some lunch?" he asked.

"Huh? What time is it?"

"It's two o'clock. I thought you might want to take time to eat and take a shower before the kids showed up after school."

"I've slept a lot today."

"Yeah. Nice work if you can get it."

"Is Sylvie downstairs? I can't believe we did that to her. And she's the only one of us that has to work today."

"She's here. She looks pretty rugged, but at least she's upright."

Polly pulled her legs out from between two cats and sat up on the edge of the bed. "I'm pathetic."

"Yes. Yes you are."

"We are never going to speak of last night again, deal?"

"No you don't. You can't make me do that. I've never been quite that entertained."

"You want entertainment, you should have been there for the rest of the night."

"That might have been too much for my poor, innocent ears."

"Yeah. Whatever." Polly stood up and when she wobbled, Henry grabbed her arm.

"Are you going to be okay?"

"I just need a shower. What did you bring me for food?"

"Ice cream."

"That sounds good. Anything else?"

"I asked Lucy at the diner what would make a good hangover meal..."

"You did not." Polly put her hand on the door frame into the bathroom and turned to glare at him.

"She said you needed to rehydrate."

"Oh, good heavens, you did."

"There's a big salad out here for you."

Polly went in to the bathroom and turned on the shower. "That sounds wonderful. I'll get cleaned up. Did you see Stephanie when you went to the convenience store to get ice cream?"

"No, she's not there any longer. I thought you knew that."

"I figured she had two weeks."

"Honey, she's downstairs working."

Polly poked her head out of the bathroom. "She's what?"

"Downstairs. They let her go when she told them she was quitting, so Jeff brought her right in."

"Wow. I have one bad night and the world changes around me. Are you leaving to go back to work or do you get to stay?"

"I wanted to make sure you were alive, but I have to go back. While you're in the shower, I'll take the dogs outside."

"Thank you." Polly stepped into the shower, stood under the hot water and moaned. "Yeah. That's the good stuff," she said. After the hot water loosened her muscles, she scrubbed herself clean and stepped back out.

They had gotten up at seven thirty to Lydia poking around in the kitchen. No one could believe she was so alert. Even worse than Lydia was Andy, who came downstairs a few minutes later, completely fresh and alive. She'd had the least to drink and said that she didn't get hangovers very often. That hadn't gone over well with Beryl, who could barely move. She'd stuck her hand out for a mug of coffee and then flopped into one of the kitchen chairs and watched while Lydia and Andy cleaned the kitchen.

When Sylvie came down, they made toast and had cereal, and then the five women tore through the house, cleaning and organizing as fast as they could.

Polly was home by nine thirty, took the dogs outside and called Henry to let him know where she was. As soon as that call was finished, she crawled into bed and fell back to sleep. She felt much better now - ready to take on the world.

Henry came back in with Han and Obiwan, who ran over to Polly to see if there was anything she wanted to share with them from her salad.

"Ken Wallers is downstairs in the office," Henry said.

"I wonder what's up."

"He was talking to Jeff and Stephanie."

"Oh no. There couldn't be something wrong with her on the first day of work, could there? Hopefully this doesn't have anything to do with the convenience store."

"I don't know."

"Do you think I should check it out?"

"It's your business. If the police show up, you should probably know why."

"You're right. If I hadn't been sleeping, I'd have been downstairs anyway." She jumped up from the table and glanced back and forth from the dogs to the salad. "Yeah. I don't trust you two." She put the salad in the refrigerator and gave Henry a kiss. "Are you heading back to work?"

"I think so. Will you call and tell me what's going on?"

"Absolutely." She kissed him again, this time much more slowly. "You know. I missed you last night."

"I missed you too. It was strange being in bed by myself with all those animals."

"Thank you for taking care of me today."

"This? This was no big deal. But I do want the rest of the stories from last night. Promise?"

Polly thought back to the fun they'd had. "I promise. Beryl fell out of bed. It was awesome. You'll laugh and laugh."

He headed for the back door and Polly went out their front door and down the steps. No one was in the front office when she turned the corner, but she went in and checked Jeff's office. The conference room door was closed and she softly tapped on it and then opened it.

Jeff was sitting beside Stephanie, whose eyes were red from crying. Ken Wallers was across the table.

"What's going on?" Polly asked.

Ken gestured to the seat next to him, "Come in and sit down, Polly."

"Is Stephanie okay? Is she in trouble?"

"She isn't in any trouble," Jeff said, patting the girl's hand. "But she's not okay either."

"This is a terrible way to start a new job," Stephanie said, trying to stop her tears. "I'm so sorry."

"Will someone tell me what has happened?"

Ken said plainly, "Stephanie's mother has been killed."

"Oh, honey, I'm so sorry!" Polly said. "Do you need to go home for the funeral?"

Stephanie gulped back sobs. "No. I'm not going back there. Ever."

Polly looked at her and then at Ken. "You said she had been killed. Do they know who did it?"

Ken glanced over at Stephanie as if for permission and when she nodded, he said. "Stephanie's father."

"Oh," Polly's voice broke and she jumped up out of her chair and ran around the table to gather Stephanie into her arms. "I hope he dies a terrible death in prison. He deserves it."

"What do you mean?"

"He's why I left and came here with Kayla. We ran away. But Mom told us to go. She made us leave."

Polly was certain she didn't want to hear the rest of this story. It was going to be appalling. "Do you want to talk about it?"

The girl fell into Polly's arms, sobbing and shaking her head.

"What do we need to do?" Polly asked Ken.

"Nothing right now. It was very clearly murder at his hand," he said. "Neighbors heard screaming and yelling and called the police. When they arrived, he was still sitting over her, the knife in his hand. He said that she had attacked him and tried to play it off as self-defense, but he has a long history of abuse. He's been arrested several times for battery and the police came into that home quite often."

He said quietly, "Records show that you called several times when you were younger and then again just before you left."

"He raped me over and over," Stephanie said quietly, her face still buried in Polly's chest. "I tried to call the police in the beginning, but Mom couldn't handle it. Then I tried to call when he was starting to look at Kayla. That's when I told Mom that we were leaving and I wasn't telling her where we were going so he wouldn't come looking for us."

"They never filed a missing persons report on you," Ken said.

"How did you find out about this?" Polly asked him. "I would have thought that local news, wherever it was, wouldn't have made it this far."

"One person knew," Stephanie said. "But after I called to tell her that we were here in Bellingwood and safe, we never talked again. I didn't tell her what my address was or give her my phone number. I didn't want her to have to lie."

"Who was that?"

"A neighbor a couple of doors down - Mrs. Jennings. She was probably the one that called the police. She knew that he hit Mom but I never told her what he was doing to me."

"I suspect she knew," Ken said. "She talked to the police department last night and told them where you were. She thought you'd want to know that he was finally in jail and if you wanted to come home, you could."

"I'm never going back there."

"Is there anything in the house that you want?" Polly asked.

"No." Stephanie spat the word out. "He owned everything in that house and always made sure we knew it."

Ken spoke up. "Someone from that police force might need to talk to you. Especially if your father insists that he killed her in self-defense."

"Did they see how big he is and how little she is? Even if she did try to kill him because she'd had enough, he could have controlled her until the cops got there. He just lost control all over again and this time it went too far. I was always worried that he'd kill her someday, but I was afraid I'd still be in the house and then I would never be able to get away. And I wasn't leaving without Kayla."

"Oh, Stephanie," Polly said again.

Stephanie started to cry again. "Mom sacrificed her life so me and Kayla could get out of there. She knew he'd hurt her bad when we left, but she told us to go anyway. She gave me some money and told me that I was supposed to find a small town. Not a big town or a city. But a small town because people would take care of us."

"How long have you been here?" Polly asked

"Just after that big tornado last summer. We lived in a wrecked home until I had enough money to rent that trailer."

"And no one knew?"

"One lady knows. She helps us with food sometimes and she got some clothes so Kayla could start school. Then I told her that I didn't want any more help. I had to do this by myself. I wasn't ever going to rely on anyone again."

"Who is it that knows?" Polly was sure she knew already, but needed confirmation.

"Her name is Andy something."

Polly sat back, a bemused look on her face. "Andy Specek?"

"Yeah. That's her. She came into the convenience store, so I got to know her. One day she saw me at the grocery store. I didn't have enough money and she paid for our food, then she asked me some questions and I ended up telling her everything. She's so nice. Did you know she was a teacher? She was the first person to even care that I was here."

"She is a wonderful person," Polly said. "She's one of my best friends and her husband works for Henry."

"That's right," Stephanie said. "I remember her telling me that."

Ken stood up. "I'm very sorry to have had to tell you this today, Stephanie." She nodded and he walked to the door. "I'll be in touch if we need anything else. Otherwise, you're in good hands here. Polly and Jeff are good people." He grinned at Polly and left.

"Is this too weird?" Stephanie asked. "Are you sure you want me to stay here now?"

Jeff finally spoke up. "What do you mean?"

"Are you sure you want me around?"

He took a deep breath and let it out in something that sounded like a growl. "Stephanie. All I can do is be thankful that you were here today and not anywhere else when you found out about this. When you come to work at Sycamore House, you become part of a big family. We watch out for each other and when things like this come up, we have a tendency to step in and make sure you're safe while you deal with it."

"How are you going to tell Kayla?" Polly asked.

"She's coming here after school with Rebecca. Is that okay? I know that we didn't talk about it first."

"Of course it's okay."

"I can't believe Mom is dead," Stephanie said. "It's my fault."

Jeff took her hand. "It's not your fault. It's your father's fault."

"She made us leave. We talked about it the last night he raped me. When he was done, he went in to her room and beat her up. He told her that she was worthless and he would rather be dead than have sex with her and that it was a good thing she'd had two girls. We were the only reason he stayed."

Polly and Jeff looked at each other. Neither of them had any idea what to say, so they just held on to Stephanie while she talked.

"When he went to work the next morning, I told her that we were all leaving. I had a car because I worked on the other side of town. I'd already picked out Bellingwood. I loved the name of the town and I remember watching old episodes of MASH. Radar loved his family in Iowa so much, I thought it had to be a good place.

"Mom said she couldn't leave, but I had to. She called the school and told them that Kayla had a family emergency and I was picking her up."

Stephanie sobbed into Polly's shoulder again, then straightened up. "I really did beg her to come with us. I didn't want to leave the house. I knew he'd hurt her, but she told me that if she left with us, he'd never stop looking. And if he tried to file a missing person's report on me and Kayla, she'd call the police and cancel it. When I tried to tell her where we were going, she shushed me. She didn't want to know, just in case the beating got so bad she blurted it out. We cried a long time, but she told me that it was the only courageous thing she would ever be able to do. She hadn't been able to protect me, but the two of us could protect Kayla."

Polly didn't know why these people kept coming into her life, but she was glad she had resources to help when they did. She took a breath and asked, "Do you want anyone with you when you talk to Kayla or would you like to be alone with her?"

"I can't believe I told you so much," Stephanie said and turned to Jeff. "I'm so sorry. I'm really a good employee. I don't like dragging my personal life into things."

"Please don't," he said. "No one is exempt from bad things in their lives. You shouldn't have to apologize when they show up in your face. This doesn't change my opinion of you at all." He thought about what he'd just said. "I take that back. It *has* changed my opinion of you. You're amazing. You are the courage that your mother wanted to have. You've not only made a safe home for your sister, but you also kept her in school and held down a job."

"I'm glad to be here. We were at the end," Stephanie said. "If it weren't cold out, they'd have turned our heat off by now. Hopefully with the extra money I'm making, we'll finally catch up."

Polly realized that was an easy fix. She wondered how many others were in the same situation. Jeff didn't want her offering to take away Stephanie's independence, but she could at least do something about their desperate financial situation.

She heard noise in the main foyer and poked her head out of the conference room door. Rebecca, Kayla and Andrew were coming into the office.

"Hi kids," she said, closing the door behind her. "How was school today?"

"Is Stephanie here?" Kayla asked. "She said I could come over because she started working here today. I drew a picture at school to congratulate her."

"That's wonderful. She's in the other room right now and I think she wants to talk to you. Andrew and Rebecca, would you go upstairs and take the animals outside? Henry did a while ago, but I'm sure they're waiting for you to show up. You know how much they love you."

"Did you see Jerry Smith's black eye today?" Andrew asked Rebecca as they left the main office.

"Yeah. What happened?" she asked.

Polly missed the rest of the conversation when they got too far away. She wondered what happened, too.

She knocked on the conference room door and opened it slightly, enough to peek in. "Kayla's here. Do you want us in there or not?"

"Can Jeff stay?"

"Absolutely. I'll be in my office if you need me." Polly pushed the door open and Kayla started through it.

When she saw her sister's red face and puffy eyes, she stopped. "What happened?" she asked. "Are you fired or do we have to move? What?"

Stephanie patted the chair beside her. "No. I'm fine and we can stay. Come here and sit beside me. I need to talk to you."

Kayla looked up at Polly and hesitantly entered the room. Polly pulled the door shut and went into her own office and sat down. Those girls had a lot to deal with right now and she was thrilled that Stephanie preferred Jeff's presence to hers. Those two would be working together every day and the sooner she trusted him, the better.

There was still enough time to call the local electric company.

The only information they would give Polly was how much Stephanie was behind. It was less than two hundred dollars. Polly asked about others who were in that much trouble and after the representative gave her recommendations, she took care of those and asked that it all remain anonymous. At least it was a start.

The next call was to Henry. He answered on the first ring. "Is everything okay?"

"I love you, Henry."

"I love you too. What's going on?"

"Everything is okay. At least it's all okay here in Bellingwood. Stephanie and Kayla's father killed their mother last night. He's an abuser and he raped Stephanie. She ran away with Kayla before he could start on her sister."

"No," he gasped. "Those poor girls."

"I know. But do you want to know the best part?"

"There's a best part?"

"Okay. It is for me. I was in there as a soft shoulder to cry on when she talked about it, but she wanted Jeff with her when she talked to Kayla. He's doing the rescue, not me. He knows that I'll do whatever he needs me to do, but he's got this."

"You're a funny girl."

"What do you mean?"

"Most people would have to be involved because they couldn't let a rescue like this happen without their input. Not you. You are just as happy to have someone else take care of it and back them up when they need it. You're an amazing woman, Polly Giller."

"You're a crazy man. I want to help her, but she wants him and I'm perfectly happy to let him. I have enough other things to deal with."

"Like I said, you're amazing."

She was embarrassed. "Stop it. Anyway, I wanted you to know what was going on and I especially wanted you to know how much I love you. I appreciate that you are honorable and have integrity and would never consider hurting another human being, much less your daughter or your wife."

"The thought of that makes me shudder," he said. "I am always amazed at humanity's capacity for harm. We can come up with the most horrendous things to do to each other."

Polly interrupted. "But then I think of you and realize that we have an even greater capacity for love. You teach me that every day."

"So... ice cream sandwiches tonight?"

She laughed. "Stephanie isn't working up there anymore. You're going to have to... oh, and that's the other crazy thing."

"What?"

"Andy knows all about her. When she started telling me about this lady in town who had helped her with groceries and got her going, I just figured it was Lydia. No! It was Andy."

"Hmm," Henry said. "I didn't put that all together. Len said something last summer about a young girl that Andy was helping. He was building a set of steps. That must have been the steps that went up into the trailer."

"We have the best people in our lives, don't we," Polly said, her throat clenching as she tried to hold back tears.

"We really do. Okay. I'm going back to work and I'll be home with plenty of ice cream bars. It sounds like we might have to pass them around."

"I love you, Henry."

"Love you too, sweetums."

"Goofball."

CHAPTER THIRTEEN

"Taking a break from your regular job?"

Polly was surprised to see Stu Decker walk into her office.

"Hey Stu," she said as she stood and shook his hand. "What are you doing here? And no, I haven't found any more bodies."

"For which we're grateful. We have enough going on right now."

"How can I help you?"

"Jeff said he would make a copy of the information he was given by Albert Cook, the guy who was killed last week."

"When did you ask him for it?"

"This morning."

"Okay," she said with a chuckle. "That just tells me where I need to look for it. He's in the conference room right now."

"I'm sorry. I should have let him know for sure when I was coming."

"It's no big deal. Let's look out on Stephanie's desk first."

"I should have just had him email it to us, but I knew I'd be in town this afternoon."

"Really, not a problem. Let me check."

Polly went out to the main office and found a neat stack of folders on one corner of the desk. She flipped through them until she pulled out a manila envelope tagged with Stu's name.

"I think this is it," she said, handing him the envelope.

He opened it and pulled out two sheets of paper. "Thanks. That's it. How are you doing after everything that happened last weekend? I know you've found bodies before, but this was intense."

Polly sat back down at her desk. "Honestly, I haven't had time to think about it much this week. I was a mess Saturday night, but then, just like it always does, life took over and I lost control of everything."

He smiled at her. "You do tend to run on the edge up here."

"Hey!" It was only a weak protest, but Polly didn't think it was fair to let that one go. She leaned forward. "I have a question."

"Shoot."

"How's Aaron doing?"

Stu peered at her, trying to uncover her motives. "This case really has him worked up. He knew the guy, you know. They were supposed to get together this week."

"Okay, but where does he know this guy from?"

"Sorry, I figured you already knew that. It was when he was living in Atlanta. This guy was on the force with Aaron."

"Aaron was on the police force in Atlanta? I had no idea."

"Yeah. That's where he grew up."

"And he moved to Iowa? I wonder why?"

"I don't know. He never talks about it. Something happened with a case, I think."

"And you don't think it's all connected?"

"It's not." Stu sounded really certain of that.

"So, Aaron's been acting like a jerk for a month or so, one of his old co-workers comes to Bellingwood and is killed by a sniper, you tell me that he left that place because of a case, and you aren't asking questions as to how these things might be related?"

Stu shook his head and smiled patronizingly at her. "We've asked all the questions. There's nothing there."

"Really. Nothing there. And who says that there's nothing there? Aaron?"

"Yes, but the Iowa DCI has been involved in the investigation too and they aren't finding any connections."

"Who's the lead? Aaron's buddy, Digger? Those two go way back."

Stu sat up straight, his jaw grew stiff. "I don't know what you are insinuating, but I don't like it. Aaron Merritt is not involved in this murder. I thought you were his friend."

"Don't get all defensive," Polly said. "I'm not the only person who is going to ask questions. Have you come any closer to finding out who the shooter is?"

Stu didn't relax and Polly knew she'd crossed a line. "Look, Stu," she said. "Aaron and Lydia are my friends and you know that as well as anyone, but something is going on. If it were anyone else, you'd be all over it."

"But it's not anyone else. It's Aaron. He has more integrity and honor than anyone I've ever met in my life. He's not involved in this man's death."

"And that's all you're investigating - this Albert Cook's death?"

"What do you mean?"

"What if he was killed because of something that happened when they were both in Atlanta? What if there's some connection?"

"If anything comes up while we're investigating the shooting, we'll make sure there aren't any loose ends, but right now, there's nothing else."

"Every good crime show would have you checking into the cases those two men worked together when they were in Atlanta."

"But we aren't a crime show and Polly, we're in Iowa. How exactly would you want us to go through those records?"

"They aren't digital?"

"Who knows? It was thirty years ago. I don't know if they've gotten scanned into the system. And I'm not going to start bringing things up that don't have any bearing on this case."

"I think you're being stubborn. How could they not have

something to do with this case?"

"You don't think that Albert Cook could have just been in town to visit Aaron. Maybe to spend time with an old friend?"

"Well, no." she said.

"If you must know, we have emails going back about six months between those two men, setting up a time for them to get together. Albert's wife died last summer, his kids are all across the country, he was retired and he reached out to Aaron. I guess he was like Aaron's mentor. Polly, we've asked all these questions."

"Okay, but still, there's something odd going on with Aaron. And it just can't be this random."

"Yes it can. Spend time in my shoes and you'd be surprised at how random things can really be sometimes."

"And I'm guessing you don't want to admit how often random circumstances usually end up being connected."

He grinned. "You've got me there. Some of your cases have been really out there."

"That's what I mean."

"Don't try to make more out of this for Aaron than it already is. He's pretty upset that his old friend came into town and was killed."

"So, I'm asking again. You've got nothing on who did it?"

"It's probably someone from out of state."

"Well, duh. It's not like we have a state filled with highly trained snipers. I don't know anyone who is."

Stu took a breath and looked at her. "Aaron is."

"The one man in town who is a sniper and it's my friend," she said. "You really aren't making this easy on me."

"That's not my job," Stu said, glaring at her, "My job is to follow an investigation and that's what I've been doing all week long. But it wasn't Aaron. Don't ask me to explain how we know, but we do."

"I don't mean to sound like I'm accusing him of the murder."

Stu looked at her skeptically.

"That's not it at all," she said. "Aaron wouldn't kill someone like that. Especially not in his home town. He's not that stupid. But I just can't believe that this whole thing doesn't have some connecting point."

"Anything's possible, but there's nothing there." Stu stood up. "Don't bother Aaron with this. He's got enough on his plate. If you start doing your investigating thing..."

"What, it might make him even more distant and morose?" she asked.

"Just leave it alone. We're handling it."

"Aaron's bad mood is rubbing off on you."

"Let us do our job, Polly. This one time. Just let us do our job." He spun and walked away before she could say anything else.

Polly smacked her fist down on her desk. This was the second time she'd gotten frustrated with these men.

Rebecca and Andrew came running into her office and jumped into the chairs in front of her desk. They both started talking at once.

Andrew: "Eliseo asked us..."

Rebecca: "Can I..."

The two kids looked at each other and giggled. "You go," Rebecca said.

"No, you go," Andrew repeated.

"One of you, go," Polly said.

Rebecca put her hand over her mouth and pointed at Andrew.

"I'm going," he said. "Eliseo said that since it was such a warm day, we could go for a wagon ride. Can we? We're going to take hot dogs and chips and stuff for s'mores and make a fire. Can we?"

"Of course you can," Polly responded. "That sounds like a blast. Who's going?"

"Me and Rebecca and Jason for sure. He said that if Kayla was here, she could go and there was room for Stephanie and Jessie too, but she's probably working."

"I don't know how much she'd like climbing in and out of that wagon," Polly said. "She's pretty pregnant."

"Do you and Henry want to come?" Rebecca asked.

A flash of something went across Andrew's face.

When Polly said, "No. I think it would be more fun if it was just you kids with Eliseo," his face brightened up again. That was it. He just wanted to play without much adult intervention tonight. That made sense. And she was thrilled that he wanted to do something with the horses and with Eliseo. Any opportunity to get both of the kids playing outside was one she'd grab.

"Have you asked your mom, Andrew?"

"She said it was okay. She'll let us do anything with Eliseo. And she won't be done working until late anyway."

"Then, yes. Rebecca, you make sure you have your warm clothes on. I know it has been a nice day, but it could get cold."

"He's going to put blankets in the back for us."

"Warm clothes," Polly said again. "And mittens and a hat."

The conference room door opened and Stephanie and Kayla came out, both looking drawn and defeated.

"Do you guys want to go on a wagon ride tonight?" Andrew asked, jumping out of his seat when he saw them.

"Maybe not tonight," Jeff said. "But another time."

Kayla perked up, but then she remembered that she was supposed to be sad and her shoulders drooped again.

"Just a second guys. I need to ask Jeff something."

Polly stepped into the outer office after he had ushered Kayla and Stephanie into his office and shut the door.

"What's up?" he asked.

"Can you ask Kayla again if she'd like to go?"

"She's been through a lot this afternoon. The girls want to go home and rest."

"Okay. She just seemed to perk up at doing this."

"I know. But Stephanie needs her as much as anything."

Polly nodded and said, "You're right. I'll ask Eliseo to do this again soon. Maybe she can go that time. They are staying in town, aren't they?"

"Oh yes. Neither of them want anything to do with their old home."

"I can't thank you enough for being with them this afternoon. That was over and above for you."

"No problem. You've been training me for the last couple of years. It was my turn to take care of people."

"You were exactly the right person to be in their lives."

"Yeah. I know. Gay man. Can't be much safer than that, can you?"

Polly felt the laugh begin in her belly. "You are such a nut. But, you're right. And Stephanie picked right up on that."

"She held on to you while she sobbed."

"Because I walked into it and held her. She never really let go of you. I hope that you'll be able to deal with this and maintain a good working relationship with her without her falling in love with you."

Jeff leaned in and whispered. "I've dealt with girls who've had ridiculous crushes on me before. Gay men are always safe for girls who need love. They move on when they finally manage their emotional baggage. We become great friends after they realize there will be nothing more."

"Someday I'll tell you about my gay crush."

He stepped back. "You too?"

"You have no idea. I had no idea. Sal tells me I was blind as a bat - that it was obvious to everyone but me. But I'd fallen in love with him and was not going to be denied."

"This is a story I want to hear someday."

"When we're drinking wine... a lot of wine." Yep, she might have a problem. The thought of wine should have put her off after last night, but no, she was ready to do it again. Maybe not tonight, but someday.

"I want to get the girls out of here. Can you manage..." he nodded toward her office.

"Oh yeah. Sorry." Polly stuck her head in the doorway. "Kids, why don't you go upstairs and get ready for your wagon ride. Kayla and Stephanie won't be going tonight."

Rebecca pulled Andrew out of his chair and ran for the steps. As they went upstairs, Polly heard them chattering away at each other.

"Thanks," Jeff said. "It always amazes me how kids can just

move on. When did we lose that?"

"I think it was junior high. Everything becomes so much more important. And by high school, the angst is enough to kill you."

"That's why I was in drama club. We emoted all over the stage so we could..." He grinned. "No, I was still filled with angst and drama."

Polly went back into her office as Jeff escorted Stephanie and Kayla outside and to Stephanie's car. He handed something to Stephanie as she opened her car door. The girl tried to push his hand back, but he pushed forward and she bowed her head and nodded.

She pulled her phone out and texted Henry. *"Don't bring ice cream. No one will be here but you and me."*

"Do you want to go out or stay in tonight?"

The idea of sitting in her own living room with no one around but her husband and her animals was rather appealing. *"Stay in?"*

"I hoped you would say that. Do you want to cook or have me pick something up?"

There wasn't anything in the refrigerator upstairs worthwhile. She needed to make a grocery store run this weekend. *"Pick up?"*

"Call an order in to Davey's. Put candles on the table. Wine? ;)"

The smiley winkey face cracked her up. *"How about no wine?"*

"I thought so. You'll never make a good alcoholic with that attitude."

"Whatever. See you later."

She didn't have it in her to do busy work in the office and besides, the work day was nearly over. People had been streaming in since she'd come down the stairs, preparing for the evening. She was done.

"I'm going back upstairs," she said to Jeff, stopping in front of his office. "Thanks again for taking care of things."

"No thanks necessary."

"You were awesome."

"My head hurts."

She chuckled. "Of course it does. That's what happens when you get all involved with people. They make your head hurt."

"I have to be here tonight. But what I want to do is go home and go to sleep."

"Ummm... I don't know how to help?"

"Maybe Sylvie has some aspirin. Or wine." He gave her an evil grin.

"Yeah. You go ask her for wine and see what she says."

"You guys really tied one on from everything I've heard."

"What did you hear?"

"Nothing much. Just that you tied one on. I haven't gone near Sylvie today. She's been like a bear with a thorn in its paw."

"That's a lion with the thorn."

"Whatever. She's not friendly. I hope it was all worth it."

"It was so worth it, but I don't think any of us ever want to do that again."

He waved her away. "I'll quit complaining. You go away and I'll talk to you later."

Polly went upstairs and opened her front door to chaos on the floor.

"I don't know what to wear," Rebecca said. "This coat is too hot and should I wear my ski pants?"

"You nut. I don't think it will be *that* cold tonight. Here, let me help." They finally got Rebecca appropriately dressed, much to Andrew's delight.

"Took long enough," he said.

"You'd better not complain about getting cold," Polly said. "Or I'll never let you live it down."

"Mom has my stuff downstairs."

"Good. What time did Eliseo say you'd be coming back?"

"By eight. You don't have to worry about me, though. He's taking Jason and me to our house."

"And I'm going to sleep in Mom's room tonight, if that's okay," Rebecca said.

"Really? No kids in my house tonight? What am I going to do with that? I'll miss you."

"Well..." Rebecca started.

"Oh honey, I'm kidding." Polly hugged her. "Spend time with your Mom and I'll see you in the morning."

"When we go to Beryl's house?"

"Any time in the morning is fine. Just come upstairs whenever you want. If we're not up, you can occupy yourself."

"Can we go now?" an exasperated Andrew asked, tugging at Rebecca's arm.

Rebecca rolled her eyes at Polly. "He gets so impatient."

"Have fun," Polly said, holding the door open for them. She watched them run down the steps and then closed the door.

"We have the house to ourselves tonight," she said to Obiwan. He followed her out into the kitchen. "Henry said candles. I can do that."

Jessie came in through Henry's office door as Polly was setting the candles up. "Romantic dinner tonight?" she asked.

"The kids are all going out on a wagon ride and I figured you were working the reception."

"Absolutely. This extra money is all going into my apartment fund. I'm going to be able to afford to put the first and last month down with no problem. And I'm also saving for a bed and things. You've really helped me by letting me live here."

"You might as well get the best start you can with this new baby. It's going to be pretty crazy for a while."

"I wish I could find a roommate. It would make it so much easier."

"What about one of your friends?"

Jessie shook her head. "They've all got their own stuff going on. Boyfriends, girlfriends. And some of them I would never live with. They're psycho."

"I get that," Polly said. "Something will come up."

"I was kind of thinking that we might stay here for a month, but not much longer. I'll have enough money to buy a couple of things. Especially if I check out some of the thrift stores."

"Henry's building a crib for the baby."

"I know. That's so awesome. It will be really special." Jessie's eyes filled. "You two have been so great. I don't know what I'd do without you."

"I'm glad we can be part of it, sweetie. You've been a great help with the kids and I know that Marie thinks you are doing a wonderful job working there."

Jessie brushed the tears from her eyes. "I cry all the time. It's so stupid. I need to change my clothes for working in the kitchen. I'll see you later tonight. Have fun with Henry."

"Thanks." Polly went back into the kitchen, checked the time and made the call to Davey's to order supper.

CHAPTER FOURTEEN

Sanity by pizza. Polly dropped into her regular chair at Pizzazz.

An unfamiliar waitress approached the table and asked Polly what she wanted to drink. The question confused her so much that she looked up in surprise and said, "I don't know."

"Okay. I'll come back in a while. Will there be others joining you?"

Polly shook her head to clear the cobwebs and then put her hand out to stop the girl. "I'm sorry. I know what I want. Where's Bri?"

"She took the night off," the girl said, chomping loudly on a piece of gum. "Something about a baseball game or football or I don't know what. So do you know what you want?"

"Yeah. We're here every Sunday night and Bri just takes care of it, so I'm afraid I lost my mind for a minute. There will be four of us." Polly paused to take a breath and the girl cut in.

"I'll be back with menus."

Polly opened her mouth to say, "No wait," but the girl was already three tables away, heading for the front of the restaurant.

Sal and Joss came in the front door and waved to Polly before wending their way through the tables.

"Where are the drinks?" Sal asked. "They're always here."

Polly rolled her eyes. "New waitress. Bri is at some baseball football thing."

"Really!" she said with a laugh. "Interesting rules."

"She's bringing us menus. Heads up!" Polly grinned across the table as the girl dropped menus in front of Sal and Joss.

"Four, you said?"

"Honey-chile," Sal said, her voice dripping with Southern charm. "We don' need menus. You mus' have us confused with northenuhs who read."

"You don't read?"

"Only if someone makes it worth my while and honey, you ain't gonna be the one to do that."

"Uh."

At that, Sal snapped the other menus up from the table and put them in a stack. "We're regulars here every Sunday evening and our order is pretty simple. I'm guessing your cook knows exactly what to do and I wouldn't be surprised if it was already in the oven."

"Okay. Can I take your drink orders then?"

Sal was on it. "Two diet cokes, a regular coke and an iced tea. There should be an order of cheese bread and I have no idea what pizza we order every week. It just comes out. I'm sorry. I don't mean to be snippy. It was just surprising to have to think about this."

"I'll ask Sonny. He probably knows." She picked up the menus and scooted away just as Sylvie sat down.

"New girl? Where's Bri? She's never gone." Sylvie said, pulling off her scarf and coat.

"Bri's at some baseball football thing. We forgot what pizza we order."

Sylvie laughed. "I have no idea. How did you fix it?"

"We hope Sonny remembers," Joss said. She leaned over toward Sylvie. "Would you like me to order a glass or two of wine for you?"

Polly laughed. "How did you hear about that?"

"What? What does she know?" Sal asked.

"These two got blasted Thursday night and couldn't make it home. I hear there were shenanigans."

"No shenanigans," Polly said. "But yes, I will admit to the drunk on my butt thing. A girl can't get away with anything in this town. Does everyone know?"

Sylvie shook her head. "Enough. I heard about it all weekend and they were still teasing me about it this morning at church."

"How come I never get invited to these parties?" Sal was indignant.

"It wasn't going to be that kind of a party," Polly said. "We were just going to have dinner at Sylvie's house. Then it got out of hand. Sylvie's a wonderful host."

"Henry told Nate you were down on your knees begging to spend the night."

"I seem to remember abasing myself," Polly said. "If it had been anyone but Henry and my friends I would have been embarrassed. Now it's just a silly story."

"That sounds like fun," Sal said. "If I remember right, getting Polly drunk is hilarious."

"Okay, I'm a little goofy, but you're the one who throws herself on strange men when she's drinking." Polly looked at the other two. "And I mean that literally. Not just once, but at least five different times. Sal gets happy drunk and flings herself into the laps of strange men. Whether their girlfriends or wives are with them or not. I pulled her out of several bars before she got thwopped with a purse."

"That's why I don't drink any longer," Sal said.

"It's a good thing."

The waitress brought their drinks and a basket of cheese bread. "Your pizza will be out in a few minutes. Sonny knew right away what your order was. It was already in the oven. Sorry about that."

"No problem," Joss said. "Thanks."

"I usually work the lunch hour during the week. I don't know any of these night things."

"Really. We're fine. You're okay. Ignore our crazy lady." Joss looked at Sal, who put her hands up in a 'who me?' gesture.

"I wish Bri would have left me a note about you. I would have read it and known."

Joss nodded.

"It's really confusing to come into someone else's shift and figure out what they usually do."

"I'm sure it is," Joss said.

"Do you need any more napkins or anything? Lemon wedge for your tea? Did I bring enough straws?"

"We're fine, honey," Sal said. "We'll let you know if we need anything. Thanks, though."

She hesitated at the table a moment too long and finally broke and moved away.

"What did you do to her, Sal?" Sylvie asked. "Did you break her?"

"I don't know. I was a little flippant, but..."

"So," Polly interrupted. "Have you signed papers for the building across the street? I haven't heard anything else about it. Are we moving ahead?"

Sal took a deep breath. "I'm scared to death. I keep putting it off, hoping that it will just happen without any intervention on my part."

"That's effective."

"Can you take care of it?"

"I'm sorry, what?" Polly put her drink down to turn her full gaze on Sal. "Are you serious?"

"Maybe. Kinda. I have the financing worked out, but I'm paralyzed at the thought of pulling the trigger. I'm driving Mark crazy. I call him all day long when I'm thinking about it. Then I avoid it at night by writing. I'm not sleeping at all."

"What do you need me to do?"

"I need you to put the papers in front of me and make me sign them. Then I need you to design the place with Henry and make him start working on it. I need you to do everything. I'll just pay the bills."

"When did you get this pathetic?"

"When I moved out here and had to make big decisions by myself. You won't believe it, but Daddy always took care of things. When I decided where I wanted to go to college, he took care of the paperwork and all I had to do was go. When I got my first job, Daddy made sure I had the paperwork for that, too. I just went where they told me and once I was there, I knew what to do."

"How in the world did you ever make it out to Bellingwood?" Joss asked, incredulous at the thought.

"Daddy helped me find a moving company. I paid the bills and they packed everything up and brought it out."

"You are so accomplished and smart and articulate and..." Sylvie started. "I would never have thought this about you."

Sal scowled. "There are a few things that terrify me. If Polly hadn't been here already, I would never have considered coming. She's the one who gave me courage to do what I did in college."

"You did a lot without me," Polly protested.

"All of that was stuff that built on things I'd already done. It's the big, wild decisions that incapacitate me. I'm so afraid that I might be making a huge mistake."

"But you won't know unless you try," Polly said.

"I know that! Why do you think I want you to help me get this started? It's a great idea, but I need you to push me off the starting block."

Polly gave her a gentle shove.

"Yes. Exactly. So now that I've admitted my darkest secret to you, will you help me?"

"I guess so," Polly said with a laugh. "When do you want me to start?"

"Tomorrow morning? I'll come to you with all of the paperwork. My lawyer has already looked at it. Changes are made, things are approved. I just need someone that I trust to force me to do it. And then, help me start the rest of the process."

"I will absolutely be that person for you. But what about Mark?

Why aren't you asking him to help?"

"Maybe I'm not ready to let him see my foibles yet."

"Now's as good a time as any," Joss said.

"Not on this. He said he supports me, but I..." Sal stopped, pursed her lips and looked around the table. "I want him to be proud of what I've done. He's made such an impact in Bellingwood. Everybody loves him. I don't want to take anything away from that."

Polly put her hand on Sal's back and rubbed. "You nut. Don't you realize that you are this mysterious East coast woman who came in and swept their favorite pretty boy off his feet? Women are jealous, men are curious, and kids just gawk at you when you walk past in your four inch red stilettos. You have totally added to Mark's mystique just by being here. When the rumors start that you're buying a building downtown to put a coffee shop in simply because you want a place to write, that's going to rock their little worlds."

"Exactly how are those rumors going to start?" Sal asked.

With a wicked glint in her eyes, Sylvie said, "We're going to start them. A little here, a little there and you're going to have to buy a blond wig and big sunglasses."

Joss and Sylvie began moving things around the table and Polly realized that the waitress was standing behind her with their pizza.

She put it down and brandished a spatula. "Who can I serve first?" she asked.

"Oh, hand that to me, dear," Sal said. "We take care of ourselves." She took it from the very surprised girl's hands and slid slices of pizza onto each of the plates.

"Can I refill your drinks?" She looked down at their full glasses. "Oh, I guess not. If there is anything else I can do for you…"

"We've got this," Polly said. "No worries. You're doing fine."

The waitress hovered for a few more moments, unsure as to what to do next and finally flitted away to another table.

"If she's sticking around on Sunday evenings, we're going to have to re-train her," Sal said.

Sylvie waggled her finger. "You be nice."

"I'm being nice. I'm just saying. She needs to take a few cues from the customers. If they don't want her hovering helpfully, go away."

"So," Joss said. "A coffee shop and what else?"

Sal pointed at Sylvie. "A bakery. Maybe. Are you two still on board with that?"

"I think so," Sylvie said with a sigh.

"Absolutely," Polly said. "That's how you have to handle those questions from now on, Sal. With full assurance. It's going to be a coffee shop and bakery and it's going to be awesome. Once we get the paperwork finished and we figure out what it's going to look like on the inside, we are going to need a name. We want to draw attention while it's being built out and we're going to have to ask Jeff to get involved. He knows everyone in town."

"And you all thought I was just being a scaredy-cat," Sal said. "I know this girl. Once she gets started on a project, she's unstoppable."

Their waitress silently slipped in beside Sylvie and replaced her empty glass with a fresh one, scanned the table and moved away.

"See," Sal whispered. "She figured it out. Maybe I'll steal her for the coffee shop."

Sylvie shook her head. "You're weird. You don't even know her name."

"Shoot me now," Joss said under her breath.

"What?" Sal asked.

"Short lady coming in the front door. The bane of my existence. I promise you, if she sees me, she will come right to the table and the first thing out of her mouth will be something wrong with what I'm doing at the library."

"Good evening, Mrs. Mikkels," the woman said. "I see you are out with friends."

"Hello, Lorna. How are you this evening? Do you know Polly Giller from Sycamore House?"

"I know of you, Miss Giller. Are you planning to do something with that land behind your hotel? It is quite overgrown."

Polly stood up and put her hand out. "Lorna?"

"Lorna Bender. This is my husband." She stood as if waiting for an answer and ignored Polly's hand.

Her husband, who was only a few inches taller than she, but bent at the shoulders, nodded and took Polly's hand to shake it.

"Well?" she asked again.

"We don't actually own that land," Polly said, returning to her seat. "It's part of the winery."

"Then nothing will ever happen with it," the woman said in disgust. "Those three don't know what the meaning of real work is."

"Are you out for the evening or picking up pizza to take home?" Joss asked.

"Floyd, get a table. Not too close to the front door though, it's cold." Lorna turned back to Joss. "I was in the library yesterday afternoon and had to ask three children to not play in the reading lounge. I thought your assistants knew better than to allow that."

"Were they playing or reading books?" Joss asked.

"It doesn't matter. There is a room for children. If they take up all of the chairs, where will other people sit?"

"Was someone unable to find a seat?"

"Not while I was there, but it shouldn't happen in the first place."

"Some of the older children like to be able to read in a quiet place. The staff knows to keep an eye on them. I think there are plenty of comfortable places to sit in that room. We've never had a problem."

"I'll be bringing it up at the next board meeting, then. We need to institute a policy ensuring that children know their place. If you aren't going to take care of it, someone will."

"Mrs. Bender. You hired me to *ensure*..." Joss put extra emphasis on the woman's word, "that the library is a place where all of the people in Bellingwood feel safe and comfortable. The children are part of Bellingwood and in many cases they bring their parents in rather than the other way around. I am not about to institute a policy that will make it more difficult for them to read."

"We'll see," the woman said. "I need to make sure Floyd places our order correctly. I will be in Tuesday afternoon to discuss this again."

"I look forward to seeing you then," Joss said. She waited until the woman turned her back and then drew her hands into claws and raised her upper lip.

Polly chuckled. "It seems like you have her well in hand."

"For goodness' sake," Joss said, exhaling loudly. "I don't know why she thinks that she has the run of the place. She and her husband donated money to the foundation, but it's no more than many other people. For some reason, she believes that entitles her to complain about everything and demand that we adhere to her outdated opinions. Would you believe that she insisted we not use her money to bring computers into the library? And movies. She complains about movies. Apparently, we are only supposed to provide books and should be pickier about who we provide them to."

"Speaking of computers and kids, what do you think will happen to kids who went to the library on Mondays?" Polly asked.

"If I didn't have to think about utilities, I'd open the place anyway. But people like Mrs. Bender would find a way to shut me down. I don't know what else to do. The kids loved having a place to come read and we have some great after school activities. Her group calls us overpaid babysitters, but it's an opportunity to build more readers. Drives me nuts."

"What if we opened up Sycamore House on Mondays? If the kids need a place to go, we could add more books to the lounge. Maybe bring older kids in to help with homework in the classroom and open the computer room."

"That sounds fabulous, Polly," Sal said. "I'd come in and help with that."

Polly turned her body toward Sal. "You'd what?"

"I'd help."

"We're pretty slow on Mondays in the kitchen," Sylvie offered. "Rachel and I could come up with healthy snacks. If we did it just one day a week, it would be something different for the kids. Andrew would love this."

"Now I just need someone to be in charge of it," Polly said. "And depending on how many kids are interested, more volunteers."

"I'd be interested," came a timid voice from behind her.

Polly looked up as the waitress replaced her empty glass with another drink.

"In volunteering after school on Mondays?"

"Sure. Or working there. I finish my teaching degree in May at Iowa State and I don't have classes on Mondays. I work here until two, but then I'm free."

"What's your name?" Sal asked.

"Melissa Bradford."

"Any relationship to Lisa Bradford, my mailperson?" Polly asked.

The girl smiled. "That's my mom."

"Isn't that a small world. I tell you what. Why don't you think about it tonight and come by tomorrow. Do you have time in the morning before you have to be here?"

"Sure. I don't have to be here until ten thirty."

"Can you come by at nine?"

"Okay."

"Look the place over and then think about what types of things you might do with a whole bunch of kids. Think about plans for a small group - say five or ten, and then consider what might happen if you had thirty or forty kids show up. All ages. If you come up with something interesting and creative, maybe we can create an internship for you. If there's enough interest, maybe it can be a paid internship."

"Really?"

"Why not."

"Thanks." She held the bill in her hand, hesitating as to whether she wanted to put it down.

"Don't even think about it," Polly said, taking it from her. "You haven't got another job yet. We're all working women here. We've got it."

"Thank you. I'll be back in a while. No hurry."

"Well, well, well," Sal said. "I thought about hiring her at the coffee shop and Polly beat me to it."

"It might not even work out. But at least she's interested." Polly looked at Joss who was quietly laughing. "What are you laughing at?"

"I keep hearing your friends say that you try to solve every problem Bellingwood has. They weren't kidding."

"Shut up. I have this huge facility and my dream is that it is filled every waking hour of the day. If I have to bring kids in to make noise and fill it up, then that's where I'll start."

CHAPTER FIFTEEN

Polly sent a text to Lydia, while waiting for Melissa Bradford to arrive. *"Do you have time for lunch today?"*

Jeff hadn't been at all surprised when Polly sat down across from him in his office to talk about opening the classroom area up to kids in the afternoons. He promised to start on insurance and licensing questions right away. Not only would this be good for the kids, but it would be an opportunity to expose a much larger group of people to Sycamore House. Within an hour, he'd already scheduled a meeting with Joss and the principal at the elementary school. Closing the library on Mondays had upset many routines and the school was scrambling to provide a safe place for their children.

"I'd love to, but can't get away until one o'clock," Lydia texted back.

"That's perfect. Where?"

"Can we find some place a little less noisy than the diner?"

Polly grinned. The diner was packed every day for lunch. While that was great for business, they desperately needed a few more restaurants in town. She'd heard rumors that there might be a Mexican restaurant and maybe a Chinese buffet opening in the next several months and hoped either of those would be true.

"Come here. Either we'll do takeout from Sylvie's kitchen or we can make sandwiches upstairs."

"Thank you. I'd love to. See you later dear." Lydia texted just like she spoke. She couldn't help herself.

Melissa Bradford came bouncing in the front door and Polly got up to meet her in the main foyer.

"Good morning," she said with a smile.

Polly gestured to the lounge and classroom area. "Let me show you around."

"I've been here for a couple of wedding receptions," Melissa said. "And last night I asked Mom to describe things so I knew what you had."

She followed Polly into the lounge and then into the other three rooms. "Can we have access to the auditorium too?" she asked.

"Sure," Polly said. "Especially if the kids need to have something active to do."

"That's what I was thinking. We can play games to exercise their big muscles because they'll have been sitting all day."

"That makes sense."

"I'm excited about this opportunity, Miss Giller. There are so many things we can do, whether there are only two kids or two hundred."

"Two hundred kids?"

"You could, you know."

"That would be a lot of children. I don't know if we're ready for that."

"Most of the kids have someplace to go, but if they started having fun here, you never know."

"Let's hope that doesn't happen for a while."

"I was thinking that we could ask for volunteers and solicit some of the businesses. They could give us supplies and maybe even donate money since you're donating the building. Right?"

"Right. It would be great if this became self-sustaining. But Jeff is the one who would help you with that. He knows everyone in town."

"Dad said that the hardware store would be a supporter and Mom thought that the General Store would do it too. She's friends with Tim's wife."

"Follow me. Jeff Lyndsay would like to meet you. It sounds like you've got great ideas." Polly took Melissa into the main office.

"Hi Stephanie," Melissa said, stopping at the desk. "I didn't know you worked here now."

Stephanie smiled at the two of them. "I started last Friday."

"This has to be way better hours."

"It is. Better money, too."

"I'll bet."

Polly looked back and forth between the two girls. "You know each other?"

"She was my coffee supplier," Melissa said. "The first place I go when I get back in town after class."

"He's free," Stephanie said, nodding at Jeff's office.

Polly aimed Melissa that way and realized that she was going to have to get used to having someone else manage interactions with Jeff. Things were growing and getting busier and she was going to have to act more like an owner than she was used to.

"Jeff, this is Melissa Bradford and she has great ideas about the Monday afternoon program for kids."

He stood and put out his hand and then gestured to the seat in front of his desk. "Are you staying, Polly?"

"Do you need me?"

"I think I've got it."

Polly ducked out of his office and back into hers. She'd been awake on and off through the night dreaming up plans for Sal's coffee shop and wanted to start sketching things.

She was head down and focused on her work when she heard Stephanie say, "Just a second, I'll check with her."

"Miss Giller?"

"It's Polly. Please."

"There's someone to see you. Are you available?"

Lydia poked her head in the door and smiled.

"Is it one o'clock already? I haven't been paying attention to the time. Wow, how did that happen?"

"No honey, it's only eleven. You're okay."

"Stephanie Armstrong, this is Lydia Merritt, one of my closest friends."

"Nice to meet you, dear. Are you working here now?"

"Yes ma'am," Stephanie said. "Excuse me." She slipped back out and Lydia closed the door.

"I'm sorry to be here so early, but one of my ladies forgot to tell me that her daughter was spending the week, so I don't have to drive her around. I wanted to see if you would rather go to Boone or Ames for lunch."

"Ames?" Polly brightened up. "Bagels? Can we do bagels?"

"Of course we can. Are you sure I'm not intruding?"

Polly looked down at her sketch pad. "This? I was working on some ideas for a building up town that Sal is buying. She wants to put a coffee shop in."

Lydia tried to look at the sketches upside down. "That's a wonderful idea. Can I see what you've done?"

"It won't make much sense yet. I'm still trying to map out the space. We might put a bakery in the back."

"Would Sylvie take that on, too?"

"We're still talking about it. She says she can do it with some additional help here. It will take time for things to get really busy, so we can grow into it."

"I wouldn't count on it taking very long. Bring your pad. I'll drive and you can tell me all about it."

Polly grabbed her jacket and thought about Obiwan and Han. They'd be okay if she got back in a couple of hours.

"I'm going out to lunch with Lydia," she told Stephanie. "Call if you need me."

Stephanie nodded.

"Are you sure I'm not bothering you?" Lydia asked as they walked out to her Jeep.

"You aren't at all."

Lydia moved things out of the front seat to make room.

"How are things at home?" Polly asked, once they were on the road.

"He's trying to come back, but something is really upsetting him. I just wish he'd talk to me about it."

"He hasn't said anything about the man who was killed? That he knew him when they lived in Atlanta?"

Lydia visibly flinched. "He knew the man from Atlanta?"

"Yeah. What does that mean?"

"I have no idea, but why wouldn't he tell me? Damn it, Polly. Things are so out of control. I don't understand this."

"He never told you who his mentor was? I got that out of Stu Decker."

"Sure. He talked about him years ago, when we were first going out. But it was no big deal. We haven't talked about those days in years. Even when we're with his family, no one talks about the days he was on the police force. I just assumed it wasn't important. He was only a rookie."

"I don't want to turn into a conspiracy theorist or anything," Polly said. "But I'm just not buying that this isn't all connected. Aaron didn't tell you that Albert Cook was coming to Bellingwood? Stu says there are emails between the two of them going back about six months."

"Why does he know that?"

"Because they want to investigate everything. But I don't buy it. How can this not all be connected?"

Lydia drove past the Iowa State University stadium. "You know more than I do. No one in Aaron's office talks to me now unless they're looking for him."

"I might have trapped Stu. He thought he was asking me questions about the shooting."

"You're an evil woman, Polly Giller."

"He got really defensive when he thought I was accusing Aaron of killing that Albert Cook."

"I would have too. Aaron would never kill anyone like that."

"But did you know that Aaron is a trained sniper?" Polly asked.

"Sure. He's very good." Lydia gripped the steering wheel. "Oh."

She came to a stop at the light. "You don't think."

"See. No, I don't think that at all. But it really pissed Stu off when I brought it up. He knows that I love you and that I consider Aaron a friend. Why would he react to me asking questions? I'd never accuse Aaron of that."

"Because everything has been out of control lately," Lydia said as she turned the vehicle onto Lincoln Way. "There's no way they don't know that something is wrong with Aaron. He can't hide it."

"Stu told me that the DCI is involved and found nothing. It just doesn't make sense to me."

"Digger has been here as long as Aaron. They go way back."

"You don't think he'd cover things up."

"Oh, dear, I don't know what to think any longer."

Polly sat in silence until Lydia parked behind the restaurant. "Lydia?" she asked once the Jeep was turned off.

"Yes dear?"

"How long are you going to allow this to go on?"

"I don't know what you mean. I'm not allowing anything."

"Yes you are," Polly said, turning in her seat to face Lydia. "You are the strongest woman I know. You deal with things right up front. You face everything with courage. But not this. You're lying down and playing dead."

"What should I do? This is Aaron. I either trust him or I don't. And when I stop trusting him, we're done."

"Maybe he needs you to do something other than blindly follow along. That doesn't eliminate trust, does it?"

"Okay. What would you have me do?"

"I'm not sure. I believe that Stu and everybody else is hiding something. Maybe it's for our own good, but you and I both know that secrets never work out well for anyone. I think this has something to do with Atlanta."

Lydia pulled her phone out and fiddled with it, passing it back and forth between her hands. "How hungry are you?"

"I'm fine."

She backed out of the parking space and drove back out onto Lincoln Way, headed to Duff and turned north.

"Where are we going?"

"I need someplace quiet. There's a park on the north side of town. It's time to get some answers. If we have to drive through McDonalds because we're in a hurry, we'll eat hamburgers."

"Okay. How are you getting answers?"

"I'm going to make a phone call. If she doesn't answer, I'll call her brother. And if he doesn't answer, I will call the other brother."

"Aaron's siblings?"

"Yes. I'm absolutely certain that his sister knows what's going on. She's older than him and there was always something between the two of them. Something I couldn't know. But it all happened long before I was part of the family and as long as it didn't crawl out and bite me, I didn't figure that I needed to worry about it."

Lydia pulled into the park and drove until she found a place to park facing the South Skunk River. The river was frozen, but still beautiful.

"Sit still," she said. "We'll see how this goes."

She scrolled through her contacts and finally pressed a few buttons and then put the phone to her ear and waited.

"Helen?" she finally said. "Yes. It's me. Lydia."

She listened. "Oh, the kids are all good and the grandkids are adorable. Things are fine. But Helen, I have a different problem. It's Aaron."

A pause. "No, no, no, he's healthy. Nothing like that. But I need to ask a huge favor of you."

Polly could hear the voice speaking in the background, but it was too muffled to distinguish words.

"Aaron has been distant for the last month or so," Lydia said. "I've never known him to be like this in all the years we've been married. And Helen, last week a man named Albert Cook was killed here in Bellingwood. They don't know who did it, but rumor has it that it was a professional... a sniper."

Lydia glanced at Polly, then said, "Helen? Are you there?"

More muffled speaking and Lydia replied. "I just need information. You don't need to come to Iowa."

Her eyes grew wide and her mouth dropped open, then she said. "I understand. I will meet you in Des Moines tomorrow. No. I won't say anything to him. I'm sorry. I didn't mean to upset you."

Another moment of listening. "That sounds fine. I'll be ready for you. It will be good to see you again, too. Goodbye."

Lydia swiped to end the call and put the phone in her lap.

"What?" Polly asked.

"She's coming to Bellingwood. Tomorrow. Now I really don't know what to think about this. I assumed she would give me advice on how to talk to Aaron."

"What else did she say?"

"That I'm not supposed to tell Aaron she's coming because he'll try to talk her out of it and be very angry with me."

"We don't have any more information than we did before."

"She knows something, but didn't want to talk about it on the phone. She said we all needed to be face to face. And she said that Aaron has done nothing wrong, but he needs to tell me everything now. It's over... whatever that means."

"I guess we wait until she gets into town."

Lydia put her hand on Polly's leg. "Can she stay at Sycamore House?"

"I'm sure Aaron would love that," Polly said sarcastically. "But yes, I know there's a room available in the addition. Are you sure?"

"Aaron and Helen have a... let's call it a volatile relationship. They love each other dearly, but can set a room on fire with their sparks. If she says something is black, he explains in no uncertain terms that it's gray and she doesn't understand how color works. There's no one else on the planet who sets him off like she does."

"I'm surprised you called her."

"There is also no one else on this entire planet who understands him like Helen does and she is the only person I would trust to have his back no matter what. They may drive each other out of their minds, but she loves him more than I do."

Polly sent a text to Jeff, telling him that she had a guest who needed one of the rooms in the addition. Sycamore Inn had changed how they did things. There were still a few long term guests that requested a room at Sycamore House, but after the experience with the punks in the band last summer, he'd gotten choosier about who stayed on-site.

He responded in the affirmative.

Polly sat back and said, "We've got a room. Just bring her over when you get into town."

"Thanks. I think she'll love the place. She's into old buildings and antiques and all that."

"What does she do?"

"Helen's independently wealthy. Her husband made money before he died. They invested it and now she lives well. She travels and is involved with one of the big children's shelters in Atlanta. I think that's where she spends most of her time and energy."

"No kids of her own?"

"They never got around to that."

"Does she come to Bellingwood very often?"

Lydia shook her head. "No. Like I said, she and Aaron are oil and water. It just got to be too difficult. I think all of our kids have trekked down to Atlanta to see her over the years. They love Aunt Helen and she spoiled them rotten. She's quite a character. I think you'll love her."

"A character like Beryl?"

Lydia backed up and turned to head out of the park. "That's interesting. Yes. She's like Beryl. She's outspoken and doesn't care if people are annoyed with her for saying what's on her mind. She's not nearly as creative, but she's as passionate about what she loves. Helen isn't a small woman. She looks like a military matron. Her hair is always pulled tightly into a severe bun, she has a blocky face and wears wire rim glasses that do nothing to make her beautiful. Imagine Aaron's eyebrows on a woman." She chuckled. "But when she sees a child, everything about her becomes soft and warm. I always thought my children would be afraid of her because she seems so formidable. The first time they saw her, Marilyn was only four. She ran up to Helen, took her hand and waited to be lifted into Helen's arms. I was shocked, but every single one of the children loved her immediately."

"She sounds pretty amazing," Polly said.

"She's always just been Helen. The woman is definitely a force to be reckoned with. If we're going to confront Aaron, I'm glad she'll be here and on our side."

"Me too. Even when Aaron is all droopy and out of sorts, he still scares me."

Lydia laughed. "He's not all that scary. What he's doing now is weird and has me pretty well freaked out, but he isn't scary. Now what do you want to do about lunch?"

Polly looked at the time. She really needed to get back and take care of her dogs. "What if we got takeout? I have a couple of dogs who are going to be desperate to see me."

"I forgot about them!" Lydia exclaimed. "I'm sorry."

"No," Polly said. "Don't. I usually make sure there's someone around to take care of them, but Henry is on a job site out of town and I didn't think to ask anyone else."

"What if we run in and get sandwiches to go. It will only take a few minutes."

"That's perfect." Polly reached out and took Lydia's hand and gave it a squeeze. "Now that you've talked to Helen and have started to be proactive, you sound better."

Lydia pulled back into a parking spot at the bagel shop. She turned off the Jeep and reached over to draw Polly into a hug. "I feel better. Thank you for pushing me to do something rather than let it continue to fester. There has to be an end to Aaron's craziness and it's time for me to put the finish line out there in front of him. No more wandering aimlessly. Come on, I'm buying lunch."

CHAPTER SIXTEEN

"Over achieving again, I see." Henry walked into Polly's office.

She looked up, startled to see him. "What are you doing here?" she asked.

"Better question. What are *you* doing here?"

That didn't make sense, so she subtly turned to look at the time on her computer. "How did it get to be five thirty?"

"Tick, tick, tick," he said, tapping at the invisible watch on his wrist. "What are you working on?"

Papers were scattered across her desk, covering everything. Polly made a half-hearted attempt to straighten them up and then pushed them away.

"I'm frustrated with the coffee shop and bakery. I don't know what I want yet. So, it's a mess."

He pulled a chair around to sit beside her and picked up several sheets. He put them down and picked up a few more. "You really are all over the place with this, aren't you?"

"If someone just gave me a hint - a name or a style, anything - I could focus. Right now all I'm doing is being frustrated."

"Maybe you should stop for the day. Rebecca and Evelyn are

taking Sarah out for dinner, the office is dark, and Sylvie and Andrew are gone. Jessie is out with some friends. It's just us."

"Just us? Really? What should we do?"

"You know what I think we should do." He brushed his hand across her shoulder, and caressed her neck.

Polly's body reacted with a shiver. "You always think we should do that."

"Are you complaining?"

"Nope, not at all."

"That wasn't what I was thinking, though. Let's get the dogs and go for a drive."

Henry never wanted to just go for a drive. He had something in mind.

"Where are you taking me? Do I need to get dressed up?"

"No. Just wear warm clothes and we'll want to take the leashes."

Polly gathered up the paper that had been spread out and piled it into a relatively neat stack. She turned her monitor off and grabbed her phone. "I don't need anything else?"

"Nope. I'll feed you."

"This sounds like fun." She took his hand as they left the office and walked up the stairs to their home. Sometimes she still called it her apartment, but more often than not, she thought of it in terms of their home. Henry was part of every single inch of it. Even when it had just been her apartment, it was filled with him. He'd built everything.

She opened the front door and stopped. "We aren't going out, are we?" she asked.

"I lied."

"I'd have gone anywhere with you, but this is perfect."

Henry had found many candles and candlelight filled the living room. She could see it flickering around the corner of the doorway into the media room and dining room as well. "Where are the animals?" she asked. "Candles seem dangerous."

A small bark answered her question. They were locked in her bedroom.

"Can we let them out?"

He chuckled. "Sure. I just knew that they weren't safe with unattended fire." He drew her close and kissed her lips, then trailed kisses down her neck.

"Ohhh, you *were* thinking about that."

"Are you?"

Polly put her hands on his upper arms and pushed him back so she could look into his eyes. "Henry, I love you. There is never a time that I don't want to be thinking about that."

"That's a strange response, but I'll take it."

"What made you do this?"

He took her hand and led her to the sofa. "I started thinking about you today and how much you do for everyone. We stopped in Ogden for lunch. A woman from Fraser heard us talking about Sycamore House and stopped me. She said you saved her life."

Polly dropped her head. No one was to know about that except Aaron.

"Do you do that type of thing very often?"

It hadn't been a big deal. The woman had three children and last fall she was in danger of losing her house. Polly and Lydia had been talking about something else when Aaron came in, upset at having to deliver a foreclosure notice. It still startled Polly at how small the amounts really were in the middle of Iowa, but it was enough to put a young, single mom over the edge. She'd been out of work for a few months, gotten behind, and had never been able to catch up.

"It just happened," Polly said. "It's no big deal."

He leaned forward and kissed her. "It's a big deal to her. She gave me this." Henry reached over and turned a piece of paper right side up. "She's had it in her car for months, hoping to get down here to meet you, but at the same time she was embarrassed to face you."

Polly picked up the hand drawn picture of three kids and their mother in front of a trailer. The sun was in the sky, grass was on the ground and smiles were on each face. "That's sweet," she said, her eyes filling with tears. "Aaron wasn't supposed to tell her who did it. She needed help and I could do it."

"Is this the first time?" Henry asked quietly.

She shook her head. "No. It's not. Does that upset you?"

He gestured around the room at the lit candles. "Not at all. I'm proud of you and it's this type of thing that makes me fall in love with you more and more. I thought about it all afternoon and I just wanted to spend some time with you this evening telling you how wonderful I think you are."

Another yip and scratching at their bedroom door startled both of them out of the moment. "We'd better deal with that before your dog damages the door," Polly said.

"My dog?"

"Yes. Your dog. Obiwan would never do anything so heinous." She stood up and crossed the room to open the bedroom door. Two dogs came barreling out at her and right behind them were two cats that were incredibly miffed at having been confined to a single space.

Henry had gotten up and was standing in the doorway to the dining room. "I picked up dinner, too."

~~~

They were snuggled on the sofa in front of the television when the front door opened.

Rebecca called out softly, "Polly? Henry?"

"We're in here, honey." Polly said, pausing the movie.

She came bouncing in and sat down on the chair next to Henry. "We took Mom out for pizza. That was fun. Mrs. Morrow said that we should go out more often so Mom can get some fresh air. Isn't that great? She's better!"

Polly forced a smile. Rebecca wanted nothing more than for her mother to be healthy. She wasn't. It was one thing for the girl to manage her grief while her mother showed signs of deterioration, but renewed strength and vigor would only give Rebecca hope and that hope was going to be crushed. Polly knew this because she'd been through it as a child with her own mother.
~~~

"I'm glad you are having fun with her. Mrs. Morrow is pretty terrific."

"She said that after school tomorrow we should go downtown to find a dress for Mom for the Valentine's Day party. We're going to look at the antique store. Won't that be cool? There are some great old dresses there and Mrs. Morrow said she saw something that would be perfect and it won't cost very much either."

Polly drew a sigh of relief. She no longer needed to worry about the yellow dress.

Henry put his hand out much like he did with Polly, waiting for Rebecca to take it. "Did you take pictures tonight at dinner?"

"Mrs. Morrow took some of the two of us. It was great. She said she would print them out and I should draw some frames." Rebecca looked at his hand and finally put hers into it. He squeezed and she smiled.

"That's great." He turned to Polly. "I never thought about having Rebecca draw frames for pictures. Maybe we should do that with a picture of Han."

"What about Obiwan?"

He brushed her away. "Oh, that old dog? He's just common place. Han is the hot new thing around here." He winked at Rebecca. "Don't you think?"

She took her hand back. "You're weird and you're trying to get me in trouble with Polly. It won't work."

"Why don't you get ready for bed," Polly said. "I'm glad you had a great evening and it sounds like Mrs. Morrow has a busy week ahead for you."

"It's gonna be great!" Rebecca jumped up and ran out of the room. They heard her open and shut her door and then open it again and run across the floor to the bathroom.

Henry took Polly's hand. "Stop it."

"What?" she asked, surprised.

"Stop worrying about what's coming. Let her have what's happening now. These are the memories she needs to keep."

Polly swatted his belly with the back of her hand. "You shouldn't read me so well."

"I watched that look go across your face. Evelyn Morrow has been through this a number of times with patients and their families. You let her take care of this. Your job will come when Sarah is gone and Rebecca needs to be comforted."

"That's going to be horrible."

"And you will make it easier for her. Then as time passes, she will find it easier and easier to deal with her memories and grief. But let her have this right now."

"I know," Polly said. "I kept my mouth shut, but it's going to break my heart."

He pulled her close and she snuggled in against his chest. "I love you with all of my heart, Polly Giller."

The front door opened and closed again and Polly sat back up. "We're in here," she called out.

Jessie walked in. "Romantic night in?" she asked.

"Henry did it," Polly said, turning around to look at Jessie. "Come over here," she said.

Jessie hesitated in the doorway.

Henry sat forward and turned around. "What happened?" he asked.

Polly jumped up and ran across the room to Jessie, pulled the girl's hair back from her face and swore. "What happened to you?"

"I really don't want to tell you," Jessie said.

"Who hurt you?"

"I asked for it."

Henry had come to stand beside Polly. "Screw that. Nobody asks to be hurt like that. Who did this?"

Jessie sagged into Polly's arms. "I've done it again. Why can't I just find a nice guy like you?"

Polly led her to the sofa and said, "Henry, would you get a warm, wet cloth?"

He left and Polly sat down next to Jessie and took her hand. "I didn't even know you were dating. You should have told me."

Jessie gave the bathroom a furtive look. "He's going to come unglued."

"Why?" Then it suddenly occurred to Polly. "Is it someone who works for him?"

"I don't want Henry to hurt anybody because of me. It was all my fault."

"Jessie, I don't know how I'm going to get through to you that getting hit is never your fault."

"He was drinking and I said something to piss him off. I should have known better. He's gotten mad before and..."

"You've been hit before?"

"Never on the face. He usually just yells at me and one time he punched my arm." She brushed her fingers across her upper arm. "But he's a really nice guy."

"That's crap. Do you ever hear Henry yelling at me for no reason and have you ever seen him hit me?"

"No, but you're nicer than me."

Polly couldn't help it. She let out a laugh. "That's also crap. I push Henry's buttons all the time. I infuriate him." She sighed. "Oh honey, I wish I could make you understand that nobody deserves to be abused."

Henry came out of the bathroom and handed Polly a wet washcloth. She dabbed at the red mark on Jessie's face, bringing tears and sobbing.

"I'm such a screw-up," Jessie said through her tears. "How am I supposed to raise a daughter when I can't even find a good guy?"

"You're going to be a good mom," Polly said.

Jessie broke down again and Polly held her while she cried. Henry gave Polly a questioning look over Jessie's shoulders and all Polly could do was mouth "Later."

"I'll be in the other room," he said and walked out.

"Why didn't you tell me you were dating someone?" Polly asked.

"He told me that we shouldn't talk about it... because of our jobs and everything. And tonight he begged me not to say anything. He said that if I loved him, I'd keep this just between us. That it was private and stuff."

Polly took a shuddering breath. "Have you told this boy that you aren't going to see him again?" Polly asked.

"No-o-o-o."

"Why not?"

"I like him. He's cute and it doesn't freak him out that I'm eight months pregnant."

"So that's the requirement for a good man now? Seems like your standards are pretty low."

"You don't know what it's like. No one wants to date a girl with a kid."

"Because you've met everyone?" Polly was frustrated.

"Well, no."

"Honey, I know that you are freaked out and upset right now, but you have got to understand that you are worth so much more than this. Even if you never meet a man and get married, that's better than taking abuse from some jerk."

"No it's not. I just want someone to love me."

"I love you. Henry and Rebecca love you. Your parents love you."

At Jessie's look of disdain, Polly pressed forward. "I know. Your mother has a hard time showing it, but she does love you."

"Then why do I keep hooking up with boys that treat me like this. No nice guy ever wants to go out with me."

"I know you don't want to hear this, but you're in too much of a hurry. You are only twenty-one. You have decades in front of you. People are going to come in and out of your life. Some of them will be jerks, some of them will be ehhh, and some will be wonderful. But you don't have to settle for a jerk because you think there isn't enough time to wait for someone wonderful. What if I'd settled when I was twenty-one? I'd have completely missed out on meeting Henry."

"Yeah? Did you have jerks in your life?"

"Oh honey, I had one of the worst jerks in my life and I had a hard time getting rid of him. I'm just saying that you don't have to settle. It doesn't matter if you're pregnant or if you have a child. When the right person for you shows up, you won't have to worry about whether or not they're going to hurt you."

"When am I ever going to learn?"

Polly gave a slight chuckle. "I want to give you a piece of advice and I want you to hear this clearly. When anyone ever tells you that you are to keep your relationship a secret and that no one is supposed to know what happens between you, that's a clear signal he's a loser. There's a big difference between privacy and secrecy. You don't know what happens in our bedroom because that's private, but there is very little that I'm ashamed to talk about in my relationship with Henry."

She thought about it. "At the beginning, I guess we didn't tell people because we didn't want them all up in our business, but that probably wasn't the right thing to do. It got weird after a while and it's not like people didn't know anyway. Just know that if a boy wants you to keep things secret, you need to ask why. If he's hiding you from someone, or if he's hiding from somebody, it's bad."

"That makes sense. It's going to be hard to break up with him. I see him all the time."

"Tell me who it is."

Jessie dropped her head. "I really don't want to get him into trouble."

"He hit you, Jessie. He's in trouble. He should have been in trouble with you. Don't protect him."

"Cody Clark."

"How long has he been working for Henry, do you know?"

"He came on after I started working there. When things got really busy last fall."

"Okay. What does your day look like tomorrow at work?"

Jessie shrugged. "I don't know. It's a normal day."

"Let me talk to Henry. I don't think you need to go in to work until he's dealt with this."

"Is Cody going to lose his job?"

Polly scowled. "What do you think? If the jerk can't keep his hands off of you, who knows what else he thinks is okay to do. Henry doesn't need someone like that working for him."

"He's going to hate me."

"Maybe, but honey, you should hate him first. He doesn't

deserve anything from you."

Jessie sat for a minute and then her shoulders drooped. "I was going to have a date for Valentine's Day. I guess that's out the window."

"The things we worry about," Polly said, rubbing Jessie's shoulder. "I'd rather you have a great life before Valentine's Day and for that entire year after Valentine's Day. One evening shouldn't define your happiness, okay?"

"I guess I'll tell Sylvie I can work, then." She perked up. "More money for my apartment fund."

"There ya go." Polly hid the shudder that went through her at the thought of Jessie living on her own. She knew it was going to have to happen someday and probably sooner rather than later, but this was now the third really bad decision she'd made regarding men.

"I'm going to change," Jessie said, interrupting Polly's train of thought. "Do you care if I watch television?"

"That's fine." Polly watched her walk out of the room. Being a mom totally stunk.

She went into the living room and found Henry and Rebecca on the couch with Han and the two cats. Rebecca was showing him something in one of her books.

He looked up. "Everything okay?"

"We need to talk."

"I was afraid of that."

"Rebecca," Polly said. "Jessie is going to change and watch some television before she goes to bed. I'll bet she could use a friend. Do you mind hanging out with her?"

"Really? How long do I get?"

"How about another hour." That would get Rebecca to bed only a half hour past her regular bedtime. It seemed okay for tonight.

Polly took Henry's hand and led him into the bedroom, closing the door behind them, locking the animals out in the main room.

"This seems serious," he said.

"You have to fire Cody Clark. Tomorrow."

He pursed his lips together, walked over to the desk and sat down in the chair.

"Henry?"

"Don't talk to me right now."

"Do I need to leave the room?" She stood in silence, waiting for him to settle down. The man just didn't react visibly. If he hadn't said anything, she would never have known how angry he was.

He took a deep breath. "That's who hit her?"

"They've been dating. There's been some verbal abuse before this and he slugged her in the arm once."

"I put him in front of her. I entrusted her to my guys. He's a punk, but he was always willing to be the one to go back to the shop for things. I know his parents." His jaw started working back and forth.

Polly nodded and waited.

"Do you have any idea how much I want to yell and swear right now?" he asked.

"I can only imagine."

"He hasn't hurt her baby, has he?"

"No," Polly shook her head.

"I'm going to scare that little..." He stopped and gave her a sheepish grin. "I won't use the word. But he's going to be very scared."

"That's not going to change his behavior. You know that, right?"

Henry held his hand out and Polly crossed the room to take it. He pulled her into his lap and buried his face in her shoulder. "I know this isn't my fault," he said. "But I wish I could have protected her from this."

Polly pulled back and looked at him. There were tears in his eyes. "Oh honey. As much as I love that girl, she would have found him on her own. I'm going to make sure that she's still seeing her counselor. We have to find a way to break this pattern for her."

"She needs a good man."

"No. What she needs is the confidence that she is okay all by herself."

"I love you so much."
"I love you too, you big softie."

CHAPTER SEVENTEEN

"Little elves are in our house. Do you smell that?" Henry asked.

"It smells like breakfast. Who's cooking in my kitchen?"

He chuckled. "Maybe we should get up and see."

"Don't wanna. Wanna stay in bed. Will you stay with me?"

"I'd love to, but I have to work," he said. Then he turned to look at her. "I know you. You never want to stay in bed. What are you trying to avoid?" he asked.

"Everything. There is nothing out there that I want to deal with today. I don't want to have to deal with Aaron's sister and whatever horrible thing she's going to tell us when she comes to Bellingwood. I don't want to have to deal with Jessie and her inability to make abusive men go away. I don't want to look at Stephanie and wonder why any father would choose to hurt his daughter or why a mother wouldn't protect her kids. I don't want to do anything. I just want to stay in bed. Please stay here with me. Please?"

Henry brushed a lock of hair away from her face, caressed her cheek and leaned in for a kiss. She shut her eyes and waited.

"What?" she demanded, opening her eyes again. He was

grinning down at her.

"You're gullible. We have to get moving."

Polly swatted his arm. "You're a rat!"

He kissed her lips and unfolded himself from the animals on the bed. "I'll take a shower. You check on our kitchen and make sure there aren't strangers out there cooking eggs and sausage." Henry stopped at the bathroom door. "And don't worry about the dogs. I'll take them out."

Obiwan was already on the floor and the cats had leaped to their perches on the cat tree. Poor Han was still too small to negotiate the bed. He looked over the edge and then back at Polly, pleading for some assistance.

"Yeah, yeah, yeah," she said, picking him up. She gave him a quick kiss on the nose and put him on the floor. He nearly wagged his tail off his bottom in glee and ran underneath Obiwan's chest to get to the door first.

Polly grabbed her robe and opened the door into the main room, waiting while all four animals raced to escape. Both of the other bedroom doors were open and she heard giggling in the kitchen.

"What are you two doing this morning?" she asked when she walked into the dining room.

Rebecca was putting plates out on the table. "We made a plan last night."

"You did. What kind of plan was that?"

"You always make breakfast for us, so Jessie and I decided it was our turn."

"That sounds wonderful. Thank you. How is everyone doing this morning?"

Jessie turned from the stovetop. "I'm doing fine. Thank you for listening to me last night. Rebecca and I talked about it. She told me that I have to be nicer to myself and not let boys define me."

"She said that?"

"Yes I did," Rebecca said, standing a little straighter.

"That's good stuff. Where did you hear those words?"

"Some girls at school were talking about boyfriends and our

teacher said it."

"Mrs. Hastings?"

"Yeah. She got mad because they were more interested in boys than in being smart. She said that girls can be anything they want to be and if boys got in the way they weren't worth it."

"She must have been really mad."

Rebecca giggled again and stood in front of the cupboard where the glasses were. She pointed and Jessie pulled four down for her. "Brooke told Shelby that as long as she married someone with a good job, she didn't need to worry about knowing English and Math and stuff." She gave Polly a look of contempt. "They get bad grades and don't care. It's more important for them to talk about..." Rebecca put her hands on her hips and swung them back and forth "makeup and new clothes and the right tops to wear with skirts."

"Good for Mrs. Hastings, then."

"We're only in sixth grade," Rebecca said in protest. "It's not like I'm going to get married next year."

"I'd hope not!"

"I don't ever want to get married."

"Ever?"

"Maybe someday. But I want to go to France. Ms. Watson said she'd take me."

"She did!"

"She said that every artist should see Paris in the springtime."

Polly chuckled. Beryl was laying it on a bit thick, but as long as she had Rebecca's attention, that was fine.

"So, no marriage."

"At least until after I see Paris. And maybe Rome and Cairo and London."

"Is Beryl taking you to those places?"

"She said that if I go, she'll go."

"I'm fine with all of that," Polly said. "Boys can wait until we're ready for them. Right?"

"We're starting a girl's club," Rebecca said. "Me and Jessie and Kayla and Stephanie if she wants to come. I think we should invite Rachel, too."

"How about me?" Polly asked.

"You don't count. You're married."

"But I'm a girl."

"No, this is for us single girls."

"I see."

Rebecca looked up. "Do you think Ms. Watson would come?"

It was all Polly could do not to laugh out loud, but she contained herself. "I think she would be honored. It's great that you want her there. Not Sylvie?"

"She's got boys and everybody knows that she and Eliseo are going to end up together."

"It sounds like you've got this all figured out."

Rebecca shrugged and Jessie winked at Polly, then turned back to the scrambled eggs.

"I think it's a wonderful plan. Where are you going to meet?" Polly asked.

"Jessie and I haven't figured out all the details yet. But the first thing we're going to do is make a pact to say nice things to each other. Because we don't need boys to tell us how great we are. We should do that for ourselves."

"You *are* great," Henry said, coming into the room. "What are we talking about?"

"It's nothing." Rebecca ducked behind the peninsula to get silverware.

"I'm taking the dogs out. How much time do I have?" he asked.

Jessie opened the stove and closed it. "The timer says seven minutes, so maybe ten before it's on the table."

"We'll be back long before that. Have you fed the dogs?"

"I took care of it," Rebecca announced.

"I'm going to work today," Jessie called after him. "Cody isn't going to scare me."

"You won't even see him. I can promise you that," Henry said over his shoulder as he passed through into his office, the dogs close on his heels.

"Jessie, you don't have to go in," Polly said. "You know that, right?"

Jessie glanced at Rebecca, who stood and waited for her response and said, "Yes I do. It's time for me to figure this out. I have a baby coming and last night it hit me that it's not just about me anymore."

Polly took a seat at the table and smiled when Rebecca handed her a mug of coffee. "Thanks, sweetie. You two sure know how to take care of me."

"I'll be right back," Rebecca said to Jessie and ran out of the room.

"It sounds like you two had a great talk," Polly said.

Jessie took toast out of the toaster and spread butter on it. "It isn't just about the baby, you know."

"What do you mean?"

"When a twelve year old girl has to tell me I'm worth it, something's messed up. I realized that I'm important to her too and she shouldn't see me bruised and beaten because I'm too chicken to wait for the right person in my life."

Polly felt tears threaten. "That's really wise, Jessie. It takes most people a lot longer to figure that out."

"She has so much to deal..." Jessie stopped when Rebecca came back into the room.

"I made up names for our group last night." Rebecca held up a piece of paper and then put it down in front of Polly. "I was so excited I couldn't go to sleep."

"Girl Power. Girlfriends. Girl's Rock. Girl Talk. It's a Girl Thing. Syc Sistahs. Bellingwood Belles. Sycamore Chicks." Polly read them out loud. "These are fun names."

"I'm going to ask Kayla to help me come up with some more." Rebecca looked at Jessie. "Do you have any ideas?"

"Not yet, but I'll give it some thought today. We can discuss it tonight."

Rebecca stood at the end of the peninsula. "I wish Kayla was still here when you got home from work. But Stephanie and you have the same hours."

"Maybe you should all go out to dinner sometime this week,"

Polly said.

"Could we? Maybe tonight?" Rebecca lit up and then she stopped. "Oh no. Not this week. Mom and I are going to be busy. Maybe soon."

"You'll find a time. But it would be fun for you to have an official planning meeting."

Obiwan and Han dashed into the kitchen hoping to find one last morsel of food.

"Those were some busy dogs this morning," Henry said. "You'd think they had never marked their territories. Every single leaf and clump of grass under the snow was a target, but they're good to go for the next half hour." He sat down beside Polly. "Food in. Poop out. It's a cycle."

She chuckled and put her hand on his, then pushed the piece of paper over in front of him.

"What's this?"

"The girls are going to start a club. All about supporting each other. They want Beryl to join them."

"Really!"

"I think it's great. I'm a married woman, so I can't go."

"That probably leaves me out, too."

Rebecca put a plate of food in front of him. "You're silly."

"That's me." He snaked Polly's coffee mug away from her and took a drink.

"Hey! Get your own."

"Too many people in the kitchen. I'd step on someone."

Jessie came over with two more plates and said, "I've got it. You go ahead and sit down, Rebecca."

"What's your favorite name on there?" Rebecca asked Henry.

"Syc Sistahs. Is that Sycamore House?"

"Uh huh."

"That's my pick."

Rebecca turned to Jessie. "Cross that one off."

"No respect," he said, laughing. "Absolutely no respect."

After everyone left the house, Polly finished cleaning the kitchen. Luke leaped up onto the counter and batted at the suds in the sink. When he got bored, he jumped across to the other side and wandered around the counter to the end of the peninsula to watch her work.

"Kind of the long way around, bud," she said, drying her hands on a towel. "Do you want to hang out in the bathroom while I shower?"

It was a ridiculous question. She and Henry had given up shutting doors. The animals would have none of it. Dogs whined and whimpered, cats poked their paws underneath and meowed until someone let them in. It just wasn't worth it. With everyone gone, she left all the doors open and once Luke and Leia identified where she would be for the next few minutes, took off to explore the outside world from their perches.

~~~

Polly was sketching on a pad and looked up when she heard a quiet tap on her door frame. Papers covered her desk and she didn't even bother attempting to straighten them.

"Hey Jeff, what's up?"

He entered and shut the door behind him, then sat down. "I need to talk to you."

That worried her. "Sounds serious. Is everything okay?"

He chuckled. "Sorry. It's fine. Didn't mean to scare you. But I want to talk to you about next week."

"What's next week?" Polly sat back in her chair and opened the calendar on her computer. There was nothing there. She pointed at the screen. "See? I'm learning."

"It's been two years and I've done nothing but harass you about it. It's about time."

"Whatever. Tell me what you have next week."

"I'd like to take some time. Since it's just after Valentine's Day, there's nothing much happening here."

"Of course. Absolutely. Are you going home?" She bit her lips closed. "I'm sorry. None of my business."

"We're friends. It's always your business, but yes... and no. We
~~~

got a call this morning that Stephanie needs to go home to Ohio. The prosecutor wants to talk to her about pressing charges against her father. Since it's not far from Columbus and my family, I thought I'd go with her and stop and say hello."

Polly looked up quizzically. "You're sure you want to get this involved in her life? It's pretty messed up, you know."

Jeff gave Polly a look she could only describe as cross-eyed. "This?" he asked. "Coming from you?"

"Hey. Everyone is always trying to force me to look at things reasonably, I thought it was only fair that I do the same to you. But really, are you sure about this? You don't even know her all that well."

"I know her well enough. She needs a friend."

Polly slowly nodded. "First of all. Of course you can have the time. Let's get that out of the way. I wish you didn't even feel like you needed to ask my permission. You know better than anyone what goes on here and what needs to be done. Let's just say that you shouldn't ask me, you should just give me plenty of notice."

"Thanks. We can talk about that another day."

She scowled at him. "I was afraid it wouldn't be that easy."

"Anyway, we're going to leave early Sunday morning. We should get into my parent's place that evening. Once she tells the prosecutor that she's coming, they'll set a meeting for Monday. If everything goes as planned, we'll come home on Wednesday or Thursday."

"That sounds like a whirlwind trip. You don't want more time?"

"She doesn't want to be there much longer than that. But I'm going to make sure that if there's anything she wants out of that house, anything at all - we can get it taken care of."

"Do whatever you need to do. I'm grateful you stepped into the middle of this, though. You're probably the only person that Stephanie feels safe with."

He grinned at her. "See, there are some advantages to hiring a gay man."

Polly scowled at him. "Let's just say there are advantages to hiring you. However, with what her father did to her, it's going to take time before she really trusts men at all. And she'll never understand why her mother didn't protect her, especially when she finally got it together to protect Kayla. There isn't anyone here that she'll feel completely safe with. "

He opened his mouth to speak and Polly started to laugh. "What?" he asked.

"I figured you were going to give me trouble because I accused you of being trustworthy when she doesn't trust men."

"It might have occurred to me, but I get it. I'm no threat to her in any sexual manner at all."

"Yes. That. Thanks for bailing me out there."

"This is why I love you, Polly Giller."

"What do you mean?" she asked.

"You don't worry too much about labels or anything. You just say what's on your mind."

Now she was worried that she'd said something wrong without realizing it. "Was I offensive?"

"Not at all. In fact, the farthest thing from it. But most people won't just be up front with me about what's right in front of them. They hem and haw, avoiding the obvious."

"You mean the gay elephant in my office?" Polly laughed out loud, then said, "That would mean I had a problem with it or was embarrassed by it. Why should I be? You're just you."

Jeff squeezed his side and said, "I'm not so sure I like being called a gay elephant."

"Come on," she protested.

"You're so easy. I get it and I'm just giving you trouble."

"Exactly." He stood to leave. "Since Sarah is feeling better, she's available to answer phones."

"I can take care of it for a few days and it isn't like I can't reach you immediately if I have a question."

Jeff opened the door. "We're on, Stephanie. It's a road trip."

She came to Polly's door. "Thank you. I can't believe that this is how I'm starting my employment with you."

"What about Kayla? Is she going with you?"

Stephanie looked up at Jeff. "Well..." she started.

"I forgot to ask that," he said. "Would you consider letting her stay with Rebecca?"

Polly nodded. "I'm glad to have her stay with us, it's just that the last time she woke up with a nightmare and the only way to deal with it was to have you pick her up. This is a long separation for the two of you."

"I don't want her to have to go through everything. She wasn't involved." Stephanie shuddered violently. "Dad didn't have time to get to her."

"Rebecca would love to have her stay with us. Tell me what I can do to make it easier on her."

"I'll talk to her this week. Help her understand that it's going to be okay. Maybe I can bring a present back for her," Stephanie looked up at Jeff again.

He shrugged. "Sure. There are wonderful places to go shopping out there. Have you heard of Easton Town Center? It's huge. We could lose ourselves there for weeks. And you know me, I love to shop."

"Please don't get lost for weeks," Polly said. "I couldn't take it."

Stephanie smiled. "I can't afford that. Don't worry, I'll make sure that she will be okay with it. She has to be."

"We'll do our best," Polly said. "Jeff, can you stay here a minute? I have a couple more questions."

He gave Stephanie a smile, then shut the door again. "What?"

"Does she have a cell phone? Make sure that's taken care of before you leave. Kayla should have a way to reach her sister while she's traveling."

"Okay. Good idea."

"And the next thing. You're not going to like this, but Stephanie is crushing on you. I can see it in her eyes when she looks at you."

"I know," he breathed. "It's not the first time a messed-up straight girl has thought I'd be perfect for her future. Don't worry. I've dealt with this before. She'll be okay. And besides, I'm her boss. We'll make sure the boundaries are well-defined."

"Good."

"I'm rescuing her. It's the right thing to do, but until she gets some balance in her life, she's not going to know what's up and what's down."

Polly glanced at her computer, then asked, "Why aren't you flying out?"

"She doesn't have that kind of money and won't let me give it to her."

"Talk to the prosecutor. If they ask her to come out to give testimony, there's probably a stipend. It would make your trip go faster and you two would have less travel time."

"Thanks. That's a good idea." He winked at Polly. "You're a smart woman."

"Sometimes. Get out of here so she doesn't think I'm yelling at you for something."

"Got it." Jeff opened the door and said so Stephanie could hear him, "Man, if you want to beat me, at least use a pillow, woman."

Polly looked at him in shock and he chuckled. "Just kidding."

She flung an eraser at him, he ducked and it landed on the floor of the main office.

"That was pitiful," he said.

"You're useless."

CHAPTER EIGHTEEN

"Look at this," Jeff said as he walked into Polly's office carrying his tablet. "You won't believe what I found."

"A baby camel swimming in the Des Moines River," she said.

He'd been so focused on what was on the tablet, he didn't realize what she said. She watched his face turn to incredulity and then he rolled his eyes at her.

"No?" she asked.

"You're a strange woman. Anyway, there's a bakery in eastern Iowa that's gone out of business. They just closed the doors. No auction, no nothing.

Polly perked up. "Ovens?"

"Yep. Everything we need. They even have display cases and bread racks. I thought Sylvie and I could take a road trip tomorrow since Wednesday is her slow day. Rachel can take care of the groups that will be in here and I'm ready for Saturday night. Stephanie will answer the phone and forward anything important to me. We'll be gone nearly all day."

"I keep telling you that you don't need to justify things to me," Polly said. "Now, how exactly did you find out about this?"

He laughed and preened. "It's all about who you know."

"I get it," she said. "You know everyone, but seriously. How did you find it?"

"My next door neighbor in Ames. It belonged to her parents. When her mother died, her dad just closed the doors and never went back inside. He ran the kitchen, but she ran the show."

"And you just happened to mention to her that we were thinking of putting a bakery in here at Bellingwood."

"We had dinner," he said. "We talk about a lot of things. Anyway, she called her dad today. If we're interested, all we have to do is make him a reasonable offer and haul the stuff away."

"Unbelievable. I don't know how you do it."

"I just pay attention."

"We aren't going to be ready for a while, you know," she said

Jeff brushed Polly's concerns aside. "If necessary, we can rent storage."

"And Sylvie's good with this?"

"She loves the idea of having a working bakery to start from," he said. "We can talk about adding other appliances once she gets everything installed."

Polly smiled. "You are amazing."

"I keep telling you - I need a raise."

"How about I double the raise I gave you last week?"

He just shook his head at her and grinned.

"Let me know what happens," she said. "I know you've got this."

"Thanks. I'll call you tomorrow." Jeff looked out the window behind Polly and said, "Who's that with Lydia?"

She spun in her chair. "Hmm, must be Helen, Aaron's sister."

"Aaron Merritt has a sister?"

"She's in town from Atlanta. Do me a favor. Don't say too much about this yet."

"Because that woman can hide?"

"I'll tell you all about it later. Just keep it quiet for now."

"You owe me, Polly Giller."

"More than I'll ever be able to repay you. Thanks."

Jeff was out of the door and back in his office before Lydia and Helen made it to the front door of the building. They came inside and Lydia waved at Polly through her office window, then breezed past Stephanie and into Polly's office, closing the door.

Polly stood and put out her hand. "Hi. I'm Polly Giller."

"This is my sister-in-law, Helen Oswald," Lydia said.

The woman took Polly's hand into her firm grip and gave it a quick shake. "Nice to meet you, Miss Giller."

"Please, it's Polly. Have a seat." Polly gestured to the chairs in front of her desk. "Are you staying with us tonight?"

"If it's not too much trouble."

"We're glad to have you. Honestly, I'm just thankful you're here."

"Lydia has told me a little of what she's been going through." Helen turned to her sister-in-law. "I wish you'd said somethin' earlier. We might could've fixed y'all up before things got to this point."

Might-could? Oh Polly was going to like this woman. She was exactly as Lydia had described her. Grey-black hair pulled back in a severe bun, horn-rimmed glasses, built like a Mac truck. Polly had no problem imagining the woman in grey shorts and a shirt, running a girl's dormitory in the middle of Russia, commanding respect and quick obedience with every snap of the finger. But when she smiled and even when she spoke, her soft southern accent and twinkling eyes gave away the soft heart she carried within. She was dressed in blue jeans, tennis shoes and an oversized plaid shirt, and had taken a blue woolen pea coat off when she entered the building.

"Does Aaron know you're in town?" Polly asked.

"Not yet. Lord a-mercy, don't you want to be in the room when he sees me?" The woman started to laugh. It came from deep in her belly, low and resonant.

"I don't know. That scares me."

"That little boy has you intimidated, does he? My goodness, the stories I could tell."

This would be the only time that Polly would hear someone

refer to Aaron Merritt as a little boy and it warmed her heart. It wasn't often that she wished she'd had siblings, but every once in a while, when she saw sisters and brothers tease each other and then support each other, it made her wistful.

"So, Miss Giller," Helen started.

"Polly?" Polly pleaded.

"We'll work on that."

Polly wasn't sure whether Helen meant that she would work on calling her by her first name or that she would change Polly's insistence on being so informal.

"All of this is yours?"

Polly nodded. "We've worked hard to bring it all together. Things dropped into my lap when they were most needed."

"Lydia tells me you have horses?"

"Those are part of the story of this place," Polly said. "I knew I wanted a horse, so we came up with a crazy idea to have a barn-raising. Before it was finished, there were four Percherons that needed a new place to live. When I realized I was in over my head, a man showed up who became our groundskeeper. He knows more about horses and animals than I will ever be able to learn."

Helen was nodding as she looked around. "Pretty nice woodworking. Someone fall into your lap there too?"

"That's her husband," Lydia said.

"But he was my contractor first. He did the renovation of Sycamore House. He's pretty amazing."

"How'd'ja find yourself a single man with talent like that in a small town in Iowa?"

"Like I said, things worked out."

"You must have a fairy godmother."

"Polly makes her own wishes come true," Lydia said. "She's been a godsend to Bellingwood. There isn't much that frightens her and she'll dig right in and work until things are done."

"Will y'all show me around? I'd like to see the rest of this place."

"I'd love to. Let's get a key to your room and I can take you up there," Polly said. "If you want to rest or unpack, we can explore at your leisure."

"Don't need leisure. God above gave me time on earth to get things done. I'm not about to go wastin' it on leisure. I don't know when he'll see fit to take me home." She glanced over Polly's shoulder. "You have children here?"

Polly turned and looked out to see Rebecca, Kayla and Andrew running across the parking lot to the front door.

"Their families work here during the day, so the kids hang out upstairs in my apartment."

"I'd like to meet 'em." Helen walked out of the office.

Polly jumped up and followed, only to discover that Helen had stopped the kids before they could run up the steps.

Helen sat down on the fourth step and looked up at Andrew with rapt attention. Polly got closer to hear him telling her about dinosaurs. Before she knew it, Rebecca was digging into her backpack and pulled out a notebook, handing it over to Helen.

"She's kind of a force," Polly said quietly to Lydia.

"She is that, but look at her. This is where she really lights up. Kids get her. More than anyone else, they love to talk to her."

"What do you want to do this evening?" Polly asked.

"What do you mean?"

"For dinner. Do you want to deal with her and Aaron tonight?"

"I'm going to have to sometime," Lydia said with a sigh.

"What if she spends the evening here," Polly offered. "I'd love to invite her up for dinner. I can show her Sycamore House... maybe take her on a driving tour of Bellingwood."

"It's been a long time since she was last in town. I don't think my youngest was even born then."

"You do whatever you want, but if you aren't ready to have the Aaron and Helen confrontation, I wouldn't mind getting to know her. How long will she be in town?"

"She's leaving on Sunday. I asked her to stay for Valentine's Day." Lydia turned a very sad face to Polly. "I hate to admit it, but I'm being a complete chicken about this. I don't want to have to face Aaron if he tries to avoid telling me I'm his Valentine."

Polly nudged her friend with a shoulder. "Here's hoping things are straightened out before then."

"What are they doing?" Lydia asked, watching Helen head up the steps.

"Apparently, the kids are taking her to the apartment. Is she okay with dogs and cats?"

"She's had both at one time or other. Should we help?"

Polly took Lydia's arm. "Nah. Let's leave them to it. I think we should bother Sylvie. Jeff tells me they're taking a road trip tomorrow to look at items for a bakery."

"You're going ahead with it?"

"Unless Sylvie tells me no, I think we have to. Have you tried to get into Joe's lately for breakfast?"

"No. But I hear he's busy."

They stopped in front of the counter and waited for Sylvie to turn.

"Hello there," she said. "What's up?"

"Do you have any of the good coffee?" Polly asked. "And maybe something sweet?"

"Come on in. The coffee is hot and we always have sweet things."

Lydia and Polly passed through on their way to the large table in the back. Rachel brought a thermos and two mugs over.

"Thanks dear," Lydia said, reaching to pour the coffee.

"How are things with your boy?" Polly asked.

Rachel shook her head and dropped into a chair beside Polly. "He drives me nuts. He was busy all last weekend. Said he had things to do. He wasn't even in town for most of it. He and Doug were in Des Moines all day on Saturday."

"Weren't you working?"

"Yeah, but I always go upstairs when I take a break. This time I had to walk his stupid dog instead."

"I'm so sorry," Polly said, with a laugh. "What do you think he was up to?"

"I don't know. Probably some stupid game store. I told him that it was okay if he played more games with Doug. I just wanted some of his time. He probably took me up on it. Men are idiots."

"Yes they are, dear," Lydia agreed. "And they don't get any better when they get older. So you need to figure out if you can live with this or not. What you have in front of you is what you will have for the rest of your life if you decide to keep him."

"You and the Sheriff are good, right?" Rachel asked.

"Most of the time. It's not always easy, though. There are plenty of times I'd like to boot his butt to the curb."

Rachel's eyes grew big and she gave a pained chuckle. "Really?"

"Really. But we get through those times and even though they're tough and make me angry, the good guy I married shows back up and things are normal again. Do you love this boy?"

"I really do," Rachel said.

"Can you put up with the odd things he does? The games, the animals, his music, his friends?"

"I already do."

"And you aren't trying to change those things?"

Rachel gave Polly a guilty look. "I might be."

"I wish I could tell young men and women that changing the person they fell in love with does exactly that. They're no longer the person they fell in love with."

"But..." Rachel began.

"Honey, take it from me. After thirty years of marriage, you force them to change at your own risk. They'll either do it and resent you or they'll do it and become someone you don't recognize."

"But he needs to grow up."

"He'll do that with or without you." Lydia took another drink of coffee. "Listen to me. You didn't ask for my advice. Just love him and be who you've always been with him. He'll figure it out."

Polly ran her hand up Rachel's arm. "You've got this. Be confident."

Rachel smiled at them both and stood up. "Thanks. I think I need to be more patient with him."

"That's easier said than done," Lydia said in a mumble.

Sylvie traded places with Rachel and put a platter of bars in front of Polly. "You have choices."

"What's here?"

"Some people call these zebra bars, but I kinda like the idea of Panda bars. More cheesecake than brownie. Here are caramel apple crumb bars and double chocolate chip cookies."

"One of each, thank you," Polly said and reached for a napkin. "Jeff says you're taking a road trip tomorrow?"

"Isn't it great?" Sylvie said. "His friend said it was a busy bakery and her dad was very clean. I was worried when Jeff said that he closed it and walked out, but she didn't mean that. He shut the doors and cleaned it out. But he did quit selling things the day his wife died. They'd been running that place together for thirty years."

"That had to have been hard," Lydia said. "Everything can change just like that." Her eyes filled. "One minute things are going along like they do every day and the next minute you're alone."

She brushed away the tears. "Were you serious about inviting Helen to dinner tonight?"

"Of course," Polly said.

"I'm going home. I have some things I need to take care of."

Before Polly and Sylvie could ask any more questions, Lydia had cleared the kitchen door and was on her way out.

"I'll tell Helen you've gone home," Polly said quietly.

"Who's Helen?"

"Aaron's sister. She's upstairs with the kids right now."

Sylvie creased her brows. "Upstairs? When did she meet the kids?"

"When they walked in the door. She's some kind of pied piper. I watched it happen and still couldn't believe it."

"This is Aaron's sister?"

"Uh huh. She works at a children's shelter in Atlanta."

"Crazy."

"I know. So, you said that they'd had the bakery for thirty years. Is the equipment that old?"

"No. They upgraded five years ago and his wife just died a year and a half ago. Jeff's friend said that when he meets us there, it will be the first time he's set foot in the door since the day he left."

"I'm surprised he's willing to sell."

"I think that his kids have been pushing him to deal with it."

"Where are you going?"

"A town east of Waterloo. Strawberry Point."

Polly chuckled. Small town names were wonderful. "That's adorable!"

"I know. I'm going to take pictures of that strawberry."

"There's a strawberry?"

"It's supposed to be the world's largest."

Polly laughed. "Who knew?"

Sylvie picked up a cookie and put it on Polly's napkin. "Thank you for letting me dream about the bakery. I'm excited."

"I was worried that I might be pushing you into something you weren't ready for."

"But that didn't stop you," Sylvie said with a laugh. "Did it?"

Polly nodded. "It's the right thing to do, though. Right?"

"Oh Polly," Sylvie said, reaching out to squeeze Polly's hand. "If I hadn't wanted to do it, I would have said so. It's intimidating, but I can't let that stop me."

"Whew," Polly said. "So, will you make lots of pastries for me? There were a couple of bakeries in Boston that made the most amazing brioche and croissants. I miss those. And the fruit tarts? My goodness. Please tell me you're going to try wild and crazy things."

"I guess. I want to try many things, but we have to think about items that will sell."

"Trust me, if you are baking, people will try anything. But I don't think you have to make everything every day. I was only able to get fruit tarts at one of the bakeries on the weekend and they only baked brioche on Wednesdays."

Polly's mouth started to water and she licked her lips. "And sourdough bread. Tell me you can get your hands on a starter and make sourdough. Please, please, please?"

"You make bread. Why don't you do it yourself?"

"Because every time I begin a starter, I am obedient and take care of it for about three days. Then I forget and I forget again and before anyone knows how bad it has gotten, I've tossed the entire thing out and washed the jar. I'm terrible."

Sylvie looked over her shoulder and pointed at the counter. "Rachel? Could you hand that jar to me?"

Rachel brought the large crock over and put it in front of Sylvie, who lifted the lid. A strong smell of yeast wafted to Polly's nostrils.

"This was my mother's," Sylvie said.

"Have you been holding out on me?"

"I didn't think it was that big of a deal. I used it at home. But when we moved into the new house and you started talking about a bakery, it occurred to me that I should use it here, too."

"Why haven't I known about this?"

"Because I didn't think it was that big of a deal," Sylvie scolded. "Weren't you listening?"

Polly pushed her lower lip out into a pout. Sylvie shut her eyes, shook her head and stood up, returning the crock to its place. She reached into a drawer and drew out a bag of bread, then picked up a tub of butter and a knife and came back to the table.

"Try this," she said and handed Polly a slice.

Polly took a bite of the bread and moaned. "You really have been holding out on me. I want this every day."

"No butter?"

"Why would I want to alter the flavor? This is amazing."

"You really think so?"

Polly pushed the slice toward Sylvie and said, "Taste it."

"I know what it tastes like. It's my bread."

"No. Taste it like you've never had it before." She kept pushing the slice toward Sylvie's face.

Sylvie obediently took a bite. "It's sourdough bread. That's all."

"You won't be able to keep this in stock. Oh please, please, please make me some bread."

"Take this. I was planning to bake on Thursday."

Polly took the bag of bread and tucked it under her arm. "I'm not telling anyone that I have this. It's all mine."

"You're an odd woman, Polly. It's just bread."

"How am I going to get this through your head? It's not just bread. It's amazing. You need to quit protesting and say, 'Thank you, Polly.'"

"Thank you, Polly."

"That's better." Polly took another bite and rolled her eyes back in her head. "Amazing."

CHAPTER NINETEEN

Yipping, yapping, and thunderous noise down the back steps announced the arrival of Andrew and the dogs. Polly wasn't surprised to see Kayla, Rebecca and Helen Oswald with him.

"Mom!" Andrew yelled as he came into the kitchen.

"Dogs," Sylvie said firmly.

Andrew put his hand on Obiwan's collar and Rebecca reached down to pick Han up into her arms.

"Mom, you have to meet Helen. She's the Sheriff's sister!"

Sylvie stood up to shake the woman's hand. "I'm the boy's mother, Sylvie Donovan," she said looking down at her son.

Helen smiled. "I assumed as much. He's told me all about you. You've made your son very proud." She turned back to the kids. "Are you ready to show me around?"

"We can go outside this way," Andrew said, heading for the back door of the kitchen. "This place is great. Did you know that those stairs we just came down were boarded up? I have to show you the office Henry made for me." He opened the door and held it for Rebecca and Helen.

Obiwan dashed outside as Helen turned back to Polly. "I

understand I've been fobbed off on you for the evening. I can make my own way if you have other plans. Just point me to a restaurant and I'll take an evening stroll."

"I offered," Polly said. "It will be fun to hear stories of Aaron's childhood without him here to hush you up."

Rebecca stood in the doorway, holding Han. "I wish I could be there, but Mom and I are eating together. She feels really good."

Kayla said nothing and Polly wasn't sure what to do next. She was sure that she could stop in the office and invite Stephanie and Jeff to join them.

"It doesn't matter to me where I cook dinner. I could use this kitchen and we could all eat at the table back here," Polly said, and then she looked at Sylvie. "Can I?"

Sylvie laughed. "Of course you can. It's your kitchen. But I have a better idea. Andrew, would you like to stay for dinner too?"

"Could we? That would be awesome!"

"We'll make a party of it. I'll call Eliseo and invite him to join us."

"Rachel?" Polly asked. "Do you want to ask Doug and Billy? If we're cooking a feast, we might as well feed everyone."

Rachel nodded shyly. "I'll call him."

"It seems we're fixin' to have party," Helen said. "Let's walk these animals. You two have to show me everything you think is special about Sycamore House." She followed the kids outside and pulled the door shut behind her.

"How many are we cooking for now?" Polly asked, trying to count in her head.

"I'll call Eliseo and alert him," Sylvie said. "Do you want to invite Jeff and Stephanie? What about Evelyn and Sarah?"

"Only you could think that it's okay to whip together a dinner for nearly twenty people," Polly said. "I'll see who I can add to the list."

"We'd better plan to eat in the auditorium. We can't put seventeen people at this table."

"Let me make sure." Polly took off and headed for the addition and Sarah Heater's room. She tapped lightly at the door and heard a quiet, "Come in."

"Sarah?" she asked, opening the door.

"Hi Polly." Sarah stood up and crossed the room to greet her. "Look at me," she said, sweeping her hands up and down. "I'm in great shape today. I feel good, I'm dressed and walking." She sat down at the desk near the door, breathing heavily. "But it's not without its effort."

"You look wonderful." Polly bent over to give her a small hug. "Rebecca is ecstatic that you are doing so well."

"We were supposed to go shopping for a dress this afternoon, but after the doctor's appointment today, I'm exhausted. I know she was disappointed."

"There's always tomorrow."

"I feel silly buying a dress at this point in my life."

Polly sat down in a chair across from her. "Oh no, Sarah. You should enjoy every minute you have with Rebecca and with us. If a dress helps make it more fun, that's what you should do."

"I try to tell myself that, but spending money on me is not something I've ever done."

"Then that's the wrong way to look at it. You are spending money on something that will bring joy to Rebecca. She wants desperately to be with you and the Valentine's party on Saturday night will be fun for both of you."

Sarah smiled. "You do have the best parties here. I wish I'd known about them back when I was healthy. It would have been great fun to swing around on the dance floor with a gorgeous young man."

"Speaking of parties, the Sheriff's sister is staying here this week and we're hosting her for dinner tonight. She spent time this afternoon with Andrew and Rebecca and if you'd like to join us, we're serving dinner in the auditorium. Are you up to it?"

"If I go slowly."

Polly looked around the room. "I can push you down in the wheelchair. Save your energy for dinner."

"That's a good idea. Maybe Rebecca would do that."

"I'm sure she'd love to. Is Evelyn here?"

"She's next door." Polly had insisted that Evelyn have the room next door to Sarah's even though she had an apartment in town. That way the two women could have privacy whenever possible. It had become a communal room for the nurses who cared for Sarah, but generally, Evelyn could be found there.

"I'll invite her too."

"That would be nice. She's a wonderful woman."

"It seems that way."

"No, she's really something. She allows me to talk through my fears. I'm not worried about Rebecca anymore. I know that you and Henry love her and she'll find happiness with you when I'm gone, but Evelyn and I talked about those ugly realities. She just isn't scared of anything and she lets me ask the strangest questions."

It broke Polly's heart that anyone had to face their own imminent death. She wanted to fall asleep one night about eighty years in the future and not wake up. She didn't want to know it was coming, her life on earth would just be finished. Hearing Sarah talk about Rebecca in the future without her mother also destroyed Polly. Yes, she loved the girl like her own, but given a choice, she'd rather see these two in their own home, living a big life with a future stretching out for decades.

"I'm glad she's here for that. I don't mind answering questions, but some of that stuff is way over my head."

Sarah leaned forward. "I don't want a big dramatic sendoff, but I would like you there to take care of Rebecca when it finally happens. Do you mind?"

"Of course I don't mind," Polly replied. They'd approached this question off and on throughout the last months, but this was the first time Sarah had just put it out there. She really was getting more comfortable with the thought of actually dying.

"That's enough of that," Sarah said. "Ask Rebecca to come get me when it's time for dinner, if you would. Tonight will be fun."

Polly stood, bent over to hug Sarah once more and said, "I'm so glad you two are here. It's been wonderful getting to know you."

"Thank you, Polly." Sarah took Polly's arm to steady herself as she stood and then walked back to her bed. "I'm going to rest before we eat."

Polly left the room and knocked on the next door, "Evelyn? It's me. Polly."

The door was quickly opened, "Is everything okay?"

"It's fine. We're serving dinner to a crowd of friends in the auditorium tonight and would like to invite you to join us. I just left Sarah and she's planning to be there. Will you?"

"I'd be honored. Thank you. I'll make sure Sarah is there."

"She asked that I send Rebecca. Maybe the wheelchair?"

Evelyn nodded approvingly. "Very good idea. We'll be ready."

"Thank you." Polly left the addition and headed for the office. Two down, three more to go.

Jeff was bent over Stephanie's desk and they were looking at the computer screen. He glanced up, "Hey, Polly."

"You two. Dinner in the auditorium. It's a plan," she said determinedly.

"Tonight?" he asked.

"Yes. Don't tell me you have plans. You never eat with us when we do spontaneous meals."

"Wow. Direct orders and guilt. All in one breath. That's impressive."

"Come on. Please?"

He chuckled and said to Stephanie, "Shall we?"

"I don't know."

"Kayla has been having a wonderful time with Helen Oswald. She's the reason we're doing this. She loves the kids and they love her. Please?" Polly asked again.

"You'd better say yes," Jeff said. "Once she starts pleading, there's no stopping her."

Stephanie looked at Polly, concern on her face.

"Jessie will be there. You know her from working at the convenience store, don't you? And Rachel. Doug and Billy are about your age, too. It will be fun," Polly said. "Say yes. You'll have fun, meet a few people, and Kayla will have a good time, too."

"Okay. But we can't stay too late."

"You come and eat, then you can leave whenever you like."

"Okay," she said tentatively.

Polly smiled and left the office, but hadn't gotten all the way out when she heard Stephanie say to Jeff, "I'm never going to lose weight if you keep feeding me." Yes, Jeff was the perfect person to be in Stephanie's life right now. She just needed to know that she was okay, no matter what size she was. He'd do that easily. The poor girl needed to learn how to dress for her size and he'd take care of that, too, slowly but surely. Polly hesitated, waiting to hear Jeff's response.

"You're a beautiful girl, Stephanie Armstrong and don't you forget it. However, I suspect that eating regular healthy meals will be better for both you and Kayla. You can't tell me that you weren't living off hot dogs and other things from the convenience store."

"I know. You're right. Thanks."

Polly nodded and smiled to herself. Sometimes she was more fortunate than smart when it came to the people who had dropped into her life.

~~~

"That was too much food," Henry said, leaning back in his chair and draping his arm across Polly's.

"Sylvie is amazing."

"I still can't believe she did that with no notice," Evelyn said. "When I lived next door to her, she used to bring food over sometimes, usually sweet treats. She's really come into herself, hasn't she?"

Polly nodded. Between her kitchen and the Sycamore House kitchen, they'd come up with enough ingredients to make up three pans of lasagna. Sylvie had made a pan of incredible vegetable lasagna using frozen slices of eggplant from Eliseo's garden last fall. Polly had the hamburger and ricotta to make a regular pan and they'd come up with a chicken lasagna with
~~~

white sauce. Sylvie had cranked out sourdough rolls with garlic butter and a quick run to the grocery store gave them ingredients for a tossed salad. Rachel and Sylvie's baking experiments provided sweet treats and everyone was enjoying dinner together.

Jason and Eliseo had pulled together two of the circular tables, making it possible for the entire group to eat together.

"Eliseo asked me to join him for a ride tomorrow morning," Helen said across the table to Polly. "Those are some mighty fine horses you have down there. They won't be intimidated by my size... not a one of them. However, those purty little donkeys saw me comin' and scampered out to the field."

"They did?"

Helen laughed. "No, they were as friendly as could be. Even when they discovered I wasn't carrying treats." She leaned forward to catch Stephanie's eye. "Your Kayla here should ask Eliseo for riding lessons. She's a natural around those animals. Just like her friend, Rebecca." Helen looked pointedly at Andrew. "You like to act as if you're scared of those big horses, but I think that's all made up." She spoke in a stage whisper. "He just doesn't want to show up his big brother."

"I don't like Nan," Andrew said. "She *does* scare me."

Jason said, "You just need to spend more time with her. She's not scary."

Polly was so thankful that Jason had finally settled in at school. He had gotten involved with FFA and had also found a kindred spirit in the school's shop teacher. She was waiting for him to find a girlfriend. He had rid himself of the gang he'd started the school year with and become more comfortable in his own skin. Now he was back to the loving boy she knew so well. He laughed easily and oh my goodness, he was turning into a good looking young man. He continued to fill out, but it was all muscle from working at the barn. Sylvie tried to keep his hair cut short, but those dark waves grew out before she could manage it. Polly had to admit it, if she was in high school, every time he brushed the hair back from his face, she'd have swooned. What in the world were the girls thinking? Why weren't they throwing themselves at him?

Jessie had commanded everyone's attention when she walked in the front door. She walked with the swagger of a pregnant woman who was getting tired of it and dropped into the first chair that was pulled out for her. Jeff had come in with Stephanie, taken in the room and sat so that Stephanie would be beside Jessie. He'd engaged the girls in conversation until they were talking together about babies and little girls, apartments and Stephanie's job at Sycamore House. There. That was a friendship ignited. The two would be good for each other. At least for a while.

Polly smiled to herself. Those two had both come from difficult situations. She hoped they would support each other.

Rebecca bounced around the room - spending most of her time making sure that her mother was comfortable and had everything she needed. It didn't matter that Evelyn was nearby, Rebecca insisted on being the one who did the work. Helen Oswald had taken time to sit beside Sarah, talking to her about her daughter and what a wonderfully talented girl Rebecca was.

"You're just watching it all happen, aren't you?" Henry asked Polly. He'd sat up so he could lean in and speak quietly in her ear.

"It's pretty cool, isn't it?"

"What about those two?" he nodded toward Rachel and Billy.

"Lydia talked to her today. I think she'll give him a break. She just needs to let him figure this out on his own."

"No, I meant the other two."

"Doug and Billy?"

"Yes."

"What do you mean?"

"Watch Doug."

Polly did and didn't see anything. "I don't know what you mean."

"He knows something is up. Something is going to change. He's so antsy, he can't stand it."

"How do you see that?"

"I'm just that good."

"So I didn't ask," she said, lowering her voice. "What happened with that Cody kid?"

"I fired him."

"He didn't ask why?"

"Of course he did. He was all innocent about it. Like he doesn't know she lives in my house!"

Polly put her hand on his knee to bring him back down. "What did you say?"

"I told him that if he ever went near her again, I would know. That I know everything and have people watching her all the time." He chuckled at his lie. "I told him that she's part of my family and he crossed the line. Then I told him that I was going to register a complaint with the police department so they'd have a record of his behavior."

"You can't do that. Jessie has to."

Henry scowled at her. "I know that. You know that. Dimwit doesn't know that."

"Oh," she chuckled. "I get it."

"I grabbed his shirt and pushed him up against a cabinet and told him that if he ever came near her or anyone else in this town with a raised fist, I would make sure that he spent the rest of his life fighting off unwanted attention from big burly men in Anamosa. That scared him. But, the worst thing I did?" He waited for her to pay attention.

"What's that?"

"I made him sit there while I telephoned his mother and told her what he'd done."

"You didn't!" Polly looked up, worried that people had heard her. They were busy with their own conversations."

"Yes I did. Right there in front of him. I told her that I was firing him because he'd hurt Jessie and that I was keeping an eye on him and he'd better not hurt anyone else. And then I gave her Jessie's therapist's name and told her that he needed counseling because this was a terrible way to start a life."

Polly's mouth dropped open and she stared at her husband. "I have no words."

"Neither did she. At first she was angry and defensive, but she knows me and I suspect she knows her son. When I hung up, young Cody wasn't much more than a stain in the chair. I told him I'd send his final check and that this was a wakeup call. He'd best figure it out. He left. I felt better."

"I love you," she said to him.

"You would have done the same thing."

"I don't know that I would have thought to call his mother. That was a nice touch."

"I wanted to punch his arrogant face." Henry's teeth were gritted. "Then I wanted to push him into the sander. I made all sorts of horrible plans for that boy today, but I kinda figured you might not want to have Aaron call you to hire a lawyer for me."

"Thank you," she said. "I appreciate that. Still... the mom? Good job."

Helen stood up with her plate. "It's been nice to meet y'all, but I've had a busy day. What say we help our wonderful hostesses and clean up so they don't have to."

Polly, Sylvie and Rachel were waved back to their seats as the others quickly cleared the tables. Finally Sylvie could stand it no longer. "They don't know how to run the dishwasher," she said. "At least let me be the boss in my kitchen."

Rebecca and Evelyn took an exhausted Sarah Heater back to her room, but not before she grabbed Polly's hand. "This was a wonderful evening. Thanks for letting me be part of it."

Polly hugged her again. "I'm glad you were here. You know she will always be loved by tons of people, don't you?"

"That's what I saw tonight. Thank you."

"Get some rest. It sounds like you're going to help me in the office next week when Jeff and Stephanie leave town."

"I'm looking forward to it. Thanks again."

The mood in the kitchen had erupted into play and fun. Sylvie didn't stop the water fight that broke out, she simply tossed towels at them from her perch on the counter top. Stephanie stood apart, trying to understand what was happening in front of her until Doug mistakenly threw an entire pitcher of water down her front. She looked at him in shock and the look on his face was priceless.

"I'm sorry!" he exclaimed. "I was aiming for Polly, but I had to move to miss Andrew. I'm so sorry." He grabbed up one of the towels and started patting at her chest. In a split second, he started to laugh hysterically and handed her the towel. "Oh god, I'm so sorry." He turned to Polly. "Help me out here, will you?"

"Me?" she asked. "You were aiming for me. This is your doing."

"But I barely know her. What a first impression. Help me!"

Stephanie's shock was quickly replaced with laughter as she tried to blot up the water. The adults in the room had stopped for just a moment to see how she would respond to Doug, but when she relaxed, so did everyone and they went back to what they were doing.

The kitchen was finally clean and Sylvie said, "I think it's time that my boys get home. There is still school tomorrow and it's getting late."

"We should go too," Stephanie said to Kayla. "Thank you for inviting us. This was fun." She stopped by the stool Jessie was sitting on. "We should do lunch sometime."

"That sounds great."

Sycamore House cleared out, Helen was shown to her room and Polly asked Rebecca and Jessie to send the dogs down for one last trip outside before bedtime. She and Henry stood in the back yard as Han and Obiwan wandered, sniffing and romping in the last bits of the melting snow.

"That was a good evening," he said, pulling her close for warmth.

"I always say we should do it more often, but then we get busy and it never happens."

"Maybe spontaneity is what makes it work."

"You really are perfect, you know that?"

"I'm what?"

"Everyone tells me you're perfect. Maybe too perfect."

Henry wrinkled his nose and stuck his tongue out at her. "Does that help?"

"Yes. Could you keep it like that forever, please?"

CHAPTER TWENTY

"I've got it!" Sal said, rushing into Polly's office.

"Where'd you come from?" Polly asked, bewildered.

Sal slapped a piece of paper down on her desk. "I've got it!"

"You've got what."

"The name for the coffee shop. Sweet Beans. It's perfect!"

"Okay, Sweet Beans. That sounds great."

"No, it's not just great, it's perfect."

"Tell me why it's perfect."

"Because that's what I called my dachshund when I was young. Some friends of his bred them and he wanted me to experience the entire journey. He and Mom thought it would be a good way for me to learn how to take care of someone other than myself. So, the day after she was born, he took me over to the house and I saw this itty bitty baby dachshund and I told Dad she looked like a bean. That was her name. She was always Sweet Bean after that. But, beans ... coffee. You know. And sweet works perfectly for all of the pastries Sylvie is going to bake."

"Then it's perfect. I agree." Polly was glad to see her friend excited about this. "Now, what do you want the decor to look like? Beans or dachshunds."

Sal finally took a breath and sat down. "So you're fine with the name?"

"Of course I am. It's a great name and the story is even better. Whatever happened to her?"

"She got diabetes and died the week before I graduated from high school."

"That's horrible."

"It was pretty awful. I'd been taking care of her for four years - giving her insulin shots every day. We got really close. Finally it just took her over and we couldn't keep up. I sat beside her all night long and Dad told me in the morning that it was time to let her go."

"How did you even get through the rest of that week?"

"I just existed."

"You never talked about this and you haven't had a dog since I've known you."

Sal shook her head. "I just couldn't. But Mark says I should get a dog to keep me company when I'm writing."

"You really should. Would you get another dachshund?"

"Maybe," Sal smiled weakly at Polly. "I do miss her."

"What are you waiting for? We should go to the shelter and see what they have."

Sal chuckled and took out her phone, swiped it open and after another couple of swipes, showed Polly a picture.

"Who's that?"

"They have three dachshunds." She swiped through the pictures from a red to a black and tan, to a cream colored long-hair. "I've been watching for the last couple of weeks. Those first two just showed up yesterday."

Polly snatched her coat from the back of her chair. "Let's go now."

"No. Not now. You have work to do and I'm in the middle of an article. I just had to get out of the house to tell you my idea."

"Come on. You need one of those babies. Today."

Sal gestured for Polly to sit back down. "Let me talk to Mark about it again. Not right now."

Polly dropped back into her chair. "You don't want to let the right one get away, you know."

"I figure that whoever is there when I'm ready is who I'm supposed to have in my life. It will work out."

"Okay. So back to decor at the coffee shop. What are you thinking?"

"I want it soft and warm, not cold and warehousey. People should be able to talk to each other without sound echoing through the room. Soft, comfortable chairs in corners and at side tables holding lamps and maybe piles of books. Wouldn't it be awesome to have a big bookshelf along one of the walls filled with things that people can read? If they take a book home, no big deal. Or maybe other people would bring in some of their old books."

"Who's going to manage that?"

"I don't know. But let's put a bookshelf on the inside wall anyway. We'll figure out the details later. I want rustic dark wood. Not polished and probably on the darker side."

Polly opened her browser and did a search. "What about this?"

"That's it! It's not like red mahogany or cherry. I don't want those. What is that?"

"It's called knotty alder and it can be a dark stain. It's what our front door is made of."

"Perfect. I love it. And I want oddly shaped tables. Not those four by four pre-made things that are in every restaurant. And do you think that the chairs can all be different?"

"Sure. We might have to hit some thrift stores and antique shops."

"You have a truck. We could take Joss and go shopping some Saturday."

Polly just smiled. Now that Sal had found her name, she was jumping on board with the project. "What about on the walls and maybe in the shelves of the bookcases?" she asked.

"You're going to think I'm weird."

"That's just putting words in my mouth. Go ahead, what are you thinking?"

"Since it's named after my dog, what if we used old pictures and statues of animals. And what if we put a computer screen on one wall that scrolled through adoption pets from the shelter."

"That could work," Polly was taking notes as fast as she could. "Dogs playing poker?"

"My mother would just die. She'd think those type of things were so déclassé."

"So no?"

"So, absolutely yes! I want the kitschiest things we can find and I want to tuck them into nooks and crannies all over the place so that when people look up from their work or their coffee, they see silly and interesting pieces."

"You know pieces like that will get stolen."

Sal waved her off. "This is Iowa. No one would ever do that out here, would they?"

"In a heartbeat."

"I'm not going to worry about it. I'm just going to have to trust. Besides, it isn't like I'm going to have hundreds of people in and out of there during the day."

"You never know! It could become the hottest thing in the Midwest."

"Now you're just scaring me. That's not very nice, you know."

Polly smiled. "It will be fine and this will be fun. You want eclectic and comfortable, soft and warm, puppies and kittens. Are you pregnant?"

"Stop it!" Sal exclaimed, horrified. "Don't even hint at that thought."

"We'll talk about that later," Polly said. "But Sal, you have to know that I was ready to design with chic elegance. Something that looked like you. This looks like me."

"Because I like being around you. You make it easy for people to be who they are. You make people comfortable to try things and do things. Did you ever think about that?"

"Whatever." Polly rolled her eyes. "You know I'll help you put together whatever it is that you want."

"This is what I want." Sal chuckled. "I wonder how much of this kitsch is already in people's homes. What if we had a fund raiser a couple of months before we opened? We could have it here. People would bring their crazy animal and pet-themed items as the donation and for every one they bring... " She thought about it. "Wow, that could get expensive."

"What were you thinking?"

"I could donate five dollars to the shelter. But, that's not how I want to do this."

"It depends," Polly said. "Figure out what you want to spend on that type of decor. Make a budget."

Sal started to laugh. "Me? Budget? There's our first problem."

"Okay. We can work on that, too. But once you figure out what you're going to spend, you can decide whether you want to spend it to support the shelter or on EBay or in a thrift store."

"You're right," Sal said, sitting up a little straighter. "I can make any decision I want to."

Polly nodded. "It's really strange to realize that you're an adult, isn't it."

"No kidding. I mean, I go through every day doing all of the adult things I'm supposed to do, and then something happens and I realize that there isn't anyone else around to tell me what to do. It's all on me." She leaned forward conspiratorially. "It's kind of freaky. I haven't grown up enough to have that kind of responsibility."

"Do you remember my first jar of macadamia nuts?" Polly asked.

Sal shook her head. "Um, no? Your first jar? You remember that?"

"Yeah. It was our senior year. I was working part time at the library and it was the first time I had extra money. I remember standing in the grocery store and looking at it. I wanted them so bad. Mary always told me they were too expensive. Every once in a while she slipped a jar in my Christmas stocking. That only made me want them more. But that day, I splurged my extra money and spent nine dollars on nuts. I didn't tell anybody."

"So you think I should remember?"

"I shared them with you. You had brought a bottle of wine back from your parent's house and we sat around putting makeup on."

"I let you put makeup on me?"

"Okay no. You got drunk and dolled me up. I thought we were being so grown up that night. Wine and macadamias and you turning me into a… I don't know what."

"I remember doing that, but I didn't realize those were so special to you."

"I didn't want you to know," Polly said. "It felt so good to be independent and make decisions and drink wine. It was a perfect night."

Sal started to laugh. "You are such a weirdo."

"Hey, it was one of my moments, don't take that away from me."

"I never would," she replied, shaking her head. "I guess I'm glad I was there for one of them. You seem to have been around for most of mine." Sal looked up at the clock on Polly's shelf. "Look at the time. I need to get back to work."

"Sweet Beans," Polly said. "I'm on it."

~~~

"Polly?"

She looked up to see Stephanie standing in her doorway.

"Yes, what's up?"

"Mrs. Oswald wondered if you had a few minutes."

Polly pushed back from her desk and stood up. "Sure. Thank you."

Stephanie stepped back and Helen Oswald came in, grinning from ear to ear. "You run a wonderful establishment, my dear."

"Thank you." Polly gestured to the chairs. "Please have a seat. How can I help you this morning?"

"I had a ride this morning on the back of your Nat. I don't know if I've ever been on the back of something quite so wide." She gave a wicked giggle and placed her fingers over her lips.
~~~

"That sounded naughty."

Polly just chuckled. "It does take some getting used to. I 'd never ridden a regular sized horse, so I had nothing to compare it to, but I do remember feeling like I might never walk normally again."

"I enjoyed spending time with Eliseo. He's a good man and you are fortunate to have him."

"I am fortunate to have everyone that is here."

"It seems like the good Lord put the right people in place."

"I agree." Polly wondered where the conversation was going. Helen didn't seem like the type of person to randomly engage in small talk.

"You might wonder why I'm here this morning. I received a call from our Lydia. Would you be free for luncheon?"

"Certainly." Then Polly stopped. Jeff and Sylvie were off site today and she hated to leave Stephanie alone. "Wait. No, I probably shouldn't. Stephanie has only been here for a few days and I don't want to leave her alone."

Helen nodded, looking off to the side while she considered Polly's words. "Lydia specifically asked if me to invite you."

"Why don't we have lunch upstairs?" She knew there was chili in the freezer and she surely had sandwich ingredients.

"We don't want to put you to any trouble. Especially if you must pay attention to the comings and goings of your people."

"It won't be any trouble. Let me call Lydia. The two of us can work this out in no time."

Polly picked up her phone and quickly made the call.

"Hello dear," Lydia said. "Did Helen speak with you about lunch?"

"Yes, but I can't go out. Jeff and Sylvie are out of town today. I don't want to leave Stephanie here alone."

"That makes sense, but I'm sorry to hear it."

"But what if you were to come here? I wouldn't be too far away from the action if we ate upstairs in my apartment. I have chili in the freezer and we can make sandwiches."

"Are you certain?"

"Of course I am."

"Let me see what I have here. We'll make it a potluck."

"If you're digging into your refrigerator, it will be a feast."

"If you are certain this will work..."

Polly interrupted her, "Lydia, it will be great. I just don't want to get too far away. Nothing is going to happen, but I'd hate to not be able to be here and have the place explode."

"Thank you so much, dear. I will be over for lunch. Let Helen know that we have this well in hand."

"I'll do it. See you later." Polly put the phone back down on her desk and said, "I knew we could work it out."

"You two are quite good friends, aren't you," Helen said.

"I don't know what I would have done without her. She's taken care of me through the strangest things and keeps me sane when all I want to do is run screaming through the town."

"She's one of the most stable women I've ever known."

"You know, most of us believe that her stability is because of the relationship she and Aaron have."

Helen nodded. "They've always been a good team."

"That's why we're so worried. Lydia is falling apart at the seams because he has quit talking to her. She says he's never done this before."

"He's protecting people he shouldn't be concerned about. You know Aaron. His honor would never let him go back on a promise and he made several long before he met Lydia. They're coming back to hurt him now and he's caught between a very big rock and a very hard place."

"And you know what's going on?"

Helen brushed back an invisible strand of hair, then took her glasses off and rubbed her eyes. "I was a large part of it. He thinks he needs to continue to protect me. But I don't need his protection. I can handle my own troubles."

Polly smiled. "I've known you less than twenty-four hours and it seems to me that you can handle your own and anyone else's you choose to manage. How much younger is Aaron than you."

"Tut, tut, young lady," Helen scolded, shaking a finger at her.

"You mustn't ask those types of questions of a lady."

"I'm sorry," Polly said with a nervous giggle. "I didn't mean to ask that. It's just that you are obviously the older sister."

"That I am. But not by much. Enough, though, that I can still tell that boy what to do and expect him to obey."

"That's something I'd really like to see. I've never seen Aaron as anything but in charge."

"Years of practice and self-denial taught him that. Getting beat up by his older sister helped, too."

"You beat him up?"

"Goodness Gracious, yes. He was a horrible child. Mother told us that we weren't allowed to hit or slap or kick. However, we were often encouraged to wrestle out our frustrations. I was old enough that I could take him down in a flash. I sat on him, just to stop him from picking at me. That all changed the summer before he entered high school. I realized he was within months of being able to take me out, so I just stopped, hoping he'd forget those years of torment."

"I'm guessing your hope was in vain."

"He never said anything," Helen mused. "He never threatened me or warned me or anything."

"So you didn't see it coming."

"No, ma'am. Father set up a wrestling mat in the basement for the boys to work out and build up those wonderful Merritt muscles. They had a mighty nice weight set and all of them were taking martial arts. One night on summer break, Aaron asked me to step in to practice with him. I was as naive as a newborn kitten. He took a stance, asked me to rush him and before I knew what happened, I was flat on my back, out of breath. He stood over me and put his hand out to help me up. He said nothing, didn't laugh or taunt me. I stepped back, still not understanding what just happened. Aaron practiced a few more moves and then told me he thought he might have done something wrong and would I consider trying it again. He hadn't hurt me, so what did I have to lose?"

Polly shook her head slowly, knowing where this story was

going.

"Yes. Exactly. He flipped me over and I was on my back again. This time, though, he dropped down and straddled my stomach so I couldn't move, then grabbed my hands. I was out of breath and both of us were laughing. In fact, I remember worrying about whether or not I was going to wet my pants. The next thing I knew, he took my right hand and made me swat myself in the face. I was furious! He asked if I wanted more and made my left hand swat myself. I couldn't make my arms resist. I was out of control and both of us were laughing uncontrollably. I realized he was paying me back for years and years of sibling torture and wasn't letting up until I knew exactly what I was receiving."

"How did you get out of that?"

"I cried because I knew I was going to wet myself. When he saw the tears come, he knew he'd gone too far and jumped up. By that point, I couldn't move I was laughing so hard."

"You didn't."

"Oh lordie, yes I did."

Polly let out a snort of laughter. "I can't believe you just told me this story."

"I don't know whether it was harder on me or on him, but both of us learned lessons that day."

"I guess so," Polly said. "The first was not to trust a brother on a wrestling mat."

"You know, I always heard them say 'fool me once, shame on you - fool me twice, shame on me.' I learned that lesson. You can get me once, but I will never let you get away with it a second time. And as for trusting a brother on a wrestling mat, he learned about consequences of tormenting your sister to the point of ... well, that. He had to clean the mat, not me. Dad heard the entire thing. After I'd finally slunk away, he carried a bucket in filled with hot soapy water and a scrub brush."

"These are the stories I want to know about Aaron. I hope you have many, many more."

"I do, that's for certain-sure, but look at me takin' up your time. I'll meet you upstairs for lunch. I'm going to take a walk. If I am going to have wounded muscles tomorrow morning, I should see the place today."

She left the office and Polly sat back, imagining a young Aaron Merritt looking at his sister in horror. Yes, that would take her through the rest of the day.

CHAPTER TWENTY-ONE

"Nothing from Jeff and Sylvie yet?" Polly asked Stephanie, walking out of her office.

"They're in Strawberry Point. Jeff called about fifteen minutes ago. They're meeting his friend's father after lunch."

"I hope it's a good day for them." Polly stood in the doorway to the hallway. "I'm taking the dogs out and then having lunch upstairs with Lydia and Helen. If you need anything, call or come get me."

"You really have a lot of things going on."

Polly nodded. "I guess we do. It's kind of fun, though."

"Rachel invited me to have lunch with her in the kitchen. Will it be okay if I'm not in the office?"

"Of course," Polly said. "You know how to turn on the voice mail system, right?"

"Yes, that was the first thing Jeff showed me last week. All I have to do is..."

"No, I believe you've got it. Jeff's a great teacher."

"He's been so good to me. I can't believe he's taking me back to Ohio. You two shouldn't have to do this. You barely know me."

"It might take time for you to fully understand, but once you come to work at Sycamore House, you become part of the family. We'll give you all the freedom you need, but we're there when you need us."

Stephanie ducked her head, a smile on her face. "It's so different than anything I've ever done before."

"I hope it's a good different. Okay. I'll be gone for a while, but don't hesitate to call me."

"Have a good lunch."

Polly went up the steps and snagged two leashes just as the dogs came out of the bedroom to see who was in their house. At the sight of what she was holding, Han bounded across the room and tried to leap in her arms. Obiwan ran over and stood in front of her, his big ole tongue hanging out and his tail wagging his whole body.

"From the looks of it, you two are desperate for a walk. We don't have much time, but let's wander down to the barn and see what's up with the big boys."

She took them back down the front steps and out the main door. The weather had been absolutely wacky lately. One day it was nearly fifty degrees and the next it was in the teens. Fortunately, it was relatively warm today, but she was tired of hanging fog and grey skies.

The snow in the pasture had given way to mud, but the horses didn't care. She chuckled when she watched Demi on his back, rolling around. Ahh, that would be something for Jason to deal with this afternoon. Nan and Nat were actually scampering around the back end of the pasture and all of a sudden, Nan took off and ran toward... her! Nan was happy to see her. She came rushing to the front and then looked straight at Polly and let out a whinny.

"Hello girl," Polly called back. "Are you having a good day?" Nan shook her head and called again. "I know!" Polly said. "It's a great day to be outside." The other three horses joined Nan and watched as Polly and her dogs walked across the yard. Han and Obiwan were preoccupied with their own sniffs and smells so she couldn't move as quickly as she wanted, but she finally hooked both of their leashes onto her left hand and reached up to rub Nan's face with the other. She moved on down the row, taking a minute with each of the horses.

Eliseo poked his head out of the door to Demi's stall and said, "Hello there! I couldn't figure out what all the fuss was."

"This is new," Polly said. "Nan came running to greet me."

"Maybe she misses you."

Polly started to apologize and he put his hands up, "No. I didn't mean it that way. It's good for her to react this way to you."

She backed up and rubbed Nan's face again. The horse reached down and nuzzled Polly's shoulder. "I wish I had a treat for you. You have no idea how wonderful this moment is."

Demi reached across and nipped at Nan's shoulder, distracting her. Then he took off and she chased him across the pasture, the other horses running after them. Polly looked for Tom and Huck only to discover that they were inside with Eliseo. Wimps.

"Let's see if we can get their attention on the other side of the barn," Polly said, guiding the dogs back toward the main street.

Helen Oswald was walking up the sidewalk past the barn as Polly emerged.

"Hi there," she called out. "A beautiful day for a walk. I saw your horses chasing after you a few minutes ago."

Eliseo came out as they were talking. "Hello ladies, it's a wonderful day, isn't it?"

Polly glanced up at the sky. "You're a good man," she said. "I want sunshine."

"If we don't have sunshine, at least we have melting. What do you think, one more good snow before the season is over?"

"I'm such a pessimist about winter," Polly responded. "I figure it will torture us until June."

He smiled at Helen. "Are you going back up to the house? I'll walk with you."

Polly split off from them and started walking south when a red car sped past her, its tires squealing as it tore into the driveway of Sycamore House. She spun around, clutching the two leashes in her hands as she watched it race toward Eliseo and Helen, picking up the pace as it aimed straight for them.

Eliseo turned to see what the noise was and as Polly watched in shock and amazement, he pulled Helen away from the path of the oncoming car, tossing her aside as if she were a child. The driver of the car spun his tires, flinging gravel up as he raced on around the driveway and out the other side. He came to a short stop as a car passed in front, going north. The driver turned south again, heading back the way he had come. Polly was terrified he might make another pass through the driveway and fumbled in her pocket for her phone. Instead, he tore past her, gaining speed. Within seconds, the car crested the hill at the south end of her lot and was gone.

Polly ran as fast as Han would let her. Eliseo was just starting to sit up, his hand reaching out to Helen. Blood covered his face.

"What in the hell was that?" Polly asked, panting from both fear and exertion.

"Ms. Oswald, are you okay?" Eliseo asked.

The older woman rolled over, her face scraped and her hands raw and bloody. Blood was seeping through a rip in her jeans and one of her tennis shoes was three feet behind her.

"Bless your heart, you're something else," she gasped. "No one's ever tossed me like that."

Polly knelt down. "Can you stand?"

Helen flexed both of her legs and then rolled her shoulder and her arms. "I seem to be in one piece, though I lost a dad-burned shoe."

Eliseo stood up and groaned. "That's going to leave a mark," he said. He walked over to her tennis shoe, picked it up and handed it to her.

"Your face is a mess," Polly said to him.

"It was the gravel he spat up at me. Do you have any idea what that was about?"

"We need to call the Sheriff."

"Don't you dare," Helen demanded. "That will just get Aaron all worked up."

"Then I'm calling Ken Wallers at the police station. Someone needs to know what just happened."

"He'll tell Aaron," she muttered.

Polly took her phone out. "I've found that it's easier for me when they know what's happening here. I run into enough trouble that I don't need them to think I'm hiding things."

"Are you ready to try standing up?" Eliseo asked, putting both of his hands out.

"I'd like to tell you that I can do this by myself," Helen said, "but I'd be lying to us both. My legs feel quite shaky."

"It's shock. Let me help you."

"I think I'll let you." She took his arm and started to lift herself from the ground, then released him and sat back down. "A few more minutes," she said. "There isn't enough strength in me right now to do much of anything except sit here."

"The ground is cold. We should get you inside as soon as possible."

"Just one more minute. I won't freeze to death in one minute."

Eliseo took his coat off and wrapped it around her shoulders.

"You're a gentleman," she said, pulling it close. "That's helpful."

Polly stood up as she reached the police office. "Bellingwood Police, how may I help you?"

"Hi, this is Polly over at Sycamore House. Can someone come visit me?" She gave a slight chuckle.

"I suppose so. What happened today?"

"I hate to say that it was a murder attempt..."

"Oh Polly."

"I know, right? But someone in a red car just sped into my driveway and tried to run down Sheriff Merritt's sister and Eliseo."

"The Sheriff's sister and you're calling us?"

"She doesn't want him involved."

"He's going to get involved sooner or later."

"Oh Mindy, I know that, but could you send Ken or one of the guys over for now?"

"Sure. I'll see who is in your neighborhood. Where will they find you?"

"I'm not sure. Just ask at the front. Someone will know where we've landed."

"Take care of yourself. I'd hate to lose our entertainment."

"That's not funny."

"Well. It really is." Mindy chuckled on the other end as she hung up the phone.

"Someone will be here in a bit," Polly said. "Can we get you inside now?"

She stood on one side of the woman as Eliseo stood on the other and they helped Helen get to her feet.

"This is embarrassing," she said, wobbling between them.

"I'm just glad you're okay," Polly said, holding her with one arm while trying to maneuver the dogs with the other.

They got to the side door of Sycamore House and stopped while Eliseo opened the door. Polly reached down and unlatched the leashes, letting both dogs run inside. They knew where they were and there was no one around for them to bother.

"Let me knock on Evelyn Morrow's door," Polly said. "She's a nurse and can check you out to make sure that everything is working properly."

"Everything's working just fine," Helen said. "Now that I'm up and moving, I'm embarrassed. I should change my clothes."

"Nope. Both of you are getting checked out by Evelyn. I insist." Polly put her hands on her hips and stared both Eliseo and Helen down.

Interestingly enough, they followed her meekly to Evelyn's door. Polly knocked. "Evelyn, it's me, Polly. Are you available?"

The door opened and Evelyn Morrow started to speak and then saw the two wounded people beside Polly.

"Oh dear. What happened? Come in here right away and let's clean you up."

Knowing Evelyn had things in hand, Polly realized that she needed to take care of a few things, including her dogs.

"I'll be back in a few minutes," she said and trotted out of the addition into the main building. "Obiwan, Han, where did you end up?"

"They're in here," Stephanie said, stepping into the foyer from the office. "Did they get lost?"

Polly chuckled. "No, they knew just where to go. Jeff has treats for them in his desk."

"Sorry, boys." Stephanie said. "I don't have anything for you."

"I'll take them up to the apartment. Say, Ken Wallers is going to be here in just a few minutes. If I'm not back, would you tell him I will be?"

"Is this about that car speeding through the driveway?"

"Did you see that?"

"I looked through your office window. That was crazy."

"Yeah. He tried to run Eliseo and Helen Oswald down."

"He what?"

"They're back in Evelyn Morrow's room. She's dealing with their injuries."

"Injuries? How bad?"

"Just scrapes and cuts. Thank goodness. I'll be right back down."

Polly slapped her thigh and said, "Come on boys, it's time to go home."

"Is it always like this?" Stephanie asked quietly.

"Oh honey, you'd be surprised. We can always hope that it will quiet down, but better to be prepared for anything, right?"

"Uh huh." Stephanie didn't sound like she was ready to accept Polly's pragmatism.

"Let's go. Obiwan. Han. Follow me." The dogs followed Polly up the steps to her apartment. She opened the door and they went inside, then turned around and wagged at her.

"You are so spoiled. Yes, I have treats. Let's find them."

At the word, they ran for the kitchen, stopping in front of the cupboard that held their food and treats. Polly walked in and realized that Lydia would be here any minute. She hadn't taken the chili out of the freezer, she hadn't found sandwiches. Nothing. This was turning into an interesting day.

Polly handed each dog a treat and took her phone out again,

dialing Lydia.

"Hello dear. I'm just ready to pull out of the garage. Do you need me to pick something up?"

"We have a problem."

"What's that?"

"Somebody just tried to run Helen down in my driveway."

"What? Is she hurt?"

"She's got some scrapes and cuts. Evelyn Morrow is looking at her right now."

"Who was it?"

"I have no idea. Eliseo was walking with her. Lydia, I've never seen anything like it. He saw the car coming and tossed her like she was light as a feather. Her injuries are more from him getting her out of the way than anything else. He got hit with the gravel the car spun up at him."

"We have to talk to Aaron. Don't you think it's all connected?"

"Of course I do, but no one will listen to me."

"I will. And I think Aaron will now, too. We had a long talk last night. Well, I talked and he listened. But he came to bed with me for the first time in weeks."

"Does he know Helen is in town? She wouldn't let me call him so I had to call Ken." Polly looked out the kitchen window and saw Ken's car pull in. "In fact, he's driving in right now. I should go downstairs."

"I'll be right there. After we speak with Helen, we'll make the call to Aaron. Thank you for taking care of her."

"I don't have anything made for lunch, I'm sorry."

"That's the last thing we need to worry about. We'll be fine. Go talk to Ken. I'll be there soon."

Polly pushed her way past the dogs, who were wagging in front of her, hoping for another treat. "You know better," she said. "Stop begging." She bent down and scratched both of their heads, then planted a kiss on Obiwan's nose. "I need to go, but I love you."

She ran back down the steps and saw Ken step into the office.

"Ken," she called out. He stepped back out.

"Hi Polly. I understand you've had some trouble here today. I'm not sure if you hate me or what."

"What do you mean?"

"Mindy said someone tried to run down Aaron Merritt's sister and you called my office?"

"It was what she preferred."

He shook his head. "It's never easy with you, is it? Tell me what happened."

"We were outside. I was taking the dogs for a walk and she was returning from one. Eliseo had come out and the two of them were coming up the driveway to the house. I was going to walk around the barn on the sidewalk. All of a sudden, a red car came barreling into the driveway, aiming straight for them. Eliseo tossed her out of the way and avoided the car, then it went on through, turned south on the highway and sped off. It happened so fast."

"What kind of car was it?"

She gave him a sideways glance. "You're asking me?"

"It was a shot in the dark. How many people were in the car?"

"Just the driver. But I did see that it had Polk County plates."

Ken took out a notebook and wrote that down. "Anything else?"

"Nothing. Now it feels like I was watching a movie. I didn't move. I didn't do anything. But I don't think there was really time. It happened and then in a split second it was over."

He smiled and nodded. "Yeah. That's about right. Where is Eliseo?"

Polly gestured to the addition. "They're in Evelyn Morrow's room. She's doing first-aid. Eliseo got cut up by flying gravel and I think Helen landed pretty hard when he tossed her out of the way."

"Tossed her?"

"That's the only description I have. That man is strong."

"Let's hear what they have to say." He waved her forward. "After you."

Polly knocked on Evelyn's door again and Eliseo answered.

"Hello Chief," he said.

"Polly says you've had some excitement. Can you tell me about it?"

"I don't know if I can tell you very much. I didn't see anything other than a car ripping down the driveway coming right at us."

"You don't know what type of car it was either?"

"Sure," Eliseo said. "It was a Toyota Avalon. Probably only a year old or so."

"The first two letters of the license plate were X and K," Helen said. She stood up from the chair at Evelyn's desk and walked across the room. She was much more sure of herself. "Hello. You must be the local police. I'm Helen Oswald."

Ken put his hand out to shake hers. "Ken Wallers. You're Aaron Merritt's sister?"

"I am. We aren't involving him in this yet. Can you live with that?"

"Not really. He and I have a strong relationship. I'm not comfortable with holding this back from him."

"Just for today. That's all I ask."

"Why?"

"Because he and I need to spend time working through things before he has to worry about a hired gun."

"Hired gun?" Ken looked at Polly and then Eliseo. "What do you mean hired gun?"

"More than likely it is coming from the same person who hired the sniper to kill Aaron's friend. I thought maybe I'd gotten out of Atlanta without... well... let's just say that eyes and ears are everywhere."

She sat back down at the desk and put her arm out. Evelyn had barely begun to clean the dirt and gravel out of the abrasion.

"I'm at a loss," Ken said. "That's not my favorite place to be. Would you mind explaining yourself?"

"I'm sorry, sir," Helen replied. "I can't speak to this until I talk to my brother. That's why I asked Polly not to involve anyone in law enforcement."

"Helen?" Lydia's voice came from the doorway. "Helen, how

badly are you hurt? Polly called. I was already on my way."

"I'm bruised and battered, but I'll live. Eliseo is my new hero."

Lydia turned to him. "You wonderful man. You're like an angel sent to Sycamore House, aren't you."

He chuckled. "Something like that. Seeing as how there is a lot happening here that I don't need to know about, I'm going to go back to work." He put his hand out. "Ken, if you need anything more from me, you know where I'll be."

Ken Wallers just nodded and continued to nod after Eliseo left the room. Finally he spoke. "Ladies, I need answers."

Lydia took his arm. "They'll come. I promise. But Helen can't speak about any of this right now. Will you please trust me?"

"Lydia." Ken scowled at her. "You know I can't..."

"Yes you can. Pretend you didn't come over here today. Aaron will reach out to you in just a couple of days and tell you everything."

"But..."

"Please. I know it's a lot to ask. But you know that I wouldn't unless it were desperately important."

He took a deep breath. "I don't like this."

"Trust me," she said. "I don't either. It needs to be over, but not right now. Please?"

"If I don't hear from Aaron by Friday, I'm calling him. One way or other this will all come out."

"That's fair," Lydia said. "Will we see you at the dance Saturday night?"

Ken looked at her and smiled. "You're not an easy woman to push around, are you?"

"Why, Chief Wallers, I have no idea what you mean." Lydia batted her eyes and smiled back at him. "Will you be there?"

"We will." He touched her arm and then brushed past Polly. "It's always going to be something over here, isn't it?"

"I'm sorry. I shouldn't have called."

"You should always call. You did the right thing. Now we wait for the rest of it to come together."

CHAPTER TWENTY-TWO

"Ain't nothing all that wrong," Helen Oswald protested when Lydia offered her arm as they were heading up to Polly's apartment. "I'm not broken, just battered."

"I know dear, but you must understand what a shock it was to me."

"Let this old woman keep her dignity." Helen looked terrible. She had bandages on her hands and forearms, her left cheek and another on her forehead. She limped slightly due to the battering her leg had taken when she landed on the gravel.

Polly held the door open at the top of the steps. "Aaron is going to be horrified when he sees you."

"We mustn't speak of such things. Lunch first."

Polly had no idea what she was serving today.

"I know that look," Lydia said. "You're worried about feeding us.

"I'll figure it out. Both of you have a seat out here." Polly shut the front door. "I know you aren't an invalid, but you've had a wild day between riding that big horse and being attacked by a crazed driver."

Helen dropped onto the sofa and moaned. "That's better. I must admit I'm fearful of tomorrow morning. If you don't hear from me, send gorgeous firefighters to help me out of bed, will you?"

"That sounds good," Polly said. "You two stay here and I'll forage. Iced tea to drink?"

"Sweet tea?" Helen asked.

"Ummm, I have sugar."

"You northerners don't know how to brew a good ole pot of sweet tea. How did Aaron ever survive up here?"

"He drinks coffee now," Lydia replied. "I'll get your tea. Don't you dare move."

Obiwan had planted himself in front of Helen, waiting for attention while Han followed Lydia to the kitchen. Leia rubbed her face against Helen's leg. Polly smiled. Her animals were friendly, no matter what.

"What are you going to tell Aaron?" she asked Lydia when they got into the kitchen.

Lydia shuddered. "I don't want to think about it. He'll be furious. He was already angry that I called her. We managed to get through that, but this is going to tip him over the edge. I didn't put it all together until last night, but he's carrying guilt about her. I wish they would just tell me what happened all those years ago. It's kept them apart for too long."

She poured out three glasses of tea and Polly handed her a tray. "You go on ahead. Give me a few minutes to make up sandwiches. I'll be right out."

Lydia started for the door and then turned. "I've lost my mind. There is a basket of food in the back of my Jeep. I sliced beef from a roast and have salads and dessert."

"Just hanging around your kitchen?"

"Leftovers. I still can't manage to cook for only two people. I'll be right back."

Polly heard the front door open and shut and stood in front of the refrigerator. She took out bread and cheese, mayonnaise and mustard and put them on the peninsula, then opened a cupboard and pulled out potato chips and crackers. That was about as far as she could go.

Her front door opened again and she heard Obiwan let out a bark. Han ran out to see who had come in and then Polly heard a male voice.

She got to the living room in time to see Aaron on one knee in front of his sister, pulling her into a hug. Lydia came over to stand beside Polly. "He heard it on the scanner and thought maybe he should check it out. Mindy from the police station gave us up. At least Ken's off the hook now."

"I bet we're not," Polly whispered. "Let me take that." She put her hand out for the basket.

Before she could get out of the room, Aaron stood back up and turned on them. "You weren't going to tell me about this?"

"Now Bubby," Helen said, reaching out to touch his arm. "It's not their fault. I made everybody stay quiet. Polly wanted to call you and by the time Lydia arrived, I'd already made the decision."

"Bubby?" Polly asked.

"Don't change the subject." Aaron's tear-filled eyes flashed with anger. She'd never seen him like this.

"Aaron Burr Merritt, you stop it right now." Helen rose up from the sofa and grabbed his arm, pulling him back to her. "You have no right stalking in here like a bear with a sore paw. Especially after everything is said and done. You certainly don't need to make it worse than it already is. Miss Giller has been gracious and helpful. Behave yourself."

He wrenched his arm away from her and stepped forward.

"I'm not going to tell you again," she said, in a tone of voice that Polly never wanted to have turned on her. Fire and fury filled the woman's words and Aaron relaxed his posture.

"He hurt you," he said.

"Polly's man hurt me. He's the one who tossed me like I was light as air. And yes, I could have been killed, but just because you are upset doesn't mean you can take it out on your wife and Miss Polly, here. Do you understand me? I want a response from you, young man."

"Yes ma'am," he said meekly.

"What did he say?" Polly mouthed to Lydia.

Lydia motioned to the kitchen with her head. "Let's make sandwiches while these two talk."

Aaron turned and sat down across from his sister. He leaned forward, his face a mixture of fear and pain.

"Is he going to be okay?" Polly asked once they were back in the kitchen.

Lydia shook her head and opened the basket. "I don't know. He finally told me last night that some things had happened before he came to Iowa. He couldn't tell me about them back then and he didn't think that he dared tell anyone about them now. Whatever it is, he thought he'd left it behind him and now it's come into his territory and it scares him."

"I would never have thought anything could scare Aaron."

"This has." Lydia reached across and took Polly's hand. "But last night I felt like we were heading back to normal. Even if this is hanging between us, at least he was talking to me again."

"I'm glad. Does he have any idea how much he's hurt you?"

"That's not important."

"Yes it is. He shouldn't get away with that."

Lydia stopped assembling the sandwiches in front of her and caught Polly's attention. "You know as well as anyone that sometimes people need to get through the things that are in front of them. His actions weren't intentional, they happened and spun out of control. I can't punish him for that. You wouldn't either."

"You're a good woman, Lydia Merritt."

"We do what we have to do. At least I didn't have to string him up and hang him out to dry."

"No punishment?"

"I'd have punished him if he kept this up or if it happened regularly, but not this. He has enough to deal with."

"Still... you're a good woman."

Lydia grinned. "He and I will find an interesting way to get through the apologies and recrimination. He'll do it to himself. Who knows, there might be a trip to sunny Florida before the winter is over."

"I love you," Polly said with a chuckle. "Aaron will hate that."

"Exactly."

They carried food into the living room to find Leia curled up in Aaron's lap and Luke doing his best to look inconspicuous on the back of Aaron's chair. The two dogs were pressed against either side of Helen.

"It looks like my animals have found their warm bodies for the day," Polly said. She picked Leia up and put her on the ground, knowing Aaron wouldn't move and disrupt the cat. Luke bounded down to join his sister and see what she might be getting. Polly snapped a finger and Obiwan jumped to the floor. Fortunately Han was just as curious as Luke and followed suit.

"Are you going to tell us what's going on yet?" Polly asked, passing around plates and napkins.

Aaron shook his head. "I can't. I just can't."

"But it's all connected, right? The murder of your friend, your bad attitude the last couple of months and now the attack on Helen?"

He leaned forward and took a sandwich from the platter, sat back and looked at the expectant faces. "I really can't talk about it."

"We should probably give up," Lydia says. "He's the interrogator in the group and doesn't bow to pressure very easily."

"Unless there's fried chicken involved," Polly said.

Helen asked, "Fried chicken?"

"It has to be Lydia's fried chicken and there has to be a very good reason for me to spill my guts," Aaron said. "No regular fried chicken will do."

"Do we have anything more to worry about here? Is Helen's life still in danger?" Polly continued to press.

Helen patted Polly's arm. "I can find another place to stay. I would hate to put anyone else in danger. Especially with these sweet children you have here."

"No, that's not what I meant at all," Polly said. "Worse things have happened to me here. We just manage our way through it. I'm worried about you. What can we do to keep you safe?"

Aaron took a deep breath. "They know where I live or I'd ask her to stay with us."

Lydia's eyes flew open and she gasped. "Are we in danger?"

"I'm sure we aren't, but if you wanted to spend time with Marilyn in Dayton, I wouldn't protest."

"And leave you alone in that house? Absolutely not." Lydia frowned. "I'm not going to Dayton. I won't put anyone else in my family at risk." Then she had a thought. "Have we been at risk all these years?"

"Oh no," he assured her. "Not at all."

"Then how long? Since your friend was killed?"

He gave a slight shrug. "More so since then, but I can't believe they would take it that far. You're innocent and know nothing about any of this."

"But whoever this 'they' is, they don't know that. For all they know, you've told me everything."

Aaron put the plate with his sandwich back down on the coffee table. "No, that isn't true. Your life has never been in danger." He turned to Helen. "Who did you tell that you were coming to Bellingwood?"

"No one!" she exclaimed. "There wasn't time. I spoke with Lydia the other day, made my reservations online, called Julie at the shelter to tell her I had a family emergency, asked Bob and Bonnie next door to take care of the animals and left."

Polly jumped up. "The cameras. We still have those cameras hooked up. I never think about them, but they would show that car. Maybe you could get the license plate number and figure out who was driving."

Aaron nodded. "Since you got Ken involved, you should probably contact him to take possession of the video."

"Really?"

"Just call him, Polly."

She went into the other room and made the call.

"Hi Polly," Mindy said. "Is everything okay?"

"Can you patch me through to Ken Wallers? I think I might have video from this morning and I need to tell him that Aaron knows everything and is here at Sycamore House."

"Sure. Just a second."

Polly waited and soon enough, Ken came onto the call. "What's up?" he asked.

"First of all. I'm sorry about earlier. I shouldn't have put you in that position."

"If you recall, you weren't the one who did, but thank you. That can't be the only reason you're calling me."

"No, Aaron is here. He knows everything now. While we were talking, I remembered I have video. He says you should have it."

"Is he sure?"

"I guess. He told me to call you."

"If this is linked to his case, it should be his."

"Do you want to fight with him? Because I sure don't."

Ken chuckled. "I suppose not. I wonder what he's trying to do here, though."

"Are you available? I can download video for you."

"How about I meet you in your office in a half hour. I have a few things to take care of first."

"Thank you."

After all of the arguing Polly had done regarding the installation of cameras at Sycamore House, she was now glad they were there. She still hated the idea of surveillance, but when it came to the safety of her friends, she'd get over it."

"He's coming in a half hour," she said, going back into the living room. "But he didn't understand why you want him to take it."

Aaron nodded. "This is all much too close to me. I want to keep things as aboveboard as possible. It's already too convoluted for my taste."

He stood up, his sandwich still uneaten on the plate in front of him. "Helen, I want you to stay inside until this is over. If Polly's information is good, we should be able to handle this quickly."

"Between those big horses and the fall, my body will rebel against any outings," she said. "But what about you and Lydia?"

He stepped over in front of his wife and held out a hand. She took it and stood up. "I was serious about you staying away from the house," he said. "If you won't go to Dayton, would you consider staying here with Helen?"

"I've spent too many nights sleeping away from you," Lydia said. "I'm not doing that any longer."

Aaron set his jaw. "I would rather you slept away from me than for you to be collateral damage in this mess. Please do this for me. Let me take care of you again."

Lydia turned to Polly. "Do you have one more room?"

"Of course I do. You can have the room next to Helen's. Do we need to take you home and pick clothes up?"

"Can I do that?" Lydia asked her husband.

"I'll take you home and bring you back. Plan to be away for a couple of days, would you? Hopefully it won't take any more time than that."

She started ticking things off on a mental list, using her fingers, yet not speaking, then said. "I have a busy day tomorrow. Will you be okay if I do my regular errands? There are two women that haven't gotten groceries for two weeks. I can't ask them to go any longer than that."

"Can you call someone else?"

"I can ask Andy," Lydia said. "But I'm going to go out of my mind, sitting still all day long. Will you fix this as fast as you can? I don't need Polly to see me at my daily worst. And I definitely don't want her to see me when I'm bored."

He chuckled. "I've never known you to be bored, Lydia. No matter where you've been stuck. You always find something that you can do."

"Are you sure I can't stay at home?"

"Please do this for me," he begged. "I know I don't have a right to ask much of you after all I've put you through these last couple of months..."

"Stop it. We'll deal with that when this is over."

He looked down and whispered, "What does that mean?"

Polly started to laugh. "Oh, you're going to pay for it. No one tortures Lydia Merritt and gets away with it for very long."

"What is this going to cost me?" he asked.

"Time," Lydia responded. "Lots and lots of time. But we'll talk about that later. You take me home and then I'll come back to Sycamore House like an obedient wife." She winked up at him and leaned in to draw her husband into a hug. "I'm so glad you're talking to me again, even if you're telling me to live somewhere else. You're back to normal."

Aaron held her close and rested his cheek on the top of her head. Polly felt like she was intruding on a very intimate moment and slipped over to sit on the sofa beside Helen. Obiwan and Han jumped back up onto the couch, Han nuzzling Helen's hand.

He finally released his wife and said, "Helen, will you be okay up here until Lydia comes back?"

"I'm fine." She scowled at him. "I've lived a lifetime without your assistance, I think I can sit around a piece."

Polly stood up and walked over to the front door with Lydia and Aaron. "Come find me when you get back and we'll settle you in the room upstairs."

"Thank you for everything," Lydia said and reached out to hug her. She whispered in her ear. "Don't expect to see me for a while. I need to..."

Polly stopped her. "Don't say it. I'll see you when I see you."

She shut the door after them and turned back to Helen. "I should go downstairs and wait for Chief Wallers. Do you want to stay up here with the animals or what? The kids will be here soon and I know they'd like to spend more time with you."

Helen nodded. "I don't want to face those stairs again. If you don't mind, I'll stay right here on your sofa and let these warm fuzzy things keep me company."

"Feel free to wander. You found the bathroom yesterday?"

"I did, honey. Thank you. I'll be fine."

"Television is in the other room."

"I'll be just fine right here. Thank you for everything."

Polly left the apartment and went downstairs to her office. This really was one of her more crazy weeks. Things needed to slow down.

CHAPTER TWENTY-THREE

Polly was awakened again by Henry whispering, "Someone's cooking in our kitchen again."

"Oh for heaven's sake," she said. "Who is it this time?"

"You go see. It's probably one of your friends."

Polly looked at the clock. Six thirty. Last night, she'd jokingly told Lydia that if she was desperate to make breakfast, she could use the kitchen, not thinking for a minute the woman would take her up on it.

She stretched her legs and snuggled closer to Henry. "If it's Lydia, I'm praying for a quick end to this siege."

"Siege?"

"Yeah. People stuck here because they can't go anywhere else."

"That means you're going to have an exciting day." He tickled her side and sang mockingly, "I get to go to work. I get to go to work."

"If I call you in a panic will you meet me for lunch?"

"I'd love to, but I won't be in town today."

"You're a fink. Maybe I'll call my friends and make them come over and play."

"First you have to get out of bed and see who is in our kitchen."

"It's Lydia. I just know it."

He gave her a push. "Go. I'll do the doggy thing this morning after my shower. You feed them and make nice with your guests."

"Fabulous. They're your guests too. You married me for better or worse."

Henry reached around Polly and turned her so she was facing him, then planted a kiss on her lips. "If this is the worse, I'm in pretty good shape."

Polly sat up on the edge of the bed, feeling on the floor with her feet for slippers. They'd had a nice evening with everyone who was at Sycamore House. There had only been eight, so they ate dinner in the downstairs kitchen and watched the sun set through the large windows facing the western horizon. The oranges, reds and pinks shone through the trees, making a beautiful setting.

They'd laughed at stories Helen told of her childhood with Aaron and their other two brothers and then Helen did something that Polly had never thought of doing. She pressed Sarah Heater for stories of Rebecca's infancy and her own childhood and youth. Rebecca listened with rapt attention and Polly took the opportunity to record it with her phone. Sarah talked about grandparents and cousins, people that Rebecca might like to find when she got older. For that time alone, Polly was grateful that Helen Oswald had come to town.

"You're not moving very fast," Henry said from the doorway to the bathroom.

"I know, I know. Here I go." Polly pulled on her robe and followed by the entire menagerie, went out into the main room and then into the kitchen.

Sure enough, Lydia was hard at work.

"Good morning," she sang out. "I have coffee ready for you. Sweet rolls are in the oven and as soon as I start seeing faces, I'll cook eggs and sausage. I made up a fresh pitcher of orange juice. Is there anything else you'd like?"

"That's plenty," Polly said. "You didn't have to do this."

"I stopped in to say good morning to Helen. She isn't moving very well. I asked her what hurt more and I think it was the ride on that big Percheron yesterday. I'll take breakfast over to her."

"How are you this morning? Did you have trouble not being at home with your husband?"

Lydia winked. "You'll never guess who came to visit me in the middle of the night."

"He did not."

"Yes he did. It was the sweetest thing. He said he missed me."

"So after two months of pure hell and you're just letting him go back to normal?" Polly raised an eyebrow. She would never let Henry get away with this.

"Oh dear, this isn't back to normal. He's doing his very best to make up for everything. We'll talk through it as it comes, but there's no sense stirring up a nasty fuss over something that's already happened. We have to make the best of what we can with the present and plan ways to never let it happen again in the future. That isn't going to be something we do in one or two days."

"You're really just letting him get away with it?"

Lydia spun around, a frying pan in her hand. "Not on your life. But I'm also not going to reject his attempts. That's not the way to handle a man like Aaron. He needs positive reinforcement. We have plenty of time to work on the rest of it."

Polly shook her head. "It makes no sense to me."

"Of course it doesn't. You and Henry don't have the same relationship that Aaron and I have, why would you expect to do things the same way? This is what works for us."

Han gave a little yip.

"Oops. I'm supposed to feed them. I'm a bad mom."

"Let me get out of your way," Lydia said. "I'll finish setting the table."

Rebecca came into the kitchen and said, "Is it Saturday?"

"No honey, why do you ask that?" Polly asked.

"Because it feels like Saturday."

"That's just because Lydia is here. You're up early. Why don't you go get ready for school and maybe you can run down and spend a few minutes with your mom before breakfast."

"That was pretty cool last night," Rebecca said.

"Hearing your stories?"

"Yeah. Do you think she has more like that?"

"We'll have to ask her and see. Why don't you ask her to write out some ideas and we can ask her about them another time."

"Great!" Rebecca ran out of the room.

"That was a wonderful thing Helen did last night," Polly said, weaving through the animals to get back into the dining room. "I don't know why I hadn't thought of doing that."

"Did I see you recording it?"

"I loaded it onto my computer last night. One of these evenings we'll watch it with Rebecca again. I think she heard some of those stories for the first time last night. I don't know about you, but that's how I know my family's history. Dad told stories over and over and over again until they were anchored in my mind."

"We didn't do enough of that with the kids. At least they're taking lots of pictures and movies with their own children. Those will help them tell the stories."

"Good morning, girls," Henry said as he came into the room. "It sure smells good in here."

Lydia beamed. "I like being able to make big breakfasts. I miss it now that my kids are all gone. My favorite days of the year are when they fill up my house and want to eat my cooking."

"Come on, boys," he said. "Let's get out and back inside before the food is gone. I don't want dry toast because you made me miss out."

"You have a wonderful man there," Lydia said as he crossed into the office, heading for the back stairway.

"Sometimes I wonder how I got so lucky. He should have been snatched up by a woman by the time I found him," Polly said. "But there he was."

"Just waiting for you to show up."

Jessie came around the corner, rubbing her eyes and clutching her robe around her seemingly ever expanding waist. "Am I late?"

she asked.

"No, in fact you're still early."

She dropped into a chair at the end of the table. "This baby kept me up all night. I didn't think I ate anything that should have upset her. But wow. Moving and kicking. This is going to be a long day."

Lydia walked over and rubbed Jessie's shoulders. "These last weeks seem like they go on forever, but honey, before you know it, you'll be in the delivery room wishing they had lasted a little bit longer and yet desperate for it to be over so you can hold your baby. Right now everyone is taking care of you, so enjoy that as long as you can. When the baby comes, the focus changes and you'll just be the mom of a new baby."

"That's a good thing, right?"

"Oh yes, dear. I guess what I'm trying to tell you is that the whole experience is a good thing. Enjoy each of the moments. Take time now to enjoy being pregnant. Enjoy the attention and care you're receiving. When the baby arrives, enjoy all of that. Each one of those moments. Think back to the last seven or eight months and all that has been happening. Make sure you know your memories."

"Like Sarah talked about last night?"

"Just like that. Someday you'll want to tell those stories to your children."

~~~

Polly called her friends and both Joss and Sal showed up. Joss knew a good thing when she heard it. Lydia offered to spend time with Cooper and Sophia who had turned into very active crawlers. Since there was nothing happening in the auditorium and the floor was carpeted, it was the perfect place for two little ones to chase each other.

Sal was ready to talk about the coffee shop. Once she'd settled on a name, she wanted to put plans into place. Sylvie and Jeff were excited about the bakery they'd seen the day before and
~~~

were hunkered down in Jeff's office working on a proposal. Helen Oswald had begged off any excitement for today. Her legs hurt so bad she just wanted to sit in her room.

Sarah Heater was in the office working with Stephanie on some of the details regarding the filing system she'd built.

Everyone was head down when a rather attractive young man walked into the office. Polly was surprised that she hadn't seen him come past her office, but at the same time, she and Sal were looking over plans for the shop.

"I'd like to see the manager," the young man said to Stephanie.

"He's in a meeting," she responded. "Could I help you?"

"I'm interested in booking this location for my wedding next year and would like a tour. Can you do that for me?"

Stephanie turned to look at Polly, who nodded at Jeff's office.

"Just a moment, let me see if I can interrupt him." Stephanie knocked on Jeff's door and slipped inside. In just a moment, Jeff came into the main office.

"How can I help you?" he asked.

"Like I told the girl, I'd like a tour for a future wedding. You have rooms here where we could stay after a reception? I'd like to see those too."

"I'm sorry, our rooms are filled right now, but I'd be glad to show you the rest of the facility. When are you planning to be married?"

The young man's face registered surprise and then relaxed. "It won't happen until next year. If I like what I see, we can talk about dates."

"Okay. We can do that. Let me just get a couple of things and I'll be right with you."

Jeff and the young man left the main office and turned toward the auditorium. Polly looked down at the papers on her desk, then back up.

"He's familiar to me," she said.

"Who, the rude boy who wants to get married?" Sal asked.

"Yes. I don't know where I've seen him before. It's fuzzy."

"Is he from Bellingwood? I've never seen him before."

"No, I don't think so. Where else would I have gone that I'd recognize him. Boone? Maybe he works down there somewhere."

She pushed a sketch over in front of Sal. "I was thinking we could put the bread racks here behind the counter. And a pastry display case right there."

Sal nodded. "Do you think we might do create a sun porch in the winter and open air space in the summer? I can't figure out how we could do both things, but it would be really nice if we didn't lose all of that space outside when it rained or got too cold."

"This is driving me nuts," Polly said.

"I'm sorry. Am I asking too much?"

"No, no. That's not it. I've seen him before and it wasn't that long ago. Why do I know him?"

"The number of people you see on a weekly basis is big, Polly Giller. It could be anything."

"But I should know this." She tapped her tongue. "It's right there."

Jeff and the young man walked past and into the classrooms and lounge area. He was barely paying any attention to Jeff, but looked at everything, taking it all in.

"Crap," Polly said under her breath. She jumped up and shut the door to her office.

"What?"

"I know where I saw him."

"Where? Why are you shutting the door? What's going on?"

"He was driving the car that ran down Eliseo and Helen yesterday. What in the hell is he doing back here today, acting like this?"

"Calm down. Are you sure?"

"Of course I'm sure. I watched the video yesterday afternoon before I gave it to Ken Wallers. That's the guy."

"Then you need to call someone."

"I don't want him to know what I'm doing."

"You mean, like shutting your door in a hurry?"

"He didn't see me. He was in the computer room. I checked." Polly took out her phone, started to dial and then put it back down on her desk. "Who do I call?"

"Call Aaron Merritt. He can call Chief Wallers."

"Right. That's what I'll do."

A knock at her door caused Polly to drop the phone back on her desk.

"Yes?"

Jeff opened the door. "Polly, this is Jerry Costanza. He'd really like to look at the rooms in the addition. Do you suppose you could..."

"No. We can't," she said. "Not today. There is too much going on."

Jeff looked at her quizzically and she gave him a slight, gritted teeth, shake of the head.

"Okay," he said and turned back to the young man. "I don't think it will work out today. Rooms will be open early next week if you would like to come back. I'd be glad to show you the rest of the facility at that point." He pulled the door shut behind him.

"Jerry Costanza?" Polly hissed at Sal. "Does he think we're idiots?"

"What do you mean?" Sal asked.

"Jerry Seinfeld, George Costanza. Please."

Sal chuckled. "That didn't even occur to me. But you're right. It's kind of lame. Are you calling Aaron?"

"I don't want to call. I don't want this guy to hear me."

"So, what are you doing?"

"I have texting. Aaron will figure it out. Now keep talking about the building or something. Just make noise like we're in here working."

"Because I really am in here working?"

"Whatever. Just give me some cover."

Sal stood up and bent over the desk, riffling through the sheets of paper. "Cover like this? Is he looking at my ass yet?"

"Holy cow girl, you're a nut." Polly said, laughing. She quickly pressed keys on her phone. *"Aaron, the guy who ran your sister down is here at Sycamore House checking things out. What should I do?"*

"What do you mean?"

"He's asked for a tour from Jeff, purportedly for a wedding reception next year."

"Are you sure?"

"I saw him on the video yesterday. I'm sure. Should I try to keep him here?"

"I'm in town and I'm on my way over. Don't do anything. If he tries to leave, let him. Where's Helen?"

"Upstairs in her room. Lydia is in the auditorium with Joss and the babies. The rest of us are in the offices."

"I'm driving into your driveway in back. Can you unlock it for me?"

"The kitchen door is unlocked. Anything else I should do?"

"Sit still. Don't make a scene. I've called for backup."

"You can sit down now," Polly said to Sal. "Aaron is here. He's coming in the back. We aren't supposed to do anything."

Another knock at Polly's door made her jump. "Come in," she said.

Sylvie walked in. "Do I need to shut this? Jeff's in his office with the Costanza fellow. Kind of a funny name, don't you think?"

"No, that's fine. It can stay open." Polly wasn't sure how much more she should say. It was probably better to just let everyone remain clueless for now. That way no one would do anything to make him nervous.

She heard Jeff say, "Thank you for stopping in, Mr. Costanza. Please let me know if you need any other information."

"I have everything I need."

Jerry Costanza, or whatever his name was, left the office and turned to the left, heading for the side door and the addition. Where was Aaron?

Polly jumped up out of her seat. There was no way she was letting him get into that addition and search for Helen. She rushed past Sylvie and Sal and dashed into the foyer just as he had his hand on the door to push it open.

"Excuse me, Mr. Costanza?" she called.

He didn't respond immediately, but then turned.

"Yes?"

"I didn't get an opportunity to properly meet you. My name is Polly Giller and I'm the owner of Sycamore House." She put her hand out as she strode across the floor to meet him.

"I see," he said, unsure as how to proceed. He finally did what was ingrained in everyone and put his hand out, taking hers and shaking it.

"Did Jeff talk to you about our catering service? I believe we have one of the best chefs in the region working for us here." Once she had his hand, Polly drew him back into the main building.

"He did. I even met her. Thank you." His eyes grew hard and he gripped Polly's hand, drawing her in front of him.

"What?" she gasped.

"Let her go," came Aaron's firm voice.

"Oh crap," Polly said under her breath.

"That's right, oh crap," Jerry Costanza said. "It looks like you're taking a walk with me."

Polly tried to sense whether or not he was carrying a gun. She'd taken punches before and knew she could live through that, but she'd obey if there was a gun. He had one hand in hers and his other hand was reaching up to grab her chest. In an instant, she made a decision and picked her foot up, jamming it back down on his foot. She leaned forward, bit his hand, and twisted at the same time.

"Bitch!" he yelled, releasing her. He turned to run for the door, but she stuck a leg out and tripped him. He didn't fall to the ground, only tripped across the floor, staying on his feet. It gave Aaron enough time to move in.

"Stop right there," Aaron demanded.

"You're a fool," the man said. "You want to let me go."

"No, I'm sorry. I don't. You've threatened too many people in my territory. This ends now."

The man dropped to his knees. "You know better than that. There is no end to this."

"It's ending for you today. And if you're smart, you'll talk to me so that we can finish this."

Aaron pushed him down until his face was on the floor, kicked his legs apart, and zip tied his hands behind his back. He patted him down and didn't find a weapon. Polly took a deep breath, glad that she'd not made a horribly stupid decision.

She looked back at the office. Sal, Sylvie, Jeff, Sarah and Stephanie were all standing there staring at her.

"It really sucks getting taken down by a girl, doesn't it?" she asked the man lying prone on the floor.

He didn't respond and Aaron shook his head. "You're going to scare me to death for the rest of my life, aren't you, Polly?"

"Maybe?"

Stu Decker and another deputy came in the front door and rushed over to Aaron. Stu pulled the man up from the floor. "Anything special?" he asked Aaron.

"Just take him in for now. Polly recognized him from the video yesterday. I suspect that will be an easy match. He's part of it."

"Got it, boss. You coming down to the office?"

"I'll be there in a bit. I need to breathe. Polly did it again."

"Hey," she protested.

"Hey whatever," Aaron said.

Stu grinned as he walked the man out. "I'm sorry we were late to that party." He nodded to the group standing in front of the office and went on out the front door.

CHAPTER TWENTY-FOUR

"I'm never going to win with you, am I? When are you going to let me be the tough guy?" Aaron asked Polly.

She glared, giving him her most rotten evil eye. "But he was getting away!"

"I could have handled it. It's my job."

"Look, he didn't freak out until he saw you come around the corner. We were just chatting up until that point. And..." she glared at him. "By the way, I handled him. I'm getting pretty good at this self-defense stuff."

He laughed. "You were lucky. That kid was a thick-headed thug. He didn't know what he was doing."

That surprised Polly. "You mean that wasn't the assassin?"

Aaron shook his head. "No, Polly. If he'd been a trained assassin, you would have been dead in a heartbeat. The man who killed Albert was in and out of town that same day. He didn't stick around for a week and a half just to try to run down my sister. I'm guessing this poor young man works in an office during the week and got sent to reconnoiter. He's less qualified to engage in hand to hand combat than you are."

"I think you just insulted me."

"You're lucky and manage to get in a few good pot shots every once in a while, but you'd be no match against someone who knew what they were doing." He looked up in thought. "However, it might be interesting for you to train with some of my people. None of them can believe that you are capable of doing damage, even after we have proof of it. Would you want to come down and work out with us?"

"Are you serious?" she asked.

"I might be. If I thought for one minute that this was the last time you'd get into a skirmish, I'd let it pass, but with you, I never know what's coming next."

"Will you teach me how to use a gun?" she asked as they walked back to the office.

He stopped mid-stride and looked at her sideways. "Now it's my turn to ask. Are you serious?"

Polly cackled. "Nope. Not at all. I'd shoot myself in the foot. Pretty sure of that."

"Thank goodness. Telling Lydia that you were packing would only be detrimental to me and I am not ready to walk that path any longer."

"I'm surprised she isn't out here checking on us."

He put his hand on her back. "That's the reason it took me a bit longer to get to you. I stopped in the auditorium and told her and Joss to stay put with the babies. I need to tell them that all is safe."

Polly looked into the office as they walked past and waved. From the looks on everyone's faces, she knew she had some explaining to do. At least there weren't any visitors and guests here today. That might keep Jeff from taking her to task about her impact on the reputation of Sycamore House. She wished he would quit blaming her for the things that happened. It just wasn't her fault.

"Are you ever going to tell us what's been going on?" Polly asked.

Aaron took a deep breath, blinked and said, "It isn't safe yet. We're closer. Getting our hands on this young man is going to give us some leverage."

He pushed the door open to the auditorium only to find it completely empty. There were no babies, no adults, no nothing. "Where would they have gone?" he asked.

Polly texted Lydia, *"Where did you go?"*

"Upstairs to your apartment."

"Do you want us to come up or do you want to come back downstairs?"

"We'll be right there. Is everyone okay? I saw the deputies drive in and then I watched them drive away."

"Come down. We'll tell you everything. Well, what I know, at least."

She put the phone back in her pocket and said, "They went upstairs."

"She's a smart woman."

"Yes she is." Polly put her hand on Aaron's forearm. "You have been a terrible husband these last couple of months and you owe her an explanation for all of it. If it hadn't come to a head and your sister hadn't come into town, how much longer would you have let this mess go on between the two of you?"

He dropped his head and pulled away from her.

"Aaron, your wife can't function if she's worried about your marriage. The two of you provide a foundation for each other. Surely you see that."

"All I ever wanted to do was keep her safe. That's all."

"So this was about keeping Lydia safe?"

"Of course it was."

"That's crap and you know it."

He frowned at her. "What do you mean?"

"You've been in a dark place. You've been afraid of something. If you had simply wanted to keep her safe, you would have been proactive. That's what you do. You don't sit and wait for things to fall apart until they can't get any worse. You fix it and make everything right."

"It wasn't possible. The only thing I could do was..." Aaron paused. "That's enough. I can't talk about it to you and besides, I hear babies."

Joss and Lydia came back into the auditorium, each carrying a baby.

"Did you catch the bad guy?" Lydia asked.

"One of them," he said. "And I think you need to have a talk with your friend about her behavior when the bad guys show up."

Polly coughed and said under her breath, "Throwing me under the bus?"

Lydia picked right up on it. "What did she do?"

"Why don't you ask her?" Aaron slid Polly an evil grin.

"What did you do, Polly?" Lydia asked, passing Sophia to her husband. "Here, I think you need a baby fix. She's just been changed and she could use a big, teddy bear hug."

"I didn't do anything," Polly said. "I was talking to that young man when Aaron turned the corner."

"And ask her what she did when he tried to use her as a shield?" Aaron asked in his best high-pitched baby voice, smiling and messing with Sophia.

"Polly!" Lydia exclaimed. "What am I going to do with you?"

"Aaron assures me that the kid was probably an office worker and any foolish woman could have taken him."

"That's not what I said. You have great presence of mind and handle yourself very well in tense situations," Aaron said.

"He also said that I should come down and train with his deputies," Polly said with a grin. "But I think he might have been teasing me."

Lydia nodded with enthusiasm. "It would certainly make me feel better if you had self-defense training. That's what it would be, right Aaron?"

"Uh huh," he said, cooing at the baby. "Self-defense. Absolutely."

"Aaron, are you paying attention to me?"

"No, ma'am."

The door opened and they all looked up to see Helen limp into the auditorium.

"Your friends told me you were here," she said, looking around. "Is there a chair in this place? I can barely lift my legs and the rest of me feels like it's been run through a wringer washer. I had no idea it was going to be so dangerous to come tell my brother how to run his life."

Aaron passed Sophia back to Lydia and went off in search of chairs. He came back with four in his hands and quickly set them up, gesturing to Lydia and Joss to sit after he'd helped Helen.

She beckoned to Lydia. "Can I hold her?"

"She's not a lightweight. Are you sure?"

"Babies are good for the soul." Lydia stood and placed Sophia in Helen's arms. The child was quickly enraptured with the woman, who then slid off her seat to the floor and said to Joss, "Go ahead. Put your son down. There's a great big room here for them to explore. I'll keep an eye on them."

"But you're..." Aaron started.

Helen waved him off, "Leave me alone. I'm not an invalid. By the way, you goin' to tell me what those sheriff's vehicles were doing in the parking lot and why you're here at this hour of the day playing with your wife?"

"I'm not playing with my wife," he said defensively.

"Tell me." Helen got up on her knees and crawled to where Cooper had face planted into the carpet. She picked him up and put him on his bottom.

Polly shook her head at the woman. She just didn't give up.

"I'm waiting for a confirmation call from Digger on his identity, but I suspect he works for..."

"Oh, for heaven's sake," Helen spat. "Just say his name. No one up here knows who he is and it isn't like the entire community is terrified of Voldemort. Say his damned name."

"Helen," Aaron said warningly.

"Don't 'Helen' me. Price Sutton. That's his name. It's time you quit being scared of him."

"It isn't just me that I'm concerned about. He had Albert killed and sent someone after you."

"I'm sorry your friend was killed, but you need to find a way to end this. It's been thirty years and you left home. I'm tired of him controlling our lives."

"That was the deal we made."

Helen sat back and watched the two children in front of her crawl to their mother. "I remember that day," she said. "It was the early eighties. Nobody thought much about the future, except that it was coming up someday. We were young, invincible and twenty-fifteen was so far away it didn't register as real. We weren't even thinking about the new century. You didn't have a wife or a family, you barely had a job. Mom and Dad were still alive. Our future was way out in front of us. These girls," she pointed at Joss and Sylvie, "weren't even born yet."

Aaron nodded.

"Aaron. The future is right now. Accept that everything is different and you were not the one who reneged on the deal. Sutton did when he sent a man to kill Albert."

"He thought we were going to expose him."

"He didn't know that. He panicked. And it's because Ludders was released from prison. Sutton didn't think about the future back then either. All he could see was that he'd gotten away with it. Jeff Ludders took the fall and went away for what we thought was a lifetime. But it wasn't, was it? Not for any of us."

Polly desperately wanted to ask questions, but all she could do was watch the interaction between Aaron Merritt and his sister.

"Digger is working with the FBI," Aaron said. "I'm not saying anything until Sutton is either in custody or dealt with. As soon as they confirm the identity of the kid who was just here, it will move forward. Until then, you all don't need to know anything."

"Digger?" Lydia asked quietly. "He knows about this?"

Aaron nodded again. "He knew thirty years ago."

"You told him and you couldn't tell me?"

"Honey. I couldn't. He was working for the FBI in Atlanta when it all went down. After I came to Iowa and found a good life, he called and asked questions, wanting to be back in the Midwest." Aaron turned to Polly. "He grew up in Minnesota. He applied at the Iowa Division of Criminal Investigation and the rest is history."

"You knew Digger from back then?" Lydia asked, still in shock.

"I'm sorry, honey, yes. We didn't talk about it much."

"Apparently not."

"You're going to owe her a vacation in Hawaii, maybe even Australia," Polly muttered.

A knock at the door made them all jump and Sal poked her head in. "I'm sorry to interrupt, but Mark called and wants to have lunch. I'm taking off." She held up a folder. "We'll talk more about this later, okay Polly?"

"I'm sorry," Polly said, jumping out of her chair. "I didn't mean to run out on you."

"Of course you did. Quit apologizing. We all know that sending bad guys to jail is kinda your thing... that is, after finding dead bodies. We're all just sorry we missed the excitement. I think you should start a self-defense class here during the week. Teach us all about your tricks to turning men into gibbering fools."

"You're teasing me, right?"

"Not really," Sal said with a straight face. "You have no fear when it comes to hurting a man who is intimidating you. That's one of those things that most of us don't think of doing. Men are supposed to protect us poor, sweet women from the rougher things in life."

"Okay, okay. That's enough."

"I'm actually serious," Sal said. "Women aren't taught to do damage to men who hurt them. You're kind of my hero."

"Whatever. You go have lunch with your pretty boyfriend and oh, by the way, what are you doing about those puppies?"

Sal winked. "They might be a Valentine's Day present for Mark. How do you think he'll react to that?"

"I think that if he's smart, he'll consider them the best present ever."

"That's what I'll tell him." Sal leaned in and waved. "I'll see you all Saturday night."

Polly hugged her. "Have a good day and thanks for being here this morning." She watched Sal walk away and turned back to the room. "I left in a hurry. They're probably wondering what's going on."

"I should take these two home so they can get lunch and a nap," Joss said. "But I will admit that the action here is better than anything daytime television offers."

"You watch that stuff?"

"Uh, yes. What else am I supposed to do? Some of those people are my best friends during the day."

"You need to invite me over more often," Polly said.

"Don't you give me any trouble. Oprah, Ellen, Walker and Chief Gillespie and Olivia Benson take good care of me."

"Chief Gillespie?" Aaron asked.

"Television show," Lydia said. "In the Heat of the Night."

Joss was surprised. "You watch it too?"

Lydia smiled and winked. "Sometimes, but don't tell anyone."

"If y'all are taking these sweet babies away, someone is going to have to haul my butt off the floor," Helen said. "Lordie, I might have made a terrible mistake getting down here."

"Thank you for entertaining them," Joss said. "We never have this much fun when we're at home."

"You look like you're a wonderful mama." Helen picked up Sophia and held her up to Lydia. "Those chunky, brown cheeks and deep, dark eyes would make it difficult to deny her anything."

"I had to be firm right up front or these two would have ruled the roost," Joss said. She brought the car seats over and once Cooper was tucked in, she took Sophia. The little girl protested, but when she was placed in front of her brother, she gurgled and reached out for him.

"Do you ever think they're actually having conversations with each other?" Polly asked.

"All the time. Sometimes I'll hear noises from them in the middle of the night. When I go in to check, they're just lying in their crib, chattering away at each other. It's back and forth too. It isn't like they are both making noise at the same time. It sounds like a conversation." She smiled. "I'll be honest, it freaks both me and Nate out. He tells me I should be worried that they're planning a takeover."

"Let me help you take them to your car," Aaron said. "Do you have a jacket?"

"It's in the hallway on the bench," Joss responded. "Thanks for an interesting morning, Polly."

Polly hugged her. "I'm sorry it got weird."

"You're fine. Where else am I going to get this kind of excitement?"

"Great. I'm your entertainment and excitement now."

Aaron picked up the two car seats and waited for Joss to hold the door open for him.

Helen waited until the door had closed before saying, "My puny bones are useless. Can you two at least get me into a chair?"

Polly looked at Lydia and they both chuckled.

"I'm sorry," Lydia gushed. "You poor thing. I thought you were staying up in your room today."

She and Polly reached down and lifted Helen to a standing position.

"What was I thinking," Helen moaned. "I should have stayed up there, but when I saw the sheriff's vehicles come in and leave, I hated to be missin' the action."

She hobbled over to one of the chairs. "Did you get a name on the young man who was here this morning? And what was he doing?"

"He said his name was Jerry Costanza," Polly said. "He wanted a tour so he could book a wedding reception here sometime next year."

"That was a convenient excuse to case the joint. Aaron put that all together, right?"

"What do you mean?" Polly asked.

"If he was casing the joint, who was it for? Why did he need the information?"

"We're asking those questions," Aaron said, coming back into the auditorium. "It worries me too."

"Good. I knew you'd be smart about this."

"Of course you did. When I leave today, are you two," he looked at Polly. "You *three* ladies going to play it safe around here or do I need to send an unsuspecting deputy up to keep an eye on you?"

"We'll be good," Lydia said. "I promise. You won't let me go home yet?"

"Not yet. But soon."

"There are comfortable chairs in the conference room," Polly said. "And the television works, too. Unless you want to go back upstairs."

"I'm not ready for that much solitude again," Helen said. "Do you have a deck of cards in this joint? Maybe we could talk your staff into a game of strip poker."

"Helen!" Aaron said.

"If it were one of Lydia's church meetings, it would be much more fun. Can't you just see all of those wrinkled, old faces in shock as they try to imagine each other without any clothes?" She cackled as she thought about it.

Lydia tried desperately to suppress a grin and failed. Even Aaron had to put his hand over his eyes as he shook his head.

Polly put her arm out to give Helen leverage as she stood back up from the chair. "Have you met Lydia's friend, Beryl Watson?"

"No!" Lydia cried. "They can never meet. The universe couldn't withstand the cataclysm."

"Who's this Beryl Watson? Is she as great a gal as me?" Helen asked.

"I'm leaving now." Aaron bent over and kissed his wife. She wrapped her arms around his neck and made a waving motion behind his back to Polly and Helen.

"We should leave first," Polly said in a stage whisper.

"They never could keep their hands off each other. I could tell you stories of the days before they had children." Helen's gave her a grin. "Let me tell you about the time they stayed in a hotel near a golf course. Which hole was it, Aaron? Was that why they started lighting it at night?"

"Stop it, you old lady," he said, taking Lydia's hand. "If you start telling stories, I have plenty that will embarrass you."

"He does, you know," Helen said, her arm through Polly's. "I was a girl with three younger brothers. I had to learn how to hold my own."

"I think you succeeded."

"Years and years of practice, my dear. Years and years of practice."

CHAPTER TWENTY-FIVE

"Can you give me a minute?" Aaron asked Jeff. He'd walked back into the office with Polly, Lydia and Helen. "I'd like you to tell me what you can about your visitor."

"I probably gave him more information than he gave me," Jeff said.

"Tell me what he was interested in."

Polly didn't hear anyone object, so she followed Aaron into Jeff's office and sat down on the sofa. When he looked at her and grinned, she just shrugged her shoulders.

"He was upset that I wouldn't let him tour the addition," Jeff said. "He wanted to see the rooms over there - said that he and his fiancée might want to spend the night after their reception. We've actually had several couples do that so I didn't think anything of it.

"What else?" Aaron asked.

"He wanted to see the whole place. He took pictures and said he was sending them to his girlfriend."

"He sent pictures out?"

"Sure," Jeff said nonchalantly. Then he stopped. "Crap."

Aaron stood. "I'll be right back."

He left the office with his phone at his ear.

"What do you think?" Jeff asked Polly.

"He's having them check the guy's phone. If he was sending pictures to someone, they aren't done up here yet."

"Do you think it's safe for us to be here? Maybe I should send Stephanie home."

She nodded. "If they aren't comfortable here, it's better that they go. I'll pay them anyway."

Aaron came back into the office. "Do you have anything going on here this afternoon or evening?"

"No," Jeff said. "Why?"

"Polly, I want you to lock the doors. Don't let anyone in unless you know them or they have an appointment."

She sat forward. "Jeff and I were just talking about it. Should we send people home? And I have to get the kids this afternoon from school. What about taking the dogs out?"

"I think you're safe, but do what you need to do."

Sylvie stood in Jeff's door. "I'm not going anywhere. If Polly is safe here, then I'll be fine. And besides, I have to prep for Saturday night. I can't afford to sit at home, staring at the television."

"There won't be any random violence. I'm certain of that," Aaron said. "Helen and I are the only targets this person is interested in and in just a short period of time, we will have this dealt with. Jeff, is there anything else that comes to mind regarding your visitor?"

Jeff shook his head. "No. Nothing else. I gave him brochures and pricing information. He was very polite."

"They always are," Polly muttered. "Right up until they go all serial killer on you."

She got up and followed Aaron out of the office. "Do you think we need to worry?" she asked.

"Not really, but it can't hurt to be safe. Can you lock the doors from here?"

Polly nodded and swiped her phone open and proceeded to click the doors locked from the app. "Here," she said. "Let me email you the key. That way you can get in and out."

"I already have it."

"Sure," she said, shaking her head. "I knew that. I'm a bit flustered by all of this."

He put his arm around her shoulder. "It's all going to be fine. Sutton has to know by now that everything is erupting. His days of calm are over and he'll either have to deal with it or go away and hide."

"What?" she asked. "When will you tell us?"

"I don't know why I still feel as if I need to keep everything quiet. It's just been second nature for all these years. Until someone with more clout than I have tells me that it's okay to tell people, I just don't feel comfortable. There are lives at stake out there and if Sutton decided to do something stupid, people other than me and Helen would be at risk."

"Okay. I know I'm being a pain about this. Sorry."

"I get it. These last couple of months have been strange."

They walked through the kitchen and he tugged on the door leading outside, then they walked through to the garage.

"I should have talked to Lydia all those years ago," he said. "But I thought it was behind me. It never occurred to any of us that it would come up again. When Albert called last summer, I still couldn't imagine that it would affect me. But the more time passed and the closer it got, the more I knew this had the potential to go south and I was going to be dragged into it. I shut down." He shrugged a shoulder. "That's all I can say. I just shut down. I didn't see a way to make it better. I worried about Helen and I couldn't talk to anyone. I didn't want to call her to make sure that she knew to be prepared. Polly, you don't know how powerful some of those people are and how deeply they have tentacles in the politics and life of Atlanta."

She wanted to interrupt and ask questions, but if he finally started talking, she was just going to follow him around the building and listen.

"Albert told me he was coming to see me. I don't know why. There wasn't any reason for it. We weren't going to fix things from here. Maybe he needed to make sure for himself that I was doing okay."

"Did you and he stay close through the years?"

"No," Aaron said. "It was too difficult. I left town and he left the force. He was so angry he couldn't see a way around it. I think he stayed in contact with Helen at the shelter. Every once in a while she mentioned that he was helping out with the kids. He was disappointed that we'd been allowed to just leave. No one wanted to take care of us. It was easier to let us go. I was young enough that it didn't matter. I could start over. He had a family, but in the middle of it all, his first wife left him and took their boys. I would never have known where she was except I had to let her know that he'd been killed."

"He never saw them again?"

"I don't think so. It was part of the price he paid."

"What was your price?"

He glanced in the vicinity of the offices. "Helen. She was angry with how things were handled. I was furious that she couldn't understand my choices. We both felt like we were betrayed by the other one. Lydia took the kids down to Atlanta several times to see the family, but I stayed here. When Dad died and then Mom a couple of years later, I went back for their funerals, but I lost my family. I did the right thing, though, even if she didn't like it."

"Did she know everything?"

"She knew enough. In fact, she was the catalyst. But she had no idea how much her actions would cost. She did the right thing too, though. The cost was worth it."

He tugged at the front doors and said, "It never occurred to me that you would end up in the middle of all of this. For the last two years I've tried to protect you from the absurdity of your own life and then, mine sideswiped you. That nearly destroyed me, you know. How was I ever going to explain to Lydia that you were in danger because of choices I made before she'd even met me."

"How did the two of you meet, anyway?" Polly asked. She didn't want him to stop talking.

Aaron smiled. "It was a blind date for me. But not for Lydia.

That woman picked me out and told one of her friends to set us up. She didn't ask, she told the friend."

"Someone I know?"

"No. Nena Mack. She lives in Washington. Got married, he worked for a little programming company that exploded in the nineties. But back then, Nena was dating a boy whose brother was a deputy."

"Where was your first date?"

"I took her to State Fair. It's always been her favorite thing to do in the summer." He released a breath that sounded like a laugh. "Actually, I didn't take her. She took me. I'd never seen anything like it. She loved the entire experience."

"Did you ever camp down there?" Polly asked. "I have friends who used to do that."

"When we had young kids, we spent the whole two weeks. I rented a camper and off we went. Lydia was in heaven. There was nothing too big or too small for her to experience. We don't spend enough time doing that now. If we can get down for a day, it's a big deal."

"You should go with your grandkids. They'd love it."

"Maybe when they're older. Lydia will tell me when she's ready. You know, after that first date, she told her friend that if I asked her out again, she'd marry me."

"I take it you asked her out."

"Nena called me and told me that I'd better not screw this up. So I didn't. I called Lydia the next night and asked her to dinner. That night she took me to Davey's and she never let me out of her sight again. We were married five months later and Marilyn was born less than a year after that."

"Lydia's never really talked about this."

"All you need to do is ask. She tells these stories all the time, but I think she believes that she's worn them out and no one wants to hear them any longer."

"I loved hearing my dad tell stories of when he and Mom were dating. You could feel them falling in love with each other."

"I fell in love with that woman the first time I met her and then as I experienced her enthusiastic joy while she dragged me around those State Fairgrounds, I knew I couldn't live without her. She was like no one I'd ever known. I moved here after experiencing the worst lows of my life and one day, there was a light and she wanted to be with me. I couldn't marry her fast enough."

"Five months is a short time to plan a wedding."

"That's what her mom said, too. Her Dad offered me two thousand dollars to elope. But Lydia had it well in hand. I gave her a ring, she said yes, and flew into a frenzy of activity. It was a simple wedding. We got married and had a small reception at the church. Nothing like what you serve up here at Sycamore House."

"Some of them are ridiculous," Polly said. "You saw how I did it. Simple. I couldn't go through what these brides and their families create."

They were standing in the lounge across from the offices. Polly would have loved to sit, relax and listen to Aaron talk. But she knew that if she interrupted him, he'd take off and the moment would be gone.

"As long as they're happy," he said. "Marilyn's wedding was an extravaganza. That's the only word I have for it. Lydia had a ball. I wondered if she was making up for her modest wedding, but no, that woman always knew what she wanted. She and Marilyn spent a year planning and honestly, it wasn't as expensive as I feared."

He looked off toward the addition as if he could see Lydia through the walls. "She's always taken care of me. No matter what. Our family had everything it needed and more, but she wasn't reckless or out of control. I couldn't have asked for a better life."

"So far," Polly said.

Aaron smiled at her. "Of course. So far. Don't worry, Polly. I'm not going anywhere. You live much too risky a life for me to let anyone else take care of you." He patted her shoulder. "Except for Henry. That man is a saint. I'm not married to you and some nights I stay awake worrying about what you've gotten in to. He has to live with you every day. I don't know how he goes to work in the morning."

"Stop it," she brushed him off. "It's not that bad."

"It would be for me. You're a menace to strong hearts everywhere."

Polly had subtly guided Aaron back into her office as they talked and gestured to a chair. He hesitated and then sat down.

"I guess I'm not going anywhere and at least this way I can see out into the parking lot," he said.

"Nothing is going to happen. You've got the bad guy."

"No, we just have a minion, but if we're lucky, he's not a bright minion and will give us what we need."

Aaron's phone rang and he looked at it curiously. "Sheriff Merritt speaking."

All of a sudden, he looked up at Polly and motioned for a pen and paper. She shoved those at him and he wrote, "Call Stu. Tell them to trace this call. I need to know where he's at."

"That's not going to happen, Price. It's all over," he said.

Polly dialed the main number for the Sheriff's office. The voice on the other end of Aaron's call was loud, yelling.

"Boone County Sheriff," a voice said.

"This is Polly Giller. Can I speak to Stu? Aaron needs a trace."

"Just a moment."

In a split second, Stu was on the line. "Aaron's number?"

"Yes. I think it's that Price Sutton. Aaron wants to know where he is."

"It's already going through. Tell him we'll call back when we have information."

"Thanks, Stu."

"Is everything okay up there?"

"Just peachy," she said. "We thrive on insanity around here, you know."

Polly thought she heard a chuckle, but he said, "Tell Aaron I'll call."

While she was talking to Stu, Aaron left the office. She figured he would come back when he was finished. This was probably as good a time as any to let Henry know what was going on, but when she looked at the time, she realized there was only a short time left to pick up the kids from school.

She grabbed her coat and keys and walked out, stopping to tell Stephanie where she was going.

"Gonna get the kids," she called out to Sylvie as she ran through the kitchen toward the garage. "Back in a few." She pulled up short at the back door and ran back to the stairs.

"Obiwan! Han! Come down here!" Both dogs came running through the house and down the steps. She grabbed two leashes from the hook inside the door and they followed her into the garage. Obiwan jumped up into the cab, but Han needed help. He was trying to grow into his feet, but hadn't gotten there yet.

Polly had hoped that he was going to be a small dog like his mother, but he was starting to fill out and grow. When they saw his feet growing faster than the rest of him, she and Henry had become concerned. They were running out of room on the bed. What kind of dog had hooked up with the poor mother of this litter?

Sylvie's dog, Padme, was not as thick as the three males. Eliseo's pups were growing too. She couldn't just get lap dogs, she had to have dogs that took the entire chair.

Andrew, Rebecca and Kayla were already crossing the street in front of the elementary school when Polly drove up. She honked and they stopped to wait for her.

"In the back seat," she said. "We're taking a side trip today."

"Why are the dogs here?" Kayla asked.

"I thought it would be fun to take them to the park for a romp."

"Isn't it too cold?"

"You all have your coats and mittens. The dogs would love to play in some of this snow. Come on, it's an adventure."

Kayla didn't seem thrilled, but when Polly glanced in the rear view mirror, she saw Andrew's face alight with excitement. Rebecca pulled a piece of paper out of her backpack and handed it to Kayla.

"Where did you get this?" Kayla asked in a whisper.

"I saved it. You should show Polly."

"I threw it away."

"I know. It's cool, though. Show Polly."

"Show me what?" Polly said.

Kayla took the paper from Rebecca and pushed it down in her opened backpack. "Nothing."

"It's something. Rebecca thought it was important enough to save it. Show me."

"Okay," Kayla huffed and pushed the paper over the seat toward Polly.

Polly glanced at it as she turned into a parking space. She'd come up to the newly restored baseball fields. They'd been destroyed in last summer's tornado, but several fundraisers put together enough money to build new bleachers and a brand new snack shack. They'd finished it just before the season ended last fall and the community was already abuzz with excitement over a new season.

The snow on the ground had been trampled by people and animals, but there were plenty of new scents for the dogs to have a blast.

She snapped leashes on the two dogs and they followed her out of the truck.

"I get Obiwan," Andrew said and took the leash from Polly. "Kayla, you take Han. He likes you. Come on, Rebecca, let's run!"

Polly looked at the sheet of paper that Kayla had handed her. The pre-printed handout asked the question "Who inspires you?"

Kayla had written her paper about Rebecca and gotten an A. Of course Rebecca pulled this out of the trash. This was something Polly wanted to keep for the girl forever. Kayla told of how Rebecca took care of her mother even when she couldn't stay with her every day and how she was a great artist and a good friend. Polly breathed back tears when Kayla talked about missing her own mother and that when Rebecca's mother died, she'd make sure that Rebecca was okay because that's what friends did.

It occurred to Polly that so much had been happening this last week she hadn't taken enough time with Rebecca. Polly thought back to the year after she'd lost her own mother. So much of it was a blur. Her dad and the woman who practically raised her - Mary, and her husband, Sylvester, were the only people who really came into focus. There weren't any friends who listened or let her talk about her mom. Kayla and Rebecca were lucky to have each other.

Polly leaned against the truck and watched the kids and dogs in the snow. Kayla fell down once and Polly started toward her, but the girl stood up, shook herself off and ran after Obiwan. She caught up to him and threw herself at him, hugging his neck. He gave her a sloppy lick on the face and she rubbed it off. When she turned toward Polly to find Han and Rebecca, she had a look of pure joy on her face. She chased the smaller dog and picked him up, then started walking back to the truck.

"Have they done their business enough?" she asked.

"A few times," Polly said. "Are you ready?"

Obiwan was meandering, sniffing and lifting his leg, with Andrew and Rebecca following behind. They were both panting from the chase and their faces were bright red from cold and exertion.

"He's good to go," Andrew said.

"Then I vote we head back to Sycamore House for hot cocoa."

They piled back into the truck. Somehow Han had managed to squeeze himself between Rebecca and Kayla, perfectly happy with the attention they offered.

CHAPTER TWENTY-SIX

Kayla, Rebecca and Andrew were settled upstairs with homework and hot cocoa. Polly stopped in the main kitchen on her way back to the office, but Sylvie and Rachel were both head down in a frothy concoction at the stove top, so she slipped on through.

She had just settled at her desk when Helen Oswald stormed in. "Where's my brother?"

"I don't know," Polly said. "I just got back from picking up the kids. What happened?"

"That son of a bitch. I'll kill him myself."

"Aaron?"

"No, not Aaron. Price Sutton. You won't believe what he had the audacity to do."

Polly shook her head. It seemed better to just let Helen storm for a few moments.

"He's shutting down the shelter. He's trying to intimidate me."

Aaron walked in and said, "What happened?"

Helen spun on him and jabbed a finger in his chest. "Fix this. Fix this right now. I got a call from Fuller at the shelter. They were just served an eviction notice. He's not even giving them ninety days."

"Who? Sutton?"

"Damned right, Sutton. He owns that building."

"Helen, I would have expected you to move out of his building."

"Don't give me that. We did. Twice. Each time he ended up buying whatever building we were located in. If that jackass thinks he's going to intimidate me, he has another think coming. I'm done. I've played the game far too long. I don't care who this exposes, he's not hurting those children. He has no right."

"Calm down." Aaron pulled out a chair and tried to move Helen into it.

"I will not calm down."

"Helen. You're in the middle of Iowa. You can't do anything from up here."

"Yes I can. There are a million reporters in that city that would like to hear from me about this. I don't care how old the scandal is, some of those people are still in power and they won't like the press. He has pushed this too far. First a murder and then attempted murder and now this. I was willing to be patient right up until this point."

"Helen."

She jerked the chair so hard that Polly flinched.

"Stop it!" she yelled.

Aaron shut the door and sent a look of apology at Polly. This wasn't her fight. She was only an observer.

"Helen. This isn't the right time or place."

"When's the right time? Your friend was killed. I was a target. How many more people have to be hurt before you stand up against this man?"

"You don't understand." Aaron wilted and dropped into the chair that had taken abuse from his sister.

That was enough to calm Helen back down. She sat on the corner of Polly's desk in front of her brother. "I do understand. But it's time for this to be over and you're the only person who can stop it. When Albert was killed, you became the keeper of this secret."

"There are others," he said quietly.

"But they aren't as honorable. Their careers still rely on the secret. They've put in their time. Let them retire or face the music. He's threatening us now."

Aaron took her hand. "I know you're right. But there are some good men who got caught up in this without understanding who they were dealing with."

"They might've been naive then, but no longer. They're living on borrowed time. Sutton has been intimidating them with his threats. Make it stop now, Aaron. Please."

Aaron took out his phone and dialed. "Digger? I think it's time. When can they be ready?"

He listened and nodded, then said. "They've got an eye on him? He's going to try to do something. They know that, right?"

A few more nods. "What about the girls. What if he leaks it? They're in position?" Aaron listened again and then said, "I know. We've talked about this. It's just more than I want to be responsible for."

Polly knew that any assumptions she was making about this conversation had to be way off base, but she was about to go out of her mind with curiosity. Here it was playing out right in front of her and she had no idea what Aaron and Helen were talking about. Big city politics, girls, leaks, cops. She was sure that Digger was in touch with the FBI. That was the only connection she could make.

"I'll make the call," Aaron said. "Thanks for everything."

He put his phone down on her desk and looked up at his sister. "Two hours. I call him in two hours."

Helen leaned in and hugged him. "After all these years, that's all that is left. It will be over, Aaron. You can come home again."

"No," he said, shaking his head. "No, I can't. It will be worse now, you know. I won't be able to set foot in that city. Every cop will have my name. They aren't going to know enough details about the whole thing. They'll just know I forced some of their bosses to leave in a hurry. I wasn't on the force long enough to make friends. Just Albert and everyone thought he was a conspiracy nut."

"What about the kids at the shelter?" she asked.

"We'll work that out once he's in custody and the list is safe."

"D'ya think he made copies?"

"Probably. But they'll find them. No one wants those girls to go through any more than they did. Their lives are as normal as possible now. It's been thirty years."

"You and I both know that for some of them, time has made no difference. And for those who made a good life, they don't need to face this again."

"I don't know what you're telling me, Helen. First you want me to take him down, no matter what and now you're telling me that the girls have to be a priority."

"It's not easy. Nothin's easy. But that threat needs to be gone."

"You're right. Things are in motion now. We just have to wait."

As if she weren't even in the room, Aaron and Helen moved to Polly's office door and left.

"What?" she asked when they were in the main hallway. "What's in motion? What threat? What girls?"

Jeff came in. "Are you talking to yourself?"

"Apparently." Polly patted her shoulders. "I'm still visible, right? You have no trouble seeing me here."

He chuckled. "Yep. You're all there."

"Good. I was worried. They talked and talked, telling me nothing, then left as if I didn't even exist. It was a bit disconcerting. But it will be over in a couple of hours. I did get that much."

"You poor thing. You don't like not being part of all the excitement, do you?"

"It wouldn't be so bad if it wasn't happening right in front of me."

"We're taking off," he said.

"Who's we?"

"I'm taking Stephanie and Kayla home."

Polly looked at him quizzically.

"Her car is in the shop."

"Okay?"

"No big deal, just a few things she had to put off before."

"Jeff?"

He bent over her desk and said in an undertone, "You be quiet and don't give me any trouble. You've done more than this for people."

"Only if you stop giving me trouble about what I do."

"Deal. We'll be in tomorrow morning after taking Kayla to school."

Polly nodded and got up to follow him out of the office. She wondered how long Sylvie was staying tonight. When she got to the kitchen, Sylvie and Rachel were gone and the lights were turned off. She ran up the back steps and into the apartment. Jessie and Rebecca were watching "Ghostbusters" in the media room.

"What the heck time is it?" Polly asked.

Jessie looked up. "Hi Polly. I came home a few minutes early. There wasn't much going on. Henry told me to lock up and leave. He said he'd be here before long."

"It's empty around here and it feels strange," Polly said. "Are you spending the evening with your mom, Rebecca?"

"Evelyn said she'd be awake six thirty. Is that okay?"

"Sure."

"Is everything okay, Polly?" Jessie asked.

"It feels strange here today. Everyone is where should be, but there's usually more activity. What do you think about pizza tonight? I could order it and have Henry pick up."

They both nodded and turned back to the television. Polly walked into the kitchen and called Henry.

"Hey sweet stuff, what's up?" he asked.

"Where are you?"

"I'm about twenty minutes out. What do you need?"

"Can you pick up pizza if I call it in? It might be a few minutes. I need to check with everyone over on the other side."

"Sure. Meet you in the kitchen downstairs?"

"Thanks. I'll see you later."

"Are you okay? You sound weird."

"I feel upside down. Like something's missing. People left today and no one said good-bye."

"You don't think they're upset at you, do you?"

"No, that's not it. I just feel a little invisible."

"You aren't that. And when I get home, I'll touch you all over and make sure that all of you is still there."

"Stop that," she whispered. "There are kids in the room."

"No one is here with me."

"I'm hanging up now. I have to order pizza. You be good."

Polly headed for the front door. There were a lot of steps in this place. "I'm going over to the addition to get pizza orders," she called out, knowing that neither of the girls really cared whether she was gone or not. They were engrossed in the movie.

She placed the pizza order and told everyone when they could meet in the kitchen, then went in and turned the lights back on, set the table, and sat down to wait.

By the time Henry came in the back door, she had gone through the refrigerator and found leftover cake. Sylvie left presents on purpose for those who were always foraging. There was enough for everyone and Polly also found two opened containers of ice cream. That would do.

Henry helped her set the pizzas out on the prep table and then kissed her, long and deep.

"What's that for?" she gasped.

"You seem like you need it."

"I'll always take it, but I don't think I need it."

"Well, I do." He kissed her again and when he broke away, she stepped back, breathing heavily.

"You still do that to me," she said. "I don't care how long we've been together. You still wipe me out when you kiss me like that."

"Good. Now round up our guests and I'll get the girls upstairs. I have some things I need to drop on my desk. Are the dogs okay?"

"I think so." Polly shook her head. "I still feel dazed, but thank you."

He winked at her and as she stood in the middle of the kitchen, she realized that her heart might be racing, but her feet weren't moving.

~~~

Henry, Polly, Helen, Lydia and Aaron were still at the table in the kitchen. Rebecca had gone back to her mother's room for the evening and Jessie wanted to spend time talking to her friend in Colorado on Facebook.

Aaron looked at his phone and said, "I need to make a phone call. Might I use your offices, Polly?"

"Sure," she said, waving that way. "Then are you going to finally tell us what has been happening?"

He looked at her in confusion, gave a quick shake of his head, and walked away.

"What was that?" she asked.

"Who knows," Helen responded.

Lydia jumped up. "I'm nervous about this call he's making, so let's clean up." She picked up the rest of the paper plates and took them to the trash can. Within minutes the kitchen was spotless.

"Do you want to come upstairs?" Polly asked. "Jessie's in her room and it's much more comfortable than sitting around down here."

"Sure," Helen said. "I've had enough napping and sitting by myself today."

Lydia gave her a look.

"Well, haven't you had enough of sitting by myself with me today?" Helen asked with a laugh. "We've played cards and talked about family issues for far too long."

"Go on upstairs with Henry," Polly said. "I'll tell Aaron what we're doing."

Henry gave a cough as she turned to leave the kitchen.

"What?" she asked.

"You aren't fooling me."
~~~

She waggled her fingers at him. "Go away. Go upstairs and leave me alone. I'll be right there." Polly left the kitchen and headed for the office where she found Aaron sitting at Stephanie's desk with his head in his hands.

"Aaron?"

He looked up, his face drawn, his eyes sad.

"Are you okay?"

"No," he said, putting the phone down on the desk in front of him. "I just ruined several good men's careers and if this isn't handled well from here on out, twenty innocent women may have their lives turned upside down in the next week. I can only pray that he's a better man than he threatens."

"Sutton?"

He nodded.

"Is he responsible for killing your friend and the attempt on Helen's life?"

"He is. He hired people to do his dirty work, but he's behind it. The man was a fool. If he had left public life before this all came to a head, he would have been able to keep most everything together, but because he craved attention and couldn't imagine any life other than what he had built, he's lost it all."

"Are you going to tell me about this?"

He gave her a wry grin. "Do I have a choice?"

"Sure you do, but then you'll have to live knowing that every single time you see me, I'll be wondering why you wouldn't tell me. And every time I call you on the phone, you'll wonder if I'm going to ask you about it one more time. Is that what you want in our relationship?"

Aaron smiled at her. "I understand why your husband and my wife love you so much." He stood up and came around the desk, pulling her into a hug. "You insist on being up front about everything, don't you?"

"Well, I don't really need to know about your bathroom habits or your sex life."

"Polly!" he said, stepping away from her.

She giggled. "I said I don't need to know those things. Come on!"

"I think I can tell you my story now. Are you going to make me tell it several times or can I tell my wife at the same time."

"They're all upstairs in our apartment." She started out of the office. "Oh! Can you take Lydia home now or is there still a threat out there?"

Aaron winked at her. "The threat has passed, but we're here. Maybe we'll take you up on your hospitality one more night. It's good for her to not have to think about all of the mundane things that happen in our home. It's like a mini vacation."

"That's fine with me," Polly said. "Come on up and we'll hear all about your evil nemesis from Dixieland."

Henry, Lydia and Helen were settled in the media room watching television. Polly nodded for Aaron to join them and then knocked on Jessie's door.

"Come in?"

"Hey," Polly said.

Jessie was propped up in her bed, wearing a flannel nightgown and had her tablet propped up on her belly.

"Are you comfy? Do you need anything?"

"No, I'm good. Thanks."

"We're in the media room, so you're free to come and go in here without getting all dressed up. I don't know how long they'll be here, but let me know if you need anything."

"It's pretty much just me and the bathroom these days," Jessie said. "I know I have a few more weeks, but I'm going to be glad when this baby is here."

"I'm sure you will. Have a good night."

"Thanks for everything, Polly."

CHAPTER TWENTY-SEVEN

Luke had been weaving in and out of Polly's legs from the moment she walked in the door. She picked him up and walked into the dining room.

"Do you want anything from the kitchen?" she asked. There were no positive responses, so she carried the cat with her and took an open space beside Henry. He waited for her to settle in, then patted his leg for Han to jump up and sit on his lap.

Aaron sat back in his chair, scratched his head, then shut his eyes.

"What do I have to do to make him talk?" Polly asked Lydia.

Lydia grinned. "I don't know. We could try torture."

"No torture. You two aren't safe to be around," Aaron said, sitting upright. He turned to his sister. "I'm going to tell this story, but if I leave something out, you'll intervene. Right?"

She leaned forward and patted his knee. "It's like we grew up together."

He took a deep breath and said, "Albert Cook and I were on patrol one night when we got a call. My sister had called the precinct looking for me. She had an emergency at a children's shelter where she spent her free time and they needed the police."

"I needed you. I didn't need the police," Helen interrupted.

Aaron gave her a look. "Three sentences is all it took. Hush."

She rolled her eyes and gestured for him to continue.

"I was just a rookie, barely six months in. When we got to the shelter, Helen took me into her office where there was a young girl, not even thirteen years old. She was a mess. She was bloody and had been beaten pretty badly. When she saw my uniform, she panicked."

"I think it was your partner, not you," Helen said.

He scowled at her. "It was the uniform. Her name was Melody. I remember that much. When Helen finally convinced her that I wasn't just any cop, but that I was her younger brother, Melody started to talk. She told me things that I didn't want to know. About powerful men in Atlanta who liked little girls. The names she gave me that night were names of men in politics and in local business.

"I didn't want to hear what she said. In fact, I would have been glad to call her a liar, but Helen wouldn't let me. Especially when Melody told me that she had escaped from a house where she and quite a few other girls were kept. She said that some of the girls came from other places. They transferred the girls around, based on their age and experience."

"How long had this been going on?" Polly asked.

"About ten years. The thing is, the FBI knew about it and so did many in the police force. They'd been investigating this group of men, but hadn't been able to get anyone to identify the culprits. I called my buddy, Digger, that night. I didn't know who to trust, but I knew him. That's when I found out about the investigation. I was young and naive. If it hadn't been for Albert, I would have probably gone out waving a gun, disrupting the whole world and generally causing havoc. I was furious and disgusted and shaken to my core. Some of the men she named were people I respected.

"That night we raided the first house. I was so fired up by what I'd heard that I insisted Digger let me go along. He knew better than to refuse me. He knew I needed to fix it.

"There were eight girls living there - all under the age of fifteen. They each had a room and were..." Aaron stopped talking and then lowered his voice. "I don't want to upset Jessie. The girls were chained up in their rooms, only to be released when it was time for them to be used by a member of the circle. In each closet there was a port-a-potty. During the day, an armed guard watched as they cleaned their rooms, cleaned themselves, ate something - usually very little - and prepared themselves for more hell. Sometimes the men came after work, sometimes they showed up in the morning before going to work. It didn't matter when one would arrive, whichever girl he wanted, he took her."

Polly gulped and huddled closer to Henry.

Aaron's voice had gone flat in his recitation of the story. His eyes narrowed to slits and his fists clenched the arms of the chair.

"Over the next week, we found all of the houses. The girls were lifeless. They'd given up. One of the saddest things to see was their keepsakes – one girl had a rag doll tucked under her mattress. There were so many tear stains on that doll's body, it broke my heart. But she wouldn't leave without it. We called Helen and she organized care - both physical and psychiatric. She was the only person I trusted and I wasn't going to let this go to anyone."

Helen nodded, her eyes filled with pain for her brother. "I'd been working with homeless kids. I knew what some of those kids lived through before they got to the shelter, but poor Aaron wasn't prepared for the trauma."

"There's no way to prepare for that," he said. "We arrested as many men as we could. Asking those girls to identify their abusers was the hardest thing I'd ever done. Here I thought we'd rescued them, but then we exposed them again. I felt like we were betraying their trust. Helen and Albert tried to make me see that for most of the girls, this was a closure that would help them heal."

"Once that part of the investigation was underway, we realized that this couldn't have happened without the help of others who weren't directly involved with the abuse. There were policemen who looked the other way. And in the beginnings of the investigation some of them tried to trip us up by covering over evidence. There were young cops, my age, who didn't know any better and had gotten caught in the whole mess because their partners were receiving payoffs. In a system that big, when you've only been around for a few months, who are you to say what's tradition and what's been acceptable."

Lydia growled. "You do the right thing."

"I'd want to hope so," Aaron said. "But I was pretty naive. If Albert had been taking hush money and wanted me to look the other way, I might not have asked the right questions. I just can't be that rigid about what they did."

Polly was curious. "How does Price Sutton fit into this?"

"He worked in the prosecutor's office. The US Attorney helped the girls get new identities and leave Atlanta, but a list was created somewhere along the line with each girl's name, identity and new home. This was before computers. Sutton got his hands on the list. Then we found out he was part of the cover up. No blatant evidence that he'd been involved, but he knew about it. Two of his buddies were went to prison. Sutton took that list and promised that no one would ever see it if we all just let him go quietly."

"What?" Polly asked.

"We didn't have anything firm on him. I think he promised his buddies an easier sentence if they kept quiet. Those of us who were aware of what he did were sworn to secrecy. He swore that if his name was tied to the scandal, he'd expose the cops who had been on the outskirts of the cover up and release the names and addresses of the girls who had been involved, essentially destroying their lives."

Lydia spoke up. "You went along with this?"

"I had to. It wasn't criminal, though it was abominable, and at that point, there were quite a few good men who didn't need to be dragged through the mud. So we agreed. Albert stayed in Atlanta, but I couldn't stomach the corruption we'd uncovered any longer. I couldn't be part of a system that allowed that man to stay in power. Digger and I talked late into the night one night and I remember opening up an atlas and jamming my finger in the middle of it and saying, 'I'm moving here. Wanna go with me?'"

"Bellingwood?" Polly asked.

"Boone. I wanted to be as far away from Georgia as possible, so I started the process and moved. Digger wasn't far behind me."

"So what happened to stir this all up again?" Lydia asked. "If you'd kept it quiet all those years, why would you expose him now?"

"I'm sure Sutton has lived with this guilt, so he's paranoid. One of his buddies was released from prison two weeks ago. That's why Albert called last summer. He knew Sutton would panic. We didn't expect him to hire an assassin, but we discovered that he tapped Albert's phone and was having him followed." Aaron huffed. "He was so paranoid. Those girls are young women now - some of them around Sylvie's age. I hope they have families and found ways to deal with the horror of their childhood. The cops who had been part of this moved up through the force. I wasn't about to hurt their lives. I figure they're living with their own guilt."

"Polly?"

Polly spun around in the couch at the sound of Rebecca's voice. "Yes honey, how was your evening?"

"It was good. I just wanted you to know I'm back."

"Do you have your homework done?"

Rebecca came over to the back of the sofa. "Yes I do," she said scolding Polly with a look. "You know I always do that after school."

Polly patted her hand. "Good. Are you about ready for bed?"

"Can I get my book?" Rebecca pointed at a bookshelf behind Aaron. "I'm sorry to interrupt."

He jumped up. "You aren't at all. What book are you reading?"

"Have you read these?" she asked, slipping behind his chair to take a book. "I'm on the fifth one."

"Bobbsey Twins," he said. "No. I never read those. I liked Tarzan and I even read some Hardy Boys."

"Those are over here," she said, pointing to another shelf. "I haven't gotten to them yet."

"It looks like Polly has plenty for you to read."

"She unpacks boxes and finds more. It's pretty cool." Rebecca looked around hesitantly, then rushed over and hugged Polly.

"I'll check on you later," Polly said.

Rebecca ran for the doorway and turned around. "Good night."

They listened as she walked across the living room floor.

"She's a good kid," Aaron said, sitting back down. "And she's happy here."

Polly nodded. "She really is. We're trying to make this transition as easy as possible. I can't imagine what goes on in her head though. Waiting for your mother to die, not knowing who to obey."

"You're doing fine," Lydia said. "No one could do more than you."

"I want to finish this story." Polly turned back to Aaron. "So Sutton is paranoid and panicked. It feels like he over reacted."

"That's just what he did. When I saw Albert on the ground at Sycamore Inn, I knew it had to be Sutton. I called Digger right away. He knew that we couldn't make a big deal up here or things would unravel. I brought Stu in on it and we shut the investigation down. But at the same time, Digger and I contacted the FBI in Atlanta and they started another one down there. This time, Sutton was up for murder. We sent the evidence to them and though they haven't tracked down the sniper, they know who it is. He works out of the Atlanta area. They've tracked payments made to him from one of Sutton's accounts."

"Who was the kid that ran down your sister and Eliseo?"

Aaron shook his head. "He was the son of that buddy who just got out of prison. Sutton put him through college and hired him as an assistant. It sounds like the kid has been doing nothing except taking a paycheck."

"I didn't tell anyone I was coming to Bellingwood," Helen said. "And that kid was here the next day."

"You told Lydia."

"What?" Lydia said. "Are our phones tapped?"

"No. I've checked. But the phones at the shelter were all wired. They were keeping an eye on you, Helen. All of these years and Sutton never forgot who was involved and who might be a threat. I was far enough away, but you and Albert never left his radar. The minute you got on that plane, he put plans in motion."

"And the shelter? Can he really shut that down?"

"Help them get some good lawyers. Everything he's done in the last few days will be under scrutiny. You shouldn't worry."

"I still don't understand," Polly said. "None of this makes sense."

"It does if you lived with a secret for thirty years. How could Price Sutton believe there were actually men of honor when he, himself, had none? He'd give people up in a flash, why wouldn't we?"

Aaron took a deep breath. "You know, the worst of it? Albert had liver cancer. He was dying. That's another reason he wanted to see me. I'm almost glad that he was shot and died so quickly. He wouldn't have wanted to fade away in a hospital."

"But he also wanted to give me a piece of the puzzle that he'd held on to. He thought it would keep us all safe from Sutton."

"What's that?" Henry asked. He'd been quiet throughout the evening, but Polly could feel the tension in his body as he listened to Aaron's story.

"It was a campaign button. We found it at the third house. There was a partial print on it. That bit of a print pointed to Price Sutton. When we couldn't find any other evidence and none of the girls was willing to point the finger at him, we had to let it go. Albert was worried that it might mysteriously disappear from evidence, so he took it."

Polly looked at him in surprise. "Do you have it?"

"I do," Aaron said and took an evidence bag out of his pocket. "I'll give it to Digger next week. He knows I have it. That's the reason for the phone call tonight."

"What did you do?" Helen asked.

"I called Price Sutton just before the FBI got to his office. I told him that I had that button and with today's advances in fingerprint technology, it would place him in that house. He was enraged. He'd called earlier in the day, raving about how he wasn't going to let us take him down. He'd worked too hard to build his reputation and after thirty years, he wasn't about to lose all of that. He reminded me that he had that list and had no fear of hurting those girls."

"Blackmail," Henry said. "Nothing more than blackmail."

"I let him rage," Aaron said. "I've lost sleep these last two months, knowing that this man was going to come unglued and not knowing how he was going to do it. I thought about leaving town so that you would be safe," he reached for Lydia's hand. "And when Albert was shot, I was just finished. He'd pushed it too far, but I still couldn't let those girls be hurt. I would have sacrificed nearly anything for them. What happened to those poor children was worse than anything I've ever seen. No one should have to go through what they went through and I will protect them with everything I have."

"You could have told me about this," Lydia said. "I would have been glad to be part of this. I could have helped you."

"I know that now. But thirty years ago, you changed my life. You didn't know any of that about me. You didn't know the filth that I'd seen and the horror I'd experienced. You were my light. And then over the years, the memories faded little by little. I didn't think about it every day. We had our own children and one day I realized I hadn't thought about it for two months and then it became years and then it was something that was so far separate from what my life was now. Does that make sense?" Aaron was pleading for Lydia to understand.

"Of course it does. I only wish you'd told me last fall when your friend called."

"Looking back, I should have. I wrecked so many things by dealing with this alone." He looked at his sister. "I wrecked our relationship by running away and leaving you to deal with it."

"I didn't deal with anything. Once you were gone, I forgot about Price Sutton, except when he bought another of our buildings. I knew he was keeping an eye on me, but I wasn't doing anything to threaten him."

Aaron's shoulders sagged as he exhaled. "I can only hope that the FBI's raid was as precise as they hoped. While I talked to Sutton on his home phone and listened to him rant and rave, they jammed his cell phone, cut his computer lines and then at just the right moment, cut his power. They didn't want him transmitting anything. He's such a fool. He thought he was smarter than any of us, but that only goes so far when you lose yourself to paranoia and insanity."

His phone rang. "Just a second," he said and walked through Henry's office to the back stairs. They all waited in stunned silence until he returned.

"That was Digger. They've got him and he's babbling like a fool. I guess he doesn't know what he's saying, because he's confessing and accusing all at the same time."

"The list?"

Aaron gave a sad smile. "He carried it in his wallet. He never put it on a computer or scanned it or put it in a safe deposit box or gave it to a lawyer. Nothing. He kept it with him for all these years. The girls are safe."

"When do you have to go to Atlanta?" Lydia asked. "Surely they're going to want you to come and testify."

"It will be a few months. Why do you ask?"

"I think we should go to Florida first. Maybe take a cruise."

"You'll go with me?"

"I'm never leaving you, Aaron Merritt. No matter how hard you try to push me away."

Helen hitched herself forward on her chair. "Now that the crisis has passed, will you take me to see those grandbabies of yours, Lydia?"

Lydia pulled her eyes away from her husband. "Of course! You'll love them."

"And you," Helen said, standing up and pointing at Aaron. "Find me a date for this Valentine's Day soiree they're putting on. I don't care how young he is, but he can't be in his nineties. I need him to keep up with me."

"A date?" he squawked.

"A date. I'm going to be escorted to this event like a fine Southern lady."

He swallowed and looked at Lydia. She chuckled. "Don't look at me. I'm going to be busy with grandbabies."

"But, I don't know any single men."

"Of course you do." She got up and stood next to him. "But if you're really good to me tonight, I might whisper some names in your ear."

"That's not what I want to hear in my ear tonight."

"La la la la la," Helen said, standing up. "You two keep it down. Your room is right next to mine and I don't want to know what my baby brother is doing with his wife. Now I'm going to try to get some sleep." She put her hand out and Polly took it. "Thank you for a lovely evening."

"I'm not sure what to say right now," Polly said.

"That's the best way to leave a room," Helen replied. "With everyone speechless."

Henry scrambled up, dumping Han into Polly's lap. "I'll walk you out," he said, taking her arm. She turned and winked at Polly. "I don't suppose you'd be free Saturday night to take an old lady to a dance."

"I might be convinced to swing you around the dance floor, but my evening is already claimed."

"I was afraid of that. Good night, all!"

"We'd best be going, too," Lydia said. "Thank you so much for a comfortable place to sit and hear this story."

"Have I satisfied your curiosity, Polly?" Aaron asked.

"I think so. If I have more questions, you know I'll ask," she responded with a laugh.

"Yes I do."

She followed them into the living room and stood beside Henry at the front door as their friends went down the steps.

"Do you want to take a walk with me and the dogs?" she asked him.

"Just tell me that we'll be like Aaron and Lydia when we get old. I want to love you for all those years."

"I promise," she said, reaching up to kiss him. He pulled her in close and held her tight.

"Whoa," she said. "You've still got it."

CHAPTER TWENTY-EIGHT

"Ergh," Jessie groaned. "Can you help me? I feel like a cow. And I can't move and I can't zip anything and I can't..."

Polly smiled. Henry had been kicked out of their bedroom while the three girls got ready for the Valentine's Day party. Jessie helped Rebecca with just a hint of makeup, and the girl was walking on clouds. They'd found an adorable red velvet dress for her with crinolines and a wide, black ribbon around the waist. Polly wanted to swoon, she was so cute. Jessie was wearing a smart, black shift with red accents. She desperately wanted to wear her black boots, even though her ankles would swell throughout the evening. Polly bent over to zip them up.

"Are you sure about these?" she asked.

"Let me have one night of glamor," Jessie said. "Just one night."

"You do know that you will be 'not pregnant' soon enough, don't you?"

"Uh huh. And then I'll be toting around a baby and there will be spit up and poop and pee."

"You make it sound so appealing." Polly laughed. If Jessie wanted to see herself as glamorous tonight, that was fine.

Rebecca stood beside Polly in the bathroom, watching as she finished her makeup. "Mom looks beautiful in that dress we got her."

"I'll bet she does. You did a good job finding that."

"Can I ask you to do something?"

"Sure what do you need?"

"Can you take pictures of her and me tonight? I don't want to forget this."

Polly sat down on the counter top and took Rebecca's hand. "Of course I'll take pictures. But here's what I will tell you. There will be many things you forget over the years, but you will always remember special times. Maybe tomorrow afternoon, you should draw things that you remember from tonight."

"Mrs. Watson said that too this morning. She said that there would be pretty people here and I should try to draw some of them."

"That's not a bad idea. You know, I wish you didn't have to go through this, but you're going to grow up and be a wonderful young woman."

Rebecca squeezed Polly's hand and left the bathroom. Polly remained where she was, watching the two girls chatter and talk about what was to happen tonight. For the last couple of days, she'd been so focused on Aaron and Helen and the ugliness that had happened thirty years ago, she'd forgotten about how life just kept moving along. Jessie and Rebecca weren't affected at all by those horrible events. They had their own things to worry about and some days it was all she could do to keep up with them."

"Are you girls about ready in there?" Henry called from the living room. "We don't want to be late, do we?"

Polly jumped down and, letting Jessie and Rebecca go through the door first, followed them into the living room.

"That's more like it," he said. "Three of the prettiest girls in town and they live under my roof."

"Henry, that sounds really bad," Polly remarked.

He chuckled. "It did." He gave a slight shudder. "Now I feel like I'm some weird cult leader with my generational wives. Bleh.

Anyway, you all look wonderful and I think I'm going to quit talking now."

"Good idea," Rebecca said. "We won't tell anyone, will we Jessie?"

"I'm not saying a word," Jessie said. "I have enough of a reputation with bad boys." She patted her belly. "She'll be quiet, too. I promise."

The girls were both excited. Rebecca was practically vibrating in her shoes. Polly took Henry's arm. "Who knew that when you married me you were going to have a huge family before a year was out."

"I did," he muttered. "It's what you do. But enough of that. You're gorgeous tonight." He kissed her lips. "I'm glad we're having this party. It's the perfect way to end the strangeness of the last couple of weeks."

"This one actually hasn't been as bad as usual," Polly said. "Most of it wasn't happening to me."

"When you lock down Sycamore House, it feels like it is."

"That was two days ago. We're moving on now."

Jessie and Rebecca were standing at the front door. "I thought you were in a hurry," Rebecca said, tapping her feet. "I can hear the band downstairs. They're warming up."

Henry took Polly's hand and walked toward them. "A man can't get a break with you three. Onward."

Rebecca scampered across the hall to the addition to find her mother and Jessie left to find some of her own friends. She and Stephanie had gotten to know each other better this last week and Polly hoped they would become better friends. Jeff and Eliseo were in the auditorium making sure things were in place for the band and Sylvie was standing in front of the kitchen giving last minute instructions to her staff of waiters and waitresses.

Dusty rose and ivory cloths covered the tables, while red and white strands of lights fell from the ceiling and colored lights draped the edges of the serving tables and the stage. Sylvie's baking took center stage at each table, with cupcakes and festively colored cake balls filling the clear tiered towers.

Jeff walked across the room toward them, "What do you think?" he asked.

"You always make this room look like a party," Polly said. "Are you ready?"

"Dinner and dancing. It can't get much easier than that."

Two young men in white shirts and black pants stood in the doorway, waving for Jeff. "Excuse me," he said. "My valets are here."

"Valets?"

"We're going all out tonight. Time to raise some serious cash."

Polly nodded. They'd gone back and forth, trying to decide which charity would be the recipient of tonight's fund-raising efforts. There were so many that needed help. If she had the money, she'd prefer fully funding every one of them, but since that wasn't at all practical, at least Jeff kept having events like this. With all they'd learned about homeless youth, it broke Polly's heart to know that there were so many, even in Iowa. Like the rest of the homeless, they weren't just in the cities, but found everywhere throughout the state. She thought about Stephanie and Jessie. With just one misstep, those two girls could have been without a place to live. They wanted nothing to do with their families and were barely making it on their own.

"There but for the grace of God," she said.

"What's that?" Henry asked.

"I know that I'm fortunate. I know that. Dad took good care of me and I had a great foundation that helped me be successful, but anything could have happened along the way to make me homeless. How can people believe anything else?"

"Don't do that to yourself," he said. "We're here to have fun tonight. Come on. I hear Aaron in the hallway."

Helen Oswald gave a small wave when she saw Polly. "Hello dear. How are you this evening?"

"I'm good." Polly looked around her. "I thought Aaron was finding you a date? Did you let him off the hook?"

"Hell no. What are brothers for?"

"Did Aaron tell you who it was?"

"I'm not sure. But we're meetin' here."

Aaron gave Polly a sly grin and a wink, took his wife's coat from her and helped Helen out of hers. Another young man in a white shirt and black pants rushed up to take the coats and gave Aaron a numbered slip of paper.

"Y'all are going all out," Helen said. "This is pretty fancy doin's."

Polly said, "It's Jeff. He loves this. I just stand back and tell him what a wonderful job he does."

More and more people came in and soon the main level of Sycamore House was buzzing with conversation. As the tables filled, young people invited groups to go through the buffet. Jeff insisted that the evening be casual and people could eat when they were ready. The tables were cleared regularly and drinks were filled.

Mark and Sal sat down with Polly and Henry.

"How are the pups?" Polly asked.

Mark shook his head. "She's obsessed. Between those runts, her book, and the coffee shop, I get no attention."

"He's right," Sal said. "But it's only fair. He's gone most of the time. Calves, foals and piglets have kept him out most every night of the week. I need someone to keep me warm."

He laughed. "I should be glad it's only two puppies. It could be worse."

"Where are Joss and Nate?" Sal asked.

"I don't know," Polly responded. "I know they're coming. I talked to her earlier today. She was having a bad day with the kids and couldn't wait for the baby sitter to show up."

"See," Sal said, poking Mark. "Another good reason for me to have puppies."

He grimaced. "I prefer children, if you don't mind."

"Here they are!" Henry said. "And just in time."

Polly chuckled. Henry was right. They didn't need to get into a discussion about children with Sal and Mark. In fact, that was the last place she wanted to be. She stood and waved at Joss, who caught her eye and nodded. The two made their way to the table.

"Trouble with the kids?" Henry asked.

"No!" Joss said as Nate held her chair for her. "You won't believe where we've been."

She looked around the table and finally Polly said, "Where?"

"Right around the corner, back there." Joss pointed toward the south side of Sycamore House.

Henry laughed. "I give up. Were you just outside making out? It's a little chilly for that, don't you think?"

"No, you nut. Down the road and around the corner. You know that broken down farmstead? We're buying it so I can have a big house and lots of room. Nate's going to move his garage to the one good building on the property. I can't wait!"

Polly's eyes filled as she watched the joy on her friend's face. "We'll be neighbors?"

"Yes. You can ride Demi over to see me. Maybe we'll get a horse. And a dog and some cats."

"Whoa," Nate said. "Let Polly have the animals."

"Our children will need pets. They're good for kids," Joss argued. She pursed her lips and looked at her husband. "You don't really want to fight with me about this, do you?"

A laugh burbled from his lips. "I'm no fool. Besides, it will be a year at least before we're even in over there. Are you ready to build a house for us, Henry?"

"I'd be honored," Henry said. "It sounds like fun."

"A great big, rambling house. One that looks like it was added on to over the years. I don't want one of those pristine, pretty things," Joss said. "Can we do that?"

"We can do anything you want."

Polly saw Aaron jump to his feet and followed his eyes to the front door. "Oh my," she said, trying not to point. "That's Helen's date."

Everyone turned to look.

"He did not," Joss said.

"You know what?" Henry asked. "It's a great idea. She has no idea of his background. He's a good guy who just got lost for a while."

Sal looked confused. "Who is it?"

"That's Doug Leon," Polly said. "The guy who hoarded those items we have in the cupboards along the wall here. Look at him. He's in a nice suit and smiling."

The room had gone quiet, but soon everyone went back to their conversations. Aaron escorted Doug to their table, seating him between Len Specek and Helen, greeting both by shaking their hands.

"That has to be Lydia's doing," Polly said.

Henry agreed. "If she set it up, then he's in good hands. I think she and Andy have been part of his life since that day we discovered what he was doing. Every once in a while Len has him into the shop to help out on a project. He's a good, hard worker."

Nate bent over and said, "But he's ancient."

"So what? It's not like he and Helen are going to be married. She lives in Atlanta. Let them have a fun evening." Polly laughed. "Do you think he dances?"

"If your table is all here, you're welcome to go to the buffet any time," a young girl said to them.

"Thank you," Polly responded. "You guys go ahead. I'm going to wander.

"You always do this," Henry said as he caught up to her.

"What?"

"You don't eat. Everyone else enjoys one of Sylvie's terrific meals while you wander."

She took his hand and turned in so they were face to face, "I get too excited to eat. This is my house and these are my employees and the room is filled with my guests. Do you see Jeff or Sylvie or Eliseo eating? It's just too much for us to manage. And please, it isn't like I'm going to starve. I just need to make sure people are enjoying themselves and get a chance to tell me they're having a good time. It's my job."

"Taking care of you is full-time work," he said with a sigh.

"You don't have to walk with me. You know that. Go eat."

Henry looked yearningly at the buffet table. "Do you mean that?"

"Of course I do, you nut." Polly kissed his cheek and laughed at him. "I'm going to say hello to Lydia's table and then check on Rebecca and Sarah. I'll find you when it's time to dance, I promise."

She made her way past tables filled with people she'd spent the last two years getting to know. Some stopped her to tell her that she'd done a wonderful job with the place, another couple stopped her to tell her how terrific their daughter's wedding reception had been and she finally arrived at Beryl's side.

"How are you all?" she asked.

Aaron stood up. "Are you joining us?"

"No. I just wanted to stop by and meet Helen's date for the evening. How are you, Mr. Leon?"

He stood and shook her hand. "Fine, thank you. It's a lovely affair you're having."

"I'm glad you could make it. Are you ready to kick up your heels?"

"I don't dance very well, ma'am, but Mrs. Lydia and Mrs. Andrea have been practicing with me. They told me I needed to learn, so I've been learning. I hope this band plays something other than that rock and roll stuff. I can't dance to that."

"We'll see what we can do," Polly said. She knelt down beside Beryl, held out her camera, and said, "Would you mind taking pictures of Sarah and Rebecca tonight? I know you're a better photographer than I am and I know that you'll pay more attention than I will."

Beryl pulled Polly in for a hug. "You're a sweetheart. Of course I will. It will keep me from becoming a wallflower and you know how I hate sitting by myself when everyone else is having fun."

"We'd never leave you alone," Lydia said.

"You'd better. That man of yours should keep you on the dance floor all night - making up for those weeks and months he didn't hold you tight."

Aaron was standing behind Lydia's chair and bent over and kissed his wife on the head. She reached up and took the hand resting on her shoulder. "We'll find ways," she said.

"Enjoy your evening," Polly said. "I want to check on Rebecca's table, too."

Beryl followed and when Polly settled down between Rebecca and Sarah, said, "Look up and give me a smile, ladies," then took a picture. "I'm going to be all over the place tonight. You might want to make sure you smile all the time. She took pictures of everyone at the table. Kayla hammed it up with her sister and Beryl caught a wonderful picture of the two of them with Kayla kissing her sister's forehead.

"How are you feeling, Sarah?" Polly asked.

"I'm wonderful. Thank you for everything. This has been a good week." She was smiling and looked radiant, though Polly knew that was due to the Evelyn's use of makeup rather than her health. In truth, she was quite pale and thin. Rebecca had found a beautiful red and black dress for her mother and she'd borrowed a shawl from Lydia.

"I'm glad you're here. Let me know if you need anything."

"I have everything I need right here." Sarah reached out and squeezed her daughter's hand. "You've given me my heart's desire."

The band was moving to the stage and Jeff lowered the lights at the front of the auditorium.

"Excuse me, I'm going to find Henry," Polly said.

Rebecca ran after Polly and stopped her by taking her hand.

"What is it, honey?"

"Could Henry…" Rebecca looked down at her feet.

"Could Henry what?" Polly pressed.

"Could he ask my mom to dance tonight?"

"Are you sure she wants that?"

"Just for a minute. It's Valentine's Day. It doesn't have to be very long. Please?"

Polly wasn't at all sure what to do about those pleading eyes. She knew Henry would do whatever she asked of him, but didn't know how Sarah would react to it. "I'll ask him. But if she says no, you'll be okay with that, right?"

"She won't."

"You go on back and finish your dinner. I'll talk to Henry."

Rebecca hugged Polly tight. "Thank you for making this a perfect night for us."

Polly took a deep breath as Rebecca skipped back to her table. If this was what raising kids was like, she was going to be in trouble. How could she say ever no to that child? Rebecca didn't ask unreasonable favors, but she did make it nearly impossible to ever refuse her anything.

She stopped to say hello to several others on her way back to the table. Her friends were finished eating and opening cupcakes.

"Do you want something to drink?" Henry asked.

"No, I'm fine."

"Polly." His scolding wasn't too strong.

"Come on," she said, taking his hand. "Dance with me. Let's get this party started."

"But cake!"

She took his hand and tugged him out of the chair. "Cake can wait. Anyone else?"

Joss looked at her husband, eyes still filled with the excitement of a new home. "Please, honey?" she asked.

"As long as you don't expect me to dip you or spin you around or anything like that."

The three couples made their way to the dance floor and found that others followed them.

"When I was in high school, no one ever liked dancing unless they were a couple," Polly said.

Henry pulled her in tight to him. "It was the only time that we got to hold someone close. If we got those girls close enough, you know we could feel their..."

"You brat," she said. "Are you serious?"

"Come on, like you didn't know that."

"I'm so naive," she said with a laugh.

"We were just horny high school boys trying to figure out what came next."

"You knew what came next."

He tipped her face up to his. "I didn't know, Polly. I truly didn't know. Talk about naive. I was that boy."

"Thank heavens. I didn't like dances because I was so bad at it. It's a good thing Mark Ogden showed up when he did."

Henry coughed.

"What?" she asked innocently, dramatically batting her eyes at him.

"That was a bad weekend."

"Only because you were being a dope."

"It was still a bad weekend. I thought I was losing you to him and you didn't even know that I'd found you."

"Stop thinking about it. Look at me. I'm dancing with you and you can feel my breasts pressed up against you." Polly couldn't help herself and giggled. "That's just so weird."

The song came to an end and she said, "Would you ask Sarah Heater to dance tonight? Rebecca wants you to."

Henry glanced over at their table. "Sure. I can do that. Why?"

"I think Rebecca wants Sarah to have some good experiences. I want Rebecca to have the memories. You don't mind?"

"I'll do it now. That way if Sarah gets tired, she can go back to her room. Am I being the perfect husband?"

"You always are," Polly said. "Thank you."

She turned to see if there was anyone else in her vicinity that might want to dance with her and spied Doug Randall. She beckoned to him and he shook his head violently. She beckoned again and winked. He shook his head again. Polly finally walked over to him and bent down to whisper in his ear. "I'm going to embarrass you if you don't help me out here. Please?"

"But I don't like dancing."

"You'd better learn. Girls like it. Come on. It's easy." What was she doing offering to show him to dance? She'd come a long ways.

"You aren't going to let me get out of this, are you?"

"Nope. Come on. Do a girl a favor."

He heaved a sigh and stood up to follow her to the dance floor.

"Put your left hand here and give me your right hand," Polly said. "Now relax. You listen to music all the time. You can do this."

"You're mean."

"Why, yes I am. But see, you're fine." She moved with him and smiled when she saw that Rebecca had pulled Andrew out onto the dance floor. He shuffled along with her while she watched her mother and Henry glide along beside them. Beryl was taking pictures as fast as the camera would recharge.

Then the music stopped and everyone was turning to the corner of the room near the kitchen.

"Dude," Doug said quietly. "He's really doing it."

"What?" Polly asked.

Doug took her hand and pulled her with him, pointing to the action. "That."

Polly saw Doug's friend, Billy, down on one knee in front of Rachel. She was dressed in her chef's apron and hat, but her eyes sparkled with tears as he slipped the ring on her finger.

"Yes," she said and dropped down in front of him to kiss and hug him. "Yes, of course I will."

"It's going to change everything," Doug said.

"But for the better?" Polly asked.

"We'll see."

"I thought you liked Rachel."

"I do. I just hope he's ready for all this."

Kayla chose that moment to grab Polly's hand. "Polly, come quick."

"What's wrong?"

"Jessie needs you. She's in the hallway."

"Get Henry," Polly said to Doug and ran after Kayla. She found Jessie and Stephanie standing together. Jessie was bent over, breathing heavily.

"What happened?" Polly asked.

"My water broke. I think I'm going to have a baby. Right now."

Henry rushed into the hallway, took a look at Polly and Jessie and said, "Are we taking a ride tonight?"

Polly nodded. "We'll head for the truck. Would you go upstairs and get her go bag? And grab some clothes for me too? I've got a stack on the corner of my dresser just for this."

"I'll meet you in the garage."

"Let's go through the kitchen," Polly said. "You don't want to go back through the party."

"No," Jessie said, with wide eyes. "It was embarrassing enough that people around me saw it happen."

"Don't worry about them." Polly looked up and saw Doug standing in the doorway, his mouth open. "Doug?"

"Uh, yes?"

"Could you tell Jeff where I've gone and maybe let Joss and Sal and Lydia know too? And Evelyn. Rebecca knows she's staying downstairs until I get back."

He was still staring at them.

"Could you do that for me, please, Doug?"

He snapped out of his trance and said, "Sure. Joss and Rebecca."

"Sal and Lydia too. Thank you. Remember to tell Billy and Rachel congratulations for me."

He turned and headed back into the party.

"I think we freaked him out," Polly said. "Let's get going."

"Polly?" Jessie said, grabbing her hand.

"Yes, honey?"

"I'm scared out of my mind. I don't know if I can do this."

Polly gave an evil cackle. "It's a little late now. You have no choice. But don't worry. I'll be right there with you. We'll get through this and everything changes tomorrow. You'll see. It's going to be a blast."

ONE PERFECT HONEYMOON

ACKNOWLEDGMENTS

The photos on the cover were taken by my photographer husband, Maxim Muir in 2008.

Someone asked if I'd actually taken the trip that Polly and Henry made and the answer is yes. I'm not sure if I could have made up her responses to the sights they saw if I'd not experienced them.

Max wanted one chance at Route 66, a return to Monument Valley and Canyonlands in Utah, and I was desperate to see the Grand Canyon. We spent quite a bit more time in locations as he grabbed every opportunity he could with his cameras, but the route was similar.

You can find a copy of the blogs I wrote during the trip on my website – nammynools.com.

CHAPTER ONE

"Last one in's a rotten egg," Henry called out as he stowed the last bag behind the driver's seat.

"I'm hurrying, I'm hurrying!" Polly said.

"I'm a little surprised that we're this far into the trip. No tornados, no dead bodies, nobody falling apart."

"We haven't left the house yet," Polly deadpanned.

"I know, but I wasn't sure we'd even make it to this point."

She tossed a satchel onto the seat and climbed in his truck. "It wasn't my fault that the town tried to blow away the last time we planned a honeymoon."

"You're right, honey. Of course you're right. Now, are you sure you haven't forgotten anything?"

"If I have, in about fifteen minutes it will be too late to worry. Let's go."

Jessie ran out with a small tote bag. Polly opened her window. "What's up?"

"Sylvie nearly forgot to send this with you."

"What's in here?"

"Something fun for the trip. Have a good time and I'll keep an eye on the animals. I promise."

Polly patted the girl's hand. "I trust you. Thanks for everything."

"Are we ready now?" Henry asked.

Jessie stepped away and Polly rolled her window back up, then waved and said. "We're ready."

He backed out of the garage and Polly felt her heart lurch into her throat. All of a sudden it hit her that she was going to miss everyone, especially her animals. She'd asked Henry more than once about bringing Obiwan, but he finally convinced her the trip would be easier without worrying about a dog.

She swiped her phone open and flipped through pictures of the dog and her two upstairs cats, then smiled and put the phone away.

"They'll be here when you get back," Henry said. "I promise."

"I know. But I've never been away from them."

He put his hand on the console between them, palm up and Polly placed hers in it. "You'll be fine."

"Get me out of town and I'll be great."

The sun was setting in the west as they left town. Polly had spent a lot of time planning the trip and if they could get just south of Kansas City tonight, they would have all day tomorrow to travel Route 66. When they had originally planned to go, Nate and Joss Mikkels were going to join them and the men had looked forward to traveling the "Mother Road" in their classic cars. Two new babies in Nate and Joss's life changed those plans in a hurry. Without Nate along, Henry wasn't comfortable taking his T-Bird on an extended trip, so they were riding in the comfort of his truck.

"Should we stop in Boone for dinner?" he asked.

"You think that's safe? What if I panic and want to go back home?"

"Maybe starvation has affected my brain. Leaving after work without supper might have been a bad decision."

"Let's see what Sylvie packed." Polly opened the tote and chuckled.

"What?" he asked.

Polly drew out a stuffed donkey and put it on the dashboard. "It looks like I'm taking some of my animals with me anyway." She put her hand back into the bag and discovered a small plush black and white cat. "And one of the cats. This is going to be fun."

"Is there any food in there?"

"Sylvie's as bad as a grandmother," Polly said. "Of course there's food." She took out a container and peeked inside. "Sandwiches made with homemade bread."

"Thank goodness. I'm starving."

"No lunch today?"

"I kept working so we could get out of town tonight. Feed me, woman."

"Just a minute." Polly pulled her phone out and snapped a picture of the stuffed animals on the dashboard and posted it out to social media. "These animals will travel with us so everyone can see where we are."

"You're a weirdo, but I love you," Henry said. "Now really, you opened that container and I can smell the roast beef. Will you feed me or am I going to have to pull over and feed myself?"

She laughed. "Is that how it's going to be the entire trip?"

"Unless you keep me fed, it is. Stop teasing me!"

~~~

After they passed through Kansas City, Henry stopped to program his handheld GPS for the hotel. It was getting late and they were both tired. Polly protested a little about using the silly machine, but not much. All they wanted to do was stop for the night and get some sleep.

At about nine o'clock, the GPS told them to exit the interstate.

"This seems odd," Polly said.

"It does. But, let's see what happens."

When they left the main highway for a county road, neither of them were comfortable with the directions they were getting, but it insisted the hotel was just down the road a few more miles. When they passed through a little town and ended up on gravel, both of them were pretty sure the silly machine had sent them on a wild goose chase.

"I only see farms," Polly said. The GPS said the hotel was on the left in just a half mile. "If there's a hotel out here in the middle of nowhere, the people running it probably have axes and shotguns and we'll be dead meat by morning."

"Now you're just being silly." Henry chuckled and drove past the location. He flipped the machine at her when it told him that it was recalculating and he should make an immediate u-turn. "Do
~~~

you have the actual address?"

Polly swiped her phone open, found the address online and programmed it into the GPS. "We're really not where we should be," she said.

"I'm almost glad for that. I certainly hope this hotel is decent once we get there."

One thing Polly and Henry had decided to do on this trip was avoid major hotel chains and popular restaurants. She'd spent time researching strip motels along the route, looking for small places to stay. They finally pulled into a clean and freshly painted little hotel off the interstate. The man running the front counter came out from his apartment to check them in, his little boy running along behind him. The child looked up at Polly with a bright smile.

They got back in the truck and Polly looked across at Henry. "I didn't expect to find Muslims in the middle of nowhere Missouri. It seems like a long way from a mosque. I can't imagine not having a community around me."

"He wasn't Muslim."

"What do you mean? Sure he was."

"He's Sikh."

Polly turned in her seat to look at Henry. "How do you know this stuff?"

"I read and pay attention. It doesn't make any difference, except to them. But the turban is different for a Sikh. So is their religion."

She shook her head. "There are things about you I'm going to be uncovering for the rest of my life. You have layers and layers of stuff inside that pretty head."

"I'm an onion."

CHAPTER TWO

"Oh baby, are you ready for today?" Polly asked, poking Henry in the back.

He rolled over. "I think so. What's on the itinerary?"

"As long as you keep moving, we'll see everything."

"This is supposed to be a vacation," he moaned. "Relaxing. Where is the sunny beach and waves lapping at my feet as I take a nap?"

"You'd hate that. And you'd really hate it because I'd be constantly asking when we could leave and go see the sights."

Henry stretched, his hands bumping the headboard as he reached over her. He slid his arm under Polly's head and pulled her close. "You're right. I could never sit on a beach all day, but I was kind of hoping we could sleep in. There is absolutely no one around to bother us."

At that, Polly's phone buzzed and she started to laugh.

"It's seven thirty in the morning," he complained. "Who in the world is bothering us today?"

Polly extracted herself from his arms and sat up, then swiped her phone open. "It's a text from Aaron."

"Is everything okay?"

She put the phone back on the bedside table. "He just wanted me to know that there were no dead bodies and he was looking forward to a week of peace and quiet while I was out of town."

"You aren't going to let him get away with that, are you?"

"No, but I'm going to have to figure out how to stage a murder or something." Polly gave her husband an evil grin. "Tonight, we're going to need ketchup and one of your old t-shirts. You're going to die."

"I like it," he flipped back at her. "Text that to him about midnight and wake him up."

"Who's in the shower first?" she asked. "I'm ready to get going. There is so much to see today."

"I think you can wait just a little while longer," Henry said, pulling her back down to the bed. "And if we really have to make up the time, we'll take a shower together."

~~~

"We're coming to Carthage," Henry said, pointing at the road sign. "The Precious Moments Chapel is there. Is it on your itinerary?"

Polly grinned at him. "I know it should be. If Lydia were with us, she'd love to see it, but I have a million things I want to see today and they're all sillier than that. So ... no. Does that upset you?"

He laughed out loud. "No, I wouldn't say that it upsets me at all."

"But there's a really cool drive-in theater on the edge of town that we are going to stop and see. It's a classic Route 66 site."

"Is it open?"

Polly dropped her head. "No, it's closed for the season. But I really want a picture of it. Do you mind?"

"Oh honey, I love you. No visit to the Precious Moments Chapel, but instead, you want pictures of a closed up drive-in. Did I corrupt you by asking for a trip on Route 66?"
~~~

"Well, maybe. While I was researching and planning, I got caught up in the glory days of driving. There are so many cool things along the road to see."

They pulled into the drive-in and Henry took a deep breath. "Did you see that car?"

She turned around. "Oh, it kind of looks like Nate's."

"Good for you! That's right. It was a beauty. I should have gotten a picture."

Another couple of cars pulled in behind them and people got out to wander around the empty drive-in theater. Polly took the stuffed donkey and plush cat with her and posed them at the ticket window for pictures. The sun was shining. It was a beautiful day.

"Okay," she said. "I'm ready to get back on the road. There's plenty more to see."

"How long do we get to actually drive on Route 66?"

"Until you get tired of it," she said. "There are places along the route that we'll have to drive on Interstate 40, but we should be able to travel along a good portion of the original road.

They drove through Missouri into Kansas, and stopped in front of a beautifully restored gas station - Cars on the Route. Polly took a quick picture of a tow truck that had been dressed up to look just like Tow-Mater from the animated movie, "Cars." Then she remembered the donkey and cat and took a few with them posed on its hood. They went inside and found plenty of kitsch to buy and discovered that the tow truck outside had been the original inspiration for the character. Four women had purchased the old gas station and restored it. The original pumps weren't functional, but looked pretty cool outside after being re-painted. Across the street was an old home that everyone proudly told Polly and Henry had been owned by Ma Staffleback, a convicted murderer and madam.

Polly chuckled as she read through the information. Not everyone agreed with the claim, but at least the home had been restored and turned into a fun place for tourists. After seeing deterioration of great old buildings along the highway, she was glad to see a little life. Part of her wanted to rescue every abandoned gas station and diner out there.

They drove into Oklahoma and pulled into the world's largest McDonald's ... mostly for a potty break, but Polly figured that when in Rome, her tummy needed to be re-filled.

She guided Henry on down the highway and they pulled off in Foyil, Oklahoma, to see the world's largest concrete totem pole. The Indians from the area had nothing to do with it, but the park was filled with one man's totem sculptures, created in the forties and fifties.

The first time Henry looked at Polly like she was absolutely nuts was when they stopped in Catoosa to see the Blue Whale. "You really are taking me to exciting places today," he said.

"I thought I'd surprise you with a few of these, but isn't this fun? Can't you just imagine Route 66's heyday? Families driving up and down the highway. Vacations were a little slower and they enjoyed the trip as much as the destination. I figure that if we're going to see crazy stuff, we might as well do it right, don't you think?"

They wandered through the park toward the immense blue whale and walked into its open mouth, back to the tail.

"I wonder if people today know how much fun this is," she asked, snapping a picture of Henry posed at the mouth of the whale. "Mom and Dad used to talk about seeing crazy things by the highway when they traveled. We just don't take time any more. We're in such a hurry."

The blue whale was a huge concrete structure in a tiny pond with big slides into the water. Polly wondered out loud if people really did swim there in the summertime?

"I have no idea," Henry said. He backed her up against an inside wall, looked around surreptitiously and when he saw no one, kissed her soundly.

"What are you doing?" she asked.

"I'm thanking you for making this trip so much fun. I'd much rather be doing these crazy things with you than sitting on a beach somewhere. I truly never imagined I'd do anything like this.

You're amazing."

"We should probably keep moving if we're going to see everything today."

"I'd rather stay here and make out with you in the blue whale."

Polly kissed him again and pushed him back. "It's going to get dark. We should go."

He slumped, "You're no fun."

"I'll be fun later. I promise."

They got back on the road and watched the sun set as he drove further into Oklahoma.

"There!" Polly said. "Do you see it?"

"What in the world? It looks like a giant pop bottle."

"Isn't it cool that they're building new places along the highway? Pull off."

"I need gas anyway. Are you hungry?"

"I could eat. This place looks fantastic."

They pulled into Pops. Polly was glad they were there after dark. LED lights changed colors as they ran up and down the immense pop bottle and the building looked like an alien space ship.

Instead of pork tenderloins, Polly realized they were close enough to Texas that this was home to the chicken fried steak. There were six hundred choices of bottled soda pop and though she desperately wanted a Diet Dew, she stood in front of the soda selections and finally just shut her eyes and pointed.

"What are you doing?" Henry asked.

"I have no idea which one to try."

"I'm going to have a sarsaparilla. That seems safe."

"I'm having ..." She opened her eyes. "Capone Strawberry."

"Do you even like strawberry soda?"

Polly giggled. "It's one of my secret favorites. I never drink it, because I never remember."

They laughed through dinner and were back on the road by eight thirty.

~~~
~~~

"You haven't told me whether or not we're going," Henry said.

"If I go, I'm going to cry."

"What does that mean?"

She pointed to the exit sign and said, "You want to see it, don't you?"

"I'd really like to. I think we should."

"Then go."

He pulled off Route 66 and headed south into Oklahoma City. As they drove up to the entrance to the National Memorial, Polly felt her throat constrict. She read the words overhead and thought about the number of lives that were changed that day, and the way the country changed in 1995. Tears threatened and both of them were silent as Henry looked for a place to park. The museum was closed, but the grounds were open and quite a few people were walking, quietly talking to each other as they faced the grief they'd felt the day it happened.

Polly sat on a bench in front of the reflecting pool, trying to understand her own feelings. The immense gates at each end marked the time before and after that moment, the empty chairs on the other side of the pool signified lives that were lost.

"Are you okay?" Henry whispered as he sat down beside her.

"I knew this would be emotional, but I don't have words to describe my feelings. It's so peaceful here right now, but I remember watching the chaos unfold. All of that noise, the wailing, the crying, the screams, the fear. And with this, the healing continues. I can't imagine what this city has gone through to come to this point."

He wrapped his arm around her shoulder. "I love you, Polly Giller."

"I love you too." She leaned into him and they sat quietly, listening to the city buzz around the memorial.

CHAPTER THREE

"Vacationing with you is pretty awesome," Polly said. "I know I love you, but I wasn't sure about traveling together. This is fun."

Henry rubbed her forearm. "I'm having a good time, but I'll be honest. I wondered if we would get into the truck and not have anything to talk about."

"Like that would ever happen."

"I know, you always have something to say."

"Like this? Darn it," she said. "I forgot to send a picture of your murder to Aaron."

"It will keep. Maybe we can do that tonight. I was busy with other things last night."

That he still made her blush surprised her. "You're right. We have all week."

"What's up today?"

"Well, that depends on how much time you want to spend on the interstate and how much you actually want to drive on Route 66."

"The truck can take it. Let's see what we can see."

They headed west on a rather rough road. Henry just shook his head when Polly explained to him that it had been constructed in the early 1930s. They arrived at the National Route 66 Museum and she laughed out loud when she realized it was closed.

"Apparently we're heathens and everyone else in Oklahoma is in church this morning," she said.

"I didn't even think about that."

"It would be open if we were here in the summer - tourist hours and all." They wandered around the museum grounds. There was as much kitsch as Polly had seen anywhere along the road. Once back in the truck, she realized she was desperate for a rest stop. Just before they crossed into Texas, she pointed frantically at a sign for a rest area.

Polly went inside, looked around and took a breath. When she was finished, she ran for the truck and the bottle of antibacterial gel he kept in the glove compartment.

"Was yours as bad as mine?" he asked, climbing back into the truck. She handed him the bottle.

"The handicapped stall had a shower curtain instead of a door," she said with a shudder. "I'm ready to be back on the interstate."

~~~

Henry pulled at the exit for Shamrock, Texas. It had the feel of a perfect Route 66 location. They drove past the beautifully restored U-Drop Inn, but since it was Sunday, little was open until they found a local diner.

"Look. We fit in," Polly said, pointing at all of the pickup trucks in the parking lot.

"I'll bet there are a lot more cowboy hats in there than we see in Bellingwood," Henry remarked. The uncomfortable stares as every single person turned to look at the newcomers had Polly grasping his hand tightly. The hostess took her time seating them.

"I don't think I fit into Texas very well," Polly whispered at him across the table.

He chuckled. "We're just here for the food. Don't look 'em in the eye and no one will shoot you."
~~~

They both ordered baked steak, which came out covered with fried onions and mushrooms. The mashed potatoes were real, the French fries were homemade and there was so much food, Polly knew she wouldn't be able to finish. She was embarrassed when they both had to leave a great deal of their meal.

The rest of the afternoon was fun. Though there were plenty of boarded up buildings along the road which broke Polly's heart, she took pictures of the Leaning Tower of Texas and the Largest Cross in the Western Hemisphere. Upon arriving in Amarillo, the GPS failed them again and took them into the heart of the city as they looked for Cadillac Ranch, but a quick check on its coordinates and Polly directed them to the site. Old Cadillacs were buried nose first in the ground and people were encouraged to spray paint all over them.

They stopped at the midpoint marker for Route 66 and then late in the afternoon, just before leaving Texas, Polly pointed out the window.

"What?" Henry asked.

"The landscape. It's all changing. Look at the mesas."

"We really are seeing the country, aren't we?"

He drove on into Tucumcari and Polly guided him to one of the two hotels that she'd desperately wanted to sleep in after reading about the history of Route 66.

A delightful woman checked them into the Blue Swallow Motel, telling them all about its renovation. The rooms were fresh and clean and when Polly dropped onto the bed, she could smell that even the quilt had been freshly laundered. The toilet paper was folded into a triangle with the motel's logo embossed on it and there was even a small garage available for each room. Cars were smaller in the fifties and Henry didn't bother attempting to drive in.

Henry dropped onto a bed and said, "Can we relax tonight and do nothing?"

"You're ready to stop already?"

"I've been driving for the last two and a half days. Please?"

She chuckled. "I could have driven at any point, you know, but because I love you, I planned nothing for tonight. After dinner we can come back here to relax."

"Thank you. Maybe we can even murder me before we have some shenanigans."

"Shenanigans? That sweet old lady won't know what to think."

"That sweet old lady will be going home to her own house. She doesn't need to know what we're doing over here."

Polly pushed him back on the bed and crawled on top of him, straddling his waist. "Doing something like this?" She bent over to kiss him.

"It's a start," he said and flipped her on to her back.

"Apparently, you aren't *too* tired."

Henry bent over and kissed her until she pushed him off. "What are you doing?" he asked.

"I can't. Not on top of these quilts. Look at them."

"Woman, you are going to be the death of me. You have to be kidding."

"Put your face into that quilt and take a whiff. Does that smell like something that has been on the bed for months? No. She just washed that and I'm not going to be the one who dirties it. Ewww. I don't want to drive away from here tomorrow and have her thinking about us getting frisky on her bedding."

"But... the sheets?"

"Tonight. Maybe in the sheets. But not on top. Now, help me get the rest of the things inside and we'll go out and look for dinner."

Henry only whimpered a little before helping Polly bring in their things. He emptied wrappers and pop bottles and cleaned the front of the cab before they took off again.

After dinner, he drove back to the hotel and parked in front of their garage. For a mid-October evening the temperatures were warm and beautiful.

"Let's take a short walk," she said. "I want to stretch my legs."

Henry took her hand and they walked along the highway. All of a sudden Polly stopped. "Do you hear that?"

He stopped and listened. "What do you think it is?"

"It's over here, behind this Chinese place. It sounds like whimpering."

"We shouldn't get involved, Polly. Who knows what you'll find. And please don't let it be a dead body. We don't have friends down here."

"Whatever it is, it's alive," she said. "I have to check."

He followed her and when the streetlight no longer illuminated her path, he turned his phone's flashlight app on. He sighed when Polly knelt down at a box beside a dumpster. "What did you find?"

"Come over here," she said, looking up at him with tears glistening in her eyes. "You won't believe this."

Inside the large box was a nursing mama dog and four puppies.

"Someone just left her here."

"This is a busy place. Surely the owners know about her."

"If they do and they're just leaving her out here, that's awful. I'm going inside to check. You stay here with them."

"I'm coming with you and don't argue. The dogs have been fine until now. They'll wait a few more minutes."

Polly stood up and spun on him. "They'd better be."

She strode around to the front of the restaurant and went inside. When the hostess tried to seat them, Polly asked to see the manager. Soon, an older Chinese woman stood in front of them, hands on her hips.

"What's the problem?" the woman asked.

"There's a box with dogs back beside your dumpster. Do you know about that?" Polly asked.

"No dogs allowed. Nobody here has dogs."

"So if I take them away, they aren't someone's pets?"

"No dogs. I don't allow dogs."

"They don't belong to someone in your kitchen? Shouldn't we ask?"

"Not in my kitchen. No dogs. You take dogs away. Find them homes. Nobody here knows about dogs."

Polly looked up at Henry. "Okay. You heard her. We're taking the dogs."

They went back outside and around to the dumpster. When they got there, a young boy in a white apron came out from the kitchen door. "Are taking those? They've been here for a few days and I've been feeding the mother. I don't know what else to do."

"Surely there's an animal rescue in town, isn't there?" Polly asked.

He didn't say anything.

"Did you call anyone?"

"They're just dogs."

"But you fed her."

"Mom won't let me do anything more. Will you take them?"

Polly turned to Henry. "Will it upset you if I take her with us tonight?"

He grinned. "My life wouldn't be worth much if I was. You stay here and get to know the mother. I'll be back with the truck."

"Thank you." She kissed his cheek and turned back to the kid. "Do you know where they came from?"

"They just showed up the other night. I think someone dumped them."

"Tell your mom that they're gone. We'll take care of them now."

He nodded and went back inside, the light from the doorway shining into the alley until the door finally closed. Polly knelt down and let the dog sniff her hand, then gently rubbed the mother's head and back down her neck, checking to make sure there was no collar. "You're safe now, girl. We'll make sure you and your puppies are okay."

Henry pulled in to the parking lot and then he and Polly lifted the box into the back seat of the truck. The dog seemed to breathe a sigh of relief when she realized someone else was there to help.

"We need to get her some food," Polly said. "Something other than leftovers."

"Dog food it is," he said. "There has to be a supermarket around here somewhere."

"And a bowl for water and something to make her comfortable."

"How about we deal with the food and water tonight and then comfort tomorrow."

"Would you mind if we found a vet tomorrow too? She and the puppies need to be looked at. If she's chipped and belongs to someone, we should know that, too."

"So, we're taking these animals with us on the rest of the trip?"

"I don't know. I haven't thought that far out yet."

"Okay. I was just checking."

"What if I had said yes to your question?"

He started to laugh. "Polly, if you were anyone else, I would tell you that I couldn't believe this. But you are you. If you aren't finding dead bodies, you are rescuing someone. I suspect you are already thinking about who will be getting the puppies from this litter, aren't you."

"Shut up," she said. "And drive. I'm calling Mark."

"Call him in the morning. It's an hour later in Bellingwood. He's probably in bed."

"Do you know how much I love you?" she asked.

"Because I'm a sucker for your rescues?"

"Because you don't say no to me and you help me take care of the world."

"I love you too." Henry put his hand out on the console, palm up, waiting for Polly to grasp it. "I love you because you want to take care of the world."

CHAPTER FOUR

Every bump they hit made Polly cringe for the mama dog. She didn't look healthy and Polly wanted to clean her up and find a more comfortable container for her and the puppies. Henry parked in front of a large department store and Polly ran in to purchase supplies while he stayed with the dogs. While she was in the check-out lane, her phone buzzed with a text.

"I need you right now, there's something wrong with the mother dog."

Polly looked at the things in her cart and at the girl running the counter. "My husband is in our car outside and there's an emergency with our dog. He just texted me. I'll be right back. Can I leave this here?"

The surprised clerk began to hem and haw.

"Fine," Polly said, pushing the cart to the side. "You deal with it. If it's still here when I come back in, I'll pay for it, but if it's not, I'll want to speak with a manager." She ran out the front door to the truck to find the back door was open and Henry hunched over the box.

"What happened?" she asked.

"All of a sudden she started gasping for air. Polly, I think she died."

Polly ripped the side of the box down and put her hand on the back of the mother dog. Tears filled her eyes. "The poor thing," she said through her sobs. "It's like she waited for us. But what are we going to do with these puppies? Do you suppose there is anything in there that will feed them?"

"What are we going to do with her?" Henry asked, ever the practical man.

"We'll deal with that later. I have four puppies that need to be fed. I'm calling Mark and I don't care what time it is."

He sat back down on the seat and nodded, then dropped his head in his hands.

Polly dialed Mark Ogden's number in Bellingwood and was only slightly surprised when her friend, Sal Kahane, answered.

"Hey Polly, what's up?"

"Is Mark there? I need to talk to him."

"Is something wrong with your animals?"

"No, I'm in New Mexico and I have a dead mother dog in the back seat of my truck and four little puppies. I need to ask him what to do. Is he already asleep?"

"He's actually in the shower. He just got home." She gave a nervous giggle. "I wouldn't normally answer his phone, but I saw it was you. What happened?"

Polly explained what they'd been through and she knew her friend couldn't wait to tell everyone about Polly's escapades on her honeymoon.

"I know, I know," Polly said. "I can't help myself. But I need to deal with all of this tonight."

"The shower stopped. Let me get him for you."

Polly heard Sal and Mark talking in the background as her friend walked to the bathroom.

"Sal told me what's going on. How old do you think the pups are?" he asked after mild pleasantries.

"I have no idea. I was going to find a vet tomorrow and go from there."

"Can you send a picture to me?"

"Just a sec," Polly said. "Henry, can you take a picture of the pups and send it to Mark so he can see them? He thinks he can tell us about how old they are."

She said back to Mark. "Why do I want to know how old they are?"

"It tells me if you will be feeding them every few hours."

"I think they're older than that. Their eyes are all open and they are pretty alert and squirmy."

"Done," Henry said. "Tell him to check."

"Let me take a look and call you right back," Mark said and hung up.

Polly picked up one of the tiny puppies, who was trying to nurse again from its mother. "You poor little thing. What are we going to do with you?" She pulled it close and held it in her arms.

"They're probably flea ridden," Henry said with a voice of warning.

"I don't care. These little things are going to need a lot of love tonight."

"I'm not going to get any, am I?" he grumped. "I thought this was supposed to be our honeymoon."

"You poor, deprived man, you," Polly said. "I'm standing in the middle of a parking lot with a box full of puppies and you're worrying about not getting enough nookie?"

"Well, not really, but it does make for a good story."

Polly's phone rang and she handed the puppy into the truck to Henry. "Hey, Mark. What do you think?"

"I can't tell for certain, but those puppies are probably around three or four weeks old. They're going to need a lot of care, but at least you won't be up every couple of hours. Are you leaving them in New Mexico?"

"What do you think?" she asked. He should know better.

"I was afraid of that. You're a crazy woman, Polly Giller and I feel sorry for your husband. Pick up a windup ticking clock and some warm blankets. Maybe even a heating pad or hot water bottle. You'll need a milk replacer and some bottles. Get a big tub and line it with piddle sheets. Then talk to a vet tomorrow to make sure they're healthy. I'm sorry you have to deal with the mother tonight."

"Okay, thanks for talking to me. I'm sorry to have bothered you."

"No problem. Let me know how this all turns out and call if you need more information."

"Give Sal a hug for me."

Polly hung up. "I'm going back in to finish shopping. Will you be okay out here?"

"Pick up some garbage bags." He heaved a deep breath. "I'll deal with her when you come back."

"I'm sorry, Henry," Polly said. She gently shut the truck door and went back into the store. Her cart was still where she left it and she nodded to the girl at the counter, then went back into the depths of the store to search for milk replacer. When she had everything the pups might possibly need, she went back to the front and checked out.

"I'm sorry I was so abrupt," she said to the girl.

"No problem. Was everything okay?"

Polly shook her head. "No. My husband and I are from out of town and we picked up a dog and her puppies that had been dumped. The dog died a few minutes ago and it looks like I'm taking care of orphaned puppies tonight."

"That's awful!" the girl said.

"I'm sorry," Polly said again. "I shouldn't have put that on you. I'm just trying to process it."

"No problem."

They finished the transaction and Polly pushed the cart out to the truck. She unpacked things and ripped open packages in the parking lot and began creating a new bed for the puppies.

As soon as she had created a nest, she and Henry placed the pups in it and he pulled the box of garbage bags out of a sack.

"Wait," Polly said and opened another towel. "Rub this all over the mother so it has her scent. I don't know if that will help, but it can't hurt. At least for tonight."

He was in the process of doing just that when a man came jogging across the lot to them.

"Are you the folks that have puppies and a dead mother dog?" he asked.

Henry turned around, handed the towel to Polly and put his hand out. "Henry Sturtz. What can I do for you?"

"Let me help you," the man said. "I'm the manager here and Amy said you were from out of town. I'd offer to take the puppies, but I don't know what I would do with them either. However, I can help you with the dog. We've got a shovel and some land out back. We'll just bury her here, if you'd like."

Polly had placed the last puppy in the tub and stood up. "Really? That's wonderful."

"And tomorrow morning, you call the doc and tell her I gave you her number." He handed Polly a piece of paper with a name and phone number on it. "We're friends and she's real good about getting emergencies in."

"Thank you so much for your help," Polly said. "What's your name?"

"David. David Han."

"Let me help you take this around back," Henry said, his hand on the box. They removed the box from the truck and Polly put her hand in the towel and then knelt back down to the tub.

When the puppy with brown eyebrows nudged her hand, she whispered. "Your name is Han. I don't have names for the rest of you yet, but that man showed up just when we needed him. I'm not sure what Henry was going to do with your mama, but it was going to break his heart if he had to take care of it by himself tonight. I haven't told him yet that at least one of you will be living with us when you all grow up. And little Han Solo, I think it's you."

He pushed his face into her hand. "I know, I know. You're probably hungry, but you have to wait until we get back to the hotel. I promise, though, we'll fill your tummies tonight."

Henry and David Han came back to the truck. "I wish you the best," David said. "Where do you go next?"

Polly smiled up at him. "We were planning to be in Holbrook, Arizona tomorrow night."

"Sleeping in a wigwam?" he asked, grinning.

"I hope so."

"Thank you for your help tonight." Henry put his hand out and the other man took it. "You've made this evening much easier."

"I'm glad I was here. Call Jennie first thing in the morning and hopefully she can get you on the road. Take care of the little ones." He knelt down and touched the head of one of the pups. "I wish I could do more."

"Thank you," Polly said. "You've done so much." She put her hand on his forearm. "Really. You've helped enormously."

He walked more slowly across the lot and turned back to wave before re-entering the store.

Henry put the bags into the back of the truck and then helped Polly lift the tub into the back seat. "We're really doing this, aren't we?" he asked.

"I think so. She reached in and touched little Han. "I've already named this one. I thought the manager's last name was appropriate. Han Solo?"

"We have another dog coming into the house. I knew it. I just knew it. That king sized bed of ours isn't going to be big enough for all of us, you know."

"We'll just have to sleep extra close together," Polly said and tilted her head up for a kiss.

CHAPTER FIVE

"Are you awake?" Henry asked quietly. She struggled to open her eyes. "Polly, wake up," he said, more loudly. "It's nearly eight o'clock and you said you wanted to call first thing."

She sat straight up and blinked a couple of times. "Thanks."

"You didn't get much sleep last night, did you?"

"Not really. I was so worried about these little guys. How do you explain to a four week old puppy that its mama died?"

Henry bent over and kissed her head. "I love you. Why don't you make the call while I take my shower?"

Polly stretched, rolling her head around on her neck and looked down at the tub full of puppies. She'd spent time reading online and worrying about a million things. Had they learned how to go to the bathroom yet on their own, how bad were their fleas, how hard would it be to wean them? The bathroom question was answered about midnight. The smell coming from the tub was horrible. She cleaned it up and replaced the sheets, then did so again a couple of times through the night. Puppies needed to learn to go to the bathroom outside real soon. She and Henry were also going to have to find a laundromat today.

As soon as eight o'clock rolled around, she dialed the number David Han had given her, smiling again at his name. He had no idea.

"Good morning. Doctor's office," a bright voice said on the other end.

"Hi, my name is Polly Giller and I am wondering if there is any way you could fit me in for an emergency visit today. I have four puppies whose mother died last night and ..."

"Oh, Miss Giller, this is Doctor Jennie. David texted me late last night and told me all about you. Of course I can see you. What time would be good?"

Polly breathed a sigh of relief. Small towns existed everywhere. "Do you have any time around nine o'clock? I'd like to make sure they're doing okay as soon as possible."

"Sure, come on in."

The puppies were still asleep when Henry came out of the shower. "Do I need to know anything?" he asked.

"No, they'll be fine and I won't take long. We have an appointment at nine o'clock."

Henry's eyes lit up. "Do you think we'll actually be able to get on the road and see some sights? I had kind of given up on today."

Polly hugged him, stopping for a moment to enjoy the scent of his clean body. "You smell good," she said.

"Any other morning and we'd have to plan for breakfast at noon. But now we have to deal with puppies."

"You aren't going to be bad about this, are you?"

He gave her a gentle shove to the bathroom. "I'm going to tease you about it, but I promise, I'm not upset. Now go, get cleaned up. I'll pack the truck."

~~~

"Well, we're puppy owners," Polly said. She and Henry sat in the truck outside a laundromat waiting for blankets and towels to dry.

"It wasn't as bad as I anticipated."
~~~

"What do you mean?"

"I don't know what I was expecting, but that wasn't horribly expensive. As long as the doctor says they're healthy, I'm fine."

"I'm just glad she let us bathe them there."

Henry pointed at the front door. "Can't you just see us using a bathroom sink in the laundromat to wash these poor things?" He reached around to the back seat and scooped a freshly cleaned puppy into his arms. "They smell much better now, too."

"I think we should name that one Khan. He looks like he's going to need a little extra help growing up. The others are already bullying him a little."

"And the tan little girl?"

"Padme for now. I'll let Sylvie choose for sure."

"Ahhh, I knew it!"

Polly poked him in the side. "Stop it."

"Who is Khan going to live with?"

"I think that both he and Kirk would be great out at Eliseo's house, don't you?"

Henry turned to look at her, stroking the puppy's head. The dog had fallen asleep in the crook of his elbow. "Khan and Kirk? Don't they fight to the death in the movie?"

Polly shrugged and grinned. "Maybe."

Henry handed Khan to Polly and got up on his knees to look into the tub of puppies. In a moment, he came back out with little Han. "If you're coming to live at our house, you're going to be my dog. There won't be any of this 'mommy this and mommy that' stuff. If I have to take you to work with me, you're going to be okay with that. Got it?"

"Your dog?" Polly asked.

"Like I didn't know that one of these was coming to live with us. I just needed you to tell me which one had gotten the Star Wars name."

She leaned over the console to kiss his cheek and he lifted the puppy up between him, so she caught the puppy's side with her lips. "What the..." she said.

"I seem to remember a kiss being interrupted by a slobbery

Obiwan one night. Turn about and all that."

Polly pressed his arm down and bent in again to kiss him. This time he turned to kiss her with his lips. "I love you, Henry Sturtz," she said. "I can't believe how lucky I am to have you in my life."

Henry pointed at the clock. "Things should be dry now. I'll be right back."

"No, I'll go." She handed Khan back to him and smiled at the man holding two small puppies. "Just don't leave without me."

"Not with these babies in the truck. I refuse to be the sole person responsible for their upbringing."

Polly ran inside and quickly folded blankets and towels, as well as the few items of clothing they'd used, and dropped things in a second basket she'd purchased after leaving the veterinarian's office. The blankets were still warm, so when she got back to the truck, she wrapped the last two puppies up and put them on the floor of the backseat while she cleaned out the tub.

"We're going to have to do a lot laundry on this trip," she said.

Henry nodded and waited until she got everything situated in the back seat and then handed the two sleeping puppies back to her. She arranged them and waited for the four to snuggle together, thankful that they still wanted to sleep a lot at this age. The vet had confirmed that they were between three and four weeks old and more than ready to be weaned. Polly had purchased enough milk replacement and some wet food to start the process, still not quite believing that this was actually happening on her honeymoon.

"Well, shall we get back on the road?" she asked.

"What's next?"

"I'd thought about driving up to Santa Fe to do some shopping, but that seems ridiculous. We won't have time to do that and get back down to Holbrook. As it is we have a six hour drive."

"No shopping?" Henry's voice perked up. "I can live with that. As many times as you want to avoid shopping, I'm all for it."

"Let's get something to eat and leave town. I'm starving."

~~~
~~~

"Honey, I need some help."

Polly had been dreaming and it took a few moments for her to place where she was. "What's wrong?" she asked. "You let me fall asleep." She stretched her shoulders. She'd been in that position far too long.

"You were exhausted, but I think the puppies need attention and I'm in traffic. Anyway, you want to see this."

She looked around and gasped. Immense red cliffs had replaced the yellow mesas. "Wow," she breathed. "This is amazing."

The puppies were whimpering and yipping in the back seat so Polly took her seatbelt off and turned around to look at them. They were nipping at each other and fussing.

"They're probably hungry. Do you know how far until a rest area?"

"About ten miles. Do you want to go into the Petrified Forest tonight?"

Polly looked down at the puppies and then back at the road. She sat down and pulled her belt back on. "Okay. I'm going to sound horrible, but can we skip it? I'm absolutely exhausted and all I can think about is crawling into bed."

He reached out and took her hand. "I avoided a shopping trip today. I'll give you this. We can come back another time."

"Thank you," Polly said and breathed deeply. "The air is getting a little thin, don't you think?"

"It's definitely different than Iowa."

He drove into the rest area and Polly smiled. Everything was done in pale yellows, pinks, teals and greens. Southwestern colors filled her eyes as far as she could see. From the mesas and cliffs to the rest area, it all matched.

The puppies hadn't taken long at all to figure out how to latch on to the bottles earlier in the day and when little Khan saw Polly fill one, his little bottom started to wiggle.

"Can you believe the resilience of these animals?" she said. "Their mama died last night and here they are, letting us care for them." She handed the puppy and bottle to Henry, then filled the other three bottles.

"We could learn things from these puppies. It would be nice to not have my emotions tied up in everything I do, to accept the good when it comes and wag my tail."

"I like it when you wag your tail," she teased.

"You're a bad girl."

"You got that right, cowboy."

"We're sleeping in a wigwam tonight. I doubt that many cowboys did that."

"Then you're my brave and I'm your ..."

"You're not my squaw."

"Nope. Not even close."

Polly had settled into the back seat, trying to keep the bottles in three puppy's mouths. Little Padme wasn't terribly interested, so she picked the last two boys up and held them in her arms. "You kids are all going to be good little puppies tonight and let me sleep, right?"

"Should we put a blanket over the top of the tub so we can have a little fun?" Henry asked, turning around to wink at her.

She held the pups closer to her chest. "Hush you. There are children in the truck."

"Yeah. I was afraid of that."

The two little boys fell asleep in her arms and Polly wriggled around to put them on a blanket. She handed Padme to Henry and emptied the piddle sheets from the bottom of the tub, wiped it out and re-lined it.

"You're a good puppy mama," Henry said. "These little ones are lucky you found them."

"You aren't so bad yourself. Thank you for helping me with this."

"Honey, you're doing all the work."

"They're going to be worth it. I promise."

Henry shook his head and handed Khan back to her. "I love you."

"I know."

CHAPTER SIX

"No," she moaned as she woke early the next morning to sounds of yipping and whimpering.

"I think they're hungry," Henry muttered.

"Yeah, yeah, yeah. I know. Are you helping or am I doing this alone?"

He growled.

She chuckled to herself as she threw the coverlet back and sat up. The pups were right beside her and enough light was coming in through the window that they scrabbled toward her when they realized she was mobile.

"I know, I know," she whispered. "Give me a minute to get this all put together."

Polly knew she was lucky that they'd slept through most of the night. She quickly mixed food into bottles, then went back into the main room and sat down on the bed beside Henry. She elbowed him in the side. "Hey," she said. "I need you."

"You're a tyrant."

"Not my fault. The kids have needs."

Henry rolled over and faced her. "What about my needs?"

"You're a needy, needy man. I thought we met your needs quite nicely last night."

He gave her a silly grin. "Who gets to make out in a teepee nowadays?"

"Uh huh." Polly bent over and picked up two puppies, then tucked them in close to Henry.

He sat up. "I can't do this lying down." The puppies had been up on the bed the night before playing with each other and luxuriating in the soft blankets. Before they settled in for breakfast, they scurried around, rolling and nuzzling each other.

Polly put the other two down and scooped up one who was ready to take a dive off the edge. "You stay here. You're hungry, remember?"

Soon each of the pups was nursing down breakfast. When they looked to be contented, she cleaned the tote out. "I can't wait for them to be on a regular diet and house trained. I'm not fond of all this needy stuff."

"Hey," Henry protested.

"Whatever. At least you can feed and clean yourself."

They spent time nuzzling and loving the puppies on the bed and soon Polly leaned against Henry. "This is really kind of fun," she said. "Look at our little ones running around."

"You're a nut." He nuzzled her hair. "What are we doing today?"

"If all goes as planned, we'll be at the Grand Canyon this afternoon. I'd like to stop and buy some collars. Maybe we can start introducing that to these little guys. It would be nice to let them play in the grass ..." she stopped and hesitated. "There's not much grass here, I guess."

"If we have a big day, I suppose we should get moving."

"Just a few more minutes?" she asked.

Henry scooped up a pup and set it between them, then leaned back again. "Okay, a few more minutes."

~~~
~~~

Polly snapped pictures of the oversized concrete wigwams as they drove away. There were several classic cars strategically parked throughout the lot, drawing tourists back to the fifties and sixties.

"First stop is an old Route 66 classic," Polly announced. "The Jack Rabbit Trading Post."

"Shopping?" Henry asked, sounding quite chagrined.

"Oh come on. This is silly touristy stuff. Don't you remember doing this when you were a kid?"

"We didn't really travel all that much," he said.

"I have to get souvenirs for everyone." She turned to him. "So did you ever go to the Grotto of the Redemption in West Bend?"

He shook his head.

"How have you missed this? I'm taking you!" Polly was astounded. It was only a couple of hours from Bellingwood. "And what about Rapid City and the Badlands?"

"I'm telling you, Mom didn't like to travel."

"Wow. We have some things to do."

"I thought you didn't like to travel."

"Well, now that you have me out of the house, I'm having a great time." She giggled. "Going to Wall Drug was awesome. All of those silly souvenir trinkets. I really have to get some for everyone."

Henry pointed at a sign on the highway. "That's really sad," he said.

"There are a lot of those down here."

"It's still sad. I can't imagine how bad it must be for them to post a phone number to call if you see a drunk driver."

He pulled off when they saw the immense concrete rabbit, not that there hadn't been signs alerting them to the trading post all along the way.

"Here it is!" the sign announced.

"I think we're here. Do you want to go in while I sit with the pups?" he asked.

"They'll be fine alone if you want to stretch your legs. I'm going in and do some quick shopping. I can't miss this."

He nodded and leaned his seat back and then put a hand into the tub with the pups.

"I knew it," Polly said. "You're falling for them, aren't you?"

"Go shopping. Get me a t-shirt." he muttered.

She laughed and jumped out of the truck and ran inside, grinning when she saw the counters and shelves filled with souvenirs. This was the best part about traveling. Buying junk that you'd never buy anytime else.

As she stood at the counter, waiting to be checked out, she listened as the owner quietly and politely reminded a young man that the bottle of Jack Daniels she was selling him was the only bottle he could buy today. Oh my goodness, there was a serious problem down here.

Polly walked back to the truck a little more subdued and climbed in. "Do you want to go inside and see the place?" she asked.

"What's wrong?"

"Oh, I'm just a little shook up. See that kid there? He bought a bottle of Jack and was told it was the only one he could buy today. Henry, it's only nine fifteen in the morning."

"I know sweetie. It's a different life for some people."

"But there were even signs hanging over the liquor display and at the front counter."

"No judgment. Right?"

"I know, but it still breaks my heart."

"We're not rescuing anyone else on this trip. Got it?"

She smiled at him. "You should go inside and just see the place. I'm not going to make you spend any money there."

Henry sighed at her and got out of the truck. He was gone for several minutes and then came back with a small bag in his hand.

"What did you get?" she asked, when he was belted in the truck.

"Nothing."

"Come on."

"Nope. Not telling."

"Meanie."

"That's me. Now, where next?"

"Get back on the interstate. We're heading to Winslow."

"Is there a corner there?" he asked, laughing.

"As a matter of fact. And you're going to stand on it. Right next to the flatbed Ford."

"There's no end to what people will do to bring in tourists."

"It makes sense. We're going to be two of those tourists today."

Before the morning was out, they were parked and Polly was shooting pictures of Henry next to a flatbed Ford truck on a corner in Winslow, Arizona. They wandered in and out of several of the shops dedicated to Eagles memorabilia on their way out of town, and Polly pointed to the Southwest Indian Art Center.

"Please?" she asked.

"You have been really good on this trip so far," he said.

"I don't want to miss *all* of the potential shopping opportunities."

He pulled off the interstate and they were the only vehicle in the parking lot. Polly turned around and the pups were sleeping again. "I think they'll be fine for a few minutes by themselves. I promise it won't take long."

The weather was beautiful, so Henry cracked the windows and followed her inside. The owner greeted them and before she could look at the beautiful rugs on the walls or pottery on shelves, he took them through a verbal history of his family in the southwest, from Navajo chiefs and princesses to traders and finally his own life. When they broke away, Polly gave Henry a look.

"I'm sorry," she whispered. "But it is really cool stuff."

He put his hand on a rug, running his fingers over the weaving. "Do you want to buy some pieces?"

"Yes, I'm spending money here. Get some nice things for everyone." She stroked a small painted bowl. "Lydia would love this."

"How about I take care of the animals. I'll give them a little freedom in the truck and let them run around. I might even clean up the tub. If you need help carrying your purchases, come get me."

Polly reached up to kiss him and he turned so that she would catch his lips. "I love you," she said. "You're awfully good to me."

"You'll pay me back. Trust me."

He slipped his fingers through hers and then trailed away as he left the shop. Before Polly knew what she'd done, the owner was packing pots and vases into boxes and she needed Henry to help her carry things out and pack them into the back of the truck. She got into the front seat and found Han sitting on the console.

"What are you doing up here?" she asked. Han licked her hand when she picked him up and held him to her chest. A small peep and she saw Padme crawl out from under Henry's seat, so Polly leaned over and picked her up, too. "Is he wearing you out for the next part of the trip?"

Henry gingerly opened his front door and said, "Have you seen the other two?"

"You were supposed to be babysitting."

He climbed in and pulled the door shut and leaned up to look in the back seat. "Uhhh, they found the dry dog food."

"They what? They're eating it?"

"Khan and Kirk are giving it their best shot. It's all over the floor behind your seat. Good heavens, they're like little kids. I should have known."

"Well, put these two down and see what they do."

Padme wanted nothing to do with it, but Han sniffed around at the food and promptly sat down right on top of it.

"Well, that should cause some excitement in a little bit," Polly laughed.

"Like we haven't had plenty already? Where are we going next?"

"Not very far. There's a meteor hole down the road."

"This tourist stuff is fun. I guess I knew that America had lots of things to see, but traveling like this, with you, is pretty wonderful."

Henry drove into the parking lot and ran up to find out about tickets. In moments, he was back.

"It's eighteen dollars to walk up to the top of those steps and look at the crater. Are you ready for that?"

Polly looked at him sideways. "A meteor crashed into Arizona and they want to charge me money to walk up a million steps so I can look at a hole in the ground?"

"What if I look at the hole and take pictures and you stay here with the puppies?"

She giggled. "I get to shop and you get to do oddball sight-seeing?"

"Seems like a fair trade-off. I think it's pretty cool. How many times will I get a chance to see where something from outer space crashed into earth?"

"I guess you're the boy who wanted to be an astronaut. You go. We'll play out here. I'll probably be cleaning up after the pups again anyway."

When Henry returned, Polly had gotten the puppies settled back into the tub and was resting her eyes.

"Okay, I had to stop in the visitor's center and buy a t-shirt," he said.

"That's all?"

"I just had to have a t-shirt. I didn't want anything else."

"You're useless."

"Did you want a t-shirt? I should have gotten one for you."

"No, that's not it. You just don't seem to get the true spirit of souvenir gift shops."

"I'll try to do better."

CHAPTER SEVEN

During the trip north toward the Grand Canyon, Polly found herself transfixed by the vistas.

"Look at that," she gasped and pointed.

"I see it. What do you suppose it is?"

She rolled down the window and shot a few pictures with her phone. "We aren't there yet, but wow."

A few minutes later, she announced, "Well, we missed it."

"What?"

"The scenic overlook. That was the Little Colorado River Gorge."

"Do you want me to turn around and go back?"

"No, that's fine. Just keep going. We're getting so close I can hardly stand it."

Henry put his hand on the console and Polly absentmindedly took it in hers. They drove and drove and then Polly heard Henry audibly take a breath. He pulled into a parking spot at a lookout point. She looked up and began to sob.

"Are you okay, honey?" he asked.

"Look at that."

He parked the truck and she sat there, looking at the grand vista in front of her, tears flowing freely. Though she'd seen plenty of pictures, nothing could compare to the reality.

"Are you going to be okay?" Henry asked.

"I'm fine. You go on ahead. I'll be right there."

"I can wait."

"No really. Just give me a few moments alone."

He glanced at her again, took the camera, and left of the truck. Polly gathered her emotions and popped the visor down to look at herself in the mirror. Great. Splotchy, red face and bright red-rimmed eyes. She wasn't prepared to share her emotions with all of the people, so she put her sunglasses on. One last look at the puppies and she wandered to where Henry was standing.

He put his arm around her as they stood together, looking out over the grand vista. "Can you imagine what the first people who came across this must have thought?" he asked.

"It's bigger than I could have ever dreamed," she breathed out.

"Makes you realize how small we are."

"All of this," she swept her arm out. "I can barely form words."

"Majestic," he whispered.

"That's it," she said softly. "I will never see anything so awe-inspiring again in my lifetime."

He looked at her.

"I know, I know. I'll see more amazing things in my life, but this moment, right now, takes my breath away."

"How long do you want to stay?"

"I don't care. Do you think we'll find other places to stop?"

"I suspect so. It's pretty big." He grinned at her.

"There are a lot of people here. Let's move on."

They stopped at overlooks throughout the park. Polly began watching people. Buddhist monks at one stop, she heard people speaking German and French, and families from India and various other Asian countries. She could tell who was seeing the sight for the first time. They stood in silence, taking it all in and as they walked back to their vehicles, they would begin talking again.

It took four or five stops before tears stopped filling Polly's eyes when she saw the vista open up in front of her. She wasn't sure how she could ever process the details of the canyon with such an overwhelming vista everywhere she looked.

Henry finally pointed at the clock in the truck. "We've been here for about three hours," he said. "What if we check into the hotel and find supper. We can come back and watch the sunset."

"I'll probably cry again," Polly said.

"I'm counting on it. How are the kiddos doing in the back seat?"

She unbuckled and turned around to check on them. They were finally becoming unique to her and she knew who was who. Their little personalities were growing and it occurred to her that as she had become overwhelmed by the hugeness of the Grand Canyon, the details of these little puppies brought each one of them into focus for her. What a dichotomy.

"How are they?" he asked again.

"Oh, they're fine. They'll be ready for some play time. What would you say to just grabbing McDonalds and resting at the hotel before we come back? We can let them play in the room."

"After all the Mexican and Indian food we've had the last couple of days, I could go for something bland and unexciting," Henry said.

~~~

Sunset at the Grand Canyon was everything Polly expected. Watching the canyon walls change color as the sun lit it from different angles was glorious. From pinks and rose hues to deep purples and oranges, the place seemed to come alive. As it grew dark, Henry drove away and headed back to the hotel.

"Do you want to do sunrise too?" he asked.

"Since we're heading to Utah tomorrow, let's," Polly responded. "We can sleep another night."

"We'll just carry in the pups and a few things. That way we can get going early."
~~~

"You're the one who has been a slug the last few mornings," she said.

"I'm the one doing all the driving," he grumped.

"I told you that I would drive any time. You aren't getting away with that one."

"Not even a little bit?"

"No way. I'm perfectly able to drive this truck. All you have to do is say something."

"If you were driving, I'd have to take care of the puppies, wouldn't I."

In answer, one of them let out a small yelp, then there was whining.

"What just happened?" he asked.

"I have no idea." Polly flipped the overhead light on, quickly unbuckled her seatbelt and turned around to look in the tub. Little Khan had managed to climb up on top of his brothers and sister. In his attempt to crest the top of the tub, he'd gotten a paw stuck in the handle. Polly unstuck him and took him into her arms.

"He's fine, but I think this one should be Eliseo's responsibility," she said, turning around and pulling the belt back across her. The puppy licked her face. "Yeah, yeah," she said. 'You're cute."

Henry turned the light back off. "Have you told anyone that you are bringing them bigger presents than t-shirts and coffee mugs?"

"No," she said, dropping her head. "But surely they won't kill me."

"No one will kill you, but I'm afraid we'll end up with four more dogs in the house."

"That won't happen," she said. "I promise. They'll be with us for a while, but as soon as Mark says they can go out on their own, I'll find them families."

"I'm holding you to that."

"I kind of like this little guy, though. He's got a lot of spunk. I thought he was the runt, but all he needed was a little love."

"I thought you just said you were glad he was going to Eliseo."

"Well, yeah, you're right, but still." The puppy licked her face again. "You're going to be a challenge, aren't you?"

Henry parked in front of their hotel room and came around to unload the puppies. "I won't miss hauling them in and out of the truck every day."

"Can you believe we're doing this?" Polly started to laugh. "How insane are we?"

"Will you get the door?" he asked, jutting his hip out at her.

"What are you doing?"

"The key is in my back pocket."

"Oh." Polly laughed at him. "I thought we might be starting a new dance."

"Get the key and unlock the door. You're a crazy woman."

"You married me. What does that make you?"

"The talk of the town, that's for sure."

Once the door was shut, Polly put Khan on the floor and helped Henry lift the others out. She opened a package of piddle sheets and scattered them around.

"Doug and Billy did me such a huge favor training Obiwan before he moved in," she said. "I have no idea how to even start."

"Don't look at me. The first dog I ever spent any quality time with was yours."

"It can't be that hard. Everyone does it."

"Well, I suspect that these little guys will need to be on a more regular schedule than we can give them on the road."

Polly sat on the floor in front of the bed and Padme waddled over. Pretty soon all four puppies were playing in front of her, coming in for a little affection. She snuggled with each of them and then after making sure they'd done their business, put them back in the tub and nodded for Henry to turn the lights down.

Before long, everyone was tucked in and asleep.

"I'm exhausted," he said.

"This has been a long day."

"Are you sure you want to do sunrise?"

Polly snuggled up against him in the bed. "Yes. I want to see it one more time before we head north into Utah."

He sighed. "Okay. I was just checking."
"I can make it worth your time," she whispered.
"But I need sleep."
"Seriously?"
"Nope."

CHAPTER EIGHT

Polly poked Henry at five o'clock the next morning. "Are you sure?" he asked, attempting to sound pitiful.

"I'm sure. We said we were going to see the Grand Canyon at sunrise and we're going to do it. We can sleep late tomorrow morning."

"You're mean."

"Yes, I am," she replied. "Now, you take a shower while I deal with the pups."

"Please make coffee too?"

"My goodness, you're a whiny butt. It's not like this is going to kill you." Polly jumped out of bed and flipped on the light beside the sink.

As soon as she was mobile, she heard noises coming from the tub and when she turned back, four little noses were peeking up at her.

"I see you all," she said, smiling. "You're so darned cute I can hardly stand it. Let me make coffee for grumpy man and then it's time for your breakfast."

Henry patted her bottom as he walked past into the bathroom.

"You're still a grump," she said, flicking water at his back. "But it's going to be a great day."

~~~

They arrived at a lookout point that they'd scoped the night before. The sunrise should light up the canyon in front of them.

"I thought the park sign said sunrise was at five forty-five," Henry said.

"It lied." Now it was Polly's turn to be grumpy. She swiped through a weather app on her phone. "We're barely seeing dawn. Apparently, the sun will arrive at six forty-five."

She stepped out of the truck and quickly shut the door, pulling her jacket tight around her. It was cold this early in the morning. Henry joined her with an extra blanket, which they wrapped around themselves.

When she looked up into the sky, Polly had to rub tears out of her eyes again. "Look at that," she whispered. "Have you ever seen so many stars?"

Henry looked up into the sky and then pointed. "There's the Big Dipper, but I've never seen it like that. It's so bright. Look at all of the stars surrounding it."

He hugged her tighter. "Thank you for waking me up. We'd have missed this if we'd stayed in bed."

A few other cars had pulled into the parking area, yet there was quiet as they took in the beauty of the morning. As the sun came up, layers of pinks and blues hovered above the canyon walls until light brought them to life.

"The colors are amazing," Polly said. She leaned into his chest. "I'm so glad I got to experience this with you."

"I don't think Mom and Dad have been here yet."

"But they're so close."

"Dad said they had plenty of time to come up here, but they just haven't done it."

She shook her head. "Why would you wait?"

They stood and watched the sun rise in the sky and when the
~~~

initial impact had worn off, Henry pulled her close. "Are you ready to head up to Monument Valley? I can't wait to see those formations."

"I suppose," Polly said. "I'm a little surprised you know what it is."

"Anyone who watched old John Wayne movies knows about Monument Valley," he said, laughing.

Polly kept the blanket and jumped back in the truck, thankful they'd left it running with the heat on. She was frozen.

When Henry had buckled in and pulled back on to the road, she asked. "John Wayne movies? I didn't know that about you."

"You didn't watch those with your Dad?"

"No. Honestly, we didn't watch that much television when I got older and hardly ever when I was a kid. There was too much to do."

"Even in the winter when he wasn't in the fields? What did he do?"

"I don't know. He read books and magazines after he finished the paper. I always had school activities and homework and I also read a lot."

"Weird."

"What's weird?"

"That explains why you're a librarian."

"Maybe. So, back to you. John Wayne movies?"

"Yes. Don't make fun of me."

"I wouldn't dare. Did you watch them with your dad?"

Henry looked at her and smiled. "Dad watched the movies, but Mom was the John Wayne junkie. You know he was born in Iowa, don't you? She dragged me down to Winterset to see that little tiny house more than once. I think she was in love with him."

"That's awesome. Your mom has amazing depths."

"Yeah. I can't wait to show her pictures of this place. Before I left, she asked me if I knew what 'Fort Apache,' 'The Searchers,' 'Tie a Yellow Ribbon,' and 'Red River' all have in common."

"I suppose those are John Wayne movies."

"Uh huh. And John Ford directed them. And they were all shot here in Monument Valley."

"That's kind of strange to think about. It's a real live movie set."

He drove on for a while and Polly shut her eyes. The sun coming through her window warmed her until she could barely stay awake.

"Polly?" he said quietly.

"What? Do you need me to drive?"

"No. You have to see this. I think you'll be sad if you miss it."

She sat up in the seat and looked out at an immense plain bordered by a row of red cliffs that stretched as far to the right and left as she could see.

"Oh my," she said. "Everything out here is so vast. You look and look and there is no end to it."

"It's been that way for a while."

"Thank you. Have you seen any of the monuments yet?"

"Just some small things. We should be there any minute, though."

They crested a rise and before them were immense stone monuments jutting up from the flat plain, rising high into the sky.

"I can't imagine what the earth was going through when these things were created. And to think we're able to see it all of these millions of years later," she said.

"Look at that one," Henry said. "That's from 'The Searchers.'"

"How do you know this?"

"It's a little familiar," he said, chuckling. "As many times as I've seen that movie, I recognize these landmarks. And look there, that's where John Wayne hid in a cave."

"Seriously?"

"I should shut up?"

"No, we should pull over so you can get some photographs for your Mom. She'd be furious if you just drove past these and didn't share with her."

"How about you just take pictures and I keep going. There's no good place for me to stop right now."

Polly snapped photographs and finally emailed one to Marie Sturtz. *"Your son is in John Wayne heaven right now. We thought we'd share. Does your husband know about your crush on this man? And how come the two of you haven't traveled up here yet?"*

It didn't take long for her phone to buzz with an incoming message. *"My husband thinks I'm silly. That's why poor Henry had to watch those movies with me. You tell him to enjoy them for me. We'll get up there one of these days."*

"How are things in Bellingwood?" Polly asked. *"How's Jessie doing?"*

"She's doing great. The guys all like working with her and they know that I'll fire their rear-ends if they mess around with her. She saw Doc Mason this morning and he's pleased with her progress. She and the baby are doing fine. Obiwan misses you horribly. He's been sleeping with her since you've been gone. The cats are sleeping with Rebecca in her room."

Rebecca was still living in the middle bedroom upstairs in Polly and Henry's home. Her mother, Sarah Heater, had gone downhill due to a sudden onset of diabetes a couple of months ago and required more attentive care by a nurse. If there was one reason Polly had been hesitant to leave Bellingwood, it had been because of Rebecca and Sarah. Sylvie stopped by in the morning to take Rebecca to school with Andrew and promised to check on both before leaving in the evenings, and Jessie had assured Polly that she would be home every day after work to care for Rebecca.

There were plenty of people around Sycamore House and Polly had only worried for a very short time. Henry reminded her that she surrounded herself with good people, who kept a better eye on things than she did. She had wondered if he would be wary of leaving Jessie in charge of the household. She'd had a couple of mis-steps earlier, but he was influenced by his mother, who insisted that if you gave someone a second chance, you had to also give them enough room to grow.

"Tell Jessie to give everyone, including Rebecca an extra hug for me, will you?"

"Have a good rest of the trip and hug my boy for me."

"What was that?" Henry asked.

"I was messaging with your mom. She says everyone is fine

and I'm supposed to hug you for her."

He leered at her. "That's not the kind of hug I want from you."

"Stop it. You be good. This is your mom we're talking about."

"Yeah. That's just weird, isn't it. Fine. You can hug me later. And then we can be done with that and onto other things."

Polly swatted his arm.

The landscape had begun to change radically as they crossed from Arizona into Utah. Colors were transforming from deep reds to oranges, whites and yellows with deeper greens filling in around the sage. They drove along the San Juan River and then Henry pulled off the highway.

"What do you see?" Polly asked.

"What's that?"

She looked at the map she'd been watching. "The Mexican Hat."

"I want to see it up close. That's really something."

He drove in closer until Polly put her hand out. "Stop," she said.

"What?"

"This is as close as we're going." She looked out of her window to the loose dirt and gravel. The closer they got, the looser the rock became.

"But the truck can get us in further than this. Come on. I have four wheel drive."

"I'm not kidding. This is far enough. That doesn't look safe."

"You're no fun."

"I'm fine with being no fun. Let's stop and walk around. We've been in the truck for a long time and I want to check on the pups, but this is as far as you're driving."

He scowled at her, but stopped the truck and stretched before opening his door. The pups sensed movement and Polly lifted them up into the front seat with her. "Here, take a couple of these guys and let them get some fresh air."

Henry tucked Khan under his left arm and held Padme in his other hand. They were still quite small. "I feel like I should put them in a bag and tote them around."

"Yeah. That's all John Wayne macho," she said.

There were a couple of accidents in the bottom of the tub on the piddle sheet, so Polly changed things out and got it cleaned back up.

"How far to the hotel?" Henry asked, putting the two pups back on his seat. Khan toddled across to Polly, who scratched his head.

"I don't know. We have to be getting close. Maybe a half hour."

"I want a nap."

"And some food."

He looked at his watch. "It's nearly two o'clock. We missed lunch."

"Nap and food. That sounds like a wonderful plan." Polly put the four puppies back into their tub and smiled down at them as they played with each other. "And maybe time for the pups to play and run around the room. I'd like to have them completely worn out before we go to sleep tonight."

"Why's that?" he asked, winking at her.

"Because I'm going to sleep like a log."

"Oh. Sure."

"Did you have something else in mind?"

"Well, it's our honeymoon, you know."

"You'll try anything, won't you?"

"Are you complaining?"

Polly smiled at him. "Not on your life."

CHAPTER NINE

"Ugh," Polly said when her alarm went off the next morning.

"What time is it?" Henry groaned.

"Dunno. Don't care."

He rustled around. "It's five o'clock. Why is your alarm bothering me?"

Polly giggled. "Oops. I'd set it yesterday morning. Sorry about that."

"Go back to sleep. We're on vacation."

She picked her phone up, intending to ensure that no more alarms would bother them, but when she swiped it open, there were eight emails and four new text messages.

"I'll be right back." Polly slipped out of bed, past the puppies and into the bathroom. She sat down and opened her phone. There were messages from everyone.

"What happened" she asked herself and started with the first email from Lydia.

"Polly, I know that you are far from home and we are taking care of everyone, but Sarah Heater was just rushed to the hospital."

Polly checked the time on the email - ten thirty last night. Why didn't someone call her? It was only nine thirty out here. She read on.

"Evelyn Morrow was with her and called the squad. She contacted Sylvie, who called me and we went right up to your place to talk to Rebecca. I took Rebecca down to Boone last night for just a few minutes. The doctors think it's pneumonia. They aren't sure how she contracted it, since Evelyn has been taking such good care of her, but you know how beaten down that poor woman is. Rebecca is at Sylvie's and you aren't supposed to worry.

"I love you and I know this is hard and will mess up your vacation, but I also know that you'd want to know. Call if you need me. You know I'm up early in the morning."

Polly dropped her head down between her knees and took a deep breath. This couldn't be happening. Sarah could not die while she was so far away. Poor Rebecca trusted Polly to be there for her.

She looked upward and breathed out, "Please not now. Please."

There were more messages. A text from Sylvie told her Rebecca was staying with them until Polly got back, another from Jessie begging Polly to call when she got up the next morning, and a third from Joss asking if she could help. Emails had come in from Evelyn Morrow and one this morning from Jeff. Henry's mother, Marie, had emailed as well, offering to do anything she could.

Polly couldn't imagine living anywhere else other than Bellingwood. Her friends were her family and they took care of things before she even knew there was a problem.

"Polly?" Henry's voice came from the other room. "Are you okay in there?"

She sighed loudly, stood up, and opened the door. "It's Sarah. They rushed her to the hospital last night. Rebecca is at Sylvie's."

He reached out and took her hand. "What happened?"

"Lydia says they're sure it's pneumonia."

"She doesn't have enough energy to deal with that."

"I know. And poor Rebecca. I wish I were there to hold her."

"Do we need to just head home?"

Polly leaned into him, settling her head on his chest. "No. We're on vacation. I want to spend this time with you."

"Honey, I get it. If you want to just start driving home, we can do that."

"No. Really. Let's stick with the plan. I'll call Lydia and I can probably reach Rebecca before she goes to school. Do you want to go back to sleep or can I make the calls out there?"

"I wouldn't be able to sleep anyway. Come on out and curl up beside me while you talk to your family."

She reached up and kissed him. "This is why I love you."

He helped her get settled on the king-size bed and then reached down and picked each of the puppies up and set them beside her. Padme and Kirk weren't finished sleeping and curled up in the crook of Polly's legs, yawned and fell back to sleep. Khan and Han rustled around where Henry had been sleeping until he sat down and separated them. Their little yips and yelps were adorable.

"You two hush. Polly has to make a call."

Polly dialed Sylvie's number, praying that she was right about the time adjustment.

"Good morning, Polly. I see you got my message," Sylvie said quietly.

"I got a lot of messages. How's our little girl?"

"She's doing as well as can be expected. This was pretty scary. Especially since we woke her up to tell her that her mom was going to the hospital. That was pretty difficult for her."

"Had Sarah been showing signs of this?"

"She had a slight cough, but when she saw her oncologist on Monday, he didn't think it was anything."

"There ya go," Polly said flatly. "Do I need to come home?"

"Don't you dare. We've got this. You and Henry need this time together."

"Does Rebecca need me?"

"She has plenty of people to take care of her. We all love her and Andrew has really kicked it up a notch this morning. He's been pretty good. Actually, even Jason has been good. He told her that he'd saddle up Tom and Huck if she and Andrew wanted to ride around the neighborhood tonight."

"He's a sweetie. Can I talk to her?"

"Of course, but please don't worry. We've got this." In the background, Polly heard Sylvie talking to Rebecca and then the little voice came on the line.

"Polly?"

"Hi honey, how are you doing this morning?"

"I'm okay. Did Sylvie tell you?"

"She sure did. In fact, a lot of people contacted me last night. But I'm worried about you. I miss you."

"I miss you too."

Polly heard the girl's voice begin to break. "I'm sorry you have to face this without me."

"It's okay." Rebecca's voice hitched.

"No, it's not okay, but I'm proud of you for saying that."

"Will you call the hospital today and ask how Mom is? No one really tells me anything."

Polly smiled. It was hard to protect kids from the worst of life, but Rebecca needed to know that she could trust Polly to be honest. "Of course I will. When you get home from school, I'll call and tell you what I know. How's that?"

"When are you coming home?" Rebecca's voice quavered.

"We aren't supposed to get home until Monday night."

"Oh. Okay. I really miss you." That was all it took. Rebecca started to weep on the other end of the phone. "I wish you were here, Polly. What if she dies?"

"Oh sweetie. I wish I were there too, but I'm not. You know Sylvie loves you, right?"

"Yes."

"And Lydia. She loves you very much too, right?"

"She took me to the hospital last night."

"That's because she loves you. Eliseo loves you, Jeff loves you, Jessie loves you. I guess even Jason and Andrew love you."

"But they aren't you and Henry."

"I know, but for now they're going to have to stand in for us, okay? And I promise that whenever you want to talk to me, all you have to do is ask someone to use their phone and we'll be able to talk right away. I'm sorry I haven't talked to you much before this."

"Okay. Andrew says I have to get ready for school. Will you call me later and tell me about Mom?"

"Absolutely. Hand the phone to Sylvie. I love you, sweetie."

"I love you too." Rebecca's voice trailed off as the phone was transferred to Sylvie.

"Are you still okay?" Sylvie asked Polly.

"That was hard. I feel like I should just come home. That poor little girl."

"We've got this. Don't worry. Promise me that."

"I can't, but thank you for taking care of her."

"As many times as you've been there for my boys, of course I'll do this."

"Say, since I have you on the phone," Polly winked over at Henry. "What do you think about a puppy?"

"You know I don't have room for one of those. What are you talking about?" Sylvie used her best scolding voice.

"I also know that you're looking at houses and that you've found three you're interested in. As soon as you get into a house, you'll have plenty of room."

"That's not fair. Why do you have puppies?"

Polly explained what they'd been doing throughout most of their trip and she could practically hear Sylvie rolling her eyes on the other end of the phone.

Then she heard Andrew yell, "Is Polly bringing us a puppy?"

"No," Sylvie snapped. "Now go brush your teeth. The car is leaving in five minutes." She waited a beat and said to Polly. "See what you did?"

"You know that both boys would love it. I'm sending you a picture. I named her Padme and I think she'd fit into your lives perfectly."

"You're a rotten friend, Polly Giller."

"The worst. I'll call after school and talk to Rebecca again. Hopefully I'll know more about Sarah. Thank you for everything."

"You're welcome. Have a wonderful day. Everything is fine here."

"I love you."

"Love you too." As Sylvie pulled the phone away, Polly heard her yell, "Jason, the bus is here. Get moving. Andrew ..."

"How was Rebecca?" Henry asked. The two pups he was holding had fallen back to sleep beside him.

Polly put her hand on Han's warm little tummy. It didn't make any sense to her why people didn't want animals in their lives. A mere touch and they calmed her.

"She's pretty upset. She cried when she realized how far away I was." Polly touched Henry's cheek. "And she said the sweetest thing about you. No one in town loves her like you and I do."

He smiled up at Polly. "Well, that yanks at a man's heart strings. Are we heading back now?"

"Sylvie said we should stay here. They've got it and we're supposed to enjoy our vacation."

"Go ahead and call Lydia. See what she has to say," he said.

"Okay. Maybe she'll tell me to come home."

Polly dialed the phone and felt herself relax when Lydia answered.

"Hi there, sweetie. I'm glad to hear from you. Are you doing okay?"

"I just talked to Rebecca. She's pretty upset."

"She had a shock last night and I doubt that she got much sleep."

"Thank you for taking her to the hospital to see her mother."

"We weren't there very long. Just enough for her to give her mama a kiss and a hug. That poor woman is so weak and sick. Evelyn was beside herself that she might have missed something."

"I suspect that at this stage in Sarah's life, anything can happen and happen in a hurry."

"That's what the doctor said."

"Is she going to die this time? Do I need to hurry back?"

Lydia took a deep breath and paused before answering. "I don't know what to tell you, Polly. Pneumonia in someone that weak isn't good, but they're going to help her as much as possible. I hate the idea of you cutting your vacation short, though. You and Henry should have some time together without the problems of Bellingwood pressing on the two of you."

"I don't know what you're telling me."

"I don't either. I won't sugar coat this. Sarah isn't well, but she hasn't been well for a long time. On the other hand, she's in the hospital and they're going to do everything they can for her. I'd hate to have you end your vacation for no good reason."

"Sylvie said I should stay, but I don't think she understands how much Rebecca and I need each other through this."

"Sylvie is being practical. But, if you were to press her about this same situation involving one of her boys, there'd be no question. She'd be here as soon as possible."

"So you're telling me to come home."

"It's a decision you and Henry have to make together. Don't you have four or five days left?"

"Yeah. But ..." Polly didn't know what else to say.

"I'm sorry I'm not being more helpful."

"You want to tell me to come home, but you don't think that's fair to say. Am I right?"

"I love you very much, Polly. You'll make the right decision."

Polly chuckled. "You should have been a politician."

"I'll leave that to my husband. Let me know what you decide to do, though. Okay?"

"Okay. I love you. I'll talk to you later."

"I love you too."

Polly put the phone down on the bed and rubbed her forehead, trying to ease the rapidly building headache.

"Are we heading out?" Henry asked.

"I still don't have a good answer."

CHAPTER TEN

Polly woke back up to a sloppy lick on her face. She tried to move and found that it hurt too much. She'd fallen asleep sitting up, leaning on Henry. "Oh that's going to hurt all day," she said.

"What?" he asked, coming awake.

"We fell asleep."

"It's the puppies' fault. They were warm and cuddly."

Polly chuckled. "We need to decide what we're doing today. I'm completely at a loss. Do we head back to Bellingwood or stay here and try to enjoy the rest of our vacation?"

Henry sat forward and turned to look at her. The two puppies who had snuggled against him, bounced awake.

"How much would you be able to enjoy this, knowing all that you know?"

"Well, I'd enjoy being with you. And I love seeing the beauty around us. It's really amazing."

"I know, but your heart isn't going to be in it and honestly, neither is mine."

"I feel like this is the second time I've screwed up our vacation. I'm so sorry."

"Stop it. You didn't have anything to do with that tornado that hit Bellingwood." He stopped and looked up at her. "Or did you? I thought your superpower was finding dead bodies, but maybe it's sabotaging vacations in crazy ways, too."

Polly swatted his arm.

"And you didn't have anything to do with Sarah getting sick. Rebecca needs us to be home, so we're going home."

She leaned across the puppies beside her and kissed him. "I love you. Thank you for making that decision easy for me. I didn't want to disappoint you."

"We really are in this together, Polly. Don't ever forget that."

"I know that, but you're so wonderful to me that I hate the possibility of messing things up."

He looked around the room. They had planned to stay in this room for three nights, so had unloaded everything from the back of the truck. Polly had hoped to find a laundromat in town and take her time repacking for the return trip. Everything was in chaos.

"Don't even say it," Polly said, sighing. "It's a mess. I'll pull out enough for tonight and jam the rest in the back of the truck. We'll deal with it once we get home."

"You're really okay with that?"

"I have to be. You go first. I'll feed the puppies and try to wrangle some kind of order out here."

~~~

Two hours later, they were headed north to Moab. They'd fed and pottied the puppies, re-packed the truck and even managed to find breakfast.

"I'd really like to at least drive through the Arches before we leave Utah," Polly said.

Henry smiled. "That's my girl. A little caffeine and some food and you're thinking again."

"They had Diet Dew!"

"You haven't been able to get much of that out here."
~~~

"I've been deprived. But I'm better now."

A sign for the Arches National Park led them off the highway and past waves of rock formations. A quick check of the map and Polly announced they were looking at the Petrified Dunes. Stopping at several points along the way to take pictures, they were also able to get close to some amazing rock formation.

At one point, Polly and Henry were standing in front of a wonderful formation that looked like an elephant when a car pulled in and parents got out with their child. Polly was prepared to be pleasant and smile at them until she heard the mother screaming at the youngster. It seemed that the argument had been going on for quite some time. The peace and beauty of the moment was completely destroyed by inept parents.

"I don't want little kids," Polly said.

"Especially not if they're like that."

She scowled. "Guessing it's not the kid's fault."

"Let's move on."

They passed the Garden of Eden and stopped at another overlook. The parking lot was completely empty. Polly jumped out to wander over to a rock formation when all of a sudden fifteen separate cars pulled in behind them. As people got out, it was obvious that no one knew anyone else. It had been a completely random stop for them all.

"We attract a crowd," Henry muttered.

"And look, more great parents."

This time, they couldn't understand the language the father was speaking as he attempted to cajole a three year old out of his car seat. The mother had taken off and was at least fifteen feet away from the vehicle, watching as the poor man tried everything in his power to handle the screaming toddler.

"That's just entertaining," Polly said.

"We might as well move on."

They drove in and around the park, stopping often in order to absorb yet one more gorgeous natural structure.

Polly breathed. "Would I ever get used to this if I lived out here? It's so overwhelming. I wish I had more time. I don't think

I'm processing it all very well."

"I have a cousin who lives in Colorado and he got used to the mountains. But he says he'll never be able to live anywhere else, he'd miss them too much."

"I wouldn't want to get used to this."

"Do you suppose people would say the same things about flowing fields of corn in Iowa?"

She laughed out loud. "I doubt it, but you never know." This time Polly put her hand out on the console and waited for Henry to take it. "You know what? I miss my fields of black dirt and corn stubble."

"Me too." Henry pointed at a sign for bighorn sheep crossing. "I wonder how long we'd have to sit here and wait to see them."

"I haven't seen any wildlife on this trip. That seems weird. Signs kept telling us to watch for it and... nothing. I see more wildlife in my back yard."

"Then it's time for us to go home."

They drove back into Moab after leaving the park. It was mid-afternoon and Henry asked, "Do you want something to eat before we head out?"

He stopped for sandwiches and Polly took out her phone. It was getting late in Iowa and she'd lost track of time. Her first call was to the hospital in Boone. The nurses on the floor recognized her right away and after a few minutes of conversation she was talking to Sandi, Sarah's nurse for the day. Sandi assured Polly that Sarah was getting the best care she could and that though she was critical right now, there was no need to believe that she was going to die.

Polly took a deep breath and dialed Sylvie's phone, hoping to talk to Rebecca.

"Hi there, Polly," Sylvie said. "Lydia says that the two of you talked this morning. Are you cutting your vacation short?"

"If it were Jason or Andrew, wouldn't you?"

"Of course I would. I don't know why I should expect anything different from you. You're going to take such good care of that little girl. Where are you?"

"We're still in Moab, but we're heading home. I suspect we'll be in town tomorrow night at some point."

"Rebecca will be glad to see you. And so will your animals. I think Obiwan misses you a lot. He drags Andrew into the office every once in a while, looking for you."

"He's a good boy. Is Rebecca near so I can talk to her?"

"She's upstairs with Jessie. Do you want me to go up?"

"Oh, it's later than I thought. What are you still doing at Sycamore House?"

"There's a family reunion tonight. Jessie is watching the kids."

"I'll just call her. Thanks, Sylvie."

"I love you, Polly. We'll see you tomorrow sometime."

Polly hung up and dialed Jessie's phone.

"Polly! How are you?" Jessie said.

"I'm doing okay. How are things there?"

"It's been a little weird. And it's really weird staying in this big place by myself at night. It was one thing with Rebecca here, but now it's so empty. Doug and Billy are bringing pizza down tonight, though. Sylvie said the reunion could go late, so we're watching movies."

"That sounds great. Can I talk to Rebecca?"

"Sure. Let me get her."

"Polly?" Rebecca sounded better this afternoon than she had earlier in the day.

"Hi honey. How are you doing?"

"I'm fine. Did you talk to Mom?"

"No, but I talked to her nurse. She said that your mom is really sick, but she's going to be okay. It might take a while, though."

Rebecca whispered into the phone, "She isn't going to die?"

"The nurse said no."

"I'd really like to go see her, but I don't know who will take me."

"Honey, I'm on my way home."

"Really? When will you get here?"

"I don't know that. We're going to drive until we're tired, then get a hotel room. Probably tomorrow night sometime."

"Really?" Rebecca started to cry. "You're coming home for me?"

"Oh, honey. Of course I am. I love you and so does Henry. You need us right now and we're going to get there as fast as we can."

"Nobody's ever done that before."

Polly smiled. "Yes they have, Rebecca. All the time. People love you like crazy. Your mom has gone out of her way for you. Remember when that woman kidnapped you? Everybody was doing whatever they could to help you. Sylvie is letting you sleep at her house, Lydia took you to Boone. You are very loved, sweetheart."

"I know," Rebecca said softly. "I love you too."

"Now, Jessie says you are having pizza and watching movies with Doug and Billy tonight. I want you to have fun and don't worry about anything, okay?"

"Okay."

"Do you have your homework done?"

"Polly!"

"I know, I know, but do you?"

"I did it at school today."

"Did you really?"

"Yes. I promise."

"Good. Then have fun tonight and hopefully I'll see you tomorrow and you can sleep in your own bed."

"Thank you for coming home."

"You're welcome. Now go have fun."

Henry had come back to the car with food and they sat quietly for a moment while eating. Then he picked up a scenic byway that would take them along the Colorado River as they left the region.

"This is a perfect way to leave Utah," Polly said.

"What do you mean?"

"This is incredible."

As he drove along the river, Polly felt inconsequential and small amid the towering canyon walls. The river was quiet and peaceful and it was all she could do to keep her eyes on everything around them. They made one last stop at Fisher Tower, a lone towering structure which showed up as the landscape was flattening out again, and then said goodbye to the Colorado River as Henry turned north to pick up I-70.

"The landscape is changing again," Polly said. "No more red rocks. We weren't there very long, but it feels like I'm losing something by leaving them behind. I am going to miss all of this grand beauty."

"We still have to get through the mountains."

"It's strange to think that we'll have gone from the depths of the Grand Canyon to the heights of the Rocky Mountains in such a short time. I'm glad we did this, even if we are heading home early."

"Hauling ass," he said, laughing.

"Where shall we plan to stay tonight?" Polly asked.

"You've been so great at planning everything else, let's just stop when we're tired."

She put her phone back in her lap and running her hand through her hair, smiled over at her husband. They were going home. Everything would be fine once she got there.

CHAPTER ELEVEN

Polly was glad to have one less state between her and home as they crossed into Colorado on I-70. Now that they'd made the decision to go, she wanted the trip to be over. Dusk was settling in and she found that the Colorado River was traveling beside her again.

"Should we stop in Grand Junction for the night?" she asked, looking at a map.

"I'm not all that tired. Let's press on and see how far we can go."

"Are you sure?"

"It's only five thirty. I have plenty of hours left in me."

"Okay. Just tell me when you're ready to stop. The ski resorts are coming up next. We could probably find a fun place to sleep for the night."

"With the puppies? These hotels aren't going to be quite as easy going as the places we've been staying."

She nodded. He was right. Getting the pups to their new home was something fun to look forward to. After only a few days, she was having fun with their little personalities. Khan thought he ruled the roost, but more often than not, Padme put him in his place. She was quiet, but firm with him. Polly was glad they were so young. That meant they slept a lot. Having four highly active pups on this trip would have been more than she or Henry wanted to handle. As it was, they were quite a handful when they were awake.

"Maybe we should stop anyway in Grand Junction. Get something to eat and give the pups a little freedom in the truck."

~~~

They were back on the road, with everyone settled in. Dusk had given way to darkness and everything grew quiet.

"If you want to sleep, that's okay," Henry said. "We'll be in the mountains pretty soon."

"Have you ever driven out here?"

"No. This will be a first for me."

"I wish we were doing it in the daylight. I'll bet it's gorgeous."

They started seeing signs for ski resorts. Her friends had flown out to Colorado and talked enough about these locations that the names were familiar, but Polly had never found enjoyment in skiing. Sal told her that was because she'd never learned how to do it well.

"Have you ever gone skiing?" she asked Henry.

His laughter came from low in his belly. "No. This old Iowa boy would probably find himself rolling down the mountain in a big ole snowball before he crashed through the lodge at the end of the slope."

"Me either. Sal used to come out here a lot. I wonder if she'll make Mark ski with her."

"As fancy as he is on his feet, he'll probably be great at it. He seems like a skier."

Polly chuckled. "And what exactly does that mean?"

"I don't know. He's just one of those guys that seems like he'd like that."

"I was just wondering if there was a type."
~~~

"No. I didn't mean anything like that. Although I wouldn't hate it if he broke a leg or something."

"Henry Sturtz!"

"What?"

"He's with Sal and I'm married to you. Don't tell me you are still jealous of him. There was absolutely nothing between us. I thought you guys were friends."

"I know, I know. And we are."

"Then what in the world was that all about?"

"Don't you ever get tired of someone always being perfect? That's Mark Ogden. Always perfect. The women swoon over him and all the farmers think he's the most wonderful vet they've ever known. Perfect. It gets a little old."

"You are a crazy man," Polly said, poking him in the side. "I would never have thought you had this in you. And just so you know, all of my friends think that you're the perfect one. You never screw up. You always support me. You don't get mad when I'm a moron. You read my mind and always do nice things for me."

Henry squeezed her hand. "Well, trust me, I have to work at it awfully hard some days. You put me to the test."

"What do you mean I put you to the test? I'm not that hard to live with."

"Not that hard to live with? Sweetie, you're pure entertainment. They know at the convenience store when I'm trying to avoid a fight. I walk in and grab a box of ice cream sandwiches."

"Those are to avoid a fight?"

"Or to soothe you when you're stressed."

"See, that's not so hard. Is it bad that I don't do things like that for you?"

"I don't need ice cream when I'm stressed. I need it when you're stressed."

"Okay, so you feed me ice cream. What else do I do that puts you to the test?"

"There are people in our house all the time. I mean, All. The. Time. If it's not the kids, you have Lydia, Beryl and Andy around or you're down at the barn with the animals or playing with everyone downstairs and then I'm stuck upstairs with people you left there."

"Wait. What?"

"It's not all that bad."

"Do you want me to not have Andrew come over after school? I can work something else out."

"No. Stop it. That's not what I mean."

"Well, what do you mean?" Polly felt an argument coming on.

"Nothing. I shouldn't have started this."

"You damned well should have. If you don't like something that I'm doing, you should tell me about it right then, rather than waiting until we're finishing a fabulous vacation and springing it on me. I can't fix it now. All I can do is feel guilty that I've screwed up your life."

"Now that's not what I mean at all."

"Then what exactly did you mean?"

"This is going bad all of a sudden. Let's not do this now."

"Oh, we're doing this. Trust me, we're doing this. What the hell else do we have to do while we're driving tonight? I'm not going to let you get away with telling me you hate having people around all the time and then back away from the conversation."

She drew her hand out of his and folded her arms across her chest.

"Now you're pissed."

"Well, I thought things were okay and you're telling me that I put you to the test. Is that all the time?"

"Polly, honey, stop it. We were having a conversation and it got out of control."

"Seriously? Stop it? Out of control? Are you trying to escalate this argument?"

"Oh lord, no. I'm trying to make it stop. I'm not sure what I did to get to this point and I don't know how to escape."

Polly wanted to laugh, but she'd managed to work herself into a good froth.

"Tell me how bad things are with all of my friends around. If you want me to change things, I'll do it."

"No, I don't want you to change anything. I love you and I fell in love with you because you have so many friends. Yes, there are times I'd like to just come home and sit around in my shorts and t-shirt. There are Saturday mornings I'd like to sleep in with you and not have the whole world descend on us. Even on this trip, we haven't had any good mornings to sleep in."

"I could let you sleep in."

"You didn't hear me. I want to sleep in with you. Just hang out and be slugs for one morning. Get out of bed about nine o'clock, watch television and not take a shower. Just do nothing. I don't even care if Rebecca is there. She's a good kid. But something always comes up to wreck those days."

"I'm sorry that there's so much going on, but I can try to come up with one Saturday where we get to stay home. I didn't know that's what you wanted."

Then Polly realized that every time they'd been interrupted, he'd mentioned how badly that was all he wanted. She'd missed his cue. "Damn it," she said. "I'm sorry. I should have paid better attention. I didn't realize that was so important to you."

"No, that's not what I want. I don't want you to feel bad."

"You're always so easy going and you take such good care of everyone around you. I forget that I should pay attention, too."

Polly looked up as the interstate split in half. The westbound lanes were suddenly far above their heads. "What in the hell?"

"I know. It's the mountain passes. And we've slowed way down. There's a lot of traffic out here tonight."

She looked out the window. The river was to her right and the mountains seemed to go straight up beside her. "This is scary."

They went through a tunnel and Polly held her breath, wishing that there were a lot more daylight. The light from oncoming traffic showed her how insane the road was and she found herself gripping the door handle.

"Are you okay?" she asked. "I'm having a hard time focusing because it's so scary."

"I wish we could get through here a little more quickly, but yeah. I'm okay. It's a little intimidating in this big truck. I don't feel like I have much room for error."

"Have you ever driven in the mountains?"

"No, have you?"

"Dad took me up to Estes Park one time. Scared the living daylights out of me. He had a great time on that road. I could barely look at the scenery because I was afraid I'd fall out of the car."

"You're a nut."

"I know. Just be careful."

"I tell you what. Shut your eyes and think about how much you love me. If you fall asleep, that's okay. I'm fine with this."

"You're a better man than me."

"I hope so. I kinda like you being a better woman than me."

"You are such a goofball."

While Henry focused on driving through the mountains, Polly opened her phone and composed several texts. Whenever she got enough coverage to send them, out they went.

"What are you doing over there?" Henry asked.

"Nothing important. Just pay attention to the road."

"You're going to want to be the one to pay attention. We're coming up to Vail. It's really pretty. The worst of the craziness is over, I think."

Polly relaxed and watched the scenery pass by, the community's lights glowing against the backdrop of the mountains.

"Should we stop in Denver for the night?"

Henry reached over and patted her hand. "Let's just keep driving. If we get into Denver and I'm tired, we'll stop. By the way, how much farther do I have?"

Polly checked and said, "About two hours to the edge of the Denver area. Will my heart be in my throat the entire time?"

"We've made it this far, I think we'll make it to Denver."

"You're amazing. I might have just pulled over and waited for someone to come get me."

"And what? Airlift you out?"

"Yeah. That would have probably made it worse. Let's just promise to never drive on that highway again."

He chuckled. "So exactly how are we planning to go west?"

"I don't know, but that was scary and I don't want to do it again."

"Yes ma'am."

CHAPTER TWELVE

It took Polly a moment to discern what seemed off when she woke up and then she realized they weren't moving. She sat up and looked around. Henry had parked the truck at one end of a rest area, away from the brightest lights, and drawn a blanket over the two of them. He'd lowered the back on his seat and Polly grinned when she realized that two of the pups were snuggled into the blanket with him. What a softie he'd turned out to be.

Even though the draw of the rest area was great, Polly didn't want to disturb him by opening a door. She had no idea how long they'd been parked, but lifted the last two sleepy puppies into her lap and settled in to rest.

~~~

The next time she woke up was to the sound of the engine turning over. Polly realized that she'd gotten a little chilly and was huddled into the blanket with the pups.

"Wait!" she said. "Don't go yet."

"I'm not. I just wanted to get some heat in here. It was getting
~~~

cold." Henry had brought his seat back up and handed the two puppies he was cradling in one arm to her. "I guess it was colder than a two puppy night."

"Where are we, anyway?"

"Somewhere in the middle of Nebraska. I need gas pretty soon. Do you want to stay here or drive on down the road?"

Polly glanced back at the building and bounced once or twice in the seat, then giggled. "I think I'm fine. Let's go on. Now that we're back in the land of Diet Dew, I want one of those, too."

Henry backed out of the parking space and pulled back onto the interstate. "A big cup of coffee. That's what I need. And donuts. Probably donuts. Sugar and caffeine."

"I can drive for a while. I slept all the way across Colorado and most of Nebraska, it seems."

They'd stopped on the east side of Denver late in the evening for supper. Polly stayed awake for a while, but when the truck warmed up, her full tummy went to work and she drifted off. She'd slept five or six hours. "How long were we in the rest area?" she asked.

"Maybe an hour."

"I must have woke up when you turned the truck off."

"You were pretty dead to the world. I didn't think you'd mind."

"Thank you for driving like this. Are you sure I can't help?"

"I'm good for now, but I'll let you know."

They stopped a few times between Grand Island and Bellingwood, pulling into their garage about ten thirty in the morning.

"How about we just go upstairs and crash," Polly said. "We can empty the truck later."

Henry rolled the garage door back down. "Will anyone notice we're home if we stay very, very quiet?"

"I'll tell Jeff and Sylvie that we're back and ask them to make sure no one comes upstairs until the kids get back from school. We can turn our phones off and sleep."

"That sounds wonderful." Henry stretched and turned to look at the puppies in the back seat. "I'll take the little ones up to meet

Obiwan and the cats. Where do you want to keep them?"

"Do you care if they're just in our room for now? We can put piddle sheets down on the floor. They're getting used to those."

"We need a baby gate."

"I'm too tired to even think about that. Can't we just shut the door?"

He yawned. "Fine." He got out of the truck and came around to grab the tote filled with puppies.

Polly put her hands on the bag she carried with all of their supplies and followed him in the back door. When he went upstairs, she went on into the kitchen to find Rachel, Hannah and Sylvie standing around the prep table working on a cake.

"Hello?" she said, trying hard not to startle them.

"Polly!" Rachel cried, looking up. Sylvie had her back to Polly and spun around. "What in the world are you doing here?"

"Henry just kept driving." She shook her head. "And driving. And here we are."

"You have to be exhausted," Sylvie said. "Are you going up to crash?"

"Yeah. Can you keep everyone away from us until the kids come home from school?"

"Of course I can." Sylvie had crossed the room and pulled Polly into a hug. "Rebecca will be so glad to see you. She's a mess."

"Will you tell Jeff I'm back?" Polly heard the back door open and shut. "That must be Henry with Obiwan. I'll see you later." She ran to the back door and looked out to see her husband walking toward the tree line with their dog. He was such a good man.

When she got to the top of the steps, she stopped for a moment to rub the cats who were very glad to see her, and then went into the living room and burst out laughing. Henry had taken a shelf from one of the bookcases in the living room and set it across the doorway. Everyone but those little puppies would have no problem moving back and forth. He'd set another shelf across the doorway into their bathroom.

Polly sat down on the end of her bed and pulled her shoes off.

It felt so good to be in her own home again. The cats jumped up beside her and nudged her with their heads until she picked up Leia and then Luke. "I know, I know," she said. "I'm back. I won't go anywhere for this long again. At least not for a while." She put them down on the bed and stroked Luke's back. "But it doesn't look like you've been suffering much this week. If I know my friends, you've been spoiled."

She was rummaging around in her dresser when she heard the clatter of Obiwan's feet on the living room floor. The pups were still in their tub and for that she was grateful. The dog came barreling into the bedroom and before Polly could bend her knees to reach him, he'd crashed into her legs, his tail wagging madly.

"Hey there, bud. I missed you!" Polly finally sat down on the floor and Obiwan crawled into her lap, whining and moaning with glee, lapping her face with his sloppy tongue.

Henry stood in the doorway, watching them.

Obiwan's nose picked up the scent of the puppies and he wandered over to the tub to investigate.

"Be good, Obiwan," Polly cautioned. He looked up at her. "They're just little things. You have to be careful with them."

The dog stuck his head in the tub and nudged one of the puppies who had put his paws on the edge. The pup fell over and came back for more. Obiwan sniffed them and gave Polly a little whine.

"I know," she said. "They smell weird. But you'll get used to them." She patted the bed beside her. "Now come up here so I can take a nap. I won't sleep if I worry that you're bothering them."

"Are you going to let them out to play?" Henry asked.

"Not while I sleep. At least not this afternoon. I want everyone to get used to everyone else first."

The cats were doing their best to ignore the activities on the floor. Luke was pushing his head against Henry's elbow and Leia was trying to crawl into Polly's lap.

"I hope I'm not too tired to sleep," Henry said.

Polly pulled the covers down and tucked her feet underneath, then put her head on the pillow. "If you're still awake in an hour, talk to me. Otherwise, I'll see you later today." She turned over on her side and waited for Obiwan to tuck himself in behind her legs.

CHAPTER THIRTEEN

Easing the cookie sheet out of the oven, Polly listened as Rebecca and Andrew came flying up the back steps.

"Polly!" Andrew yelled from Henry's office. "When did you get home?"

She waited for the two kids to come in to the media room and said, "We got back late this morning. How was your day?"

"Are you tired? Did you have fun? Did you guys really drive all night long?"

"Yes. Yes. Yes."

Andrew looked at her, his forehead creased in confusion. "What?"

"I answered your questions. Yes, I'm still tired. Yes, we had a great time and yes, we really drove all night long. Except for a couple of hours when we took a nap in a rest area."

Rebecca had come running into the room with Andrew, but dropped back while he barreled forward with questions.

"Andrew, could you take Obiwan outside for me?" Polly asked.

He looked around, wanting to ask a lot more questions, but his training had been perfected by a master. When an adult asked him to do something, he just did it.

"There will be warm cookies and milk when you get back," Polly promised. "And I have a surprise for you."

That was all it took. "Come on, Obiwan. Let's go!"

The dog followed him back outside and Polly said, "Take off your coat and come help me with the cookies, Rebecca."

The little girl dropped her coat on the sofa and slowly walked to the kitchen. Rather than hugging her, Polly handed her a spatula and put the cookie sheet on a towel she'd spread on the counter beside a cooling rack. She knew that Rebecca was doing her best to contain her emotions and wanted to respect that. Their moment would come.

They worked in silence for a few moments. "What's the surprise?" Rebecca finally asked.

"You'll have to wait and see when Andrew comes back."

"Oh. Okay." Rebecca lifted a cookie to the rack and pushed it into place. Polly recognized a child with a hint of OCD when she saw one. Rebecca lined each cookie up into perfect rows and columns. One of these days she was going to offer Rebecca a bag of M&Ms. Polly had a lifetime of experience separating them into colors and then arranging them in different orders.

"I missed you," Polly said after another moment of silence. "I'm sorry I wasn't here when your mom got sick. I know there were plenty of people taking care of you, but I wish I'd been here."

Rebecca took a deep breath and slid the spatula out from under another cookie, then dropped both the spatula and the hot pad she'd been holding and turned around into Polly's body. "I was scared," she said, her voice shaking.

"I know."

She lifted her tear-streaked face up to look at Polly. "I'm still scared. No one talks to me like you do. They're afraid that they'll hurt my feelings if they tell me the truth about Mom. But I already know she's really sick."

"Oh honey, I know. I called the hospital just before you got home and she's still pretty sick. I don't think she's coming home for a while. This one was bad. But we'll go down this afternoon and then we'll see her again tomorrow and Sunday and every day until they release her."

"Do you really think she's coming back here? She can't die in the hospital. She doesn't want to die that way."

"Rebecca, you are the reason your mom is working so hard to stay alive. She's not ready to die just yet. I promise you that she's doing everything she can to get better so that she can come back. You have to trust her. Neither one of us are going to lie to you about this. I promise."

Polly felt Rebecca relax against her as she wrapped her arms around Polly's waist. That was what she needed - someone to just give her the truth. Polly set her cheek on the top of Rebecca's head and it occurred to her that the girl was growing up. She wondered how tall Rebecca's father was.

They were still holding on to each other when Andrew and Obiwan came back up the steps. He took one look at them and rather than rushing into the kitchen with the dog, sat down on the sofa, and then turned on the television.

"It's okay, Andrew," Polly said. "I think we're done. We were just missing each other."

"Did you miss me too?" he asked, a silly grin crossing his face.

"Of course I did."

"I bet."

"No. Really. I told Henry that I missed being here during the day when you two showed up. I love spending time with you."

He popped back to his feet. "So what's the surprise and where's Henry?"

"Henry went over to the shop. He'll be back later. Now, are you sure you want to see this surprise?" Even though she had released Rebecca, they were still holding hands.

Rebecca squeezed Polly's hand and said, "You're teasing us."

"Why yes, yes I am. What I'm about to show you is very special and you have to be very gentle. Got that? No loud noises, no squealing, no jumping around."

Andrew rolled his eyes. "You didn't bring back a baby, did you? Because I know that Jessie's pregnant, but you weren't, were you?"

"No. I wasn't pregnant. Trust me on that."

"So, it's not a baby?"

"Well, not quite. Follow me." Polly kept hold of Rebecca's hand and the three of them crossed the living room to her bedroom door. "Be very quiet," she said and pushed the door open.

It was all Rebecca could do to keep herself together when she saw the four puppies. She dropped to her knees on the floor, followed closely by Andrew, who sat down as close to Padme as possible.

"Where did you get these?" he asked.

"It's a long story," Polly replied, shutting the door behind her to keep Obiwan and the cats out of the room.

"Where's their mom?"

"She died, so I guess I'm their mom right now."

Rebecca giggled as Khan tried to crawl up into her lap. "Are you keeping them?"

"Henry and I are planning to keep one of them." Polly knelt down beside Rebecca to scoop Han into her arms. "This one. I named him Han."

"For Han Solo? That's funny," Andrew said. "Who's this?"

"That's the only little girl. We named her Padme. The one Rebecca is holding is named Khan and the little brat trying to chew on my shoe is named Kirk." Neither of the kids responded to the last two names and Polly realized she hadn't spent enough time indoctrinating them into all things Star Trek yet. At least Andrew recognized Han Solo's name.

"What are you going to do with the other puppies?" Andrew asked.

"I don't know yet. But I have time. I want them to grow up a little more before we separate them."

"I wish Mom would let us have a dog. But she said we couldn't until we got into a house." He ran his hand along Padme's back. "I think she likes me. I'd be a really good dog owner." His shoulders slumped. "But we have to move out of that apartment first."

Polly just nodded. Apparently, Sylvie hadn't said anything to her boys about the house search. "We'll see what happens."

"Eliseo said he wanted a dog," Andrew said helpfully. "I'll bet he'd take one of these. How big are they going to get? Do you think Doug and Billy would take another dog over there?" He turned to Rebecca. "We could give one to Mrs. Hastings. She's always talking about how much she likes animals. And maybe we could talk to some of our friends at school. Maybe Jessie would like to have one, too. You know, for when she moves out."

Polly reached over and put her hand on his knee. "I think I've got it. There are only four puppies and I'm keeping one of them here."

"Can I hold Han?" Rebecca asked. She put Khan into Andrew's lap and waited while Polly handed the little pup to her. Once he was in her arms, she brought him up to her chest and kissed his neck. "He's so soft." The puppy squirmed and wiggled until Rebecca put him on the floor. As soon as he found his feet, he tried to crawl back into her lap. "He's wiggly, too."

"They all are," Polly said. "Since their mama died, we're going to have to do all the work to take care of them."

"Do we have to feed them with a bottle?"

"Well yes, but they're old enough to start moving to regular dog food. Now that I'm home, we have a lot of training to do and you two will have to help me."

Han settled down in front of Rebecca and put his head on her ankle, promptly falling asleep. "Look what he did," Rebecca whispered. "Do you think he likes me?"

"I'm sure he does, sweetie."

"I can't move," she said, giggling.

"Nope, you're going to have to sit like that all afternoon. You don't want to disturb a puppy while it's sleeping," Polly said.

Rebecca looked up at her with big eyes. "Really?"

"Of course not, silly girl." Polly scooted closer to Rebecca and put an arm around her. "Puppies fall asleep all the time. When you're ready to move, just do it."

"Whew." Rebecca bent over and scratched behind his ears. "Your life is so great, Polly. You always have all of these animals around. They love you no matter what."

Andrew reached over and tapped Rebecca's arm. "You get to live here. That means yours is great, too."

A tear leaked out of Rebecca's eye and Polly put the pups back on the floor and stood up. "I'm going to finish baking cookies. The two of you can stay in here as long as you want. Just keep the door closed. I don't want Obiwan and the cats to come in unless either Henry or I are with them.

"You could move the puppies into my room," Rebecca said hopefully.

"I suppose I could, but then you'd never get any sleep and little girls need lots of sleep. But maybe Obiwan could stay in your room for a couple of nights."

"Really?"

"Sure. Where has he been sleeping while we were gone?"

"With Jessie. The cats slept with me."

"We'll see about reassigning their sleeping locations now that I'm home."

Rebecca slowly slipped her leg out from under Han's head, making sure that her hands cradled it until she could place it gently on the floor. When she was free of him, she jumped up and hugged Polly. "Thank you."

CHAPTER FOURTEEN

"Sweet, wonderful wife of mine," Henry said, bumping Polly's hip as he walked past her with dishes in his hands. "This has been a perfect morning. I can't believe you managed to work it out for us."

"That's what I was texting about the other night. If you wanted a lazy morning, you deserved a lazy morning. Sylvie should be here in a little bit with the kids and I told Doug he could bring Obiwan back any time after two o'clock. Jessie thought it would be cool to sleep at the hotel with a few of her friends."

"I'm just glad she's making friends in town. I'd like to not have to worry about her leaving with more losers."

"Since she's pregnant, I also don't worry about her drinking and partying. She said they were going to Ames for dinner and then come back and have a slumber party or something. I don't know what, but I'm just glad she was okay with leaving her room."

He stood behind her and wrapped his arms around her, nuzzling her neck. "Thank you for doing all of that. This was just what I wanted. And look, I didn't even have to be five hundred miles from home. Think we can get away with it tomorrow morning?"

Polly flicked some suds at his head. "Don't push it. We're going to have to get back to normal sometime."

"Give me the wash rag," he said. After she rinsed it and squeezed it out, he started wiping the counter tops. "I didn't tell you ..." he started.

"Tell me what?"

"I think Sylvie decided on a house."

"Really? Which one?"

"She asked if I could go with her today after she drops off the kids. She still doesn't want them to know. Just in case things don't work out."

"Yeah, yeah, yeah. Which one?"

"It's the old two-story on Jefferson. Actually, not too far from Mom and Dad's house. You know the one with the round opening on the second story balcony?"

"That's a beautiful old house!"

"I think it's in good shape. I told her that I'd walk through it with her before the whole process starts. Just to reassure her that it's what she wants."

Polly pulled the plug from the sink and listened as the water drained. "You know, I kind of hoped that she and Eliseo would get together and they'd end up moving out to his place."

"You just can't be happy until everyone is all hooked up, can you?" Henry tossed the wet cloth at her forehead.

"Shaddup, you." Polly tossed it back, completely missing him. The cloth landed on the floor.

"You're really bad at that."

She spun around and headed out of the kitchen.

"Hey! You're just going to leave the mess?"

"I cleaned up the mess. It's one rag. I think you can manage that."

Out of the corner of her eye, she saw him dart around the peninsula and she took off for the living room, running as fast as she dared. The cats both jumped to one of the sofas as Henry chased Polly with the cold, wet cloth in his right hand.

"What are you doing?" she gasped, coming to a stop on the opposite side of the living room.

"I thought I might teach you a lesson about flinging things at me."

Polly feinted to the left and then to the right, waiting for Henry to make a commitment to the chase. He took off and she ran again, around the sofas. "You're a crazy man!"

He cackled as he continued to chase her. "Yes I am and don't you forget it."

They ran around the room another time and Henry stopped behind a chair, laughing. Polly stopped for a second and then started running again, toward him. Before he realized what he was doing, Henry was running from her. They chased each other until Polly caught him. She pushed him over the back of the sofa and landed on top of him, then straddled his waist and tried to catch his arms. He brought the wet cloth up to wipe her face. She caught it and then looked up to see Eliseo, Jason, Andrew and Rebecca standing inside the front door.

"He was trying to wash my face with a dirty rag," Polly said, jumping to the floor.

Henry laughed and sat up, then pulled Polly down to sit beside him. "What's up with you guys today? Come on in and sit down."

Eliseo tried not to laugh. Andrew and Rebecca were still in shock and Jason just shook his head, but they all came in and sat down.

"The kids tell me you have something fun up here," Eliseo said. "I wondered if you wanted any help with it."

"Oh Jason, they're so cute," Rebecca said with a smile. Polly watched her eyes follow Jason wherever he went. Good heavens, she had a little crush on him! "Can we show them?" she asked.

"You sit here, Eliseo," Polly said. "We'll bring them out. Come on, help me with the puppies."

The two youngest followed her. She handed Padme to Andrew to hold and Han to Rebecca, then carried Khan and Kirk out. "I don't think they'll get very big. Their mother had some Labrador in her, but she probably only weighed about twenty-five or thirty pounds."

Eliseo stood up to meet her and she handed Khan to him and Kirk off to Jason.

"Have they all found homes yet?" Eliseo asked her.

She shook her head. "Not yet. I have some ideas, but I'm going to wait and see."

"I'd be interested in at least one of them. I wanted to get a dog and this seems like a good opportunity."

"What about two of them?" she asked softly. "I think that Khan and Kirk might enjoy it out at your house.

He looked sideways at her. "Khan and Kirk? From Star Trek?"

"Maybe?" she giggled. "You don't have to keep those names. They've only had them for a week. If you want the two of them, just come up with new names and we'll start using them."

Eliseo sat back down, holding the pup close to his face. Khan leaned forward and licked Eliseo's cheek and the man's eyes twinkled. "I think Khan and Kirk will be just fine.

Henry stood up, then leaned over and kissed Polly's forehead. "I need to leave for a while."

Eliseo put Khan into Jason's lap and stood up. "I'll walk out with you. Jason, come on down to the barn whenever you're ready."

"I can come down now if you think I should."

"No. Play with the pups and come down in a half hour or so."

~~~

Andrew had ridden down to Boone with Polly and Rebecca. They'd made a quick stop at the book store after spending time with Sarah. She was still quite weak and had difficulty breathing without oxygen. This had been a rough season for Rebecca's mother, but she insisted that she'd be home before Thanksgiving. She had more tenacity than Polly could believe, but it made her feel good to see the woman giving everything she had in order to have a life with her daughter.
~~~

Polly's phone buzzed with a text as she pulled out of the parking space in front of the book store. She saw that it was a message from Sylvie and went around the corner and pulled into another space to read it.

"I'm buying the house! Henry saw it and said that it was fine. There are some things we need to work on, but he offered to help. Eliseo is going to bring Jason over to see it. Can you bring Andrew? I can't wait for you to see the inside."

"We're just leaving Boone right now. We'll be there in about twenty minutes. I won't tell Andrew anything. I promise."

"I can't wait to see you! I'm so excited!"

Polly smiled and put her phone back on the console beside her.

"Who was that?" Rebecca asked.

"Oh, it was nothing."

"You were smiling."

Polly turned around and grinned at her. "Let's just say it's another surprise and we need to get back to Bellingwood in a hurry."

Fortunately the kids had new books to capture their attention and were quiet during the ride back to Bellingwood. Polly smiled at the new decoration hanging from her rear view mirror. She was going to have to take it inside, she couldn't bear things hanging there, but it was wonderful. Henry hadn't said anything more about what he'd purchased at the Jack Rabbit Trading Post and she'd forgotten about it. This afternoon, when she came out with Andrew and Rebecca, she'd discovered a crystal cactus hanging in her truck. He didn't often buy her romantic gifts, but this was perfect.

When Polly turned north off of the highway instead of into her driveway, Andrew looked up.

"Where are we going?"

"You'll see in just a minute," she said and continued down the street. She turned east on Jefferson and then stopped in front of a beautifully painted green home with burgundy trim. Sylvie, Jason and Eliseo were standing on the porch that wrapped around the front to the side of the house.

"What's this place?" Andrew asked. "Why is mom here?"

"Why don't you get out and ask her yourself," Polly said.

Andrew opened the back door of the truck and climbed down, then walked up the sidewalk to the porch.

"We'd better hurry," Polly said to Rebecca. "We don't want to miss this."

"Is this his new house?" Rebecca asked.

"I think it's going to be. Let's go."

They hurried out of the truck and got to the porch just as Andrew started jumping up and down. He ran back down the steps and grabbed Polly's hand. "This is going to be our house! Mom, Polly has puppies. Can we have one of them? You said we could when we got a house. Can we go inside? Which one is my room?"

He let go of Polly's hand and ran back down the steps to grab Rebecca's. "Come on. Let's go inside. I wonder if there are secret rooms in here. We have to explore the whole place."

Eliseo held the front door open as Andrew pulled Rebecca through and into the large front room.

"Go on in," Jason said. "We've already been through it."

"What do you think?" Polly asked him.

"It's a cool house. There's a garage for two cars and a big back yard. The fence goes all the way around, too. They built a fire pit in the back yard. That will be really awesome."

Sylvie and Polly stood in the front room as Jason led Andrew and Rebecca on a tour, through the main level and into the upstairs.

"I know this is probably too big for just the three of us," Sylvie said. "There are four bedrooms upstairs and even a room for a study or bedroom down here."

"It's perfect," Polly said. "The floors are beautiful and all of this wood work is gorgeous."

"Come on in to the kitchen. They left the appliances because they're mostly built in." Sylvie took the lead and Polly followed through what was probably the dining room into a spacious kitchen centered around a large island. Windows looked out into the back yard, a pleasant space with a few trees and a raised garden space.

"They really loved this home," Polly said.

"I know. And I think I could love it for a lot of years." Sylvie twirled on her toes. "I'm going to finally have a house all my own!"

They heard the rumbling of feet running down the stairs and Andrew and Rebecca came flying into the kitchen. "This is awesome!" Andrew exclaimed. "Jason showed me which room was yours and he said I could pick any of the other rooms. He let me pick first!"

"Which one did you choose?" Sylvie asked.

"I want the one that looks out on the back yard. There's a big tree right there and I think it would be cool to write stories in front of that window."

Jason had come into the kitchen and gave Polly a wry grin, then shook his head.

"Is that okay with you, Jason?" Sylvie asked, crossing the room to put her arm around his shoulder.

He shrugged. "It's fine. He'll be here longer than me, so he should have the room he wants. And besides, I think I'd like to be able to look out on the street. See what's going on."

"You're a good kid," Polly said. "Andrew, do you want to see what the back yard looks like?"

"I already saw it from my room. It's fine," he responded. "When do we get to move in, mom?"

"Well, it will take time for the paperwork, but sometime in the next month. You two are going to need to start packing your room."

"Yeah! Padme will be ready to go to her new house and we'll have a yard all ready for her."

"Padme?" Sylvie asked.

"The puppy. You know."

"Puppy?" She looked at Polly.

"I told you about them. Andrew decided that one is his. Do I need to fix that decision?"

"I'm taking two," Eliseo said, his chest shaking with laughter.

"Are you going to house train her before she moves in?" Sylvie asked her son.

"We can really have her? Really?"

Sylvie smiled and said to Polly. "I thought you were joking."

"Nope." Polly gave her friend an evil smirk. "It's as if it were meant to be."

"Then it looks like we'll have one more warm body to move into this house," she said.

Andrew and Rebecca ran out of the room and back up the stairs.

"It's a good thing I already planned to let him have a dog or I'd have your head, Polly Giller," Sylvie said, scowling.

"I didn't promise him anything. He made this up all by himself. You're the one who caved."

"Come on, Jason," Eliseo said, putting his hand on Jason's back. "We'd best get back to work and let these two discuss this in private."

"Aww, that's no fun," Jason said, chuckling, but he left with Eliseo.

"If you don't want the puppy, I can fix this," Polly said.

"No, I'm teasing you. I had promised Andrew and Jason that we would. And we might as well help you with all of your crazy rescues now that we have a home of our own."

Polly hugged her friend. "This is an amazing house. I can't wait to see what you do with it. Can you believe it? A degree, a career and now a house. What's next?"

"I think that's enough for now. I'd like to raise my boys in peace for a while. No extra people, no extra stress."

"Extra people are what make it fun."

"That's why you are such a great friend. You really believe that."

"Of course I do. And we wouldn't want Bellingwood to get boring, would we?"

"Since you moved in, boring no longer describes this town." Sylvie shivered with glee and looked around the kitchen. "I'm so glad you came along. Boring doesn't describe me any longer either."

Polly smiled. This was why she enjoyed her life so much. There was nothing better than watching her friends fill their lives with good things. She nodded to herself as she wondered what was going to come next.

THANK YOU FOR READING!

I'm so glad you enjoy these stories about Polly Giller and her friends. There are many ways to stay in touch with Diane and the Bellingwood community.

You can find more details about Sycamore House and Bellingwood at the website: http://nammynools.com/

Join the Bellingwood Facebook page:
https://www.facebook.com/pollygiller
for news about upcoming books, conversations while I'm writing and you're reading, and a continued look at life in a small town.

Diane Greenwood Muir's Amazon Author Page is a great place to watch for new releases.

Follow Diane on Twitter at twitter.com/nammynools for regular updates and notifications.

Recipes and decorating ideas found in the books can often be found on Pinterest at: *http://pinterest.com/nammynools/*

And, if you are looking for Sycamore House swag, check out Polly's CafePress store: *http://www.cafepress.com/sycamorehouse*

Made in the USA
Columbia, SC
13 September 2020

20716057R00224